KG 200

The Force with no Face

by

J. D. Gilman
&
John Clive

Heywood Books

First published in Great Britain 1977
by Souvenir Press
and simultaneously in Canada
by Methuen Publications.
Previously published in paperback
by Pan Books Ltd.

ISBN 1 85481 015 4

This edition published 1989 by
Heywood Books Limited
55 Clissold Crescent
London N16 9AR

Printed in Great Britain by
Cox & Wyman Ltd, Reading

1

The great B-17 was dying in the air, sinking down through the last 1,500 feet towards a glittering sea. The sandy haze of the approaching shoreline merged confusingly with the starred, cracked web and ragged holes of the Plexiglass in the broken nose-canopy.

The inner two of the four engines were silent. The outer starboard engine roared at full throttle, trying to take the weight of flying the bomber. The outer port engine coughed, screamed in agonised little bursts of power, coughed again. From where he sat in the ruin of the flight-deck, the pilot occasionally risked a glance at the oil pouring in swift, spasmodic rushes from its cracked hub, streaming over the blue-and-white United States Army Air Force star on the wing.

A glance was all he could risk. He hunched, rigid, in the 180-mile-an-hour gale blowing back through the broken nose canopy, pushing forward on the control column with his entire strength, trying to hold the nose down so that the B-17 would not rear into its final death-stall. Above the roar of the wind he could hear, faintly, the cracking and creaking as the bomber slowly broke up.

The salvo of two 88mm shells that had hit the B-17 over Wangerooge Island had not destroyed it outright, but it had made it virtually impossible to fly. The trimming knobs, by which the angle of the B-17 must be altered for landing, hung useless on a tangle of projecting wires. They were jammed in the bomb-run position, holding the B-17 irretrievably tail-heavy. No hydraulics were working, and there was no intercom. The waist and legs of the upper-turret-gunner lay there: his head and chest were somewhere in the North Sea, sixty miles out.

Back beyond those shreds of flesh, the floor of the fuselage was open to the rushing air, a hole roughly eight feet long and four feet wide having been torn by the impact of the first 88mm shell. The fuselage walls were blackened by the fierce fire which had started at once, but there were no flames now. The second shell, exploding a second or two later, just outside the leading edge of the starboard wing, had seen to that. It had half-lifted the inner starboard engine from its mounting, smashing the starboard side of the nose canopy, and created a gale through the fuselage in which no flame could live.

The rear of the B-17, however, was still on fire. The retracted tail-wheel blocked the airway between the tail-turret and the middle-fuselage, and no gale blew back there. The burning body, squat, shapeless, no longer human, of the tail-gunner sat in his seat, leaning across his two .50 Brownings, trapped for the last twenty minutes in a blaze which had already melted every meltable thing in his narrow coffin. Above this death-perch, the rudder sagged to one side. The B-17 could no longer be steered or turned.

The bomb-doors were open, though the bombardier—there was no trace of either him or the navigator in the shattered nose canopy—had pressed no button. The blast of the first shell had done the job. Across these bomb-doors, peppered with holes but by some trick of blast unshattered, lay an open plywood container in a tangle of rigging lines and billowing parachute silk. Inside the container were two more dead bodies. One was of a youngish man in a blue civilian suit. The lower half of his face had been blown off. The other was of a middle-aged woman in a grey coat, blouse and skirt. Her injuries were not visible. She lay on her back, half-out of the container, one naked leg hanging through the bomb-doors, and her dead, spectacled eyes staring upwards through the cracked lenses.

The only other man alive in the B-17 was crouched at the

open bomb-doors, looking down at the dead couple, and at the white-flecked sea below. He turned and fought his way back against the fuselage-gale up to the flight-deck. With difficulty, he forced his way into the co-pilot's seat behind the pilot, who looked briefly towards him, questioningly. He shook his head. The pilot nodded emphatically towards the control column, and the co-pilot, shuffling forward and kneeling down, helped him to hold it forward . . . with difficulty. The third and fourth fingers of his left hand were no more than bloody stumps.

The pilot took one hand quickly from the control column, felt down beside his seat, and drew out a sheath knife. It was impossible to hear a voice above the rush of the wind and the hoarse roar of the port engine through the shattered nose, but he pantomimed a carving motion with the knife. The co-pilot pushed outwards with his hands, and looked again at the pilot, who shook his head violently, and opened the knife. Wearily, the co-pilot took it in his good hand, slid out from under the control column, and again made his way down the catwalk to the bomb-bay. Fighting against the force of the wind through the open doors, he hacked at the parachute lines which held the plywood container. When, finally, the last line parted, he braced himself against a fuselage bulkhead and levered at the container with his foot. The plywood box and the dead man dropped out cleanly, vanishing into the choppy sea which was now no more than 700 feet below. The dead woman was caught for a moment, hanging from the lip of the bomb-door by one foot. The wind had torn off her skirt. For a moment she swayed obscenely, head down, in her pink underwear, until with a tremendous effort the co-pilot arched himself against the blackened bulkhead and pushed her trapped foot with his own flying-boot. Her shoe came off, and in an instant she was gone. The co-pilot, his wounded hand again bleeding badly, was near the end of his strength, but once more he stumbled down the catwalk to the flight-deck. The pilot looked at him, and he nodded. A minute later, 300 feet up, the B-17 crossed the coastline. The pilot reckoned he could hold the plane in the air for ninety seconds more.

They were dropping, faster and faster, and at a deepening angle, across a grey town, quiet in the evening light. There was a crossroads with a military lorry parked at the side. Beyond that there was an anti-aircraft emplacement, sandbagged, with a gun pointing upwards. Three or four men had come out of a nearby Nissen hut and were staring up at him. The co-pilot was mouthing something. He could not hear. The co-pilot seized an envelope from his pocket and scrawled on it in clumsy capitals "MERSEA".

Mersea . . . the pilot tried to remember the map. Beyond Mersea, there was flat ground. It offered a chance, but even as he grasped that fact, he knew they would never reach it. The B-17 was staggering to doom, 100 feet up, perhaps less. He throttled back on the port engine, allowed the nose to come up a trifle. Two fields were looming ahead, separated by a hedged lane. They were not nearly long enough to take the B-17. As soon as her broken belly touched down, she would plough along, disintegrating, burning, for hundreds of yards. He would have to go in sideways. He was no more than thirty feet up as he crossed the boundary hedge of the first field. He pushed the throttle switch of the starboard engine. It bellowed instantly on full throttle, and the sudden boost of power skidded the B-17 sideways to port. In the same instant the pilot lifted the nose, and flopped the great bomber into the field, sliding, banging, crashing its way through the hedge, across the lane, and into the second pasture. The trees at the end of the field rushed towards the nose-canopy. Great clods of earth were flung back as the shattered Plexiglass panels carved into the ground. With a tearing crack, the entire nose and flight-deck section broke away, cartwheeled twice, stopped, teetered, and came to rest upright. The remainder of the wings and fuselage of the B-17 ploughed on, sideways, into the trees. A few moments later, there was a dull, crumping roar. A hundred yards away, the B-17 blew up, sending a great column of flame and black smoke into the washed-out blue of the evening sky. Pieces of burning fabric fell into the splintered wreck of the flight-deck where it lay in the field. Strapped in his seat, the pilot beat at his neck, where his uniform shirt collar was smouldering. He pressed his harness quick-release button and struggled shakily through the gaping side of the nose-canopy. The co-pilot was slumped, unstrapped, across a broken spar. There was no danger of fire in the broken nose-canopy, but the heat rolling down the field from the burning B-17 was unbelievably fierce. There was a steady rattle of exploding ammunition. The pilot seized the other man and half-pushed, half-carried him fifty yards further back.

The co-pilot had been unconscious, but now he opened his eyes, grimaced with pain, and then smiled weakly. His hair was matted with blood and oil. His legs were spread beneath him awkwardly, at an unnatural angle. The pilot looked at them quickly. Both were broken, the right one completely shattered. There was a hopeless, gaping wound in the chest. The boy, with difficulty, was whispering. The pilot leaned down until his ear touched the boy's mouth. The co-pilot's hand grasped his own, and his voice strengthened for a moment:

"There's no other pilot . . . no other pilot alive could have managed it . . ."

From somewhere beyond the smoking hedge came the distant clanging of an ambulance bell. The pilot drew a .45 Colt automatic from his belt, slipped off the safety catch, placed the muzzle behind the boy's neck, and blew off the back of his head.

2

The first person to reach the pilot was a middle-aged man in a grey tweed suit, who burst through a part of the hedge lower down the field and ran up, wheezing loudly, to where he crouched beside the co-pilot's body. Behind him came a young girl, seventeen or eighteen years old, her fair hair tied back with a blue ribbon. As soon as the man saw the co-pilot's shattered head, he turned and spoke sharply to her.

"Don't come any nearer, Mary. Do as I tell you. There's nothing can be done for him."

She stopped, uncertainly, a few yards away. The middle-aged man turned to the pilot, who sat in the grass with his head in his hands, although through his fingers, his eyes were watching.

"Any others?" There was an accustomed authority to the middle-aged man's voice. The pilot shook his head.

"All in there," he said. He nodded to the burning skeleton of the B-17. His voice was clipped, trans-Atlantic. The middle-aged man swung round towards the bomber. In the same instant, the pilot rose and grasped his arm.

"It's no use," he said. "There's no chance at all. They were all dead, anyway, as far as I know, before I put her down."

The man nodded. He looked briefly at the USAF gold badges on the uniform tunic collar, the gold eagle's wings, the twin bars on each shoulder.

"American, aren't you, Captain, er . . ."

"Hadley," said the pilot. "Ralph Hadley. US Army Air Force."

"You all right?" said the man. "Hurt at all?"

"No," said the pilot. "I guess I was born to be hanged." He laughed weakly.

"And this poor chap?" said the middle-aged man.

"He's my co-pilot," said the pilot. "He was alive, OK, but he'd just been to the back of the ship with a fire extinguisher, and he wasn't strapped in when he hit. We turned over a couple of times. It beat his brains out. He didn't have a hope in hell."

"I know," said the other. "I saw the crash."

He held out his hand.

"My name's Schofield. John Schofield. I live over there."

He nodded towards the grey roof of a largish house beyond the trees.

"As a matter of fact," he was saying, "I'm the colonel of the Home Guard unit here. I'll get some men to guard the wreckage, as soon as the fire's out—and that shouldn't be long, because here's the Fire Service."

Two red fire tenders, followed by a white ambulance, were bumping along the field. Firemen in asbestos suits began to spray foam on the B-17. Dozens of people were streaming through the hedge, shielding their eyes against the heat from the wreckage, looking covertly at the huddled body of the co-pilot. A police car drew up beside the pilot, and an officer in blue uniform, with two silver stars on each shoulder, got out.

"Ah, Inspector," said Schofield.

"You must have got here quickly, Colonel," said the policeman.

"I was driving over to Yarmouth," said Schofield. "Down in the lane there when I heard a hell of a noise—didn't miss me by much." He nodded towards the pilot.

"You all right, sir?" said the inspector to the pilot.

"I suppose . . ." he hesitated for a moment. "I suppose . . . you're the only one?"

"That's so," said the pilot briefly. He watched the ambulancemen load the body of the co-pilot on to a stretcher.

"Can I help you, sir?" said one of them.

"No," said the pilot. "I'm OK."

"Do you think you could manage to come down to the station with me?" said the inspector. "I'll have to make a report . . . names, casualties, and so on—you know the sort of thing."

He smiled shakily at the inspector.

"Not that I'm worried about you, you understand. But there is a rule-book for these things, and I guess I'd better start to fly by it."

"I'll tell you what," said Schofield to the inspector. "Why don't you leave him with me? He can telephone from my place, and Mary can give him a hot drink and something to eat. I've got petrol and I can take him to somewhere where his unit can send transport to pick him up. It's fair enough, after all. This is a military matter, and I'm the Home Guard here. Then you can come up to the house later on and I'll give you all the details that are relevant. Be simpler all round . . ."

The pilot held his breath. There was a pause, and the inspector nodded.

"Seems fair enough," he said.

He held out his hand and the pilot took it.

"Good luck, sir," said the inspector. "If you need any other help, I'll be glad to give you a hand."

He nodded towards the ambulance, now jolting back to the lane with the body. Then he looked beyond that to the smoking pyre of the B-17.

"I don't know what you do about this sort of thing," he said. "Perhaps you'll want to take them back to the States for burial. But if they stay here, in our churchyard, I can promise you one thing. To us, they'll be like our own."

The Schofield house was the sort of house the pilot had read about in English magazines. There was a glassed-in conservatory outside, a trim green lawn which even had croquet hoops stuck in the grass. There were two big vegetable gardens—"used to be lawns", Schofield told him as the car drew up on the gravelled drive, "but, of course, we're growing all the food we can now, like everybody else." He led the way into a book-lined study, and asked the girl Mary, whom he'd introduced in the car as his daughter, to make some coffee.

"Sure you won't have anything stronger?" he asked the younger man. "I'm damned sure I would, if I'd just been through what you've been through."

The pilot shook his head.

"Thanks, sir, but no. I'd just like to telephone. The base ought to know what's happened as soon as possible."

"Of course."

Schofield pointed to the corner of the desk.

"There's the phone. I'll make myself scarce. I know you chaps have things to say you don't want everybody else to hear. Had long enough in uniform myself, though I wasn't an airman, of course. Army . . . in the last lot. Mind you, it's all the same. Never changes. Just tell them we'll drive you anywhere you like, within reason. Haven't got all that much petrol, though I get a bit extra for the Home Guard."

He went out of the room, and the pilot crossed to the telephone. He lifted the receiver, and spoke into it at intervals, as though conducting a conversation. But he dialled no number. After a little, he put the receiver back on its rest, and crossed the room to peer into a mirror. He didn't look at all too bad, he thought. There was a smear of dried blood down his left cheek, but the cut that had caused it was nothing much. His face was red and raw from the buffeting of the gale through the broken canopy, but his uniform—now that he had removed his fleece-lined flying jacket—was reasonably tidy. He felt in his pocket and took out some money—ten £1 notes. He even had a uniform hat to replace his discarded flying helmet. It was stuffed in the side pocket of his flying jacket—a precaution he'd always taken. He took it out and put it on. A bit crumpled. but the creases would lessen as it got warm on his head. In any case, he reminded himself, flying crews often wore rather odd headgear. What was it a B-17 pilot had told him the other day? He had asked why the man's hat was so battered. "That's my twenty-mission hat," the pilot had replied. "We jump on them twenty times—once for each mission."

By now the reactions to what had happened in the past hour was coming on him fast, and he was sitting in an armchair, trying to stop his hands shaking, when the girl Mary knocked at the door and carried in a tray of coffee and sandwiches.

"Would you like to wash first and have these later?" she asked him. "Or eat now?"

She was older than he had thought in the field—perhaps nineteen, but with those strangely immature, untried good looks that so many English girls had. Even as he sat there, hands shaking, he felt a tiny quiver of desire. He thought wryly, how often he had landed from a mission and gone straight to a girl. There was one, once, who had said to him: "Sex for you is like sucking your thumb. It's a comfort habit, isn't it? You've never grown up. And you probably never will." He'd found out what that one liked, anyway. She liked it quick, break-neck, galloping. He'd never had any difficulty in being any of those things, in bed or in the air. Not at all like Peter. Girls loved Peter . . . "I woo them first," he used to say. "Much better . . ." Well, Peter would never woo one again. For a moment that blond, smashed head, now on its way in the ambulance to some cold British morgue, filled his mind's eye. He shuddered.

"Are you cold?" the girl said. "It's probably shock. Here—have some coffee. I think you should see a doctor, you know."

The pilot shook his head, and forced himself to smile.

"No, I'm OK, ma'am. But I'd love some coffee. And then I'd like to wash and clean up my uniform."

She poured out a cup, and giggled slightly, stopping when she saw his face.

"I'm sorry, but nobody's ever called me 'ma'am' before. It's like the films."

He nodded, smiling. He was beginning to feel better.

"What part of America do you come from? Or aren't you allowed to tell me?" she asked.

"Why shouldn't I tell you?"

"Well, you know, security and things. 'Careless talk costs lives.' That's what we're always told."

"I guess it's hardly classified information. I come from Chicago."

"Where the gangsters come from . . ."

"Oh, Al Capone has a lot to answer for, ma'am," he said, grinning. The door opened and Schofield came in.

"Fixed up?"

"Yes, sir. I have to report to your Air Ministry in London. I don't know why, but I guess it's because the mission we were flying was kind of a joint one. They say I can pick up a train tonight at a place called . . . Colchester, is it?"

"Colchester? Yes, I can run you there. It's about twenty-five miles. There's a night train at 12.20. God knows how long it'll take to get to London . . . you know what it's like nowadays. Or rather, you don't know, I suppose. Don't take many trains, eh?"

"I guess not," said the pilot.

"And what about your people?"

"My people?"

"Out there in the field. And the other poor boy."

"My base will get in touch with your police here. I said Colchester police were handling all that. They'll be telephoning. That's OK, isn't it?"

"Couldn't be better. I'll let the inspector know. Only please ask them to decide what they want to do fairly quickly. We haven't much in the way of . . . facilities . . . for this sort of thing here. Might be difficult."

"Sure," said the pilot.

It was cold in the train, until the heating took over. The compartment he was in was lit with dim blue lights—air raid precautions, he knew. And they'd stopped for more than two hours outside Chelmsford. There had been a lot of searchlights in the sky, and some anti-aircraft fire. But he had heard no explosions. Couldn't have been much, he told himself. A couple of JU-88s from Ostend, making a nuisance of themselves. The train was crowded—mostly, it seemed, soldiers coming from or going on leave. There wasn't much talk in his first-class compartment from the four British officers and one elderly woman who occupied it. He had chosen it carefully.

London was cold and grim in the early morning. He queued for a taxi at Liverpool Street—and would have queued longer, except that a taxi-driver, seeing the American uniform, drove down past the queue and covertly beckoned him over. He took the taxi to Sloane Square, passing some recent bomb-damage and rubble in the City on the way. At the Square he got out, giving the taxi-driver the expected American-size tip. Then he walked on down the King's Road. The people he passed seemed shabby but cheerful. Even here in Chelsea, away from the centre, there were uniforms everywhere—Polish, Free French, American, Canadian, British. The whole capital seemed like an armed camp. At least half of the women, too, seemed to be in battle-dress of various colours. He walked on, down streets he had never seen, but whose lay-out he knew as familiarly as though he had been born there. He hesitated only once or twice before he found the street he sought, walking past the freshly-budding plane trees beside a row of houses fronted by a bare, concrete shelf, from which the iron railings had long ago been torn for wartime scrap. There was a house there with a shabby green front door. He lifted the heavy brass knocker and thudded it down, once, twice, three times. There was a pause, and the door opened. A woman stood there, looking out into the grey morning. She was tall, fair, still wearing the dressing-gown in which, presumably, she was cooking breakfast. From behind her came the smell of coffee. He had never seen her before, but he knew her face. She looked at him questioningly, taking in the American uniform, the graze on his face, the faint overnight stubble on his chin.

"Yes?" she said questioningly.

"My name's Hadley. Ralph Hadley. A friend suggested I should drop by next time I was in London."

"You're a bit early for a social call."

"Right off the train, ma'am. And hungry."

She laughed.

"There's not much for breakfast. Only sausage."

She watched him closely.

"Dortmund sausage?" he said, after a pause.

"It's the best," she said, evenly. "But you can't get it here now. Not since the war."

He gave an almost imperceptible sigh of relief, and she motioned him inside. He stood in a small narrow entrance hall, beside an umbrella stand which seemed, incongruously, to be made from an elephant's foot. The smell of coffee was stronger. She was looking at him searchingly, but her face was unreadable. She led him into the sitting-room.

"Dortmund sausage," he said again, and laughed. "What a way to identify a friend."

"As good as any other," she said. "So you are Telemachus?"

"And you are Cassandra."

"Was the house hard to find?"

"No. You've always been my contact, in emergency. I learned the street map by heart."

"Very thorough," said the tall fair girl, and smiled without warmth.

He said nothing for a moment, but looked over her shoulder towards the room through which he could smell coffee.

"My God, I am really hungry," he said. She went back to the kitchen. When she came back, she began to lay two places at the little dining table. He watched her and said:

"I should explain, because you'll need to know more, of course I am—"

"I know who you are," said the girl. "You aren't the only one who does careful homework, Telemachus. You're Major Rolf Warnow, Operations Officer of *Gruppe* 1 of *Kampfgeschwader* 200 of the *Luftwaffe*. And, *Herr Major*, you're a long way from home."

The pilot looked at her for two long seconds. When he spoke, his voice had the rasp of command.

"And you, Cassandra, are going to get me back."

3

Three hours before Major Rolf Warnow walked into the house at Chelsea, the dawn came up grey at the *Luftwaffe* airfield at Stavanger-Sola, beside the cold waters of the Boknafjord in German-occupied Norway. The man who stood in the broad window of the control tower had waited long after reason had told him there was little more hope . . . not because he still expected to see the graceful bulk of the B-17 emerge safely from the overcast to begin its final approach, but because it was here that news, if there was to be any news, would come first. At last he walked over to where the duty *Feldwebel* sat beside his humming radio set, and tapped him on the shoulder. The man looked up and shook his head.

"Nothing, *Herr Hauptmann*. Nothing definite, that is. But there is something which is not so good . . ."

"Yes?"

"A battery at Wangerooge claims two, possibly three hits on a single B-17 yesterday evening. They saw it going down into the North Sea, on fire."

"They were told nothing?"

"Of course not, *Herr Hauptmann*."

The *Hauptmann* sighed.

"Good, good. Let me know if you hear anything more. I shall be in the pilots' mess, or in my quarters."

"Jawohl, Herr Hauptmann."

He put on his uniform cap, pulling it rakishly over the left eye in the way that Galland wore it. The *Gefreiter* at the map table stood and saluted. He flicked a hand to his cap and went down the wooden steps into the cold morning.

Aeroplanes loomed up in the mist and light rain . . . a radial-engined Focke-Wulf FW-190 fighter, characteristically crouched on the tarmac as though ready to spring; a big, twin-engined Heinkel HE-177; a four-engined Focke-Wulf Condor, with eighty feet of wingspan. Beyond them, but in open-fronted hangars, bulked more aircraft . . . amazing aircraft for that time and that place. The *Hauptmann* had seen them often before, but again he felt an irresistible fascination as he walked down the long line of hangars. There were two bulky, coffin-shaped four-engined bombers—Short Stirlings, their Royal Air Force roundels and red identification numbers shining wetly against the drab green-and-olive of their camouflage. There was a sturdy-looking early model Beaufighter, which carried neither roundels nor the German cross or swastika. One of its 1,400 horsepower Bristol Hercules engines had been removed. Beside it stood a Spitfire—God knows, he'd faced enough of those in battle years ago. And, most impressive of all, at thc end of the line, almost lost in the misty darkness of the hangar, stood two B-17s—Flying Fortresses, as the Americans called them. They were painted a dull green, with the big five-pointed stars of the United States Army Air Force on their sides. Men were working on the bomb-bays of the nearer one. As he turned into the doorway of the pilots' mess, pushing his way through the heavy blackout screen, a small camouflaged *Kübelwagen* truck splashed by through the puddles. It was piled with boxes of captured .50 Browning ammunition. Going out to fill the turrets, he thought. That B-17 must be on stand-by.

There was no one in the pilots' mess except a waiter laying for breakfast. He walked over to the buffet table and poured a cup of coffee from the hot urn. Well, that was it, then, he thought. What an irony! Rolf Warnow, of all people, hit by an unlucky salvo from a gun on his own side. There'd never be another like Rolf. A few, a very few, might have been considered to be as good, three years ago. They were mostly twelve feet down in the Kent marshes now, or under some bit of North Africa. There's still Galland, he thought, the best of the lot. But even his wings were being clipped nowadays—after his hundredth kill the *Führer* had made him *General der Jagdflieger.* Too much paper-work. There'd been the great Hans-Joachim Marseille —158 victories, and all but four of them English or American fighters. He'd baled out over Alamein—a few seconds too late. There was Werner Molders. He'd bought it, flying in from the Crimea for Udet's funeral, crashing in a lumbering HE-111. Another irony. And now Rolf Warnow was gone, somewhere out in the North Sea . . . Warnow, only thirty-three air victories (but you could hardly blame him for that, in the circumstances, could you?). With the possible exception of Galland, Warnow was the finest fighting pilot of them all. He was one of the few the *Luftwaffe* called *Experten.* Half a dozen fliers like him would be enough for any air force in a generation.

He pulled out a drawer, and rummaged for a moment among the framed photographs that filled it. He took out two, and hung them side by side at the end of the row of similarly-framed photographs above the long table. Smiling, the dead faces looked out . . . Specht, Protze, Mueller, Gerhard, Arndt, Wessels. Each was signed: some had a motto. He added Warnow's at the end of the row . . . unsmiling, this one, the face impassive above the Knight's Cross at the collar. It was signed in a firm hand and beneath it was the motto: "The golden rule—always look behind before you attack." Next to Warnow's picture he put that of the co-pilot, young Peter Behrens, signed but no motto. If Warnow was dead, Behrens was, too. Behrens believed that Warnow could walk on water. As a matter of fact, thought the *Hauptmann*, he probably could. That motto was typical Warnow. Other men, writing in advance for that doom-laden drawer, scrawled bits of popular songs or jokes or even chunks from *Mein Kampf.* Not Warnow. He gave an order, from beyond the grave. Moodily, the *Hauptmann* sorted through the pictures waiting in the drawer, until he found his own. He was grinning inanely, he thought. The photograph was signed in a round, almost childish hand: Frido von Altmark. Beneath the signature was his motto: "And now all my wives will be widows." Oh, well, it would have to do. But he was going to miss Rolf Warnow.

KG 200 Operational Training Directive No. 101

Subject: Andromeda *Staffel*
Security: Category One
Four copies:

Oberkommando der Wehrmacht
Oberkommando der Luftwaffe
OKL Staff Ops. Branch
Gruppe-Kommandeur I/KG 200

1. *Task*
   To establish a new *Staffel* of KG 200.
2. *Operational Area*
   Eastern Front, general.
3. *Enemy Situation*
   Soviet offensives this summer have produced unexpected situations on various parts of the front. It is likely that in such situations, the need will arise to fly out or to transfer key officers, technicians or other personnel from pockets behind the front. The enemy's growing strength in the air has at times made it hazardous to conduct such operations by conventional means.
4. *Intention*
   3rd *Staffel* I/KG 200 will at once allot pilots and aircraft as a basis for the new *Staffel*, and will begin training for such operations.
5. *Method*
   Eighteen aircraft will be allotted for the new *Staffel*. These aircraft will be Soviet Petlyakov PE-2 bombers. After training is completed, nine aircraft will be stationed at the KG 200 base at Gorkum-Smolensk and nine at Simferopol, Crimea. Three aircraft at each base will be on 24-hour standby.
6. *Administration*
   a. Aircraft used in this operation will be drawn from the KG 200 pool at Oranienburg, and will be flown by pilots of the *Staffel* to Training Centre Four at Prenz-

lau. *Under no circumstances will OKL ferry pilots be used.*

b. Aircraft will be painted with the numbers, unit codes and insignia of similarly-equipped Soviet Air Bombardment Regiments stationed on their operational fronts. Markings will be checked constantly against the Red Air Force order-of-battle digest issued weekly by Intelligence Section, OKL.

c. Changes in Soviet air camouflage have recently been reported. There has been difficulty in obtaining duck-egg-blue paint of the new type for wing under-surfaces. Supplies of this paint have now been located in the *Luftwaffe Beutepark* at Oranienburg. Aircraft painted in the new camouflage will be checked against dismantled wing sections of a recently shot-down Petlyakov PE-2 before being passed as suitable for training or operations.

d. Pilots will be trained to fly alone, acting as their own navigators. This will allow three passengers to be carried in each aircraft on the return journey.

7. *Unit Code*

The new *Staffel* will be code-named the Andromeda *Staffel*. The Smolensk and Simferopol flights will be known as North and South Flights, respectively.

4

On the same morning that von Altmark waited in vain at Stavanger-Sola, *Oberst* Adolf Pertz, *Kommandeur* of *Kampfgeschwader* 200, was reading carefully through the order he had just drafted. He sat in his office inside the *Luftwaffe* compound at Hitler's *Wolfsschanze* headquarters—600 miles away from Stavanger—deep in the dripping pine forests of Rastenburg in East Prussia. Pertz was a squat, grey, middle-aged man, who wore no decorations. Neither his appointment as *Kommandeur* nor, indeed, KG 200 itself appeared in the official *Luftwaffe* list. He had held his present post for two years, and he had never, on a specific operation, disappointed the *Führer*. That, he thought, sardonically, was because he understood the *Führer* better than most people did—and better, certainly, than did the strutting, cap-tilted young fliers of the conventional *Luftwaffe*, with their Knight's Crosses and oakleaves and swords handed to them like sweets to so many schoolboys. These men had done well in battle: there was no denying that. They knew how to fight, but it was he, *Oberst* Adolf Pertz, who had learned how to make war. No girl, he knew, would ever turn her head to watch him go by, as he'd seen the young *Luftwaffe* girl secretaries look at men like Galland. There was only one love in Adolf Pertz's life, and that was KG 200. His predecessor, a man now dead, had once, in a moment of unaccustomed poetry, called KG 200 "the *Luftwaffe*'s secret heart". Pertz had liked that. He put on his gold-rimmed spectacles and read carefully through the typed transcript. He looked at paragraph 3 for a moment, frowned, and crossed out the words "at times". Then he pressed the desk buzzer.

"Have this page retyped," he said to the senior office *Feldwebel* who entered the room. "And then distribute the copies."

The warrant officer saluted and went out. Pertz looked at his watch. It was time for the *Luftwaffe* conference. He heaved himself to his feet, and went out into the outer office. Four men worked here—each of them a *Luftwaffe* warrant officer with sergeant-major's rank. All had been rigorously investigated before being given their present jobs: all received certain small but important privileges—special duties pay, extra leave. None of them, Pertz was certain, would ever say one word outside that room, about the operations or the organisation of KG 200.

He walked on through the outer office, past the sentry at the door, and out to the concrete paths of Rastenburg. It had been raining, and the water lay in deep puddles on the mud beside the paths, but now a pale sun was shining. So the *Reichsmarschall* had torn himself away from his luxurious home in the Schorfheide woods near Berlin, had he? Pertz sniffed. Goering wanted to hear about Operation *Ulysses*.

Goering was standing beside the map table at the end of the conference room. He turned his head to watch Pertz come in. Pertz looked at him closely. He wore a plain white uniform over his bulk: at his neck simply the *Pour le Mérite*, the German equivalent of the Victoria Cross, which he had won flying Albatros fighters and Fokker triplanes in 1918. He had abandoned, for this day, the scores of decorations which usually filled his ample chest. Goering, thought Pertz shrewdly, was tired of being laughed at and he'd probably by now heard the *Luftwaffe* joke about his medals—that "Hermann's worth more to the *Reich* as scrap than as a commander". Yet although this morning he seemed more alert and lucid than for many months, he showed signs of strain. He looked tired as he walked over to the conference table and flopped heavily into his specially-strengthened chair. Outside in the ante-room waited his nurse Christina

Gormanns: beside her rested his medicine cabinet, with his wide choice of pills.

Pertz took his place on Goering's left. On Goering's right was General Hans Jeschonnek, the tall, slim *Luftwaffe* Chief of Staff—a dive-bomber fanatic, a devoted admirer of the *Führer*, an able and energetic officer. Jeschonnek had believed in 1939 that it would be a short war: now he could see years of it still to come. On the other side of the table were three *Luftwaffe Obersts*—young colonels who each commanded a *Jagdgeschwader*, a fighter group of about 120 aircraft.

From the corner of his eye, Goering looked at Pertz. Not my ideal type, he thought. Not at all. And as for KG 200 . . . what would von Richthofen have said about KG 200? Mentally, he shook himself. Other times, other ways, as the French said. Today the *Reich* needed men like *Oberst* Pertz. And the planes he flew.

Ah, yes, the surprising, astounding planes he flew. Well, he, Goering, knew about them. And the *Führer*, of course. And—because he had to—Jeschonnek. But nobody else, except Pertz himself, had the whole picture. Well, in a few minutes, Pertz was going to have to show just a corner of the picture to these three young cockerels here. He tapped the table:

"Gentlemen, we are here to discuss progress on *Fall Ulysses*. But first, General Jeschonnek has something to say."

The tall *Luftwaffe* general began to speak.

"*Herr Reichsmarschall*, the situation which I predicted last month in regard to the American day-bombing is already upon us. For the first time in this war, we are beginning to undergo a round-the-clock assault—the British by night, the Americans by day."

"The Americans?" grunted Goering. "They're still not doing a great deal. They've got a lot to learn."

"They put 126 B-17s over Kiel the other day," said one of the young fighter colonels. "We got eight of them."

"Eight from 126," said Goering. "Not enough."

The young colonel began to speak, but Jeschonnek held up his hand.

"I don't think the defensive problem these B-17s give us is generally realised as yet. They fly in box formations—sometimes boxes of twelve planes. Each box contains 120 heavy machine-guns . . . ten per plane. In your day and even in mine, *Herr Reichsmarschall*, we were taught to attack from behind. Do this against a Fortress box and you hit a wall of fire. We've lost many a good man this way."

"Attack from the front, then," said Goering impatiently.

"We're doing just that," said a young fighter colonel. "But it's not satisfactory. It gives far less firing time, and once the fighters have passed the box, they have to turn again to overhaul it, pass it, and again attack from the front."

"But with the new Focke-Wulf 190, you're travelling more than 150 miles an hour faster than those damned lumbering Christmas trees."

The fighter colonel shrugged.

"The FW-190 is fine below 21,000 feet, but much less good above that. And the B-17s come in at around 23,000."

"What about the 109s—the Fs, the Friedrichs?"

"Only one cannon and two machine-guns. It takes around twenty-five hits with 20mm shells to knock down a B-17. Very hard to do that with a Friedrich on one pass from the front of the box."

"The point is," said Jeschonnek, "that the Americans are gaining confidence. And their presence alone in Britain is helping enemy morale. What's more, there seems to be remarkably little friction. The Americans and British are settling down well. Some trouble, here and there, of course, but less than might be expected. Less than we had hoped."

"What point are you trying to make, Hans?" said Goering affably. He liked Jeschonnek. Good, intelligent, hard-working . . . though, he thought ruefully, without much sense of humour. Jeschonnek took himself too seriously.

"This," said Jeschonnek. He leaned forward earnestly, his eyes staring past Goering towards Pertz.

"We must try to advance the date of *Ulysses*. Things over there are moving faster than we thought. Can we bring *Ulysses* forward, say, to the middle of next month?"

For a moment, Pertz said nothing. Then, slowly, he shook his head.

"I am sorry, *Herr General*. If we had spoken yesterday morning, I might have been in agreement. But I regret to say that we lost a B-17 yesterday, over the North Sea."

"You mean the British spotted . . .?"

"No, no. One of our own batteries, at Wangerooge. Sheer bad luck. They couldn't be told, of course. The battery commander will be decorated. It seems the safest thing to do."

"A nuisance, nevertheless," said Goering. A thought struck him.

"This B-17 . . . was it the one that . . .?"

Pertz nodded slowly.

"Then you'll be lucky to make the original date, never mind bring it forward," said Goering.

Pertz made no comment. He was not a man who wasted time on the obvious. Goering shuffled the papers in front of him.

"Well," he said, "we seem to be getting the agenda out of sequence."

He looked directly at the three young fighter colonels.

"*Oberst* Pertz," said Goering carefully, "has a report to make to me about certain operations of KG 200. These do not fall . . . within your sphere. So perhaps, gentlemen, if you would withdraw for a few minutes . . .?"

There was a scraping of chairs, three arms outstretched in salute, three clipped "Heil Hitlers", and the young colonels left the room. Goering looked at Pertz.

"Well?"

Pertz began to speak in his ponderous, rather pedantic way.

"There are three KG 200 operations on report, apart from *Ulysses*," he said. "First, Mosul."

"Operating from Simferopol?" said Goering.

Pertz nodded.

"Three aircraft of *Gruppe* 1 are ready," he said. "Two will take agents and the other carries the explosives and the money—£50,000 in British gold sovereigns. They always ask for gold, the Iraquis. The planes will be met by friends, at night."

"Where?" said Goering.

"About twenty miles north of Mosul, on the left bank of the Tigris. We had a report from Baghdad, its suitable for landing the planes we're using."

"What are those?" said Jeschonnek curiously.

"Soviet SB-RKs," said Pertz.

"Dive-bombers?" said Goering, surprised. "An odd choice."

Pertz shrugged.

"They're quite fast—nearly 300 miles an hour. Fairly short take-off and landing. They take two passengers in addition to the pilot. And best of all, we've got plenty of them—we picked up more than fifty in the first six weeks, in 1941. All standing on the airfields, not a scratch on the paint. They went straight into the aircraft booty-parks."

"So if we lose them?" said Goering thoughtfully.

"If we lose them," said Pertz, "we lose three pilots, four agents, and £50,000 in gold. But we don't lose precious aircraft that it's taken months to rebuild."

"Of course," said Jeschonnek to Goering, "they'll be bearing Soviet markings. Neither the Turks nor the British will be too quick on the trigger with a flight of Soviet bombers that may simply have read the map wrongly. The frontier's not far away."

"You're after the oil pipelines again?" said Goering.

"We plan four breaks," said Pertz, "all south of the Eski Mosul area. Well worth the effort. We're not short of friends in Iraq, even with Rashid Ali kicked out."

Goering grunted.

"The other operations?"

"Both training operations, for the moment. One's the Andromeda *Staffel*. I've sent you a copy of the order."

"The Andromeda *Staffel*, eh" said Goering. "That's what you decided to call it?"

"Yes," said Pertz primly.

For such an ordinary looking little man, thought Goering, Pertz had unexpected leanings towards the romantic where KG 200 was concerned. Andromeda . . . wasn't she the girl who was rescued by Theseus? Surely little Pertz didn't secretly fancy himself as Theseus? And he had a whole operation operating from Zilistea, in Rumania, all code-named after operas—Rigoletto, Traviata, the lot. Extraordinary . . .

"How long will it take to train the *Staffel*?" he asked.

"Six weeks," said Pertz. "But if necessary, we could be operational in four, and train the last two weeks at Smolensk."

Goering nodded.

"The other report," said Pertz, "is about a *Gruppe* 2 training operation . . . the *Selbstopfermänner*."

In spite of himself, Goering felt a superstitious prickle down his spine.

"The suicide boys?" he said. "The 5th *Staffel*?"

"The Leonidas *Staffel*," insisted Pertz. "We lost a man last week, with a Leonidas *Staffel* dummy glider-bomb. The problem is the angle of approach. They haven't solved the critical operational height to avoid the stall. He simply fell out of the sky, like a stone."

"Then he only anticipated it by a month or two," said Goering moodily. "The *Selbstopfermänner* are just human bombs."

"Human bombs that will sink battleships and take out bridges," said Jeschonnek sharply, "as soon as the aerodynamic problems are solved. The Japanese have their *kamikaze* pilots. Why not us? And don't forget—these *Selb-*

stopfermänner get anything they want—food, wine, girls, the lot. As a matter of fact, there's no shortage of volunteers."

"No doubt," said Goering.

"And, of course, above all," said Pertz, "there's *Ulysses*." Goering leaned forward eagerly.

"If we've reached the *Ulysses* part of the agenda now," said Jeschonnek, "then we should have the others in, because they're vital to the planning."

He crossed to the door and spoke to a warrant officer outside. A minute later, the three young fighter colonels trooped back into the room. Goering waited until they were seated, and then said:

"Thank you, gentlemen, for your patience. Now, Pertz, give us your report—your amended report, I suppose, in view of yesterday's unfortunate loss—on the operational state of *Fall Ulysses*."

Pertz spoke for twenty-one minutes. The young fighter commanders listened intently. Occasionally Goering made a note on a pad, but Jeschonnek, it seemed, was content to commit all to memory. At last Pertz finished.

"There must," he said, "be no mistakes. We in KG 200 will make none."

He looked directly at the three young colonels.

"I will remind you, gentlemen, that you are dealing with KG 200—the best pilots in the *Luftwaffe*."

One of the young *Obersts* began to bristle indignantly, but Goering interrupted him.

"Who went down yesterday?" he asked.

"Warnow," said Pertz. The young *Oberst* bit off his protest, and gave a low whistle. Goering looked at his watch.

"It's time for the morning operations conference," he said. "Let's go to see the *Führer* . . ."

5

"Where was it that B-17 came down last week?"

"At Mersea, General. On the east coast. Just about here . . ."

The finger of the young American staff officer prodded at the map. General Paul Hamel put on his spectacles, took a pair of dividers, and twirled them thoughtfully over the North Sea. Beside him Air Marshal Andrew Shevlin sat back. He had arrived a few minutes before Hamel, and had already been shown where the B-17 had probably flown from. On the other side of the table, a quiet, slightly-built man in a grey suit sorted abstractedly through a slim folder of papers. At last Hamel grunted and spoke again:

"What were the sightings?"

"The Royal Navy submarine *Ursa* logged him off the Horn Reef, flying pretty well due south."

"And that British destroyer?"

"The *Longbow*, General. She sighted the B-17 about thirty miles out from the English coast, flying on one engine, and on this bearing."

He drew a line on the map, and Hamel bent over it with his dividers. After a moment or two, he looked up again.

"Looks like he was flying a long dog-leg down from Norway, trying to tag on to our mission at Heligoland that day, and then flying back here with it. But where from in Norway? Sola, I suppose?"

"Surely, General. The times of the sightings sure fit. And Stavanger-Sola seems most likely, too. One of the British Mosquito boys got a couple of good obliques the other day. There's certainly one B-17 there. Look at this . . ."

The two general officers bent over the enormous air photograph prints pinned to the table.

"That looks like a second B-17, sir, in front of the hangar. See that shadow?"

"And that," said Shevlin grimly, pointing to another hangar, "looks suspiciously like the front of a Stirling."

Hamel rose and walked to the window. Through the criss-cross of tape which covered it as a protection against bomb-blast, he peered down at the Londoners hurrying across Oxford Circus in the rain. One or two of them, he noted absently, were still carrying, slung across their shoulders, the little cardboard cartons which held their civilian gas-masks.

He was standing in the room known to British and American intelligence—and to only a handful of other people in the world—as the Martian Room, situated incongruously on top of the Peter Robinson department store. The comings and goings here could be masked by the activity in the great shop below, with its staff lifts, back stairways, fire exits. This was vitally important. What was regularly discussed in this room was the coming launching of the liberation of Europe. But on this morning, that crucial day was still well ahead. Before it arrived, British, American and German blood would be spilled, mistakes would be made, lessons would have to be learned, tricks tried, stratagems defeated. The men who sat there today were concerned with the principal way in which Germany could be hammered in the meantime. That was from the air. And about the best way to do this, they differed fundamentally.

Shevlin, of the Royal Air Force Bomber Command, an officer of great experience, had served in the old Royal Flying Corps in the First World War, winning the prized Air Force Cross in 1918. Now, night after night, he sent out the streams of heavy bombers—four-engined Lancasters, Halifaxes, Stirlings—to pound the German industrial and communications centres. He believed passionately that night bombing, developed to a high point of professional expertise, could so slow and hamper the German war effort that it would shorten the war.

Hamel, of the United States Eighth Air Force, thought differently. The Eighth was now based in East Anglia, already considerable in strength, and growing steadily. Hamel was a day-bombing man. The Eighth flew the heavily-armed B-17 Flying Fortresses. He was convinced, as strongly as Shevlin was convinced about night bombing, that precision day-bombing was the ultimate weapon of the air war. Each side in this argument—an argument which, as it happened, ensured that the Germans would soon have to face sequences of twenty-four-hour aerial assaults—was, grudgingly, having to think again about its first hard position in the dispute. The Americans were finding that their losses grew as their penetration raids reached deeper into enemy territory, when the escorting Spitfires and Thunderbolts reached the end of their range and had to turn back, leaving the Fortresses to fly on alone. And Winston Churchill, who had backed Shevlin, was coming to see that precision day-bombing might have much more to offer than he had at first thought. As he stood at the Martian Room window, Hamel thought back to what Churchill had said a few weeks ago. Churchill had been blunt. Hardly an American bomb, he pointed out, had yet fallen on Germany proper. Surely it was time to switch these great American aircraft to reinforce the British night bombings? The Americans had argued, firmly and tenaciously, and they had won. For the moment, Churchill had been convinced, and President Roosevelt would not be asked to stop American day-bombing. But now they had to get results.

Hamel had already been handed the figures for the previous month, before he met Shevlin and the man in grey here today. Thoughtfully, he flicked them through his excellent memory, his eyes watchful through his spectacles. Mission 50: Antwerp; 104 aircraft despatched: 4 lost. Mission 51: Lorient and Brest; 108 aircraft: 4 lost. Mission 52: Bremen; 115 aircraft: 16 lost. Mission 53: St Nazaire; 102

aircraft: 7 lost. Thirty-one aircraft, most of them B-17s, lost between Mission 50 on April 4 and Mission 53 on May 1. It was a lot to pay for not very much activity . . . and what in hell had happened at Bremen? Sixteen gone from 115—that was about 15 per cent. At that rate he'd lose an entire bomber force every seven missions. Bremen . . . well, it had been good bombing weather, of course, and the *Luftwaffe* would know that as well as he would. But the 109s and the 190s had met them over the Frisian Islands. You'd think the bastards had got somebody radioing the position of the B-17s all the way across—directions, speed, and height. Well, had they? There'd been three—no, four—independent reports of two strange B-17s over the North Sea that day. The other crews thought they were planes aborting because of some malfunction. And it hadn't been possible, afterwards, to pinpoint just which planes they were. Understandable, perhaps. There were, after all, occasional crews who aborted a mission for, well, non-technical reasons. Wouldn't want to talk about it afterwards. But something had gone wrong at Bremen.

"Those Stavanger air photos," he said suddenly. "Was it a special job? I mean, do they know we're on to something? They'll sure have spotted that Mosquito on their radar."

"I don't think so," said Shevlin equably. "We included one photo-reconnaissance machine in a Mosquito squadron strike at shipping in Boknafjord. It only had to divert a couple of miles, and there were two strike planes with it. I don't imagine the Germans knew they were being photographed."

Hamel grinned.

"I can see only one valid reason for the Germans keeping those B-17s at Stavanger," said Shevlin. "They must be operational. I mean, they're not just evaluating them in the normal way. Why would they take them to Stavanger, if that was all they were doing? No, they'd keep them at Rechlin or Lerz, outside Berlin. That's where they've all the facilities for full technical analysis. Probably Lerz, because if I remember correctly, Rechlin's got grass runways, and it wouldn't be much fun putting down one of your Liberators, say, on grass, would it? We know they've had the odd captured plane there in the past. Obviously, they look them over—just as we do theirs at the Aerodynamics Flight at Farnborough. There was that FW-190 that landed by mistake at West Malling, for instance. But Stavanger's a different matter. And if they're operational, what for?"

"I agree," said Hamel. "About Stavanger, I mean. And we had an I-report on the day this B-17 crashed, about an unidentified B-17 that was seen by some of our crews on a mission over Heligoland. They said it tagged on to one of the rear boxes. Could be this one at Mersea."

"It was in trouble a long way out over the sea," said Shevlin. "If it was based in Germany or Norway, why didn't it turn back? Why fly to Britain to crash?"

"Well, it was hit by something," said Hamel. "We've plenty of witnesses to say it was burning when it crossed the coast. It could have been attacked by a German fighter, by mistake. If they're flying a B-17 for some kind of undercover purpose, that's the sort of thing that could happen, I guess. Or it could have had some steering trouble. There's not much left of it now—and only one body that's anything like a body. And the guy that's missing, of course. Both in American uniform, and neither of them Americans. There's only one thing certain about that ship. The last time it took off from England wasn't the day it came back to crash. It was just five months ago, and it didn't return. Until last week, that is."

"You mean, because of the serial numbers?" said Shevlin. He took a sheet of paper from his briefcase and looked at it.

"That's right," said Hamel. "There's not much left, but the serial number's still stamped on the port engine. It belongs to a ship from the 97th Bombardment Group. 'Pregnant Portia', she was called. You know the names the boys give these ships. Attacked the *Luftwaffe* airfield at Romilly-sur-Seine. We lost six that day. I guess this one force-landed and didn't burn."

Shevlin nodded.

"This is going to be difficult for you, Paul," he said.

"For us both," said Hamel. "Look at it this way. They've got one, maybe two, B-17s—and maybe more. They must have something really big going, putting these ships together again. Yours as well as ours. And that would explain some funny things that have been happening lately. We've had formations intercepted when they were well out of Freya range—the Bremen mission, for instance. That Freya radar's nothing like as good as your British stuff, anyway. We've had stragglers, B-17s, turn back, apparently 'escorted' by another B-17—and nothing seen of either of them again . . ."

"By God," said Shevlin, "it could be even worse at night. If they start tagging captured Stirlings on to our bomber streams, they'd be the best night fighters ever."

"Well, what do we know?" said Hamel. "We know a B-17 crashed at Mersea. We know it was a B-17 that didn't come back from a mission five months ago. We know it contained at least three men: we've got one unrecognisable body in the tail turret: one unrecognisable part of a body in the main fuselage: one intact body in the morgue at Mersea, carrying American identification papers, forged. We know that one of the crew, who claims to have been the pilot, walked away from the crash, showed the police and Home Guard forged papers, left—he says—for London, and vanished. We don't know what mission this B-17 was on, except that it *may* have been a B-17 that *may* have been shadowing our mission at Heligoland. Which, by the way, is in easy reach of Stavanger. We don't know why it crashed at Mersea. We need answers to a lot of questions."

The man in the grey suit stirred for the first time. He nodded to the American staff officer, who looked inquiringly at Hamel. Hamel nodded. The staff officer saluted and left the room.

"Questions and answers," said the man in the grey suit. "Those are my province."

The two air officers looked at him curiously. Each knew his name: neither would ever use it. He was the Director of the Twenty Committee, which was responsible only to the inner defence committee of the War Cabinet and to the Prime Minister and President themselves. It was this man and his committee who coordinated the activities of all Allied agents all over the world; who studied the activities of enemy agents in Britain; and who operated the growing system of double-agent—"spies" employed by the Germans who were in reality working for British Intelligence. On his committee sat the directors of MI5, responsible for security and counter-espionage, and of MI6, whose duties were espionage proper, and the obtaining of information by agents. These men were designated M and C respectively in the prevailing alphabetical code, but the man in grey was known by no such letter. He was referred to simply as "the Director". He possessed in certain matters, a priority which could override the very considerable powers of officers like the two who now listened to him. He was using the priority now.

"I agree," he said, "with the misgivings you've expressed this morning. As a matter of fact, there's some evidence that the nature of the enemy operation you speak of goes beyond even that of harassing your bomber formations. I think it is time we learned more of that operation. As you know, gentlemen"—he looked directly at Shevlin and Hamel —"in my Memorandum Number 18, I asked for two officers, one British, one American, to be seconded to me. And that is why I asked you to meet me here."

"Speaking for the Eighth Air Force," said Hamel, "we'll be happy to lend you any officer you need. Or more than one, if necessary." Shevlin nodded, and said thoughtfully:

"There's one thing that puzzles me. Your Memorandum 18 was dated nearly a week ago. We didn't get those obliques from Sola-Stavanger until the day before yesterday."

"A bonus, that crash," said the Director. We've thought for some time that something distinctly odd was going on. We've plenty of friends in Occupied Europe, but not many of them are technicians who understand what they see. However, General Hamel himself drew my attention to the interesting debriefing reports after the Bremen raid, in particular. And now come these pictures from Stavanger, after our attention is drawn there by the, er, arrival at Mersea of this B-17. Not my province, usually, but it ties up with other things that we don't yet understand enough about. However, now we've actually got a man, a face, somewhere in London. I'm happier dealing with men than with aeroplanes."

"Why are you so sure he's in London?" said Hamel. "I know he told that Home Guard it was where he was going, but . . ."

"He's in London," said the Director impassively. "And one way or another, he'll tell us what we want to know."

I'll bet he will, thought Shevlin.

"Meanwhile, gentlemen, I'd prefer that you took no action in this regard without informing me first."

He pressed the switch on the desk intercom, and said into it:

"Miss Bennett, ask the two officers to come in."

A moment later a grey-haired, middle-aged lady appeared at the door. Behind her stood two men, one wearing the blue-grey uniform of the RAF, the other the light khaki of the United States Army Air Force. She motioned them into the room. They saluted.

"Squadron Leader Croasdell," she said. "And Lieutenant-Colonel Eugene Vandamme."

6

"Both femurs extensively splintered, pelvis shattered, spleen ruptured, left kidney destroyed—probably punctured by part of a metal rod which we found bent upwards inside the chest cavity. Death was not due to these injuries, however, though he could not, in fact, have survived them for more than an hour. Death was due to a pistol shot at the back of the skull—fired, you can see—" he pulled aside the fair hair on the crown of Peter Behren's head—"at very close range. Look at that . . . extensive powder burning."

John Croasdell stared at the torn, frozen head for a moment or two, and then walked away from the table in the blue-lit morgue. Beside him, Eugene Vandamme swallowed and cleared his throat. Neither man was a stranger to the sight of death: already in this war each had seen things which would remain, more or less, at the back of his mind, for every remaining day that he would live. But there was a clinical professionalism about this police doctor that chilled the blood.

"He's interesting enough, isn't he?" said the doctor. "But I've got more here you should see. Look at this one." He pulled out a sheeted tray from the wall, and removed the covering.

"Not at her best, I'm afraid," he said apologetically. "She was only in the water twenty-four, perhaps thirty-six hours, but there's a lot of shingle on this coat, and she came in on a high tide. She was about forty-five years old."

Vandamme and Croasdell bent over the sheeted form, and turned away.

"Not many like this here," said the doctor. "They'd be a

lot more familiar with it in London and Birmingham, after the blitz."

"Familiar with what?" said Vandamme, reluctantly. What wouldn't he give right now for the biggest Martini in the history of the world.

"Blast," said the doctor. "She died from blast. Whole of the abdominal cavity is imploded, intestines turned inside out. No external injuries, though—it's a trick effect which happens surprisingly often. It's the difference in pressure between the point of an explosion and the air surrounding it. She was pretty close when whatever it was went off." He pulled the sheet a little lower.

"Both arms, both legs and spine broken, but after death, and not from blast. Typical of hitting water from a considerable height. She didn't drown. No water at all in the lungs."

"Any identification?" said Croasdell.

"None whatever," said the police doctor. "Of course, women carry that sort of thing in a handbag. And that didn't come ashore."

"Clothes?" said Vandamme.

"They're upstairs, but they aren't interesting. Chain store stuff, the sort of thing you'd expect. No mysterious foreign labels. The police have been over the whole lot, of course." He chuckled and pulled the sheet back over the body, pushing the tray back into the wall.

"We've got identification papers for this one," he said, jerking his thumb towards Behren's body. "I'm told you can take them away. But sign for them, of course. Name's Kelly. US Army Air Force. Douglas John Kelly. Or so"—he flicked them a shrewd, inquisitive glance—"it says."

A chilly wind blew down the long main street of Colchester as Croasdell and Vandamme went out and across to where the jeep was parked.

"Where now?" said Vandamme, and answered his own question. "To the scene of the crime, I guess." He was driving the jeep himself—"we'll do better not to have an enlisted man to keep checking on," he'd said, and Croasdell had agreed. They swung off along the Ipswich road, and after a mile or so turned off into the narrow lane which Warnow had smashed his way across in the last seconds of the B-17. They drove on to the rough grass of the field and got out. The deep, broad scar of broken turf and smashed saplings and flattened hedgerow stretched before them. The blackened wreck of the B-17 still lay at the edge of the far wood. It was guarded by men in khaki—British soldiers, Croasdell noticed, and not Home Guard, either. They wore the shoulder-flashes of a famous infantry regiment. The sergeant guard-commander would not accept their identification without further authority, and sent a lance-corporal to summon the officer from a tent. He came a few seconds later . . . a tall, fresh-faced captain with a single medal ribbon, who read their authorisations carefully, and at last nodded.

"Fine," he said. "My colonel was warned you might be coming today. There's been a team here from the RAF, as I imagine you know, but they swanned off about four days ago. Is there anything we can do to help? I don't know if you'd care for a spot of lunch after you've finished whatever it is you want to do? Just over there at my tent—not exactly the Ritz, but my driver fries a rather neat egg. Glad to have you, if you feel like a bite to eat . . ."

"Love to," said Croasdell politely.

"Is that boy real?" said Vandamme as they walked away.

"He's all right," said Croasdell. He felt strangely defensive. "He was wearing the Africa Star, so he must have been in the desert." Which, he thought to himself as they walked along, is more than you were, Colonel bloody Vandamme.

But even if he'd spoken his thoughts aloud, Vandamme wouldn't have heard. He was staring back along the field, a reluctant grin on his face.

"Christ," he said. "That bastard could fly. Look at it. There's hardly room to park a truck, but he brings a B-17 in over that hedge and she's stopped before she's got more than fifteen yards into those trees. I don't know how the hell he did it—and on one engine, if what they say is true.

He must have brought her in sideways. I did hear that Boeing has a guy in Seattle who claimed it was possible to do that—but he had about 2,000 hours on Forts, and I reckon he must have had a through line to God, as well. I'd sure like to ask this fella how the hell he managed it."

"He was lucky the nose-canopy came off, nevertheless," said Croasdell. Otherwise he'd have been down in the morgue with the other chap."

"Guess so," said Vandamme reflectively. "But we make our own luck in this game, some of the way, at least. Funny thing about the other guy, though. Shot . . ."

"Your wonder-pilot seems to have had a short way with a wounded friend, Colonel," said Croasdell drily.

"The kid was probably dying," said Vandamme. "And what's all this 'colonel' stuff? We can't go on calling each other 'colonel' and 'squadron leader'. I'm Gene."

"And I'm John," said Croasdell. They walked on towards the young captain's tent.

"You're right, though," said Vandamme. "It was a pretty tough thing to do. But you can see his position. He's here on some mission we don't know anything about. Wearing American uniform--so's the kid. The kid's got a goddamn hole in his chest you could put your head in, both legs smashed. If he leaves the kid, the poor bastard may talk. He may be delirious, frightened. Wonder-boy can't take a chance . . ."

With two fingers and a thumb, Vandamme pantomimed drawing a pistol.

"Bom, bom. Problem solved—and the kid's lost, what . . . maybe only a few hours of pain? A few hours not worth having."

"Would you have done it?" said Croasdell.

"Me?" Vandamme laughed uncertainly. "I guess I might . . . no, I guess I wouldn't."

"Nor would I," said Croasdell.

Both men had been cautious and wary with each other after their meeting at the Martian Room the previous day, but this brief discussion, curiously, seemed to relax them. They ate their bacon and eggs with the young infantry captain, and went down into Mersea to their second appointment of the day. This was at the police station.

The inspector carefully poured out the tea, brought in, Vandamme noted appreciatively, by a well-endowed young policewoman whom he'd like a chance to know better.

"Well, gentlemen," he said ruefully, "all I can tell you is that he fooled me. And he fooled Colonel Schofield as well—and though you might think different, the Colonel's a fly old bird. He sounded just like an American—not that I meet many"—he smiled at Vandamme—"but I do go to the films. He was pretty white and shaken up, of course, and he wouldn't have had to fake that. Colonel Schofield saw his papers and I got his name: 'Ralph Hadley, Captain'. It all seemed right—I mean, there it was, an American plane, American markings, the only survivor in American uniform and speaking like an American. Never as much as crossed my mind he might be something else."

"Not your fault, Inspector," said Croasdell. "As a matter of fact, he could probably have walked into an RAF officers' mess and been invited to stay for the night and given transport to wherever he wanted to go."

"That's so," said Vandamme. God the tea was terrible. Everybody knew the British couldn't make coffee, but you'd think by now they knew how to make tea.

"No, the only place he might have hit trouble was on a US air base," he said. "Not because we'd have been any more suspicious than you, Lieutenant—Inspector, I mean—but because he'd have had to be processed through our own routine, which might have caught him out. Although I'm not one hundred per cent sure about that. This guy was really well briefed.

Croasdell drank his tea, and with an effort, didn't make a face. Ugh . . . condensed milk, and in dairy-farming Essex, of all places. The inspector probably thought it would be a wartime treat.

"What did he look like?" he asked the inspector.

"About the same height as you and the Colonel," said the inspector. "Say five foot ten, or eleven. He was fairer than the Colonel here, about like you, sir. Well set-up sort of chap. Nothing very remarkable about him, but he seemed very tense. I don't mean nerves . . . I mean he was tense like a . . . well, like a spring's tense. As though he was waiting to do something. To jump, for instance."

"To jump?" asked Vandamme.

"I can't put it better than that," said the inspector. "It was just a feeling I had . . . that he was sort of coiled up inside."

He drank his tea, smacked his lips appreciatively, and said briskly:

"Well, gentlemen, I deal with evidence, not with vague feeling. And talking of jumping, I've got some evidence to show you."

He led the way out of the room, and down a flight of worn stone steps to the basement. There he carefully unlocked a door, and motioned them into a dark, cold room. It contained only two trestle tables, on one of which were stretched a number of long pieces of plywood, splintered and broken, but glistening with bright grains of salt.

"Yes," said the inspector, in answer to Croasdell's inquiring look, "It's been in the sea. We picked it off the shingle, about a quarter of a mile down the beach from where that dead woman came ashore. Know what it is?"

The two men shook their heads.

"It is," said the inspector triumphantly, "what's left of a . . . a . . ."—he pronounced the German word stumblingly—"a *Personenabwurfgerat*." He was reading the name from a small buff-covered pamphlet he had taken from his pocket. The cover was, Croasdell noted, stamped "Restricted".

"What in hell is that then?" said Vandamme.

"A person-container," said the inspector. "According to this, it can hold up to three people, it's one metre wide and two long, it had four parachutes, and falls at four metres a second. I must say, I wouldn't fancy trying it myself. I've never seen one before, though all the police on the coast—and the coastguard, as well—get these books that tell them what to look out for. The Jerries are supposed to use them for dropping agents—but, as I say, I've not seen one before."

"You mean that woman in the morgue came in that?" said Vandamme incredulously. "In the B-17 and all? Was there any parachute on this box?"

"No parachute," said the inspector, "but look at this." He pointed to where short slashed cords projected from the thin metal ribbing of the cage. "There were rigging lines, but they were cut. Look here, and here. He dropped the thing out at sea, before he crashed. Cut her loose, like. Probably hoped she'd sink. But she didn't."

"Jesus wept," said Vandamme. "Four parachutes and a plywood coffin . . ." He shuddered.

"You can see why they use them, though," said Croasdell thoughtfully. "You know what it's like when two or three people bale out of a plane. They land maybe miles apart. If there are two or three agents, it's probably important for them all to land together, and not to have to look for each other afterwards. So they use these things."

Vandamme tugged idly at a shorn rigging line. "Then wonder-boy was coming in on a wing and prayer, and didn't want the lady—according to that doctor, she was already dead—to be found in the wreck. So he pushed her out—a bit too near the coast."

"He probably had plenty to think about," said Croasdell, smiling. "But one thing's obvious. He must have been carrying more than one agent . . . they wouldn't use one of those *personen* what's-its just for one woman. So presumably, there are one or two others floating around. They must have gone out with her, because there were no other survivors from the crash. And the only other body—if you can call it that—was in the tail-turret. Apart from the boy in the morgue, that is. I know he was flying on a reduced crew, but he'd hardly have put an agent in the tail-turret."

"I guess not," said Vandamme.

An hour later, driving back to London in the jeep, Vandamme said reflectively: "You know, John, this whole set-up just doesn't add up."

"What do you mean?" said Croasdell. He was half asleep, huddled in a sheepskin-lined flying jacket, hunched against the cold wind whistling in through the draughty jeep-hood. As a rule, like many drivers, he disliked being driven, but he'd watched Vandamme carefully for the first fifty miles down to Mersea the previous day, and knew he could relax.

"Well, what the hell are we supposed to achieve? We come down here, and all we're finding out is what your police already know—and what anybody who can add two and two could put together. We're no nearer finding wonder-boy, and how can we be? Because he's in London, for sure, and there's no way you and I are going to spot him. We wouldn't know him if he stood next to us in a bar. So there must be something more to it than we've been told so far. I mean, you take two good men from special duties—"

"I'm attached to RAF Intelligence," said Croasdell. "Not the cloak and dagger stuff, I hasten to add, though I got the usual basic training. I've been working between Fighter and Bomber Command, on the link staff—specialist in Intelligence Collection and Action Operations. We try to provide all the necessary gen for the planners. I suppose you've got a set-up like that in your lot?"

"That's so," said Vandamme, grinning. "Meet an Assessment and Evaluation Officer, US Army Air Force. Me. I suppose we're in the same game. Though you weren't always collecting facts for planners, were you, John. You didn't get that—" he pointed to the purple and white ribbon of the Distinguished Flying Cross on Croasdell's tunic—"for collecting facts. Battle of Britain, I was told. Eight kills, all 109s."

"How did you know that?" said Croasdell, quietly.

"Oh, at Command they gave me a paper with it all on. I

know a lot about you . . ." Everything, he thought, except why a first-class fighter pilot was taken off combat flying.

"I got a paper, too," said Croasdell. "So I know that you came over from combat duty in Luzon, a few months ago. What was it—you shot down eleven altogether, in one year . . . ten Zeros and a Jap bomber?"

"About it," said Vandamme. "So what's it all about? You heard what Paul C. Hamel said? 'What you want for this mission, you get.' Paul C. Hamel doesn't throw words like that around easily. And neither, I guess, does your guy Shevlin."

"You were on long-distance flying before the war, weren't you?" said Croasdell.

"Yeah," said the other. "Trans-Arctic, 1937. Florida–Madagascar—that was a joint mission with the French Navy—1938. And the second Pan-America flight. That kind of thing. You, too?"

"I had a go at the British–Australia record, Mildenhall to Melbourne—in 1938," said Croasdell. "I had to put down in the Timor Sea. Wasn't doing too badly until then. And later I had a spell with Imperial Airways, London to Delhi."

"I guess we're both a bit on the old side for fighter pilots," said Vandamme. "I'm twenty-seven, and I see from my paper"—he grinned disarmingly, and Croasdell found, almost reluctantly, that he was beginning to like him—"that you are, as well. About the age when your reactions start to slow down."

My God, my reactions went to the cleaners a year ago, thought Croasdell. It came back, as it always did, as the road unwound in front of the jeep in the evening light. He saw the 109 jinking in front of him, bits flying off it, staggering into its final stall, yellow nose high, before it spun away in a trail of smoke and flame down to the waiting sea.

And then the wing of the Spit, weakened at the roots where the 109 had caught him with that first burst, sheered clean off, changing what a moment before was a formidable fighting machine into a helpless tangle of perspex and aluminium and steel, falling like a dead bird. It had taken him twenty precious seconds to free the jammed cockpit hood, and when he had got out, his leg had been trapped against it. Turning over and over, held on the back of the Spitfire like a rag doll, hammered by the icy wind, he had lost consciousness, only to wake as he plunged the last 5,000 of his 30,000-foot dive to the sea. He had panicked instantly, he thought, and had been within an ace of punching the quick-release button which would have shot the parachute from his shoulders and left him to fall to death. But at the last second he had found the ripcord. The next time he'd opened his eyes, he was in hospital, and Joanna had been there. She told him later that the Air-Sea Rescue boys had reached him in forty minutes, but he could remember nothing of that. He put his hand up to his face. All that was left of that little incident now was the four-inch scar on his left cheekbone, where the hood had carved into him as he dropped, finally, clear. That . . . and whatever it was that had happened to his fighting abilities. But nobody knew about that. Or did they? He'd been in hospital for six weeks, and then he'd been posted to Intelligence. Oh, it was interesting work—fascinating, sometimes. Some of the basic training—though it had been carefully explained to him that he wasn't likely to have to use it—had been a revelation. But it wasn't like being on ops.

The jeep slipped swiftly through the flat countryside as the late spring dusk deepened into darkness. There was little traffic on the road—an occasional convoy of big American trucks or British military three-tonners, shepherded by a couple of motor-cycle despatch riders, and more and more often as they approached London, a few private cars. These were rare . . . with only a handful of rationed gallons, few Englishmen took their cars out unless they had to. And driving at night was not popular, along roads where the blackout against enemy bombing had switched off every street lamp.

"Not long now," said Vandamme. "God, I'd like a steak.

They might have some at the Kittyhawk Club—they get stuff in from the States. Not much, but we might get lucky."

"I've got a better idea," said Croasdell. "What time do we see the man in grey tomorrow . . . noon, isn't it?"

"That's right," said Vandamme. He grinned to himself. They were both a bit self-conscious about the Man in Grey, as they'd decided to call him.

"Well, look," said Croasdell. "My home's near Chelmsford—it's only just up the road from here. We've got a spare room and Joanna—my wife—will give us a meal. An omelette, if nothing else—we've got some hens."

"Seems rough on the lady, turning up with a hungry stranger," said Vandamme.

"Nonsense, she doesn't see nearly enough people. She works at the local hospital—radiographer. You know . . . X-rays. That's where we met, as a matter of fact. She'd love to meet you. And we could go on to London tomorrow. We'll probably get a quieter night, with no air raid warnings." And, he thought happily, I just want to see Joanna again, even if it's only for a few hours. It had been three weeks since the last time, three weeks too long.

"We-e-ell," said Vandamme, "I guess you've twisted my arm. And I do happen to have a couple of tins of Spam in the back."

"Just the job. Spam omelette. Who could ask for anything more?"

The Croasdell house was really a cottage, single-storied, with a long, low living-room and two bedrooms opening off it. It was dark when they arrived, and only the faint chinks of light from behind the blackout at the door and windows announced that anyone was home. Croasdell rang the bell, and a few moments later the door opened. The dark outline of a woman stood there, silhouetted against the low lights in the little hallway.

"Who is it?" she said inquiringly, and then, "John, darling. Why didn't you tell me? Oh, darling . . ."

"Just an impulse to see my woman," said Croasdell, his mouth deep in her hair.

"Well, if you don't shut the front door," she said, wriggling in his arms but without much conviction, "the air raid warden will have an impulse to come round here and get me fined ten bob—no, please, John, I must—oh!" She saw, for the first time, Vandamme standing behind Croasdell. Quickly he turned and shut the door.

"Sorry, ma'am," he said. "My fault, I guess. I haven't been over here long, and I just haven't gotten used to the blackout yet."

"Darling, this is Gene Vandamme. I've asked him to stay here tonight. I said you'd knock us up a meal. Gene, this is my wife, Joanna."

She held out her hand. Hers was cool and firm. As she moved into the brighter light of the living-room, he saw that she was tall and slim, but with the kind of hips that would one day give John Croasdell a fair clutch of kids, and a lot of fun getting them. Her hair was brown, long, straight, curled under at the ends in the fashion called the page-boy bob. Her face was narrow and intelligent, and her eyes were grey. Eugene Vandamme looked at her, and for the first time began to think there must be more to John Croasdell than appeared on the surface.

"It'll have to be omelettes," she was saying. "We've got heaps of eggs, because all the hens have got spring in the blood or something. And I think I've got a bit of last week's cheese ration left."

"Gene," said Croasdell smugly, "has got Spam."

"Spam omelettes," said Joanna Croasdell.

"Who," said Gene Vandamme, looking at Croasdell and grinning, "could ask for anything more?"

They ate at a small table at the end of the living-room. Afterwards they tossed a coin to decide who would have the first bath. John Croasdell called correctly, and vanished into the bathroom.

"Never toss a coin with John," said Joanna, as Vandamme followed her into the little kitchen and picked up a towel to help her wash the dishes. "He practically always wins. If he calls, that is. I think he's got second sight or something."

"What makes you think I've lost?" said Vandamme as he joined her at the sink. She laughed.

"Well, it seems a bit much, persuading you to come here, and then sticking you with the washing-up."

"I'll never need persuading again, ma'am," said Vandamme. "And if you smile like that just once more you could persuade me to rejoin the British Empire."

"Kindly stop making love to my wife and go and have your bath, Gene," said Croasdell from the kitchen door. "She's just a simple country girl and I don't want her head turned by your fine Southern manners."

The girl was looking from one to the other, laughing.

"Story of my life," said Gene heavily. "After twenty-seven years, I meet a woman who just might understand me, and her husband tells me to go take a bath. And in any case, I come from Westport, Connecticut, not the South."

"I thought that *was* the South," said Croasdell. "Go on—hurry up, and I'll give you a game of chess. You do play chess in America, don't you? Good. There's a pair of pyjamas in the wardrobe in your room—we're about the same size. You can wear those if you like—but there's only one dressing-gown. The one I'm wearing. The living-room's quite warm, though."

"My," said Joanna. "*Two* men in pyjamas. I hope to heaven the air raid warden doesn't come round."

7

Lieutenant Robert Turner, mission navigator on Animal Crackers, a Consolidated Liberator B-24 that had taken off from Polebrook in East Anglia and was now lying in three smashed, smouldering sections at the edge of a wood outside Mannheim, was trying to stop his hands shaking. He looked round the tram as it rattled over the rails outside Frankfurt's main station. Opposite him his guard, a *Luftwaffe* corporal, kept one hand on the sling of the Schmeisser machine-pistol which hung from his shoulder, and watched him carefully but impassively. There was a muted curiosity from the handful of German civilians in the rear compartment of the lurching tram. The older ones stared at him directly, and a couple of girls clutched each other and giggled.

The reaction to what had happened in the last few hours was coming on him quickly now: he felt tired and weak and very lonely. He was pretty sure he was the only one who'd got out of Animal Crackers after the ME-110 had got her, in the last thirty seconds of the bomb run. So Ed and Jerry and Captain Villafranca and Sergeant Werth and the others were all gone. Just him left . . . to be picked up in the wood, still tangled in his 'chute, by a couple of middle-aged *Volkssturm* who hadn't been bad guys, considering that a few minutes before he'd been trying to bomb hell out of their town. There'd been an hour in the village police headquarters, followed by the arrival of the guard, and then the train—two wearying hours of that slow, dusty train—to Frankfurt. Nobody had asked him more than his rank, name and number. Not, he reminded himself firmly, that he was going to tell them one thing more. He was going to play it by the book. Name, rank and number were all that international law required, and that was all the Germans were going to get. Lieutenant Robert Turner was just twenty-two years old, but he had grown up ten years in the last four months.

The tram rolled over a clutch of points. Why are they taking me round in a tram? he wondered, and smiled weakly. It was quite a change, from Animal Crackers boring in over Mannheim at 20,000 feet, to this dirty brown box on rails outside Frankfurt. Why not a truck, though, to take him out to the transit camp, or wherever he was being taken? He looked over his shoulder, lifted his hand, and rubbed a clear patch of the steamed window. His guard stirred abruptly, leaned forward, but then sat back and said nothing. Turner peered out. It was late afternoon, about the time that the shops and offices would be closing back in England. Not many cars about here, though . . . not many vehicles at all. That probably explains the tram, he thought. They're short of petrol. None to waste on carting prisoners to camps.

The tram stopped. The guard grunted something in German, and motioned to Turner to get out. It was a coldish evening, with a little rain in the wind. Turner looked around him. The metal tram-stop sign was swinging slightly in the breeze. It said, in chipped black letters on dirty white tin: "*Kupferhammer.*" The guard spoke: "*Wir fahren am Dulag Luft.*" He looked at his wrist watch. "*Svantzig minuten . . .*"

Turner spoke no German, but he caught the words "*Dulag Luft*". Eliades, the group intelligence officer, has lectured them about *Dulag Luft*—the clearing centre for captured Allied airmen. Once more, Lieutenant Robert Turner felt very lonely. He compressed his lips into a thin line. He'd hoped he'd never see this place, but here he was. And he was luckier than Ed and Jerry, and Captain Villafranca, at that.

They walked along a dreary high-walled road, out beyond the tramlines into a territory of scattered small warehouses and drab shops, before—twenty minutes later—they came up to the grey-green gate, fringed with barbed wire, of *Dulag Luft*. The guard felt in his damp greatcoat, drew out a bundle of papers, and formally handed over Turner to the *Luftwaffe* guardroom just inside the entrance. A small, blunt-nosed *Kübelwagen* came out a few minutes later, and a bored *Luftwaffe* corporal took Turner to a wooden hut beside the main brick building. From somewhere beyond the bare room where they now stood, came the sound of running water. After a few moments, an irritable man in a white coat appeared, and made impatient signs for Turner to strip. The doctor—as Turner assumed him to be—gave him a cursory medical examination, noted the slight shake in the hands, and said something sharply to the corporal. The man went out and returned a moment later with a glass of water and two white tablets. The doctor put them on the bare wooden table and pointed to them. Turner looked at them suspiciously. The doctor smiled.

"No, no," he said, in heavily accented English. "Not worry. Is aspirin."

Doubtfully, Turner picked up a tablet and nibbled it. It *was* aspirin. His clothes, he noted, had vanished. The *Gefreiter* gave him a coarse cotton nightshirt. The doctor went out of the room, and the *Gefreiter* took him down a long passage lit by bare, low-powered bulbs. There seemed to be rooms on either side, though he could hear no sounds from them. Halfway down the passage, the corporal unlocked a door, and motioned him inside. Then the door shut, and the key turned. He looked around. It was a bare, small cell, perhaps seven feet by nine. There was a single trestle bed in the corner, and a single coarse black blanket on it. Beside the bed was a chamber pot. Nothing else . . . no brush, no comb, no wash-basin, no razor, no book, no chair, no table. Wearily, Turner lay down on the bed. It wasn't cold in the cell—in fact, the whole block seemed rather stuffy. The nightshirt scratched his neck. He felt hungry and a little thirsty, though he'd taken the chance to drink all the water that came with the aspirin. How long, he thought, as he lay back on the hard mattress and closed his eyes, was he going to be kept in this dump? And when would he get back his clothes? They were searching them, he supposed. He smiled grimly. Let them search. There was nothing to find. He'd always obeyed strictly the orders that forbade the carrying of any kind of classified material on missions over enemy territory. There was nothing in his clothes that would be the slightest use to the enemy.

"Well, what have we got?" said *Hauptmann* Franz Weber, sorting through the pile of objects in front of him. "A surprising amount, by the look of things. Nothing classified, though. He's a good young man, this one . . . obeys orders, doesn't talk. Like you, eh, *Oberleutnant*?"

The small, dapper KG 200 officer seated beside him grinned.

"I hope so, sir," he said. "Though if we get captured . . . well . . ."

"Then you have to rely on what you've been told by people like me, don't you?" said Weber jovially. "Just look at this lot. You can learn a lot from this . . ."

He picked up a small passport-sized photograph. The face of Lieutenant Robert Turner looked out from it, unsmiling.

"They carry these so they can use them in false papers—to give them a chance to get away if they're not picked up as soon as they're shot down. The various Resistance movements have channels through which they're passed over neutral borders. They tell you a bit, the photographs themselves."

He flicked through a file index and drew out a card of photographs.

"Here you are . . . see that? There's a mark on the wall behind his head. Now that's a photograph taken for the 997th Bomb Group. They're based at Polebrook. And that's where this *Leutnant* Turner's picture was taken, too. There's the very same mark. He can go on saying rank, name and number as long as he likes, but it's a seat at the opera to a *Pfennig* that he's from the 997th. And he's just back off leave. Look at this . . .'

Weber picked up two small purple tickets—torn halves.

"Cinema seats . . . the Plaza, in Piccadilly in London. Last week—they were showing, let me see . . ." He crossed the room and leafed through a file of British newspapers.

"Here we are . . . Cary Grant, in 'Arsenic and Old Lace'. I expect *Leutnant* Turner took a girl—look at them, they're half-crown seats. Expensive. May have been this girl."

He passed a picture of a smiling brunette to the KG 200 *Oberleutnant*.

"Not bad, not bad," said the *Oberleutnant* admiringly. "I really don't think she's a Polebrook girl, though. Londoner, I'd say."

"How's that?" said Weber sharply.

"Look at the background. That's a London square, you can't mistake it. I'll bet she lives there. If she was a visitor, she'd get her picture taken outside Parliament or Buckingham Palace or somewhere a bit more obvious."

"Well, well," said the other slowly. "You're learning. What's her name . . .?"

The other turned the photo over.

" 'Love and kisses from Kay to darling Bob.' Very nice, too."

"Those tickets were dated last Friday, weren't they? Here you are, here's another bill, to go with them. Lunch for two, the Trocadero. No wonder the girls like these Americans. Dover sole, a half-bottle of good German hock—a bit of pre-war stock, I suppose. Eighteen shillings the lot . . . he's got plenty of money to spend. Interesting, that . . . the price of that hock has gone up in the last three months. We found another bill from an American in February—also the Trocadero. It was only four shilling a half-bottle then. That might be worth knowing, some time. But the real goodie here is the letter. Have you read it?"

"Not yet," said the *Oberleutnant*.

"It's from his mother, in Hartford, Connecticut. All about somebody called Ezra Pramm, who's running for Selectman —that's like one of our burgomaster's councils over there. She says this Pramm is very unpopular because he opposed some road widening scheme that some of them have set their hearts on. Apparently he's going to be reported to the State Governor. That could be really excellent background information for your lot, *Oberleutnant*."

"I agree," said the KG 200 man.

"There's nothing specifically military, though," said Weber. "Look at the *Sonderführer*'s interrogation report. He tried all the traditional stuff . . . woke him from a deep sleep . . . threatened him with continued solitary confinement, kept him dirty and unshaved. It didn't work. Look at the answers, over and over again. 'My name is Robert Burr Turner. My number is 312856. My rank is lieutenant.' I tell you, he's a good boy, this one. I think we'll take him out to lunch. And we'll put on a little performance for his benefit, first."

"Take him out to lunch?" said the *Oberleutnant*. "You aren't serious?"

"Never been more so," said Weber affably. "You see, my dear fellow, a man like this Turner can steel himself against bullying and harsh treatment. But there's one thing that a naturally nice boy is helpless against, in these circumstances."

"What's that?" said the *Oberleutnant*, curiously.

"Kindness," said Weber, and chuckled.

He'd told them nothing. Nothing at all. Lieutenant Robert Turner felt dirty, hungry, lonely, tired but proud. It would take, he thought, more than a jumped-up *Luftwaffe Sonderführer* to get anything out of an officer from the 997th. There were footsteps outside. Oh, God, here he was again, with the little buff form with all the not-to-be-answered questions on it—what type do you fly? Where are you based? Where were you trained? When were you commissioned? Who is your commanding officer? How long had you been in England? He'd got to go through all that again: "My name is Robert Burr Turner. My number is 312856. My rank lieutenant." He stood up stiffly, rubbing his hand over the thick stubble on his chin. The door opened, and the bespectacled *Sonderführer* stood there, carrying his inevitable clip-board. This time, however, he was not alone. Behind him stood two officers. Wearily Turner tried to remember the rank insignias he'd been taught at Intelligence lectures during basic training. Both, he saw, were *Luftwaffe* officers—one a *Hauptmann*, a captain, one an *Oberleutnant*, about the same rank as himself. Each wore the Iron Cross. The *Hauptmann* was staring at him incredulously. He swung furiously on the *Sonderführer*.

"What is the meaning of this?"

The man stammered nervously.

"I beg your pardon, *Herr Hauptmann*?"

"This, of course."

The *Hauptmann* pointed to Turner.

"Why is this officer in this condition?"

He looked round the cell, at the filled chamberpot standing beside the bed, and his nose wrinkled in distaste.

"Has this officer been given no washing or other sanitary facilities?"

"No, *Herr Hauptmann*."

"Why not?"

"Orders, *Herr Hauptmann*."

"Whose orders?"

"*Oberleutnant* Geiger's orders, sir."

"They are countermanded. See that the officer gets a bath, at once, and a shave. And what's this?"

Weber crossed to the side of the bed, where a tin mug and plate lay beside the floor. Delicately he picked them up. A few crumbs of coarse black bread remained on the plate, a few drops of *ersatz* coffee in the mug.

"What is that?" he repeated.

"His breakfast, sir."

"Indeed?"

The *Hauptmann* turned to Robert Turner and said in excellent English.

"I must express my regret to you, lieutenant, for the discourteous way you have been treated. No one, I hope"—he hesitated for a moment—"has offered you any physical ill-treatment?"

"No," said Turner slowly.

"Well, that is something good, at any rate. You must be longing for a bath. Please take one now. And after that muck"—he pointed disdainfully to the mug and plate—"you must be hungry. Perhaps you would give *Oberleutnant* Lange"—the second man formally clicked his heels—"and me the pleasure of lunching with us? I think we can promise you something better than this. We are like you, in one respect, at any rate. We are fliers, too. We are all fliers."

"Well . . ." said Turner, doubtfully.

"Good," said the *Hauptmann.* "That's settled then."

He turned to the *Sonderführer*.

"See the Lieutenant Turner is escorted to the officers' mess in one hour's time. Is his uniform pressed?"

"I do not think—" said the *Sonderführer*.

"See that it's pressed," said Weber. "While he's taking his bath."

Four hours later, the KG 200 *Oberleutnant* sat once more opposite Weber in the latter's small office at *Dulag Luft*. Weber was pleased.

"Not an easy boy to get anything out of, that American, was he? But we managed it."

"You mean, you succeeded?" said the *Oberleutnant* admiringly. "I was told you people here were good, but I'd never have believed just how good you are. There's a lot more to these Enemy Familiarisation courses than I'd dreamed. I'll never forget *Leutnant* Turner's face when you asked him if Kay had enjoyed 'Arsenic and Old Lace', and if she appreciated that the Trocadero was charging more for hock now than it was a month or two ago."

"He'd probably forgotten he'd even got those bits and pieces in his pocket," said Weber. "That's the first rule, of course . . . make 'em think you know everything, and then they don't feel guilty if they talk a bit. Well, let's go through it. What did we get?"

"Quite a bit of slang," said the *Oberleutnant*. "Very much the sort of thing we want. You noticed he called the Trocadero 'the Troc'. I hadn't heard that before. And that other expression . . . 'couldn't care less'. That's a new one, too. And a certain amount of administrative stuff . . . they get a weekend pass every week unless they're on operations. That's worth knowing."

"Did you notice that when I was praising the B-17," said Weber, "he suddenly, just once, said something, only a word or two really, about B-24s. I don't think he even knew he'd said it—nothing like a couple of glasses of good wine on an empty stomach to numb the memory a bit, eh? And the meal *was* rather a long time coming, wasn't it?"

"It was," said the *Oberleutnant*, and grinned.

"The trouble was," said Weber, "that I didn't quite catch what he said, and I didn't want to ask him because it might have frightened him off altogether. But I'm just wondering if they're moving a B-24 wing to Polebrook."

"It could be," said the other, dubiously. "But it's not much to go on."

"Still, it's something we could put to the next man we talk to," said Weber.

"Well, I must say, I learned a lot," said the *Oberleutnant*. "He had a way of standing, with his thumbs in his belt, that looked like some kind of private unit posture. And a special salute, that curved right away down his nose. I've been practising it, in the bathroom. Very dashing. And a thirty-mission hat."

"With a slit in the peak, you mean? That's not new, of course. All the 997th people have done that for months."

"Worth knowing that they're still doing it, though," said the *Oberleutnant.* "It's just the kind of detail that makes somebody look at you hard if you slip up and get it wrong."

Weber looked at him thoughtfully.

"Well, I won't ask why you need all this stuff. You're the twentieth officer from your *Geschwader* I've put through the EF course here, and I've always believed it better not to ask. Quite apart from the fact that it's orders."

The *Oberleutnant* looked up, his face suddenly expressionless.

"You are absolutely right, *Herr Hauptmann.* It is better not to ask."

And he grinned once more.

Two hundred yards away, back in his cell, Lieutenant Robert Burr Turner lay on his bed and smoked one of the cigarettes that the German *hauptmann* had given him. Not a bad guy, he thought. And the other one, too. And what good English they spoke—especially the young *Oberleutnant*. Of course, he'd been to Princeton, which no doubt helped. He thought back to his own career at Cornell. Hell, it was a funny kind of war. One Ivy League guy fighting another. But it had been a good meal, he'd got clean white sheets on his bed, and he'd been promised soap and a razor and hot water every morning until he left for prison camp. And there was one thing he was sure of. They'd learned nothing from him. Absolutely nothing . . .

8

"If you keep moving that blackout curtain," said Hannah Walters, "we'll have an air-raid warden round here, *Herr Major*. And that's something we don't want."

If he prowls round this flat once more, she thought, I shall scream. God knows, I've lived on my nerves for the past four years, but I've done it alone. Living on my own nerves is bad enough, but sharing somebody else's nerves as well is quite impossible.

"You're right," said Warnow wearily. He came back from the window, and flopped into her only armchair. "But I've told you not to call me 'Herr Major'. We're not on parade. And in any case, someone might hear. Call me Rolf. It's my name, and it sounds like Ralph, in any case. That's why they chose it."

"I thought you were always on parade . . . Rolf," said the girl slyly.

"Not in this damned country," said Rolf Warnow. "Though, please God, one day I will be."

"You can't really believe that," said the girl incredulously. "Not that Germany will win? Don't you know what is happening? Africa, the Eastern Front. There isn't going to be any victory for Germany, not this year, next year or any other year. There might still be a peace, a peace that we could—just—accept. But no more than that, now."

"If the facts are treason," said Warnow impassively, "then I do not deal with the facts. And in any case, what about you? You are—there was the slightest tinge of admiration in his voice—"a brave woman. Why, then, do you serve? What do you hope for?"

"I serve because I must," said Hannah Walters slowly. And oh, Herr Major, she thought, if only you knew what "serving" means, and what "must" means. "And I hope, for nothing."

"Well, I hope," said Warnow, "to be Rolf Warnow once more. To fly an aircraft into attack once more. And, if I am lucky to meet the *Führer* again. You have, perhaps, met the *Führer*, Hannah?"

Slowly she shook her head.

"He is," said Warnow simply, "the greatest man in the world. Far-seeing, unconquerable. No man can be more than that."

"I suppose not," said Hannah Walters. I know what I want, and what I shall never get again, she thought. I want to be Hanna Rutenberg again, not Hannah Walters. I want to go back to where we used to live, under the lines in that house in Dresden. I want to be loved again by Papa and Mutti, marry a nice Dresdener, maybe have not-very-good sex and four sons and a daughter. But Papa and Mutti are dead, and all the young Dresdeners are dying on the Eastern Front, and all the ideals I fought for are yellow at the edges, and the situation I'm in now is one I'll never get out of. Well, there is one chance, she thought. But it wasn't one that Rolf Warnow could be expected to understand.

"When did you tell them?" he was asking. He knew the answer well enough, but she gave it, patiently again.

"Two days ago, on the regular broadcast. And I'll get their answer tonight. We can't break the routine, even for you."

"It's important," he said. "It's more important than you realise. I must get back. I must."

"That will be up to them," said Hannah Walters. And, she thought, to me, perhaps.

"What time?" he said impatiently. She looked at him in surprise.

"The broadcast, I mean. What time is it on?"

"Oh, I see. Radio Hamburg, nine o'clock. The code word for Yes is Goethe. The one for No is Shakespeare."

"Isn't it a risk, listening to Hamburg?"

"None at all. You can't hear the radio outside this room, if it's turned reasonably low, and in any case, a lot of people here listen to the man in Hamburg. Lord Haw-Haw, they call him. It isn't even prohibited to listen."

"You mean . . .?"

Hannah Walters laughed, and went over to the mirror, picked up a brush, and began to brush her blonde curls.

"No, Rolf, they're not getting ready to rise against Churchill. Most of them listen to laugh. They joke about it when they drink in the pubs."

"I see," he said.

No, you don't see, she thought. You're the kind that will never see anything except what you want to see. She was still smiling at this when she felt his hands grasp her waist and slide up to her breasts. His mouth rasped the back of her neck. He took her so completely by surprise that for a moment she didn't move as he pulled her back against him, his hand at the buttons of her dress.

"I want you," he said, from behind her head, "now."

Her dress was half off already. She pushed at him furiously with closed fists. His other hand was down between her thighs, pulling at her suspender belt.

"What do you think you're doing, you fool? Get your hands away. You're not flying one of your bombers."

He was bending her back across the bed in the corner of the room, and now her dress was up round her neck, and he was snatching at it with his right hand. His fingers grasped her painfully. Damn him, he was tearing her dress.

"Look out, clothes cost coupons here, and I can't get any more for a month. Are you mad?"

Maybe she was herself, she thought almost hysterically, worrying about coupons in the middle of a rape.

His knee was forcing open her legs, and the muscular weight of him was bearing her down. She began, belatedly, to try to reason with him, but his mouth came down on hers while he pulled at her clothes, and she could not speak. At last he took his lips away. His trousers were unbuttoned now, and she knew she couldn't hold out much longer.

"If you don't get off me . . . I'll scream."

"You won't," he said hoarsely.

It was too late, anyway. He was pinning her like a struggling butterfly to the bed. Somehow, there seemed to be none of her left . . . She was all Warnow, piercing, heaving, straining, gasping. God, he was hurting. I'm a long way from being a virgin, she thought dazedly, but I never thought it could be as bad as this. She clutched his shoulders, more to save herself pain than anything else, and he sawed away above her until he was finished. Then he pulled away and lay with her in his arms, his face damp with sweat. Neither of them said anything for a couple of minutes, and then he said softly:

"I needed that."

She was crying a little, and was furious with herself.

"You great clumsy fool," she said.

"You enjoyed it," he said. "You know you enjoyed it."

She swung from the bed in one quick angry movement.

"Enjoyed it?" she said. "Enjoyed it? A Saxon farm labourer could do better."

"Have you had many then?" he asked sullenly. "Farm labourers, I mean?"

She said nothing, but began to smooth down her dress.

"Anyway," he said, "As I said before, I needed it."

She looked at her watch. She was struggling for composure.

"It's time for the broadcast in a quarter of an hour," she said viciously. "Or would you rather go to bed again, and miss it?"

He sat on the bed, buttoning up his trousers, and running a comb through his thick fair hair. She went into the bathroom, shut the door, and began to wash herself. His voice came through the door.

"You know what we in the *Luftwaffe* call a girl like you?" he said. "A mattress. There are three grades—*Offiziermattrasse, Feldmattrasse*, and just *Mattrasse*."

She said nothing, peering in the mirror. Her mouth felt swollen where he had kissed her—if you could call it that, she thought.

"I grade you as *Mattrasse*," he said. "I could have had as good a time with a watermelon."

At two minutes to nine, she switched on the radio, flicking down the band from the BBC to the Hamburg frequency. They were in the closing moments of some concert —it sounded like Beethoven, she thought, but she could not be sure. At nine o'clock precisely came the English language announcer's voice:

"Gairmany calling, Gairmany calling . . ." Curious how he stretched that vowel, she thought. She had met him once, before the war. Joyce, his name was, William Joyce. He'd been a member of the British Union of Fascists then, and she'd been at school in Edgbaston. They'd lived in Birmingham, well, just outside. Her father's firm had bought the house when they sent him over from Dresden. Five years . . . five years with all those stuck-up little English misses at that stupid school. Some of them, she supposed, weren't too bad. But the arrogance of them . . . the highest compliment they thought they could pay was to say wonderingly: "But you talk just like one of us. You're exactly like us." Well, that's what she'd been since the *Abwehr* recruited her in 1938. One of them, with a new British identity, ration-card, national registration, job, the lot. And a radio transmitter, stuck there in the locked wardrobe. Thirty-seconds transmission, three times a week, she'd been told. Nobody can get a fix on a transmission as short as that. And if there's something big to report, use one of the optional methods, not the radio. Thirty seconds. She'd taken no notice of that. Radio-location techniques were improving, for all she knew. So twenty seconds had always been her maximum, just in case. Not that it had helped, in the end.

". . . more trouble between the local British people and the American airmen in East Anglia," Joyce was saying. "There is a joke in the army camps there—the British army camps. There are, they say, three things wrong with the Americans . . . oversexed, overpaid and over here. There were fights yesterday in Ipswich—oh, yes, good British people, Gairmany is watching. And why do you despise the Americans? For the same reason that we in Germany, too, despise them. Where is the American Goethe, where is the American Mozart, where is the American Milton? A nation without tradition, without past, without future . . ."

She switched off the set. Warnow was looking at her inquiringly, anxiously.

"Well, you heard," she said sharply. "Goethe. He said Goethe. That means they have ordered me to try to get you back."

He was transfigured.

"Good, good," he said. "And make it soon. I can't get out of this uniform soon enough." He glanced contemptuously at his US eagle's wings and his captain's bars.

"You realise," said Hannah Walters softly, "that if you are found in that uniform, you could be hanged. As a spy."

"You, too," he said. His eyes met hers, and for one of the first times since they met he smiled.

"It seems we share something, after all," he said. "Even the code names—I, Telemachus, you Cassandra."

"Cassandra is not my code name," she said impatiently. "Not my personal code name. I use it only for *Fall Ulysses*, as you use Telemachus."

"What do you know of *Ulysses*?" he said. His voice was almost too casual.

"I know *Fall Ulysses* exists," she said swiftly. "I know that it is Priority One. I have been told that, under certain circumstances, men and women bearing certain code names may ask for help. And that's all I know."

He looked at her for a few seconds.

"It is as well," he said at last. Not a man to give away

secrets, she thought. That kind of man she had learned to recognise. Yet, perhaps, there was a little over-confidence, a little euphoria, about him now he had learned she must help. For he was talking.

"When *Ulysses-Tag* arrives, the British and the Americans will get a shock they will never forget. Something the history books will argue about long after our victory."

He smiled again, and pushed his hand through his hair. To her astonishment, behind the anger which she felt for him, there came a momentary stab of understanding. He was, she thought, like a child—utterly wrapped up in himself and this war. He was Warnow and Warnow's mission. Anything else was there to be used—his friends, she herself, her body, everything A thought came to her.

"They were all dead, in the crash?" she said. "All dead . . . immediately?"

He did not answer.

"Not . . . all . . . dead?" she half-whispered.

"There was one," he said. He was trying to keep his voice dispassionate. "He was almost certainly dying."

"And . . ."

"There was no alternative. I would have killed myself, too, had it been necessary."

"I see . . ."

His face was pale. His hands trembled slightly. Again she felt that unexpected twinge of comprehension and compassion. He was vulnerable, then, this iron major. And she knew he meant what he said. He was ruthless with others, but with himself, too.

"How can you do it?" he asked. "The Channel? A boat, perhaps?"

"Do you know anything of boats?" she said.

"No."

"Then you would drown very quickly. The Channel isn't a ditch."

He rose and walked to the window, remembering in time not to pull aside the blackout.

"Then how . . ."

"We will see. First I must acknowledge my orders."

She crossed to the wardrobe, pulled out the transmitter on its drawer, and switched on. The set hummed faintly as it warmed up. She sat down, connected the Morse key, and sent three words:

"Cassandra. Telemachus. Goethe."

Eight seconds, she thought. Not bad. He was standing beside her, his lips silently mouthing the Morse.

"Goethe," he said. "You sent 'Goethe'."

"Now they know I've received my orders," she said. He sat on the edge of the bed.

"How are we going to do it?" he said. She thought wryly afterwards that it was probably the "we" that finally melted her anger. Anyway, she would have to reassure him. They were going to have difficult days together, and there should be something more between them than the memory of her role as *Mattrasse*. Impulsively, she crossed to where he sat.

"I'll start working it out tomorrow," she said. "Meanwhile, it's time for bed."

He crossed to the kitchen door, beyond which waited the narrow camp-bed she had put up for him when he arrived.

"Not there," she said. "Here." She patted her own bed. He paused, astonished, then walked back and held her against him.

"Women," he said. "I shall never understand them."

"No," she said, "you never will."

He was gentler this time, almost considerate, but, she thought, still not very good. She supposed that a man so self-absorbed could never be good. She lay there, eyes open, afterwards, thinking. Once he stirred and cupped his hand for a moment on her bare breast.

"Thank God," he murmured sleepily, "that Hamburg said 'Goethe'."

Yes, they had said "Goethe". And that meant: "Give the subject all the assistance he requires."

But, she thought, staring into the darkness, there was something Rolf Warnow didn't know. A lot, in fact, he didn't know.

They had radioed "Goethe". But they had also sent "Mozart". And "Mozart" meant: "If the security of the operation is at any point endangered, you will kill the subject." The subject in this case being Rolf Warnow.

Winston Churchill sat in the War Cabinet Room, fifty feet below the back of the Treasury building which faced St James's Park, and looked broodingly at the men who ran Britain's war. Not the whole War Cabinet was there that morning, but there were enough members and enough of those outsiders whom the Prime Minister had christened "Constant Attenders" to fill the tables in front of him. On his left sat Clement Attlee, the Labour leader, who was Deputy Prime Minister in the Coalition Government. On his right was the Cabinet Secretary, Sir Edward Bridges, and beyond him his senior military adviser, General Sir Hastings Ismay. Round the table bulked some of the others who had responsibility for vital sections of the national war effort . . . Ernest Bevin, Minister of Labour; Lord Woolton, Minister of Food; Herbert Morrison, Home Secretary—and charged with London's defence; and, on Attlee's left, the tall debonair figure of Foreign Secretary, Anthony Eden. Immediately in front of Churchill were the Service Chiefs: Admiral Lord Louis Mountbatten, Chief of Combined Operations; General Sir Alan Brooke, Chief of the Imperial General Staff; Air Chief Marshal Sir Charles Portal, Chief of Air Staff.

Deep down beneath the Horse Guards Parade, with layers of reinforced concrete above their heads, and the duplicated winding cables of every essential service weaving above them, the War Cabinet met once or twice a week.

They met in this underground bomb-proof room—carefully constructed before the war—where daylight never penetrated, and where seven electric lamps in their white shades blazed above the green-covered tables. To get to this inner brain of Britain's war planning meant passing through a complex of steel, air-lock-type doors, and through an interlocking system of Grenadier Guards and Royal Marines sentries. Just along the passage was the even more secret Map Room, where relays of officers kept simultaneous watch on the movements of all convoys, and all British and enemy warships, across the world. And beyond that was the little austere room where, from time to time, the Prime Minister slept.

Churchill looked absently at the small brown board which he kept propped in the middle of the War Cabinet table.

"Please understand," its white letters said, "that there is no depression in this house, and we are not interested in the possibilities of defeat. They do not exist."

He spoke directly to the Chief of Air Staff.

"Finally," said the Prime Minister, "I am profoundly disturbed by the reports I have received regarding the ways in which the enemy is using captured aeroplanes. Who is responsible for dealing with this new development, and what instructions have been given him?"

"At the moment, sir," said Portal, "the security services are dealing with it. There's been little for the RAF to get hold of to date—the chief brunt seems to be falling on the Eighth Air Force. Shevlin met Hamel the other day—I think you saw the minute, sir?"

Churchill nodded.

"Then you'll know that they've both been asked to hold their hand, for the time being, until we know much more."

"Could we not annihilate these . . . these tiresome Trojans at their home bases?"

"We could, sir, when we find some of their bases. And certain bases we've heard rumours of—and I wouldn't put some of these reports higher than rumours—aren't the easiest of targets. Roumania and the Ukraine, among other places."

"I have been informed that the most recent incident originated from Stavanger."

"That's probably so, sir—and Stavanger isn't any great problem. We could use a couple of Mosquito squadrons, from Leuchars. But security have asked us not to act, for the present."

"The Director is a very devious man," said the Prime Minister thoughtfully. "No doubt he will have sound reasons for such a request. However"—he scooped up a pile of papers and deposited them in front of Sir Edward Bridges—"I shall rest content, for the present. Bridges, pray attach a green sticker to that file—'report in three days'. Thank you, gentlemen."

Frido von Altmark strapped himself quickly into his seat in the ME-109 G, and closed the canopy. His mechanic Muller waited on the starboard blue-grey wing. Altmark checked his fuel gauges, set his trimmer to one-third flaps, and leaned down and pumped the orange primer-handle on the cockpit floor. Then he raised a hand and shouted "*Los*". Outside on the wing Muller waved in reply and began to crank . . . louder, louder, louder. When the sound of cranking became a high-pitched whine, Muller shouted "*Frei!*" There was an answering wave from Altmark as Muller jumped clear of the wing. Altmark pulled the black starter handle below the fuel gauge, and the 1,500-horsepower Daimler-Benz engine stuttered, coughed, roared. Smoke belched from the six exhausts. The three blades of the propeller blurred into invisibility. Altmark took off his brakes and started to taxi.

He looked back at the control tower for a moment, turned on to the runway, once again checked his engine instruments, and shoved down the yellow lever on the throttle control. The 109-Gustav leaped forward as though suddenly released, rolling faster and faster down the concrete . . . 100 . . . 200 . . . 300 . . . 350 yards. Ground speed 100 miles an hour—

Altmark pulled lightly on the stick and the fighter rose smoothly into the air. A slight bank to starboard, and up with the wheels. Now he was climbing steadily through the grey overcast of the late Norwegian afternoon, out over the North Sea. He pressed the two firing buttons. A rhythmic thumping vibration told him the 20mm cannon and the two 12mm machine-guns were working. Automatically, he ran his eye over the circle and bars of the electric light image on the gunsight. A voice in his radio headset crackled:

"Sector Berta-Ludwig eight. Two Mosquitoes moving west. Sector Berta-Quelle ten: one Mosquito, turning north-west. Distance six miles."

That single Mosquito interested him. Much the same had happened last week, during the Tommy strike at the two ore-tankers in Boknafjord. Three Mosquitoes from a force of nine had moved out a couple of miles from the others, and one of them had made a slightly unexpected pass, a mile out from Sola. Now here were three more—and one of them, again, not so far from Sola. Was it just chance—an enterprising pilot looking for targets of opportunity? Or was it, just possible, photo-reconnaissance? There was nothing to see at Sola now, he knew. Only the sort of aircraft that might be expected . . . a couple of Heinkel IIIs and a Condor. All else was safely under wraps. But he'd like to get that Tommy, nevertheless.

Six miles . . . it was a lot to make up, and the Mosquito probably had a seven mile-an-hour edge on his Gustav, anyway—especially if it *was* photo-reconnaissance, stripped for speed.

"One Mosquito, Sector Anton-Quelle three, turning west," said the headset. Altmark made up his mind. He couldn't chase. All he could do was fly the single leg of the triangle of which the Mosquito was now flying two. If, indeed, that *was* what it was doing. He climbed high above the overcast, out into the sunshine of 20,000 . . . 23,000 . . . 25,000 feet. Ten minutes later, almost unbelievingly, he spotted the Mosquito, a minute dot to the east, 800 feet below him, flying steadily on a converging course. Altmark's port wing dipped as he banked, and then straightened as he went into the dive. The Mosquito saw him four seconds later, and dived, too.

I've got a fly one here, thought Altmark. You could rip the wings off a Gustav if you dived it too steeply and too long, and here was this Mosquito getting down to sea level where the pilot could use his edge of speed. "You're not going to get away with it, my little Englishman", he said aloud. "Because I've got four seconds start into the dive, and I'm moving just a little bit too fast. But I'm only going to get one chance."

There was a thin trail of bluish-black smoke behind the Mosquito, diving on full throttle and no more than 2,000 feet up, as Altmark came into firing range. Staring into the rectangular glass panel in front of his head, he watched the coloured electric light-ring and the range bars slowly closing. He was 200 feet away, and the Mosquito was beginning to draw clear, when he pressed the twin firing buttons and a stream of shells and bullets hit it just behind the cockpit. Without wavering in course, the Mosquito went straight into the North Sea at 350 miles an hour. Von Altmark pulled up gradually, easing back on the stick, worrying about the Gustav's wings. Then he banked, and swept back above the dark patch on the white-flecked sea. No parachutes, of course . . . not a chance at that height. Nothing at all, in fact. Poor damned Tommies.

"*Achtung, Elbe One,*" he said into his throat microphone. "One Mosquito destroyed. Sector Caesar Kurfurst nine."

The sea rescue people, he thought, might have a look. But he would be surprised if they found anything. Fifteen minutes later, he was back over Sola. He gave one victory roll before turning into the wind to land.

TOP SECRET

Headquarters: United States Strategic Air Forces Office of the Chief Intelligence Officer
MEMORANDUM

To: General Dwight D. Eisenhower (see Additional Distribution)

Subject: *Kampfgeschwader* 200.

1. This is the summary for which you asked in our conversation of 14 July.
2. In the early stages of the war, the dropping of German agents from the air in neutral and enemy territory was carried out by Major (then *Hauptmann*) Gartenfeld, who appears at that time to have been the only pilot engaged on this work. By June 1943, through the influence of Goering and Admiral Wilhelm Canaris of the *Abwehr*, Gartenfeld had been able to form his own squadron, later known as the *2 Versuchsverbände Ob. d. L.*
3. Originally there were two *Versuchsverbände*, of which the *1 Staffel* was concerned with experiment and development of aircraft types; and the *2 Staffel*, under Gartenfeld, with the dropping of agents and other irregular work for the Intelligence and other services. Gartenfeld operated on behalf of both the *Abwehr* and *Sicherheitsdienst* (Security Service), although his affiliations with the former were closer.
4. Later the HQ of the *2 Versuchsverbände* was transferred from Rangsdorf to Finsterwalde, and the combined *Versuchsverbände* were given the joint title of *Kampfgeschwader* 200, though by a curious reversal the *1 Versuchsverbände* became II/KG 200, and *2 Versuchsverbände* became I/KG 200.
5. The dropping of agents in Allied territory is carried out by I/KG 200, which operates by means of outlying detachments, there being—in general—seldom more than

a few crews and aircraft at any one base. One of these detachments—*Kommando Sued*—is understood to have been set up at Kalamaki, near Athens, with the object of establishing a chain of wireless transmitting stations in North Africa, and of eventually dropping agents there. A control station was also set up in Marseilles, but was later moved to Parma to take part in operations in Italy. There has lately been a report of a sea detachment of KG 200, but nothing is known of its functions.

6. The above information, admittedly sketchy, comes from Continental sources. Nothing more definite is known of KG 200, though there have been reports that it has been developing and expanding its activities into wider fields in recent months. Captured personnel of the conventional *Luftwaffe* appear to have no knowledge of its existence.

FRANK D. LASKER
Colonel, Air Corps
Chief Intelligence Officer

Additional Distribution: General Paul C. Hamel, one copy
AOC Royal Air Force Bomber Command, one copy

9

The Director turned back from the window, a small grey man in the grey light of a grey afternoon. Croasdell and Vandamme sat quietly at the other side of his desk, waiting.

"I've no doubt, gentlemen, that by now you're wondering exactly what you've been investigating. And you'll have guessed that it isn't simply a matter of a single Flying Fortress captured and put into service by the enemy, and crewed by enemy airmen wearing United States uniform. So let me tell you what I believe we are up against."

He paused for a moment, and Croasdell tried unobtrusively to look around him. It was a grim little room, he thought—a drab little room. It contained little more than the Director's desk, a couple of trestle tables, some green metal filing cabinets. The only concession made to the decorative arts was a coloured photograph of the King, in naval uniform, on the wall behind the desk. Another wall was hung with the *Daily Telegraph* War Map of Europe, from which a few coloured pins hung disconsolately.

The Director seemed tired. His face was drawn, with lines of strain around the small bright eyes, whose pinkish rims suggested that their owner was a little short of sleep. He pressed the buzzer on his desk, and a few moments later the grey, middle-aged woman in the outer office came in with a tray of tea. The Director himself poured the tea. It was, Vandamme noted appreciatively, very good tea, for once . . . strong and fragrant. The Director did not miss the flicker of surprise on the American's face, and said, smiling:

"It's Earl Grey—I don't know if you get it in America?"

"I can't say for sure, sir. I'm not well up in tea. But I haven't drunk it before. It's very good."

"Lord knows where Miss Bennett gets it. It's in what we call 'short supply' here at the moment. I think she's got a private key to Harrods' pre-war stocks. Thank heaven."

He put down his cup, and looked at the two men opposite him.

"I gather that each of you has seen the intelligence summary that was sent to General Hamel and Air Marshal Shevlin?"

Croasdell and Vandamme nodded.

"Then I need not waste time in going over once more the administrative origins of the enemy unit now known as KG 200. What concerns me now—and what will concern you, too—is paragraph 6 of that summary."

" 'Expanding and developing its activities'," said Croasdell thoughtfully.

"Precisely, Squadron Leader. I am beginning to be increasingly concerned about KG 200. And about the aircraft it is now using."

"You mean the B-17 at Mersea, I guess?" said Vandamme. "That ship was carrying agents, in that plywood coffin. Not too difficult for them to pick up a B-17, of course. There must be one makes a forced-landing every so often, pretty well intact."

"How many?"

"Well, an occasional one. Not many, though. Those babies need a lot of real estate to put down in one piece once they're in trouble. As that German guy found out at Mersea—even though he was one hell of a good pilot."

"And yet we're receiving reports that the enemy is operating many more—not just one or two."

Vandamme leaned forward.

"Many more . . .?"

"Perhaps twenty. Or even more than that."

Vandamme whistled.

"Those can't all come from forced-landing, then. It's statistically highly improbable. Then where . . .?"

"That's one of the things I want you to find out," said the Director.

"A good idea, from their point of view," said Croasdell. "They bring in a B-17 carrying agents. It makes a speed and height blip on our radar that's completely familiar and unsuspicious to any operator. And if they fly in at the same time as a US bomber group is coming home from a mission, it's virtually impossible to separate them from the real thing."

"And the same advantage is to be gained, of course, from using RAF aircraft," said the Director.

"Yes?"

"There is clear photographic evidence that the Germans are operating at least two Short Stirling bombers."

Croasdell watched him thoughtfully, but said nothing. After a few moments, the Director spoke again.

"We are beginning to move into the period when we, ah, shall start detailed logistic planning for the invasion of Europe. So it isn't surprising that the enemy is stepping up his Intelligence activities."

He drew a long, buff-coloured sheet of paper from a drawer in his desk.

"To the best of our knowledge"—he lifted his eyes for a moment and Vandamme had a sudden cold feeling of exactly what that meant—"the Germans have sent seventy-eight agents to this country in the past nine weeks. Thirty-two by U-boat; sixteen by boat from the Irish Republic; the rest by air. All those sent by U-boat are now in, ah, custody. Twelve of those from the Irish Republic, too—and also some of those who came by air. The casualty rate is high. I will not, of course, give you the figures for our own activities. They have no relevance for your purposes."

He put the tips of his fingers together.

"What we are seeing, in fact, is a decisive widening of the activities of KG 200. First, agent-dropping for which they are apparently responsible, is increasing. Second, they are using captured aircraft for the purpose—on what scale, we do not yet know. And third, something very odd is going on. What, for instance, strikes you as peculiar about that incident at Mersea?"

"Well, in view of what you've told us—about B-17s being used for agent-dropping—there is one rather strange feature about that crash," said Croasdell. "If the B-17 was simply being used to tag on to the end of a mission and come in unsuspected by our own fighters and radar . . . well, that's a perfectly understandable idea on the part of the Germans. But why were the pilot, who escaped, and the other bodies we found, wearing American uniforms? They weren't going to land—or they wouldn't have been carrying their agents in that *Personenabwurfgerat*. In any case, a landing would be inconceivable. So why wear enemy uniforms—and risk being hanged as spies if they're found in it? If they were simply using the B-17 as a sort of flying Trojan horse—just as a vehicle, I mean—it doesn't make sense."

The Director sat back, smiling.

"Precisely," he said. "On the basis of what we know, it doesn't make sense. Which means that we don't know enough. But first, let me tell you a little more of what we do know."

"Gartenfeld has left KG 200—at least, he has either left it or been posted to some section of it of which we're unaware. His place, in a vastly expanded organisation, has been taken by a full *Oberst*—which, as you know, is one of the most flexible ranks in the German armed forces. We do not yet know the name of this officer, though we have had vague reports that it is either Lertz or Mertz. What we do know about him is that he is not an operational flier, as Gartenfeld was, but a planner. And for unorthodox air operations, he must rank as one of the best planners in Hitler's service. And one of the most imaginative. I'll give you an example—two examples, in fact.

"For some time, the Germans have been investigating a

plan by which aircraft could bomb Washington or New York. No"—he held up a hand, laughing at Vandamme's expression—"you haven't been brought here, Colonel, to try to stop this happening. It's not a plan the Germans have yet been able to develop—the logistic difficulties, at present, are too great. But it seems certain that the contingency planning for this operation was worked out by KG 200.

"Imaginative planning, though, you'll agree. One thing this war should have taught us is that the Germans are not the rigid, hide-bound figures of our comic books. Especially KG 200. And they have imaginative weapons, too."

Again he pressed the buzzer on his desk. The grey-haired woman came in a moment later with a green box—about the size of an old-fashioned hat-box. He took from it what appeared at first to be a model of two aircraft, though, as they leaned forward, fascinated, Croasdell and Vandamme saw that it was a composite aircraft made up of one mounted on top of the other.

"JU-88 underneath," said Vandamme reflectively.

"With some kind of fighter on top," said Croasdell.

"The Germans call it the Mistel," said the Director. "Or sometimes the Huckerpack. And occasionally, appropriately, Father and Son. I had this model made up at Farnborough, from reports and one rather bad photograph sent in by a Resistance agent. So the types of aircraft used in this composite are only a guess."

"One of those ships will be radio-controlled," said Vandamme.

"Must be the bottom one," said Croasdell, "because the aerodynamics would be a lot more difficult the other way round. In any case, I imagine that the lower half is some sort of radio-controlled bomb, released by the fighter on top, and then aimed at the target. So it would be logical to have the bigger plane full of explosive, and the smaller plane to get away in. And it would make up into one hell of a bomb."

He looked at the Director, who nodded.

"You've grasped how it works, Squadron Leader. I know little of flying, but I'm told by the experts that the controls are linked, so that the pilot of the fighter flies the composite machine, stands off from the target, releases the bomb-aircraft, aims it, and tries to protect it on the way to the target."

"And the best of German luck to him," said Vandamme. "I wouldn't fancy taking off in it. I wouldn't fancy flying it, and I'd sure hate to be caught in it by one of your Spitfires or one of our P-40s, or a 1918 Spad or a Sopwith Camel, for that matter."

"Yet the Germans have already begun to fly it on test. They've already lost three KG 200 pilots, but they are learning," said the Director quietly. "They are learning because the quality of the pilots in this very unusual *Geschwader* is, frankly, superb. You've already been, in a way at least, close to one of them. The man who flew the B-17 to Mersea. Who killed his co-pilot. And vanished."

"Wonder-boy?" said Vandamme admiringly.

The Director looked at him inquiringly.

"Well, we call him that, John—the Squadron Leader here—and me, because we couldn't see how he brought that B-17 in sideways. But if he can fly that pick-a-back thing, well . . ."

Yet even this pick-a-back machine, as you call it, isn't the reason I've asked you to help," said the Director. "It's still in an early stage of development—though soon enough, when we're getting much nearer to getting back into Europe, it may be a weapon which we shall have to reckon with. Among other, ah, innovations being prepared by this versatile planner in KG 200."

"You could sink a cruiser with just a single one of those," said Croasdell thoughtfully. "Or take out a bridge."

"I showed you this model," said the Director, "because I wanted you to have a simple illustration of the skills and expertise of the people we're dealing with. People like the pilot—'wonder-boy', I think you called him—who flew that

B-17. His name is Warnow . . . Rolf Warnow. His rank is Major."

Vandamme leaned forward, his eyes fixed on the Director:

"How do you—"

"I've heard of him," said Croasdell. "He was a *Staffel* commander in Loerzer's *Fliegerkorps II* in 1940. Said to have got three Hurricanes in a day once—we used to talk about him a lot."

"He went to the Eastern Front in December 1941," said the Director. "And then he vanished. He appeared on no casualty list. No further decorations were announced. And now, suddenly he arrives at Mersea, flying a B-17, wearing American uniform. Incidentally, Colonel Vandamme, he was brought up as a boy in Chicago. His father was a German businessman who spent a lot of time in the United States and Canada. Major Warnow speaks absolutely perfect English."

"Yes," said Vandamme. "But how—"

"How do I know all this?" said the Director. "Well, you know as well as I do that I can't tell you how. But I do know, absolutely certainly, that the pilot of the B-17 was Warnow, that he is now an officer of KG 200, and that he is in London. I also know where he is in London."

"Then?"

"I don't put a hand on him because I want him to help us. Oh"—he smiled bleakly as Vandamme began to speak—"of course, a man like Warnow won't help us knowingly. But I hope that he will lead us . . ."

"Where to?" said Croasdell. Vandamme looked at him. The expression on Croasdell's face was one of those which Americans found unfathomable in British people—a carefully controlled impassivity which would mask almost any emotion. Nevertheless, he had an uneasy feeling that Croasdell had already grasped more of what the Director was talking about than he, Vandamme, had so far managed to do. What was it the preacher used to say in that little white clapboard church down the road from his home in King's Highway? "Deep calleth unto deep."

"Back to his own section of KG 200," said the Director. "Back to Stavanger, and, I hope, to very much more."

"Where the photographs came from," said Vandamme. "Can we see the new ones the Mosquito got? Do they show anything more?"

"There are no new photographs," said the Director. "The Mosquito which got the first set went out again yesterday. It failed to return, and its pilot and navigator are missing."

The Director shrugged.

"It could have been shot down by chance of course—or because it was recognised for what it was. Or it could have had engine trouble and crashed into the sea. It's a long flight. But there was no radio message."

"So we don't know if they've got more B-17s there, or not?" said Croasdell.

"I suspect there *are* more," said the Director. "We've been getting a steady stream of reports, from the European Underground and the Resistance, of German salvage operations on crashed Allied aircraft which seems to be on a scale quite unlike the normal attempts made solely for evaluation purposes."

"That might explain how they've got twenty, if they *have* got so many," said Vandamme, slowly.

"Our difficulty is that Resistance workers and other agents, however gallant and determined, are rarely technicians who understand all they see," said the Director. "They've reported force-landed or wrecked Allied aircraft being taken away by salvage teams. They can't, often, say what types of aircraft they are, even less how potentially airworthy they are. But they do know that the scale of the operation is, to say the least, unusual."

He looked searchingly at the two men before him.

"I'm sure you must realise that if the Germans are building up a substantial stock of Allied aircraft, the possibilities are daunting. I believe that they themselves have been surprised by the success of KG 200 in doing this. We know they began using one or two captured, repaired machines to watch and report on genuine B-17 missions mounted from this country. Occasionally, we know, they use the odd machine to drop agents. As you've pointed out, there is no way of distinguishing a German captured B-17 from an American one on our radar—or a German piloted Stirling from a British one. Even these activities are serious enough, but they also mean that soon American and British aircrews may have to be ordered to open fire on strange 'friendly' machines they can't positively identify. Bad for morale, of course, and the possibilities for ghastly errors are almost limitless. That isn't all, however, terrible though it is. There is also Plan *Ulysses*."

Croasdell watched him quietly. Now, he thought, we're getting down to bedrock.

"In fact," said the Director, "above all, above all there is Plan *Ulysses*. I have been demonstrating how much, or how little, we know. And now I must confess that about Plan *Ulysses—Fall Ulysses*, the Germans call it—I know almost nothing except that in some way it may involve the use of captured Allied aircraft. And that Major Rolf Warnow is engaged in it—was, indeed, engaged in it when he crashed the B-17 at Mersea."

"Why are you so sure of that?" said Croasdell. "Isn't it possible he was simply agent-dropping, in the way you've described? After all, we know there was at least one agent aboard . . . the woman whose body we saw in the mortuary at Colchester."

"And, as you have appreciated, there was probably at least one other," said the Director. "Otherwise they would not have used a *Personenabwurfgerat*."

"But Warnow?" said Croasdell, slowly, "Why Warnow?"

"Exactly, Squadron Leader. Why Warnow? Major Warnow was—is still, of course—Operations Officer of the key operational *Gruppe* 1 of KG 200. That is a very senior appointment indeed—involving active participation in the planning and execution of every operation that the *Gruppe* undertakes. It seems inconceivable that he was simply flying a B-17 here on an agent-dropping mission—a mission which, though routine, was risky. Warnow wasn't at the controls of that bomber by chance or routine. He's too valuable a man to lose on such an undistinguished mission. He was there because, for some reason, it was important to fly that machine to East Anglia—and for him, in person, to fly it."

"But why . . .?" said Vandamme.

"I don't know," said the Director, putting the tips of his fingers together. "But I have a feeling that it was what you Americans, I believe, call 'a dry run'. He was, I think, making a practice flight from which to learn more about the problems of Plan *Ulysses*. And it's likely, of course, that the agents he was going to drop were also part of Plan *Ulysses*. Nothing else makes sense. The loss of Warnow must be crippling to the operation, for the moment, at least. Yet the Germans thought the risk worth taking."

"But now you've found him, as you say you have," said Vandamme, "surely that's it? No Warnow, no Plan *Ulysses*?"

The Director smiled tiredly.

"I wish it were so easy, Colonel. Warnow's absence may well delay *Ulysses*, whatever that is. But it is hardly likely to cripple it completely. There are many good pilots, outstanding airmen, in KG 200, so there would soon be another Operations Officer for *Gruppe* 1. And another Allied plane over East Anglia, in false colours. And we might not be so lucky with this one."

"Would be another Operations Officer?" asked Croasdell curiously.

"Would be," said the Director, "because in fact that must not happen. I want Warnow to resume his post at Stavanger. I want Plan *Ulysses* to stay on schedule. I want Warnow back with his friends, and I want him to think he's done it entirely by his own initiative, courage and skill. I want the commander of KG 200, whoever he is, to think the same. That," he added, smiling, "is just a little of what I want, because I need to know a great deal more about this force with no face, and how it is planning to try to interfere with our invasion of Europe, when the day comes. That there are such KG 200 plans, I have no doubt."

Absently, he picked up the composite model of the German Mistel aircraft and weighed it in his hands.

"That is why you're here. In your present posts, you know something of Intelligence and espionage, but a great deal more about flying. I know a great deal about Intelligence and espionage, but nothing of practical flying. I need one man who understands the British side and one the American. I hope we shall fill the gaps in each other's capabilities.

"You've been chosen to spearhead and co-ordinate the Intelligence drive on KG 200 because you are exceptional pilots and also air intelligence experts, fully conversant with *Luftwaffe* operational machinery—and, added to these qualifications, you possess between you a useful combination of languages."

Croasdell and Vandamme looked at each other warily.

"You, Colonel," said the Director, "had a German immigrant grandfather. No"—he held up a hand in mock reproof—"it's nothing to be ashamed of. Our own Royal Family have similar, ah, connections. You speak German fluently, and also pretty good French.

"You, Squadron Leader, speak Norwegian—a most unusual ability in Britain. According to your records, you read it as a major modern language at Oxford, where you also became fluent in German and French—though your German, unlike Colonel Vandamme's, is somewhat accented."

"Yes," said Croasdell. "My Norwegian is, too. It's grammatical, but a real Norwegian would know the difference."

"But not a German?" said the Director.

"I suppose not," said Croasdell, almost unwillingly. He hesitated, and then added:

"I speak a little Dutch and Flemish, as well. Fairly

idiomatic, but not a great vocabulary. We used to take a holiday house there, before the war, my mother and I."

"Your mother?" said the Director.

"My father was killed in 1918, at Amiens," said Croasdell.

"Of course, I should have remembered," said the Director. "Dutch and Flemish, too? That isn't in your file. Better and better."

He looked carefully at them both.

"Between you, your languages could be of the greatest value for this assignment. In your case, Squadron Leader, your Norwegian might prove especially useful if the strong evidence that the Mersea B-17 came from Stavanger is confirmed. But first of all, I want some opinions from you both."

He pressed the desk buzzer, and the woman from the outer office came in and pinned a map to the wooden trestle table beside the Director's desk. He waited until she had left the room, and then beckoned Croasdell and Vandamme to his side.

"Please begin," he said, "by giving me a preliminary idea of what you might do, if either of you was Major Rolf Warnow, faced with the situation which I am now going to describe . . ."

The Director talked for ten minutes. Then he left the room where Croasdell and Vandamme were already busy with the map, nodded to the woman in the outer office, and opened a door into another room beyond. A foxy-faced little man, with a reddish moustache, sat at a desk, reading a file. He rose as the Director walked in.

"Good afternoon, Strongman," said the Director. "I'm afraid I've kept you longer than I'd thought I would. I had to brief those two officers. I think you'll be meeting them, some time fairly soon."

"I see," said Major Edward Butler. He was in uniform, wearing the badges of a famous cavalry regiment.

"I must say, Director," he said, "I shan't be sorry when this operation is over. Can't stand that name."

"What name?" said the Director. He looked curiously at

the small foxy man. Some people, on first acquaintance, considered Major Edward Butler an affected fool. But then, thought the Director, some people thought the mongoose was a cuddly pet. Cobras knew better. Major Edward Butler worked for MI5—British counter-espionage.

"Strongman," said Butler. "My code name, for this one. Doesn't suit me a bit."

"I shouldn't worry," said the Director cheerfully. "When I was in the field, I was once code-named Weasel."

"Hm," said the other, and laughed.

The Director nodded towards a door behind the desk.

"In there, waiting?" he said.

"Yes," said Strongman.

"How long have you been Control, with this particular subject?"

"Four months," said Strongman.

"Any trouble? Any reservations?"

"No trouble. No reservations, really, except that this subject sometimes looks at me as though I wasn't there. I like the ones I can understand more easily."

"We all do," said the Director. "Well, I'll tell you the way the operation is beginning to shape, though a lot will depend on those two out there."

He nodded back towards the room where Croasdell and Vandamme were working.

"I see it initially," said the Director, "like this . . ."

Ten minutes later, he rose, said his goodbyes, and went out. Strongman packed his files into a worn leather briefcase. Then, tucking it under his arm, he walked to the door behind the desk and opened it. The room into which it led was almost identical with the one he had left. A woman was sitting beside the desk. She looked up as he entered.

"Good evening, Miss Walters," said Strongman. "And how is Major Warnow today? Eager, I trust, to return to his—and, I suppose, your—*Führer*?"

10

Pieter Banninck bent low over his handlebars in the rain, and cycled carefully past the German 88mm flak battery at the edge of the village of Noordwelle. He went by the caped sentry who stood beside the tarpaulined guns . . . at an even speed, neither fast nor slow, without elaborately ignoring the sentry, but without paying him undue attention. The man looked up at him for a moment, but made no move to check him or to ask for his papers. Behind Banninck, their cycling jumpers sodden with the drizzle that drifted across the off-shore island of Schouwen from the grey North Sea, cycled his friends Jan Bicker and Cornelis Duck. The sentry watched them morosely. Dutch kids, he thought . . . cycling-mad. Out in all weathers, training. And for what? Another half-hour yet, before he was relieved. And then coffee in the guard-room—if you could call it coffee nowadays.

When they were half a mile from the battery, Banninck stopped and the others came alongside.

"It's somewhere down on the road towards Haamstede," he said. "Adam Steen, the postman, told me he'd heard it wasn't guarded—not even a mobile patrol."

"Can't be very important, then," said Cornelis Duck.

"We ought to have a look," said Pieter Banninck. "It might be worth entering it on the map."

He tapped his handlebars. Coiled inside the hollow metal lay the map on which Pieter and Jan and Cornelis entered anything which they thought might interest the local Resistance. Pieter and Jan and Cornelis were 14, 13 and 12 respectively, but in many respects they had already grown up. They came to the airfield nine kilometres later. There was a high hedge, and at its further side a barrier of thick barbed wire. Beyond the wire stretched three broad swathes of white paint, tapering like an A into the distance.

"They're as wide as runways," said Jan Bicker thoughtfully. And they look like runways. But they're grass . . ."

"There's something big on the other side of the field," said Pieter Banninck. "I think it's a plane. Let's go round the edge and have a look."

They cycled down the edge of the field until they reached the other side. The three leaned their cycles in the ditch, and Jan Bicker went up to the corner of the road to keep watch. There was no sign of anybody on the field, no sound of work, of engines, of movement. Cornelis and Pieter scrambled down into the dripping hedge and peered through.

"It *is* a plane," said Cornelis Duck. "A big one . . . four engines."

"It's American," said Pieter Banninck. "The kind they call a Fortress."

"Are you sure? How would the Germans have an American plane? It has no markings."

"Of course I'm sure. I've seen them in magazines. And I've seen them go over. The Germans have no plane of their own like this one."

Massive and black, the big aircraft bulked on the white-painted grass. It was staked into the grass like a tent, with cables running from pegs driven deep into the ground.

"There's something funny about it," said Pieter.

"What do you mean?"

"Well, look, the rain lies on it like it lies on a roof. It doesn't run down it quickly, like it does on a car. I wish I could get through . . ."

"Don't be stupid. Somebody'll see you. And the wire's thick, anyway."

"And that's another thing. There's nobody here to see us. Why is there nobody about? Have you ever seen an airfield with nobody about?"

"No."

Pieter Banninck scrabbled about in the ditch and picked up a jagged stone.

"What are you doing?"

"I'm going to give it a bonk."

"Don't be an idiot. There may be somebody inside it, and then we'll be in real trouble."

"I don't think there's anybody inside it."

He drew back his arm and threw the stone as hard as he could. There was a dull thud as it hit somewhere along the fuselage. Banninck picked up another, and hit the big plane again. The same thud followed. He turned to Cornelis Duck, his eyes bright with a mixture of curiosity and triumph.

"That's not metal. There was no zong like it makes when you hit metal. It's wood. That plane's wood."

"You mean . . ."

"It isn't a real plane at all. And the runways aren't real runways, just painted grass. And I'll bet there's nobody in the buildings on the other side. Because it's not a real airfield. It's an imitation airfield, and when I get home I'm going to put it on the map, and tell Frans Janssens about it. I'll bet it's important."

"It may be," said Cornelis Duck, reluctantly.

The sentry had changed as they cycled back past the 88mm battery at Noordwelle. This one was younger, keener, and he made each of them show their papers before he let them pass.

"You have," he said, "one hour to curfew. Make sure you're home by then, or there will be trouble."

He watched them cycle off, and grinned. It didn't occur to him to unscrew the handgrips and look inside Pieter Banninck's handlebars.

In so far as he could be said to smile, *Oberst* Adolf Pertz was smiling. The commander of KG 200 stumped along through the early summer sunshine which whitened the concrete bunkers of Rastenberg, across to Jeschonnek's headquarters in the *Luftwaffe* compound. A couple of black-suited civilians from the *Amtsgruppe Ausland*, the Foreign Section of the *Abwehr*, walked by in the opposite direction. ". . . naturally Turkish neutrality cannot be guaranteed," he heard one of them saying. "But . . ." They passed out of earshot. Talk, talk . . . that's all they're good for, thought Pertz. If we could win the war by talk, men like that would be our secret weapon. But talk does not win wars, even though Josef Goebbels, a man for whom he had some considerable respect, believed it had a major part to play.

Stiffy he returned the heel-click salute of the young *Luftwaffe Gefreiter* who stood, Schmeisser machine-pistol cocked, at Jeschonnek's office door. Inside, the office *Feldwebel*, a bespectacled man who acted as Jeschonnek's clerk, got to his feet as Pertz, puffing a little after his brisk walk, arrived in front of his desk.

"The *Herr General* is expecting me," said Pertz. He looked approvingly at the man's tidy desk, the neat tabulation of figures he was entering in some ledger. A man who knew how to organise himself, he thought.

"Your name?" he said sharply to the *Feldwebel*. A flicker of something which might have been alarm passed across the man's face.

"Greiner, *Herr Oberst*, warrant officer, second class."

"Well, Greiner," said Pertz, almost jovially, "how would you like to work for me? As a warrant officer, first class?"

"Of course, *Herr Oberst*."

"Good. I need men who know how to work. I shall ask General Jeschonnek to transfer you."

"Thank you, *Herr Oberst*."

And what was all that about? thought the mystified Greiner, as Pertz walked through into Jeschonnek's inner office. The old man seemed very happy today. Of course, they all said he was a slave-driver. But, he said to himself as he turned back to his ledger, *Feldwebel*, first class? Can't be bad.

Inside the office, Pertz sat in the chair which Jeschonnek had indicated, and waited until the *Luftwaffe* Chief of Staff, seated at his desk, had finished writing. He looked carefully at Jeschonnek. The man looked washed out, feverish. No joke, dealing with the *Reichsmarschall*, of course. And he'd heard that Goering had lost his temper with Jeschonnek yesterday, because he thought Jeschonnek had gone over his head to the *Führer* . . .

"I'm sorry to have kept you, *Oberst* Pertz," said Jeschonnek politely. "Now—what's your news?"

"Excellent," said Pertz. "Warnow is alive and unhurt and with . . . a friend. A friend who believes he can be brought back."

Jeschonnek rubbed his eyes tiredly.

"Good, good," he said. He rose and walked to the window, looking beyond it to the compound where the camouflaged Mercedes staff cars came and went. A big yellow butterfly was beating vainly against the inside of the glass. Jeschonnek opened the window and let it out.

What was the matter with the man? Not much of a reaction, in view of the news. Didn't he realise what it meant?

"It means," said Pertz, "that if he *can* be returned quickly, *Ulysses* is back on schedule."

Jeschonnek did not seem to hear. He walked back to the desk, and sat down heavily. He looked at Pertz.

"We shall both be at the *Führer's* conference in an hour's time, *Oberst* Pertz, so I will give you some advance information. You say *Ulysses* is on. Now I will tell you something. Operation *Zitadelle* is on. The *Führer* decided last night."

"*Zitadelle*?" said Pertz. "But I thought the *Führer* had decided not to . . ."

"General Zeitzler and General von Kluge persuaded him," said Jeschonnek.

"Hm," said Pertz thoughtfully. "What are the chances? I have already informed the *Führer* that the Russians know all about *Zitadelle*. The whole of the Kursk salient is fantastically fortified. We have enough air photographs to fill a library . . ."

"I know, I know," said Jeschonnek. "We are going to attack the Kursk salient with numerically inferior forces against a prepared, well organised enemy. I can hardly believe it. You know how many aircraft we have available for this operation? Two thousand . . . just two thousand. And the Ivans have three thousand—and the best anti-aircraft artillery in the world. And do you know what the *Reichsmarschall* said when I told this to the *Führer*? Dive-bomb them with the *Stukas*! *Stukas*! Sometimes I think we're all living in the past. *Stukas* are sitting ducks, and have been for two years. And that is what Operation *Zitadelle* at Kursk will be. A sitting duck. I was talking to a panzer general yesterday—von Mellenthin, you remember him? Did well in 1940."

Pertz nodded.

"He told me," said Jeschonnek, "that for the panzers, as for us in the *Luftwaffe*, *Zitadelle* was going to be a deathride."

"Hm," said Pertz.

Jeschonnek rubbed his chin.

"Well, we shall be hearing enough about *Zitadelle* from the *Führer* in an hour's time. And meanwhile, I must say that your Warnow news is good. But how do you hope to get him back? No, no"—he held up a hand—"I'm sorry, I don't need to know . . ."

"As I said," said Pertz, "it may mean that we can reactivate *Ulysses* on the original timetable."

"*If* you get him back," said Jeschonnek.

"We'll get him," said Pertz. "And he'll bring a bonus with him, if I know Warnow."

"I hope so," said Jeschonnek. "It's something good to tell the *Führer*, anyway. Though he'll be so full of *Zitadelle* that he'll hardly listen."

"They'll listen on *Ulysses-Tag*," said Pertz. Jeschonnek said nothing but stared at him thoughtfully. Pertz rose.

"By the way, *Herr General*."

"Yes?"

"The man in the front office . . ."

"Greiner?"

"Yes, *Herr General*. He's the kind I could use. Could I transfer him to me?"

"Greiner's useful to me, too, Pertz," said Jeschonnek sharply. "No, you cannot . . . oh, well, I suppose you might as well. I can promote the *Unterfeldwebel*. Take him, take him."

"Thank you, *Herr General*," said Pertz.

Joanna Croasdell wheeled her bicycle on to the short gravelled drive in front of the cottage. With a slight lift of the heart, she noted that the jeep was parked there. That meant John and Gene would be home again—as they'd been every day for the past week.

The pattern was always the same. Each night they drove nine miles down the road to the RAF airfield at West Murford; at dawn they came home to sleep; in the afternoon they vanished into the little spare room to work. When they weren't there, the door was locked, and John had told her firmly: "Don't poke about in here, darling, on one of your tidying-up jags—because it's all stuff that nobody else is supposed to know about. Even you." So she hadn't. All she'd heard was an occasional phrase which to her was meaningless: once she'd heard Vandamme say: "According to that guy at the OTU, the two best gaps are there . . . near Dieppe . . . and there . . . just up the Dutch coast . . ." And then John had said: "Well, he'd never try Dieppe. Not in a million years." And, when she'd taken in coffee, there'd been maps on the table, and long yellow RAF-issue rulers, and papers covered with figures.

Gene came out as she propped the bicycle against the door, seized her in an elaborate pantomime of passion, but kissed her chastely on the cheek. As usual, she felt herself blush, and hoped that he didn't notice. Not much chance of that, though. Gene was a perceptive man where women were concerned. Some girl was going to be very lucky one day, she thought, and suddenly giggled. She'd bet this month's clothes coupons that a lot of girls had been lucky already.

"What are you laughing at?" said Gene suspiciously. "Girls like you aren't supposed to laugh when they're kissed by guys like me. They're supposed to throb."

"What do you mean, girls like me?" she said, laughing.

"You know, pushovers," he said. "What we call Yankee-yums. All you British girls are the same. It's well known to all us Americans."

"John, John, he's insulting me again," she called as they went into the house, Vandamme carrying the bag of potatoes from her bicycle carrier.

"Good," said Croasdell, coming out of the spare room, and shutting and locking the door behind him. "Gene, I'll have to go over to Little Snoring tomorrow if we're going to get decent radar plots. 515 Squadron is there, and they fly Mossies. They should have all the gen."

"There's not anywhere that's truly called Little Snoring, is there?" said Vandamme. "It can't be real."

"Of course it's real," said Joanna indignantly. "It's got a gorgeous church. No, as a matter of fact, I think the church is in Great Snoring. Very near, though."

Vandamme held up his hands.

"All right, all right. I surrender. Take me to your leader."

"I'm here," said Croasdell. "Actually, she's right. It's a super church—Perpendicular, most of it."

"I guess the rest of it's horizontal," said Vandamme resignedly.

"Come on, barbarian," said Croasdell. "There's enough Scotch in the bottle for three large ones."

"Now," said Vandamme, "at last you're playing my tune."

They ate supper, the two men talking companionably while she listened. Surprising, she thought, how well they were getting on now. John wasn't, after all, the easiest of men. There was a hard intellectual confidence to him that put off some women and most men—though it had certainly attracted her. She wasn't, she considered, a very physical person. She enjoyed lovemaking—the preliminaries, especially. In fact, in some ways she enjoyed the preliminaries more than the act itself. John had been the first man she'd ever had, so she'd no basis for comparison, but he was probably a pretty good lover—even though he seemed sometimes to drift off into a sensual world of his own where she could only limp after him. Perhaps it was like that for most women. Some of her friends had told her stories that sounded very different from the sort of thing she experienced, but people always told lies about sex. She watched Gene pouring John a glass of beer. What would it be like with him? She examined the thought curiously, and found that it didn't even seem disloyal. As a thought, anyway. But John was the only man she would ever have. Or, she thought, ever really want. Fifteen thousand feet he'd fallen, so they said, before he woke and pulled that ripcord. Thank God. She'd loved him from the moment she saw him in that narrow white bed in Chelmsford RAF hospital. How could you do anything else? And he'd loved her. She knew he had—although he always said he'd married her because she was the only good-looking girl he'd ever met who knew that Plato wasn't a metal polish.

"I'll do the washing-up," she said. "You two stay here and drink your beer."

She went into the kitchen, but five minutes later, Vandamme followed her.

"I'll wipe the dishes," he said. "You've had a working day, as well."

He stood a little behind her, watching where the smooth, shining brown hair curled inwards to her neck. She turns my knees to water, he thought. The impulse to reach out and put an arm round her waist was almost overpowering. He seized a towel and began to polish a soup dish. She turned to him and said, laughing:

"Here—it's not going on exhibition, you know. All you have to do is to dry it, not try to use it for a mirror."

"I guess it's all you perfectionists," he said. "You're beginning to influence the way I do things. Like him in there . . ." He jerked his head towards the living-room, where Croasdell sat reading. She did not reply.

"I'll tell you something," said Vandamme. "That husband of your is just about the best flier I ever knew." Except one, he thought to himself.

"You've been flying together, then?" she asked swiftly.

"No reason why you shouldn't know that much, honey," he said, after a moment's pause. "Yes, we've been flying—night flying, mostly. Something I hadn't done much of. I tell you, Jo, I don't a whole lot like being flown by anybody. But I can sit back and sleep when I'm with John."

"That's funny," she said reflectively. "He said much the same about you. In bed, the other night."

Why did she have to say that? "In bed." I could easily make a fool of myself over this girl, he thought, if I'm not very, very careful.

"He said," she went on, "that if all the American pilots were half as good as you, the Germans were going to be really in trouble. He said he'd never seen anybody pick up things so quickly."

He felt irrationally pleased. Croasdell wasn't an easy man to know. You could hardly find two people who shared fewer interests than he did with this spiky, awkward Britisher. About the only thing they had in common—it was a wry thought—was flying—and the feeling they both had for Joanna. And, he reflected, I've only known her a week.

"Listen," he said. "When we go over to this Snoring place tomorrow, why don't you come along? You've a rest day, haven't you? And you could show me that horizontal church."

"All right," she said. "It's a deal. If John wants me to, that is."

"He'll want you to," said Vandamme comfortably. "Or I'll have one of my rages. Mom always said I had the worst rages of any kid she knew."

"Must have been terrifying," said Joanna.

It was a magnificent July morning—a real Connecticut day, thought Vandamme—when they took the jeep to Little Snoring, which lay fifty miles or so north of Chelmsford. Croasdell drove, and Vandamme sat in the back with Joanna. It was a long drive through the flat Suffolk countryside. Once they skirted a pool where a heron got up in front of them and flapped ahead down the unfrequented road. Then they crossed into the green, hedged world of Norfolk, pushing on through quiet villages with quiet names . . . Diss . . . Attleborough . . . Dereham . . . Fakenham, until they came down one side of the airfield at Little Snoring. Croasdell stopped the jeep at the aerodrome entrance, where a corporal of the RAF Regiment waited to check his identification pass. Beyond the guard hut, between a group of red-brick administration buildings, Vandamme could see the grey-green camouflaged shapes of several twin-engined Mosquitoes—"Mossies", as the RAF boys always called them.

"I'd better have lunch here," said Croasdell. "Gene, you take Joanna over to Great Snoring, and buy her some lunch and she'll show you around. And we could meet back here" —he looked at his watch—"at, say, half-past three."

"Couldn't be better," said Vandamme. "And she'll be the first woman who ever got me to church. Apart from my mother, that is."

Vandamme and Joanna ate a lunch of beer and sandwiches in the sunny garden of Great Snoring's old grey pub, and walked round to the church. It was quiet and still and old and, somehow, sure of itself, thought Vandamme. There was a big board inside the main building with pictures of Heaven and Hell, Death and Judgment, at which he stared a long time. About 200 years old, Joanna told him. Outside there were buttercups in the long grass of the churchyard lawn—"nobody to cut it, because all the men are in the forces or in the fields, and nearly all the women are working," she said. An old twin-engined transport lumbered overhead, only a minute or so airborne from the field at Little Snoring.

"It feels like nothing's happened here for about three hundred years," he said. She laughed.

"Just because it's old, it doesn't mean that things don't happen," she said. "Things have happened in this part of the world that have changed the whole of life in every other. Just down there"—she pointed south with a slim, brown hand—"is Thetford, where Tom Paine wrote *The Rights of Man* before he went to America to provide some of the ideas for your Revolution. And right round the corner from where we live is Writtle. That's where Marconi sent his first broadcasts from."

"You're kidding?" he said.

"I never kid," said Joanna, "because—oh . . ."

Her hair smelt of honey, and her lips tasted sweet—literally sweet, he thought later. He kissed her once, twice. His heart was pounding like a schoolboy's. She seemed to be kissing him back, too, and he was half-exultant, half-scared. In the end, it was she who was more in control of the situation than he was.

"No," she said, pushing him gently away.

"Damn it, Jo, honey," he said. "What am I going to do?"

"Nothing," said Joanna. "Nothing at all. And I'll do nothing, either."

He still held her hands in his. Gently, she took them away.

"You know," he said, "you know . . . this isn't just fooling around, for me?"

He hadn't realised he'd been going to say the words until he heard himself saying them and the moment he'd said them, they became true.

"Isn't it?" she said. "Perhaps not. Nor for me, in a way, but don't misunderstand me. Gene, you know . . . you obviously must have known I . . . like you."

"I wanted to kiss you in the kitchen last night," he said. "I damn nearly did."

"It'd have been a bit of a shock for John," she said, a litle shakily. John, John, he thought, it always comes back to John.

"I like you," she steadily. "But I love John. I'm going to have his children, nobody else's. I mean that."

Vandamme let go her hands, and managed a smile.

"That Croasdell," he said, "is one hell of a lucky guy."

That night, as they undressed for bed in the little bedroom of the cottage, John said to her: "I'm really getting very fond of Gene. He's a very good man to be with, you know. A great comfort—you know he'll always do the right thing."

She sat in front of the dressing-table mirror, brushing her hair.

"Yes," she said, "I should think he's that kind of man."

"Thank Heaven," said John, "first night home for a week. Chance for a bit of normal shut-eye."

She put down her hair-brush, crossed to the bed, leaned over him, and kissed him passionately, long and hard.

"Not just yet," she said. He regarded her with pleased surprise.

"Oh, well," he said, "if that's how you feel . . ."

Nine hundred feet below the Mosquito, a faint silvery line announced that they were crossing the long Suffolk beach and heading out to sea. Inside the cockpit—it was small but warm compared with the Beaufighters he'd been instructing on, thought Croasdell—the two small screens of the radar set glowed dimly. Vandamme sat beside him, operating the set. This was the latest of all radar sets in British night-fighters—a development of the Anglo-American Airborne Interception Mark X. To take this equipment over enemy territory, both men had been warned by the Intelligence Officer at West Murford, would mean instant court-martial.

"I'll go up to 8,000, due east," said Croasdell. "We might

get a good practice contact on one of those Liberators they send out to drop stuff for the Dutch Resistance."

"Not too close, though," said Vandamme. "We don't want a burst up our pants from some nervy tail-gunner."

The thrum of the two 1,460-horsepower Rolls Royce Merlins deepened as Croasdell edged open the throttles for the climb. Swiftly the Mosquito lifted up through the thick cloud, emerging occasionally into bright tracts of starlit sky, then slipping back into opaque whiteness. They were miles out from the coast now. Vandamme stared at the two small screens on his set, where one cathode-ray tube gave him a plan view of the radar search area in front of the Mosquito, and the other would give him the height of a contact.

They flew steadily out over the North Sea, apparently alone in a dead universe. Nothing seemed to exist outside the faint glow of the radar and the cockpit instruments. It was strangely companionable in the Mosquito, thought Croasdell—not like the Beaufighter where Vandamme would have been several feet behind him in his own cockpit.

"Not a goddam thing," said Vandamme disgustedly after a time. "Come on, John, let's go home. Two hours is long enough. I need some sack-time. Couldn't sleep last night."

"What's the trouble?" said Croasdell. He began to bank to port, turning slowly back towards the distant coast. "You drink too much coffee—you Americans. You had three cups last night—I saw you. It's no wonder you can't sleep."

"That's not it," said Vandamme. "I just lay awake, that's all."

"Hello, Big Top 18," said a voice in their headsets. "I can give you trade at 2,000 feet, 323, nine miles. Over."

"Big Top . . . that'll be a Mossie from Coltishall," said Croasdell. "Looking for the milk-train—the minelayers," he said in explanation, as Vandamme looked at him questioningly.

Another voice was crackling in the headset.

"Hello, Roundabout. Sorry, old boy, no can do. I'm on

one engine—got the starboard feathered. Just my luck. Going home now. Out."

"Big Top 18, Roger and out," said the first voice.

"Roundabout—that's the Chel station at Corton, on the coast. We must be pretty near the Mossie," said Croasdell hungrily.

"What in hell's Chel?" said Vandamme.

"Chain Home, Extra Low looking station," said Croasdell. "Put there specially to deal with these bastards." He began to turn the Mosquito sharply to port.

"What are you doing now?" said Vandamme.

"I think we might have a look for that milkman," said Croasdell. He switched to transmit and said into his microphone:

"Lighthouse One to Roundabout. We could take your trade. Over."

"Roundabout to Lighthouse One. Roger. Trade now passing out of range, 1,800 feet, 329, twelve miles. Sorry I can't do more. Over."

"Lighthouse One, Roger and out."

"We should be somewhere near that trade in about three minutes," said Croasdell. The Mosquito bored on through the night sky at almost 400 miles an hour.

"You know we've been ordered not to fight," said Vandamme, unconvincingly. I've got this guy wrong, he thought. He always seemed the kind who'd go by the book.

"Unless attacked," said Croasdell. "Remember that. Unless attacked."

I may as well find out now as any other time, he said to himself.

"I've got a blip," said Vandamme suddenly. "West 223, two miles. Two thousand feet."

"I'll come down to three," said Croasdell. "Hang on—there he is. I've got a visual."

Ahead of the Mosquito, there was a faint stabbing glow in the clouds.

"Yes, that's him," said Vandamme. "There's the bastard's exhaust."

A moment later, in full plan view like the silhouette in an aircraft recognition book, they saw the minelayer clearly —a twin-engined Heinkel 111, lumbering along at 180 miles an hour, running in to drop its mine in the Lowestoft approaches.

"One mile," said Vandamme.

Croasdell touched the Mosquito to starboard, lowering flaps as he turned to make a firing approach. They were diving now, straight at the flank of the bomber, which suddenly seemed to fill the sky like a great black shadow. Croasdell's thumb pushed the gun-button and the four Hispano 20mm cannon drummed a long burst. An edge of flame blossomed along the Heinkel's port wing, glowing steadily brighter as the Mosquito swept past and turned for a second pass. The Heinkel slipped sideways to starboard, whether deliberately or not, it was impossible to tell. A moment later, the long black fuselage seemed to fill Croasdell's gunsights again. Once more his thumb went down on the firing button. Large pieces began to fly off the Heinkel's starboard engine. The port wing was now blazing fiercely. Slowly, almost majestically, the big bomber was turning on to its back. Something hurtled across the nose of the Mosquito as Croasdell made his third pass. Mechanically, Vandamme noted that it was an aircraft door. A moment later another object followed it. It was, he saw incredulously, a man, arms flung wide, turning over and over in the starlight. he was wearing no parachute, and he vanished, plunging down through the cloud below the Mosquito. The Heinkel was now falling vertically, nose-down. High above it, the Mosquito banked back once more to watch it hit the sea, but the Heinkel was still fifty feet above the waves when its mine exploded in a great incandescent ball of fire. Vandamme looked at Croasdell and put up his thumb.

"One for the memory book," he said. "Let's go home."

11

"They could send a U-boat," said Rolf Warnow stubbornly.

"Even for you, they won't do that," said Hannah Walters. "The best pilot in the world isn't worth the loss of a U-boat. And that's what they'd be risking."

"It would be worth it, in the circumstances," said Warnow. "I tell you—you don't realise how important it is. A U-boat would be nothing . . ."

"In any case," said the girl, "it isn't that easy. The British have this coast well and truly sewn up. It wouldn't just be the possible loss of a U-boat. It would be nearly a certainty."

His conceit was almost sublime, she thought—completely invincible. In a way, it gave him a child-like quality that was irresistible. And he might be right, for all she knew. They might think it worth the gamble. She knew very, very little of *Fall Ulysses* and wished—for many reasons—she knew more. But she had to get this U-boat nonsense out of his head.

"I have a better idea," she said. "You're a flier. Then fly out."

They were lying together in her narrow bed—he seemed to want her all the time now—and his hand had been softly caressing the curling hair in her groin. She lay with her head on his chest, and his face half-buried in her blonde curls. But at her words, he sat up abruptly.

"You mean . . . of course, I've thought and thought about it. It would be absolutely ideal. But I'd never get on to an American base. Every American military policeman in England will have been warned to watch for a captain carrying papers made out for 'Ralph Hadley'. And there'll be a description of me as well. The only reason we wear enemy uniform on these trips is to take care of the immediate situation, like the one I was in at Mersea. Nobody's ever imagined that we could keep up the deception for long."

"Not an American plane," she said patiently. "An RAF one. And you'd be in RAF uniform."

Firmly, he pushed her head from his shoulder.

"I see," he said. "But how?"

"I . . . know . . . an RAF officer. A flight-lieutenant."

As she spoke, her mouth seemed to feel again the rubbing of that bristly British moustache, and the warm, eager, crude hands on her body. In spite of herself, a little quiver of distaste passed across her face. It did not escape him.

"I see," he said again. "Not very nice, eh? I was wrong about you. You are not a *Mattrasse.* It was a disgusting thing to say. I deeply regret it."

Well, she thought, that's about the nearest to a formal apology that Major Rolf Warnow has ever made, I should imagine. But she was happy he'd said it. And that he'd said it at that moment.

"I would have to get his uniform and papers, of course. And then it would be up to you. Can you fly a British machine?"

"I can fly any machine."

She pulled his head down to her lips and kissed him gently.

"I promise you, Rolf, that I will do this. Perhaps very soon, but there will be a lot to work out. I'll find out what kind of planes he flies. He's a pilot, I know. He wears"—she tapped her left breast. He laughed.

"The wings."

"Yes, wings. And then, Rolf, you'll be gone."

He drew her down beneath him on the narrow bed and straddled her firmly. She grasped him and gasped.

"Yes," he whispered exultantly. "I'll be gone. But not forever."

Oh, Rolf Warnow, she said to herself as he slid into her, I think I'm beginning to love you. But when you go from me, it will be forever.

"You've met the Royal Air Force officer in question, Miss Walters, I take it? As I suggested?"

"Yes," she said. Strongman raised an eyebrow.

"Any difficulties?" Strongman was not a sexually-motivated man, but he did not imagine that there would have been any difficulties. When somebody like Hannah Walters makes it fairly obvious to a young RAF officer that she is . . . available, he thought, there aren't likely to be any difficulties.

"No difficulties," said Hannah Walters.

"You didn't . . .?"

"No, I didn't," said Hannah Walters in a cold savage voice. "I let him fumble about a little, to get him worked up. He's worked up, I assure you. The moment I suggest my flat, he'll be mad for it. Would you like to know exactly what he's planning to do to me?"

Strongman sat back, satisfied. Outside the shadowed room, the grey light of Oxford Circus deepened into the summer light.

"No, no, of course not, Miss Walters. But I would like to know his name, and where he is stationed."

Hannah Walters told him. He wrote both pieces of information on a memo pad and put it in his desk drawer.

"You realise that when this is over, your young RAF friend could be court martialled?"

"Good," she said viciously.

"You, on the other hand, will be on your way to South America," said the Director. "Out of the war. Better than being hanged in Holloway."

"If you keep your word," she said.

"I shall. But never forget that I am your Control," said Strongman. "Co-operate, and go to South America. Disobey me, and you'll be sent for trial, and probable execution. That's always been the position, ever since we first blew your cover, Miss Walters. And you haven't minded co-operating up to now."

She said nothing. He looked at her closely.

"I hope there's no . . . emotional . . . attachment between you and Major Warnow?" he said.

"No," she said swiftly.

He looked at her long and hard. Her face was a mask. It had always been a mask, he reflected. She was a formidable human being, in her way—as good as some of his own girls. He looked at her again. Her fingers went, apparently unconsciously, to her neck, and that decided him. She might be formidable, but she didn't want to be hanged. Strongman, of course, was not a sexually understanding man. It was his one weakness.

"That's excellent," he said. "I want Major Warnow to get his RAF papers and his uniform in very much the same way that you might have got them for him if you'd still been working for Germany. I want him to think that the whole thing is one shining example of German ingenuity."

"And the plane?" she said.

"Don't worry about the plane. I'll arrange that part of it the moment you tell me the date and time of your meeting with this unfortunate young flight-lieutenant. Use the customary telephone number. All you need say is the place, the date, the time."

"Thank you," she said.

He went over and opened the door for her, and she went out, and across the outer office, where the grey-haired woman, who was always there, sat working. She went out the usual way—through the annexe used by the BBC Foreign Service. It was a building well chosen for inconspicuous arrival and departure. So many varied sorts of people went in and out at all hours that one more wouldn't be noticed.

Two elderly caretakers watched her go.

"Who's that?" said one of them.

"She's something to do with the BBC up on the fifth floor," said the other. "She's often working late. A lot of 'em do."

"Nice bit o' crackling," said the old man appreciatively. "See the way they bounce up and down. Reminds me of Jean Harlow. Cor, I could just . . ."

"You bloody couldn't," said the other scornfully. "Not if she lay on her back and said 'Have me'. Not at your age."

"You'd be surprised," said the old man, and went back to his sweeping.

Hannah Walters pushed her way through the evening crowds in Regent Street. There were uniforms everywhere: once or twice she got a long look from an assessing eye below an Army or an Air Force cap. Down at the entrance to Glasshouse Street, and all along Coventry Street, the prostitutes were beginning to gather. Some of them, she saw, were no more than fifteen or sixteen. She turned left through the big glass doors and went into the Corner House. There was a seat free at a table occupied by three middle-aged women and she took it, ordering coffee. It came and she drank it thirstily.

Well, I'm going to betray Rolf Warnow, she thought. Betray him? He wasn't going to die, of course. She was simply going to get him back to Germany. In a way, it was a service she was doing for him. Oh, for God's sake, she told herself, wearily, why pretend. She was going to betray him—in his terms, certainly. He'd kill himself and her if he had an inkling of what was being planned for him. It was obvious enough what they wanted. They thought he'd lead them to *Ulysses*. Whatever *Ulysses* was.

She didn't give a damn about *Ulysses*. They could have an operation code-named for every hero of antiquity, and Hitler still couldn't win. Germany had lost the war. They didn't know it in Germany yet—I suppose some of them do, though, she thought—but that was what had happened. That was what she must not forget. Germany had lost the war.

There was no point in facing that appalling, bone-watering, terrifying walk to the rope for a lost cause.

Was Rolf Warnow a lost cause? Don't be a fool, she begged herself. Look at the facts. What are his chances? The war may well go on another year . . . more, perhaps. He's a pilot, a special one, by the look of things. He'll be in the thick of it. He hasn't a hope. And, for that matter, he'll be better off in Germany, even so. If he's caught here, in American uniform, he'll be hanged. Her mind was made up. It was made up before she saw Strongman, but she'd had to say it all out to herself. She got up, slipped twopence under her plate, and then went back to Chelsea and Rolf Warnow. When she got there, he was lying on the bed, dozing. She kissed him on the forehead, crossed to the telephone, and dialled the number of an RAF unit in East Anglia.

"Can I speak," she said, "to Flight-Lieutenant . . . Yes, I'll hold on."

"You were given a clear, specific order, Colonel Vandamme, and you disobeyed it," said General Paul Hamel coldly. "That is a court martial matter."

"Yes, General," said Vandamme. What's got into old Ham, he thought? You'd think we'd shot down a Lancaster.

"You were instructed to confine yourselves to night training, and under no circumstances to engage the enemy," said Hamel.

"Unless attacked," said Vandamme.

Hamel slammed his fist on the table.

"You're asking me to believe that a Heinkel 111 with a goddam great mine under its belly attacked a night-fighter Mosquito that can do twice its speed? In any case—no, wait, I tell you"—as Vandamme started to speak—"don't make it worse for yourself. I've read the log of the conversation between Squadron Leader Croasdell and the radar station at Corton. So I understand, has Air Marshal Shevlin. He's seeing the Squadron Leader this morning," he added with satisfaction.

"Yes, General," said Vandamme.

"The only reason you will not be court martialled," said Hamel more quietly, "is that we cannot take you off this operation as of now. You are therefore severely reprimanded, and your record will be so marked."

"Yes, General," said Vandamme.

"Now listen to me, Colonel," said Hamel. "You are not a comic-book hero." Vandamme thought of saying, "Yes, General", once more, but decided not to risk it.

"The point is, boy," said Hamel more kindly, "that we can't afford to risk you getting killed." Not yet, anyway, he said to himself.

"As a matter of fact," he added, "it just might be that this whole thing might be used to our advantage."

"How, General?" said Vandamme curiously. "Apart from the fact that the Germans are down one Heinkel?"

"I'll assume you didn't say that, Colonel Vandamme," said Hamel. "No, I mean that it's just possible that some German agent in your area—no, I'm not kidding Colonel, there are some—is wondering what takes a British Squadron Leader and an American Lieutenant-Colonel around in a Mosquito night after night. You must have caused some talk at that RAF base—which was it?"

"West Murford, General," said Vandamme.

"That's it," said Hamel. "So we kind of hail this as an Anglo-American success. Co-operation. Night fighter teams—a try-out for night fighter teams, anyway. It isn't any sillier than some of the stuff that hits this desk. And one thing's for sure, right now we do not want any German wondering in any way whatever about Mosquitoes."

"Why not, General?" said Vandamme.

"You'll find out when we're good and ready," said Hamel. "That's a British problem, as of now. But these B-17s—these Trojan B-17s, I mean—they're our baby. Here in Eight. You know we lost a couple more of our own B-17s yesterday, to suspected infiltration of our boxes by these bastards? And the British had a Stirling shot down last night on the way to Turin—by another Stirling?"

"I didn't know, General," said Vandamme quietly.

"Well, you know now," said Hamel. "What you're doing is a hell of a lot more important than grabbing a single Heinkel. So don't do it again."

"No, General," said Vandamme. "And, General?"

"Yes?"

"Just what *does* take a British Squadron Leader and an American Lieutenant-Colonel around in a Mosquito night after night?"

"For psychological evaluation of what this Warnow is likely to do if given the chance."

"Yes, General, but . . .?"

"I've told you. You'll find out later. Now go find Croasdell. What's he like?"

"General," said Vandamme, "I'll just say that he's a regular guy."

"Hm," said Hamel.

"Two Mosquitoes?" said Air Marshal Shevlin. "And one to be written off completely?"

"Yes," said the Director.

"Well, I suppose it's worth it."

"There's a lot to be gained."

"I won't deny," said Shevlin reflectively, "that losing that Stirling in that particular way yesterday shook me a bit. The boy brought it in, you know, but it was written off. He died later. Only two survivors."

"It won't be the last," said the Director.

Shevlin got up from his chair and walked over to the window, staring across the roofs of London. On the skyline, silver dots against the haze, he could see eight barrage balloons guarding the western bomb-lane down which the Heinkels and the Dorniers had streamed three years ago.

"Of course," he said suddenly, "his Mosquito—Warnow's, I mean—won't have an operational radar set in, will it?"

"Absolutely essential it shouldn't," said the Director.

"We can fix that easily enough," said Shevlin. "Just the usual note on the instrument panel: 'Set removed for maintenance.' Or whatever. No reason he should suspect."

He walked back and sat down again.

"There are two things I don't like, Director. First, the other Mosquito's going to be equipped with a Mark X AI set, modified version. You realise that equipment is so secret that it isn't allowed—yet—to be taken over enemy territory? The Germans would probably even give Warnow in exchange for one of those sets."

"I doubt it," said the Director quietly.

"Second," said Shevlin, as though the Director had not spoken. "I don't like the business with this flight-lieutenant."

"It's got to look absolutely convincing," said the Director. "The best way to do that is to let it happen exactly as it would have happened."

"This boy is being set up," said Shevlin. "He's going to be destroyed—court martial, disgrace, the rest—for what is, after all, a perfectly natural reaction to a pretty woman. There's no way he can know she's a German agent—or supposed to be one, at any rate."

He passed his hand across his brow, and looked at the Director through his fingers.

"The flight-lieutenant will be disobeying a number of regulations when he's with the girl," said the Director. "Not least, those affecting the security of his uniform and his identity papers. A court martial would be the natural consequence. And if the *Abwehr* have any doubts whatever, it will convince them."

"Nevertheless," said Shevlin quietly, "that's the point at which I'm going to stick. No court martial."

The Director looked at him, and after a pause said evenly:

"I think we can take care of your first, very valid point about the radar set. We can have an explosive charge wired to it, with a time fuse activated when the crew . . . leave . . . the aircraft. There should be no question of anything being left, after that. Barring unforeseen accidents."

"Flying is one business, Director, where you can't bar unforeseen accidents," said Shevlin. "All right, you can have your two Mosquitoes. And your Mark X AI. And your poor damned flight-lieutenant, up to a point. But I'll deal with him—and there'll be no court martial."

The Director shrugged. Shevlin stood up.

"Well, thanks for the tea, Director. Earl Grey, wasn't it? Don't know how you get it. Go through Pink, my ADC. He'll fix it all up for you. And now I've got to get back to HQ. I'm going to have"—his lips tightened—"a short talk with Squadron Leader Croasdell."

"I got a hell of a rocket from Andy Shevlin this morning," said Croasdell, as he and Vandamme walked across the gravel drive outside the officers' mess at West Murford. "Did you see Hamel today?"

"I did," said Vandamme. "And old Ham bawled me out."

"If they do this to us for hitting a Heinkel," said Croasdell, "what do you think they'd have said if we'd missed?"

Vandamme laughed and clapped him on the shoulder. A tall, grey-haired officer, wearing RAF wings and medal ribbons from the last war, came out of the Administration Office and walked over to them.

"Gene, I don't think you've met Wing Commander Egglestone," said Croasdell. "He was on leave when we came to the station. He's station commander here. Denis, this is Gene Vandamme."

"Glad to know you," said the wing commander. "Come and have a drink."

They walked over towards the mess, and the sound of laughter and singing.

"You'll have to put up with a bit of this, Gene. They're celebrating," said Egglestone. "We had a couple of flights on Flower last night, and they got two JU-88s over the airfield at Ostend. First this month—everybody's very pleased."

"Flower?" said Vandamme.

"Oh, it's our code word for night intruder patrols," said Egglestone. "We send two or three Mossies to wait over a *Luftwaffe* airfield, and pick the Huns off as they come in to land."

"Dirty," said Vandamme.

"Ah, well, you know what they say," said the wing commander comfortably. "Never give a sucker an even break."

A roar of voices beat around them as they opened the mess door.

"Listen," said Vandamme, pleased. "They're singing 'John Brown's Body'. That's one of ours."

"Well . . ." said the wing commander. He seemed embarrassed.

A few heads turned in their direction as they walked in. Vandamme's American uniform was conspicuous against they grey-blue of the RAF tunics.

"Look, here's one of them," somebody shouted, and an officer with an immense comic-book moustache jumped on to a table , vigorously conducting with both arms. The singing swelled:

"... flying Flying Fortresses at 30,000 feet,
"We're flying Flying Fortresses at 30,000 feet,
"We've bags of point-five ammo and a teeny-weeny bomb,
"And we drop the bastard from so high we don't know where it's gone . . ."

"What the hell?" said Vandamme.

The wing commander grasped his elbow.

"What'll you have have?" he said. "We've got some good

Scotch—it came in yesterday. Three Scotches, Beckett," he told the corporal-barman. "Doubles."

The singing swelled, and the mess was now into the second verse:

"Glory, glory, shall we drop it?
"Glory, glory, shall we drop it?
"Glory, glory, what a helluva way to die.
"And we drop the bastard from so high we don't know
where it's gone . . ."

Sorry about all this nonsense, Gene," said Egglestone uncomfortably. "I think it had better stop. I had a phone call from Command just before you came, telling me I could release some news."

He picked up a heavy metal ashtray and banged it on the bar.

"All right, all right, chaps, let's have a bit of hush."

Gradually the singing died away.

"We all know what we're celebrating, don't we? Two Huns last night, marked up to us. Well, it wasn't two. It was three."

There was a roar of applause.

"Who got it, the other one?" called the officer who had jumped on the table.

"John and Gene Vandamme here," said Egglestone. "Off Lowestoft. A Heinkel on the milk-run."

There was an embarrassed silence.

"Good show," said a voice from the back of the room, followed by murmurs of approval. Men began to break up into little groups, ordering drinks, sitting down to read magazines. Vandamme and the two RAF men turned back to the bar. A moment later, there was a tap on Vandamme's shoulder. He turned, to see the officer with the handlebar moustache standing beside him.

"Can I buy you a drink?" said the Englishman.

"I've got one, thanks," said Vandamme. He felt coldly angry.

"A very large Scotch for the colonel, Beckett," said the other, unmoved. "You really must have one—I've always found it helps to numb the pain."

Vandamme grinned suddenly.

"Well, if it does that . . . but what was that all about? The song, I mean? Why all the cracks?"

"Oh, we get a bit uppity sometimes, if we've got something to celebrate. Doesn't mean anything. There's always a bit of needle between us and you Yanks, isn't there? Natural enough."

"Yes, but . . ."

"It's just that we've got this . . . thing . . . that the Forts don't carry much of a load and drop it from a long way up, if you know what I mean. Lot of nonsense, of course. It's just a different technique."

"I see . . ." said Vandamme slowly.

"Time for the news—it's started already, I think," said a voice. Someone switched on the radio.

". . . and there is still severe fighting on the Kursk-Orel front, where Soviet forces claim that they have inflicted heavy losses on German armoured formations," said the BBC announcer. He paused.

"A strong force of United States Flying Fortress bombers today struck at the aircraft assembly plants at Regensburg and Hadow, in eastern Germany. First reports indicate that very heavy damage was done to both targets, which were left burning. Twenty-eight enemy aircraft were destroyed in the air during the attack. Forty-four American aircraft failed to return . . . The Ministry of Food announces that with effect from next Monday, the cheese ration will be increased from four to six ounces. This is because of the normal seasonal increase in production—"

Someone switched off the set.

"Jesus God," said a voice. "Forty-four."

"Hadow," said the moustached officer. "That's a Messerschmitt factory, isn't it?"

"Yes," said Croasdell.

"Going out again tonight?" said the other. "What's it all about, anyway? Why are you flying together?"

"Supposed to be co-operation," said Croasdell. "Night fighter teams."

"You never know what they're going to dream up next," said the moustached officer. He turned to Vandamme.

"Why don't you come with me and meet some of the lads and show us how you play poker?" he said. As they walked over to a table, he said quickly:

"Maybe it wasn't such a very teeny bomb."

Hauptquartier

Feingeraet Untersuchungstelle 5
Mitteilungsblatt Nr. 8

To: Commanding Officer, *Lw. Bergebataillon 4*
Neustadt an Weinstrasse

1. Vital operational requirements for the salvage of enemy aircraft are not being fully met by your unit.
2. The following points have been raised by industry.
3. Fuselages have been transported without support, causing them to be damaged or pushed into each other.
4. Armament and ammunition containers have been transported still containing ammunition.
5. The taking of "souvenirs" or removal of apparatus or instruments under the guise of "safe-keeping" will not be tolerated.
6. Shields and plates will be copied, but not removed.
7. Damaged steel propellers of the Thunderbolt and Marauder aircraft can often be used again for operations, however apparently badly damaged. They will be collected and forwarded, and not kept as trophies.

H. H. STOECKLE, *Oberst*

Copies to:
Generalquartiermeister Luftwaffenbergung
Luftgaukommando: Bergestab
All salvage battalions

12

The name of the burgomaster of Seebruck was Hans Klamroth. He said it twice into the telephone, stammering a little in excitement as he identified himself to the duty officer at the *Luftwaffe* airfield outside Kiel.

"Wait a moment, while I write it down," said the bored voice at the other end of the line. Sweating slightly, for he had run fifty yards to his office, Burgomaster Klamroth looked across his work-table to the window. Sudden gusts of wind rattled the panes, sweeping in across the choppy waters of the Kieler Bucht. A rainstorm was building up, he noted absently, looking at the black pillars of cloud piling up to the east, where the Kieler Bucht merged with the Baltic Sea. The voice came back on the line.

"Now, what are you reporting?"

"An American terror-bomber, *Herr Hauptmann*."

"My rank is lieutenant. And I think you are mistaken. We have no report—"

"No, no. Not in the air . . . not flying. The bomber is here, lying on the shore, at Seebruck. A very large bomber, with four engines."

"Are there any crew?" said the voice sharply.

"There are two dead men, *Herr Leutnant*. Nobody else."

"What have you got in Seebruck? Any police or *Volksturm*?"

"There are a few *Volksturm*, if I can get them. Most are now at work."

"Get as many as you can at once, Burgomaster, and guard the plane. No one is to go near it. Do you understand . . . that is very important? No souvenir hunters. Nobody."

"Of course."

"What's the state of the tide?"

"The tide, *Herr Leutnant*?"

The voice was impatient.

"Yes, the tide. Can the sea reach the plane? How far must it be moved to be safe?"

"It's high tide here in four hours, but the weather doesn't look too good. I think the plane will have to be pulled back about a hundred metres."

"Right . . . wait . . . give me your telephone number. Please see that someone stays by the phone."

"There's only me in the office."

"Then you'll have to stay, as soon as you've warned the *Volksturm*."

"Right, *Herr Leutnant*," said Klamroth resignedly.

In the orderly room at the airfield outside Kiel, the duty officer picked up the telephone again.

"Give me the *Kommando Flughafen Bereich* at Flensburg. The duty officer."

There was a crackling on the line as an NCO answered the call. A moment later another voice spoke.

"Airfield Regional Command—duty officer."

"Good morning. This is duty officer, Kiel. Can you get hold of the *Luftgauingenieur* for me, urgently. Who's on duty today?"

"It's *Oberleutnant* Foerster. He's in the mess. But what's it all about?"

"I've got an American bomber on the sand at Seebruck and I'm worried about the tide. He's going to have to really shift himself if he doesn't want to lose it . . ."

The duty engineer officer at Rendsburg was flirting mildly with the blonde mess waitress and finishing his lunch when he was called to the telephone. When he got the news, his eyes widened in excitement. *Oberleutnant* Foerster was that formidable combination—an efficient man who was also ambitious. He thought for a few moments, and then reached for the phone again.

"Give me *Bergebataillon* 9. It's at Eutin at the moment, I think."

Twenty miles away in the headquarters of the engineering salvage battalion, the telephone rang and Foerster explained his problem.

"The damned thing's going to take some moving," he said. "If it's a B-17, and it sounds like one, it'll weigh well over twenty tons, loaded. I haven't had a chance to see it yet, but I've had a look at the Coastal Survey, and the shore-line there is open. And there looks to be a good road beside the beach. How far away are you by road?"

There was a pause while the salvage lieutenant at Eutin looked at the map.

"About twenty-seven kilometres, sir. I reckon it'll take us an hour—maybe a shade less. But you're in luck in one way."

"Oh?"

"We've got a *Bergepanzer* here—one of the old Mark III panzers with the turret off. We've been trying it out as basic recovery equipment. It'll certainly pull a B-17 for a hundred metres, if we can roll it there in time. I'll have to fuel it first, though, and I doubt if we'll get much more than twenty kilometres an hour out of it."

"Well, do your best. I'll see you at Seebruck. I'm going to get the car and zip across to Kiel and take the Storch over there. If the beach looks reasonable, I'll land."

"Right, sir."

Ninety minutes later, *Luftgauingenieur* Foerster looked down from 500 feet on the wreck of the B-17 at Seebruck. The olive-green bomber lay spreadeagled on the shore, the single blue and white star on its port wing shining in the rain. Behind it, a long deep furrow in the sand showed how the pilot had tried to bring it in parallel with the sea.

Foerster looked beyond the plane to the white line of the advancing tide. It seemed terribly near. Strong gusts of wind were shaking the fabric of the little high-winged, single-engined Fieseler Storch monoplane as it swept low above the beach. There was a clear stretch of sand and light shingle beyond the B-17, round which men were already swarming. A score or so people stood at a distance, watching, but the weather had kept most indoors. Two or three men in *Volksturm* uniform stood between them and the bomber. On the road beyond the beach, two long transporter trucks and three military lorries were parked. The engineer lieutenant from *Bergebataillon* 9 was an officer who moved quickly.

The little plane flew on down the long beach for a mile, then turned inland, following the grey ribbon of road towards Eutin. Two miles along this road, Foerster saw a moving cloud of spray on the rain-soaked highway. There it was . . . the *Bergepanzer*, a stripped-down tank with a powerful winch where the turret used to be, pounding along towards the shore. Twenty-five minutes yet, at least, thought Foerster. He tapped the Storch's young sergeant-pilot on the shoulder, and made a planing motion with his hands, pointing back towards the beach. The pilot grinned and gave the thumbs-up sign. The Storch banked to starboard, came low again over the shore, seemed to steady itself against the wind, and bumped lightly into a landing on the shingly sand, sixty yards from the B-17. Almost before they had stopped moving, the pilot was out, hammering iron staples deep into the sand to act as anchors against which to tether the little plane against the mounting wind.

Stiffly, Foerster got down from the Storch, and walked over to the B-17. All round him men were working on the long, drab-coloured fuselage—taking out the Browning .5 machine-guns, disconnecting oil and petrol lines. High on the great wings, a team of engineers was dismantling the wing-roots. Every now and then, the fuselage shuddered under the buffeting of the wind. Foerster walked up to where the *Bergebataillon* lieutenant was carefully photographing sections of the B-17. The name painted on the fuselage, he noted, was one of the usual stupid American ones: "Lulubelle". They spoke for a few moments, and then the lieutenant put the camera back in its case and led the way up into the short, spiky marram grass beyond the shore-lines. Two bodies lay there, stretched on their backs on a tarpaulin sheet. A couple of elderly men of the *Volksturm* stood there, leaning on their rifles.

"This one," said the lieutenant, pointing, "was in the pilot's seat."

Foerster looked down at the young dead face. The neck was bent at an unnatural angle.

"Broken neck, I imagine," said the lieutenant. "Lucky for us—it stopped him trying to burn the plane. I think he must have snapped it when he touched down and she tipped. He was making a belly-landing, wheels up, and he must have been doing 150 kilometres an hour. I reckon he's one of the lot that hit Regensburg—miles off course here, though."

"I wonder why he didn't bale out with the rest of the crew," said Foerster thoughtfully. "I'm told they picked up a couple near Lubeck."

The lieutenant shrugged.

"He may have been trying to help the other one," he said. "Look—" he pointed to the second maimed body—"this one couldn't have baled out. He'd got a bullet in the guts, and he was in a bad way. We found him in the waist-turret. I think the pilot told the others to go, and then tried to land it, to give him a chance. But she tipped, and he broke his own neck. And this one bled to death, anyway. You should see the mess in that turret."

There was a clatter of tracks from the direction of the road.

"Thank goodness for that," said the lieutenant. "Here's the tank. Now we might get something done, and not before time, either. Look at that sea."

The pounding line of the advancing waves was now no more than fifty yards from the plane. The *Bergepanzer*, scattering a shower of shingle and sand as it pivoted on its tracks, waddled down to the hulk of the B-17. The lieutenant ran forward and began to give orders for the fixing of the winch cables to the undercarriage housing beneath the plane's battered belly. A few minutes later, the 350-horse-power engines of the *Bergepanzer* began to roar as they took the strain on the winch cables. Slowly, with a crunching, cracking sound coming from beneath it, the B-17 began to edge forward, away from the oncoming sea. As soon as the plane was high on the foreshore, the wing dismantling teams started work again. The *Luftgauingenieur* watched for a few minutes, but he was satisfied. He turned to the young lieutenant.

"That was a first-class job. We shan't get a nasty *Mitteilungsblatt* from HQ for that one," he said. The boy flushed with pleasure. Foerster looked back at the bomber. One wing was already being loaded into a transporter.

"I'd better make my report," he said. "Well, it certainly isn't airworthy, is it? There's a lot of damage to the fuselage belly, and there's the flak damage to the tail that brought it down in the first place. And the propellers are wrecked, of course. But it's not at all bad . . . certainly capable of being repaired. I'll class it Category Two—so watch where it goes. I don't want some fool painting Category Four on that fuselage and sending it on to the dismantling plant at Grevenbroich. Here"—he took a pink form from his uniform tunic pocket, and scribbled briefly on it—"as soon as you've got the engines out of the other wing, and the wings and fuselage loaded, you'd better take the whole lot to Kiel. And I'll arrange meanwhile for the Focke Wulf people to come and look at it. I reckon this baby will fly again . . ."

He clambered back into the Storch. Thirty minutes later, he was back at the airfield outside Kiel. He walked to the communications room and asked the orderly clerk for a teleprinter form.

"To Officer Commanding, *Luftzeugruppe*," he wrote. "I have the honour to report the successful salvage of one B-17 aircraft. Location Seebruck: Category Two . . ." He added a list of details, checked a file, and allotted the B-17 a number.

An hour later, the telephone rang in the office of *Oberst* Pertz in the *Luftwaffe* compound of the *Wolfsschanze* at Rastenberg. Greiner handed him the instrument. Pertz listened.

"Excellent," he said. "We need every one we can get." Then he frowned.

"No, six weeks is far too long. A fortnight, no more."

He listened again, while the voice at the other end of the line spoke for several seconds. Then he said harshly:

"In that case, get sixty men. A fortnight. It is the *Reichsmarschall*'s order . . ."

Hauptmann Werner Lutz stared unblinkingly through the Plexiglass flight window of the B-17, watching the tops of the firs and spruce and pine hurtling towards him like the path of some great roller-coaster, while the plane followed the contours of the ground, forty feet up. Out and to his right stretched the line, also tree-top high, of the other three B-17s in his section of four. Exactly 1,000 yards behind Werner's section flew another B-17 in line abreast. The sensation of speed at what was virtually ground level was terrific. Lutz was flying at 280 miles an hour, engines on full boost. One tiny error would scatter his plane over a couple of square miles of Norwegian scrub forest.

"The lake is coming up," he said into the intercom. "Twenty seconds."

There it loomed ahead, water glittering in the afternoon light . . . a stretch of sandy shore, and then they were hurtling, for the third time this week, towards the giant moored model in the centre of the three-mile-long lake. The first of the long areas of wood and fabric shot beneath the nose of the B-17.

"On bomb-run now," said Lutz to the bombardier. "She's all yours."

"Very good," came the voice of the bomb-aimer in his headphones. He was bent, absorbed, over his instruments. "I'm counting . . ."

Behind them the second flight was crossing the edge of the lake.

"Eleven . . . bomb doors open . . . nine . . . eight . . . seven . . ."

Ahead, seemingly only just below the level of his face, Lutz saw the big whitewashed circle of the target flashing towards him.

". . . four . . . three . . . two . . . bomb goes *now*!"

Relieved of the great weight of the single bomb, the B-17 staggered twenty feet higher. Lutz eased back on the control column, climbing steadily into the pale blue of the northern Norway sky. He began to bank to port, taking the outer left position in the box of four into which the flight was now forming. Out beyond the wing he could see the second section of four, their own bomb-run just completed, beginning to climb.

"Close bomb doors."

Down in the fuselage belly, there was a purr of hydraulics.

"Bomb doors closed."

Lutz's section was now at 1,300 feet, swinging back towards the end of the lake. Eagerly he looked down at the water and its moored structure, and then swore with disappointment. Ten yards beyond the whitewashed circle on the wooden model, a slowly subsiding patch of disturbed water showed where his bomb had missed. He ran his eye along the 600-yard structure. Not one of his section had achieved a hit on any of the whitewashed circles allotted to them, though the bomb of the B-17 at the end of the line had managed to graze the edge of the wood. The second section, he noted sourly, had got three hits—and in one of them, the tailfin of the dummy bomb sprouted from the exact centre of the white target circle. That was Trobitius's section. He would have to buy Trobitius drinks again tonight.

He turned his section west, climbing to 10,000 feet. Then he took his place in the Fortress box, and began to circle, waiting for the escort squadron of FW-190s to get into position above him. As soon as he saw them, four flights of three, specks against the dazzling blue, he set course south. Those fighter boys would have had a look at the lake by now, and they'd be laughing. Let them try it, he thought savagely. Hedge-hopping and precision bombing from nearly zero feet were a bit more difficult with a four-engined bomber weighing 30 tons than with those damned gnats. He grumbled to his bomb-aimer all the way back to Sola, though he knew it wasn't really the boy's fault. The kind of problem they were facing with these practice runs was one they'd never had before. The American aircraft were bigger than any combat plane in normal service with the *Luftwaffe*—except the Condors. And, God be thanked, nobody had yet dreamed up a crackpot scheme for using the Condors in a low-level attack role. He looked down through the patchy cloud cover over the coast. There was the Boknafjord, with Stavanger and Sola coming up to the south. He turned the B-17 into the circuit until the tower at Sola cleared him to land. Then he began the landing drill with the second pilot.

"Flaps twenty."

The B-17, descending steadily, was slowing to around 170 miles an hour.

"More engine revs, please."

There was an answering thunder from the wings.

"Wheels down . . . radiators closed."

The runway appeared ahead, green markers glowing in the afternoon haze. Beside Lutz, the second pilot glanced at the green light on the instrument panel.

"Wheels locked down."

Gently, Lutz was easing the bomber in.

"Full flaps."

The nose of the B-17 lifted, and Lutz adjusted the trimming knobs. The bomber was gliding in now, beautifully balanced.

"Give me height and speed," he said to the second pilot.
"Eighty . . . 120 . . . fifty . . . 110."
"Throttles back."
The B-17 sank on to the runway, exhausts crackling. Slowly Lutz applied the brakes . . . 300 . . . 500 . . . 800 . . . 1,000 yards. The B-17 creaked to a halt. For the first time since missing the target on the lake, Lutz smiled.
"Oh, well," he said, "we flew a tidy box. And it was a good landing."
Gerhard, the Sola intelligence officer, met Lutz and his crew as they walked back to the administration buildings and the debriefing hut.
"Don't go into the mess after you've talked to me," he said. "You're all in the Special Mess again from now on. We're operational—no leave, no phone calls. Until orders."
"We're operational again?" said Lutz, surprised.
"It came through from *Führer* headquarters while you were flying," said Gerhard. Lutz whistled in astonishment.
"Well, you'll hear my opinion at the debriefing," he said. "But it seems to me that we've still got a long way to go."
He looked back at where the mechanics were swearing over the B-17.
"Those babies take some learning—the way we're being asked to use them. We were doing better until we lost Warnow, but that really set us back. It's meant re-training two whole sections."
"I know, I know," said Gerhard. "But if you're looking for a short way to trouble, try arguing with *Führer* headquarters."
Lutz opened the door of the Special Mess. Even now, after he had spent plenty of time there, it still came as a shock—the lounging men in American uniforms, the bottles of American bourbon and English gin on the bar shelves, the copies of *Esquire*, and *Life*, and *Saturday Evening Post* lying on the big table . . . even, on the walls where one might have expected to see Adolf Hitler, the pictures of

Churchill and Roosevelt. Around him, every voice was speaking English—some of them, he noticed disapprovingly, not too well. He found the triumphant Trobitius, and bought him a John Collins at the bar, while they settled down for a brief technical discussion of why Trobitius's section managed three hits to his none. Trobitius was laying it on a bit, he thought, and suddenly he wished he was back in *Luftwaffe* grey, leading his old *Staffel* in a bomber *Geschwader* somewhere where you could tell friend from foe, and didn't have to pretend. What was it the KG 200 psychologist had said? You've got to think American, talk American, fly American. You've got to do it so well that American ground control and British radar don't suspect you for a moment, so well that American fighter pilots would die to protect you. You've got to *be* Americans—until those last eighteen minutes. By God, it wasn't the last eighteen minutes that worried him, but the first five hours. He looked around the bustling mess for more congenial company than Trobitius and saw von Altmark sitting by himself, drinking rum and Coke and reading *Reader's Digest*. He crossed and flopped into a chair beside him.

"So we're operational again, Frido."

The other looked up.

"Yes, but God knows why. And there's nothing yet about targets. Not a whisper. Even in 1940, we never had security like this. How did you get on today, by the way?"

"Three misses, and one graze," said Lutz disgustedly. "And Max Trobitius's lot got three hits."

Altmark laughed.

"Well, my old Werner, he had three weeks longer with Warnow than you did. He's bound to do better, for the moment, anyhow."

Lutz shrugged. He felt dispirited.

"Warnow gone, just when he'd got the whole of *Ulysses* really rolling. It's hard to believe, even now. And yet in spite of that, we're back in the Special Mess, and operational."

"Yes," said the other thoughtfully. "It makes you wonder."

"Makes you wonder what?"

"Well, there was a sort of cat's-got-the-cream look on Gerhard's face today when he got that call from *Führer* headquarters. It just made me think a bit, that's all . . ."

Lutz picked up Altmark's discarded *Reader's Digest* and stared unseeingly at a page of photographs.

"You mean, you were wondering about Warnow?" he said at last.

"Exactly," said von Altmark.

13

"There's only one word you can use," said Vandamme, looking up wearily from a table spread with maps and papers.

"The whole organisation—you can't call it a *Luftwaffe Geschwader* in any normal sense—is like a damned octopus. Wherever you put your finger down on the map, you find a tentacle."

Croasdell nodded absently. They sat side-by-side at their desk-table in the Nissen hut room which had been allotted to them at the Eighth Air Force base at Polebrook.

"But even an octopus has a pattern," he said. "And the more I look at this one, the more I'm beginning to see the first bits of it."

He got up and walked restlessly to the dusty window. Somewhere in the distance, he heard the unmistakable howling roar of a Wright Cyclone engine, followed a few seconds later by another. B-25 Mitchell, he thought, warming up for take-off.

"Look at what we've got," he said. "There are distinct threads already visible in this whole tangle. These dummy airficlds, for instancc."

"Those cycling kids in Holland?" said Vandamme. "At . . . what was the place? . . . Haamstede."

"Yes," said Croasdell. "And pretty well the same report from Aalborg in north-west Denmark—where they've even built fake cottages exactly like those on the real field, a mile or two away. The same again from Stavanger—at least, it looks like a dummy field, though the report's a bit vague. And then there's St Manvieu—a whole French airfield layout, with *Luftwaffe* hangars and a whole system of landing lights, plus aircraft standing in the dispersal areas."

"Nothing very unusual about dummy fields," said Vandamme, dubiously. "We've built them ourselves, in the Philippines. And you've got a big one in Kent."

"It's not the fields that are so interesting," said Croasdell. "It's the planes that are on them—or rather, the planes the Germans want us to think are on them. Just look at the Resistance reports. The wooden thing those Dutch kids heaved a stone at . . . what was it supposed to be? A B-17? Aalborg . . . what did that radio message say? A wooden B-24, and a B-17 fuselage shell with wooden wings added. St Manvieu . . . two B-17s that never seem to fly, though they get towed round the so-called airfield from time to time. Almost certainly fakes. Stavanger . . . a bit vaguer, as I say, but there seem to be a couple of B-17s that never get to take-off. There *is* a pattern."

"You mean," said Vandamme thoughtfully. "That they're always—"

"They're always American aircraft," said Croasdell. "Or nearly always. Oh, I know the Rechlin and Lerz photographs show the odd RAF Stirling—and they certainly used a Stirling to interfere with our Turin mission the other night. But practically all these reports concern American planes."

"But why in hell would they want to advertise the fact that they've got American planes?" said Vandamme. "By leaving American dummies scattered round fake fields, they're going to get us really interested."

"I think," said Croasdell slowly, "that whoever's in charge of KG 200 is a very clever man. He knows we're going to find out he's operating B-17s and B-24s. He knows that, in the long run, there's no way of keeping it absolutely secret. There are bound to be incidents he can't control—wonder-boy's crash at Mersea, for instance. He knows we're going to get worked up about it—and that we'll try, one day soon, to do something. He's accepted all that. So he's trying now to do two things. First, he wants us—when we come—to bomb the wrong targets. Second, even more important, he wants us to think he hasn't got much in the way of B-17s and B-24s, and that those he has got are scattered all round northern Europe from Norway to France. So we're shown the odd dummy all over the place—just the way it would be if the real B-17s were simply being used for agent-dropping. He's trying to make us think in the way he wants us to."

"What are they being used for, then?" said Vandamme. "And how many are there—and where are they?"

Croasdell shook his head worriedly.

"I don't know. But I keep thinking back to what the Director told us, and the word '*Ulysses*' comes into my mind . . ."

"There's no doubt they've infiltrated B-17s and B-24s into our own missions," said Vandamme. "They started with the Ploesti refinery raid, using phoney B-24s. Not on a big scale —there's simply no way they could have had a lot of B-24s by August 1943. But the debriefings after Ploesti showed some very suspicious sightings. I know Intelligence reckon we lost some of our ships to 'unidentified' aircraft."

"And there've been some interesting debriefing reports from this very field," said Croasdell, jerking his thumb towards the window. "But again, if strange B-17s are mentioned, they're always in ones or twos. Never formations."

"Formations?" said Vandamme, incredulously.

"That's what I'm beginning to worry about," said Croasdell. "Formations."

He stood, packing the documents carefully into a worn leather briefcase.

"Well, we've pieced quite a bit together for the Director," he said. "Certain, confirmed bases at Aalborg, Sola, and Zilistea—which, by the way, is the Roumanian field they probably used for Trojan mission against your Ploesti B-24s."

Vandamme nodded.

"And there's that very garbled report from Germany—the agent who claims he saw nine B-17s, all painted yellow, lined up on the field at Finsterwalde. Seems a hell of a lot.

I'd guess they were really Heinkel HE-177s. They're twin-engined, I know, but in some respect they look alike."

Croasdell shook his head, as they walked over to the door.

"Perhaps. But I'm not sure, Gene. That's not the first time Finsterwalde has cropped up. There was the POW report from that *Luftwaffe* NCO shot down over Birmingham last week—that he'd seen a B-17 with German markings explode over Echterdinken. He kept grinning and saying it was one of the Finsterwalde Circus. I grant you, he was pretty shaken and didn't really know what he was saying. But it would be a funny thing for him to make up."

"Did you get any reply from the Russians?" said Vandamme.

"Not a thing," said Croasdell. "Mind you we hardly ever do. I wish we could get something, though, because I'm pretty sure that KG 200 is operating along the Russian front. The southern end, round the Crimea, anyway. There are eight separate sightings from Turkey of Russian bombers—so-called Russian bombers—going in to land at German fields in the Crimea. Mostly the Tupolov type. It looks highly suspicious. It'll be in all our interests if the Russians would let us know if they've any experiences like ours. But there's virtually no Intelligence co-operation at this level. They seem nearly as suspicious of us as they are of the Germans. Still we'll try them again."

Vandamme looked at his watch.

"Well, if we're going in to London to see the old guy, I guess it's time we got the show on the road. That drive takes longer than you think. And we can talk about wonder-boy Warnow on the way in."

"I've got the various routes marked here," said Croasdell, tapping the briefcase.

"I sure hope wonder-boy's as predictable as we seem to think," said Vandamme.

"Assuming that Warnow had an aircraft, sir, we decided

that there would be two practicable routes he would be most likely to follow," said Croasdell.

"He would be worried about the German radar, since he'd be flying one of our planes which would make an unmistakably 'enemy' blip on their screens—and the last thing he'd want would be to be picked off by some patrolling JU-88. We assume he wouldn't want to be flying longer than he could help—his natural instinct would be to get down amongst his own people in one piece as quickly as he could. Now, sir, if you'll just look at the map . . ."

Croasdell took a pencil and drew a circle on the coast of northern France. The Director bent over the map table. Croasdell spoke again:

"The Germans, we know, have a chain of radar stations, the *Himmelbett* system, right down the Dutch, Belgian and French coasts—and these stations have the long-range *Freya* sets and another new short-range precision set which our Intelligence people say is called *Wurzburg Reise.* This radar chain isn't absolutely 100 per cent. According to Bomber Command intelligence, there are two gaps which our own bomber boys try to use when possible. One's at Pointe d'Ailly, just here outside Dieppe."

Croasdell pointed to the circle on the map.

"If he crossed the coast there, low, he could make the *Luftwaffe* airfield at Elbeuf or at Evreux very quickly, and be having a celebratory drink inside about an hour from take-off. Or there's another gap, here . . ."

He pointed farther north on the map.

"It's just outside Egmond-aan-Zee on the Dutch coast. He could do the same there and take her straight into Schiphol. It'll still be chancy, unless there's some way he can let them know he's coming, because although he may slip through the radar, he'll be exposed to a lot of light flak that won't have the faintest idea of who he is."

"I don't propose," said the Director, rubbing his hands together thoughtfully, "to allow Major Warnow to get farther than the coast itself."

He looks, said Vandamme to himself, like a cat outside a mousehole.

"Given," said the Director, "that I can tell you the aerodrome he will be flying from, and the type of aircraft, and the exact weight of that aircraft, could you tell me precisely how much fuel would take Major Warnow to a point at which he would decide that he could—just—reach a beach and make a crash landing?"

Croasdell considered for a moment.

"Well, aircraft differ, just like human beings. Even aircraft of the same type obviously have varying performances. But you could get a mechanic's report—a really exact rundown on the fuel consumption of a particular individual aircraft. Then you could make a very accurate calculation of how far a given amount of fuel might take him. But there are two unknown factors."

"Yes?" said the Director.

"Well, one of them's obvious, sir, of course. If we assume that he'll go for either Pointe d'Ailly or for Egmond, we still don't know which. And the amount of fuel needed to get him just to the coast would be different for either alternative. And in any case, once he sees his fuel gauge is standing low, he may change his mind and try something else."

"And the second unknown factor?" said the Director.

"That's Warnow's own personal skill," said Croasdell. "He's a fine pilot, you tell us—and we've seen for ourselves how he managed a pretty impossible landing at Mersea. Now a fine pilot might do a lot better on an empty tank than an average pilot can manage. Against that, we might reasonably assume that he'll be flying an unfamiliar type, and won't know all the wrinkles yet. There seem to be a hell of a lot of imponderables."

The Director crossed to the taped-up window and stood in his usual "thinking" position, looking out at Oxford Circus. It was the end of the working day, and the crowds were pouring into the Underground. Back home to the week's cheese ration on a slice of toast, or scrambled dried egg, perhaps. Some of them worked long hours nowadays, he thought, and they'd be tired. There was a long, bloody road to travel yet before this war was won. He turned back to where Vandamme and Croasdell sat, waiting.

"We could give Major Warnow enough fuel on his gauge to allow him to choose one, and only one, of those routes. It would have to be the nearer, of course. Which is the nearer to West Murford?"

"Egmond," said Vandamme.

"Very well, then, Egmond it shall be," said the Director.

"But," said Croasdell, "that still doesn't solve the problem, because we aren't precisely sure what he'll be able to achieve with whatever he's given."

The Director smiled.

"You think we can't be certain that he *will* be forced to make a crash-landing on the coast? True, we can't be sure. But what we can do is to leave it entirely up to Major Warnow's abilities. Because although his gauge may tell him that he's got enough petrol for the Egmond route, it will be telling him a lie. He will be out of fuel more quickly than he imagines."

"You mean, you'll rig his gauge so that in fact he runs out of gas when he's still over the sea?" said Vandamme.

"Precisely," said the Director. "It's rather like wrestling, Japanese-style, where I understand that the object is to use the opponent's own strength against him. In this case, Major Warnow's strength is his flying skill."

"So you'll tamper with his instruments to produce an emergency for him—an emergency which only a very skilled pilot can solve, and then only in one way?" said Croasdell. His voice was impassive. Vandamme looked at him out of the corner of his eye. God, he disapproves, he thought. This edgy Britisher disapproves of handing a bum steer to another pilot. He'd blow him out of the sky if he got the chance, but he doesn't like rigging the guy's instruments.

"That's exactly what I mean, Squadron Leader," said the Director.

"And supposing Warnow isn't able to solve it?"

"Then he will die," said the Director. "But I do not think that will happen. I think he'll land on the Dutch coast—there are a lot of good stretches of sand available. I think he will bring his aircraft in without too much damage, and I think—especially in view of his own connection with KG 200—that it will look to the Germans like a gift from the gods. A brand new Mosquito, brought back by a highly experienced pilot, a man whose loyalty simply is not in doubt."

"And then?"

"And then we shall see precisely what happens to Allied aircraft when they are recovered intact, or nearly intact . . . who collects them, where they go, how they are organised, and for what purpose. And perhaps we shall learn something about Operation *Ulysses*."

Neither Vandamme nor Croasdell said anything, but sat waiting. With a slight feeling of sickness in his throat, Croasdell had realised what was coming.

"You'll have guessed just how we shall see this happen, and perhaps find what we want to find," said the Director. "As you know, we've one considerable advantage over the Germans. We have, in Europe, plenty of help. We can alert the Dutch Resistance in all the likely areas where Warnow is likely to make his crash-landing, and we can, through their eyes, see what happens. If, as seems likely, Warnow's Mosquito is taken from Holland to Occupied France, we will arrange for the Resistance Movement in each country to follow its course from man to man, woman to woman."

"It seems much more likely," said Croasdell, "that it will be taken to Germany for evaluation—Rechlin, or Lerz, perhaps."

"Even in Germany," said the Director, "we have channels of communication. Once we can say for certain—as we can here—that there will be a crashed Allied plane, in good repair, at a certain area on a certain date, we can start the ball rolling."

He paused. If, thought Vandamme, this man was ever embarrassed, he was embarrassed now. He doodled idly on a piece of scrap paper, and then went on:

"But there is one disadvantage to all this."

"Yes?" said Croasdell.

"You're aware that the Resistance has few air experts, who readily understand what they see. We need, to follow that Mosquito to wherever it's going, experienced eyes. Yours, Croasdell, and yours, Vandamme."

It was the first time, Vandamme suddenly realised, that the Director had unbent enough to address them relatively intimately, British-fashion, with just their surnames, instead of the formal "Colonel" and "Squadron Leader".

"We can get you into France, or Belgium, or Holland. And get you out. We'll put you in touch with contacts who'll take all the work off your shoulders except that of actually assessing what they take you to see. Each of you speaks German—and between you, other useful languages, too."

He paused, fiddling with a pencil on his desk, then looked up, glancing at each of them in turn.

"I realise that this is more than ever you can have imagined you would have to undertake when you first joined this project. I appreciate your experience in Intelligence has been confined to analysis and the projection of, ah, operational hypotheses. You've never been in the field, of course—no reason, until now, that you should. But not all Intelligence can be conducted behind desks, as you know. And you've each had routine basic training. Frankly, as far as I'm concerned, it's a gamble. At your desks, on this project, you've been valuable. In the field, you're unknown quantities. But nobody else can do it. So it's a gamble we need to take."

Flying Fortress BB-A-7G Choctaw Charlie drilled on through the summer afternoon sky, approaching Hanover at 22,000 feet. Choctaw Charlie was one of 303 American B-17s despatched on US Eighth Air Force Heavy Bomber Mission 77: targets, Hamburg U-boat yards, the rubber factory at Hanover, and a convoy in Hamburg harbour roads.

"Initial Point . . . now," said the co-pilot, squinting through the windshield into the black and russet columns of smoke in front. The two Fortress boxes ahead had already bombed.

"Turn right . . . right. Louis, you're three miles from target."

The pilot closed the switch which allowed the linked bombsight and automatic pilot to take over the aircraft.

"Clutch in . . . OK, Hal, you're on bomb run," said the pilot sharply into the intercom. Forward, in the nose canopy, the bombardier stared intently at the glowing indices of the bombsight as they crept slowly together.

"OK, Lieutenant."

Down in the waistgun position, Sergeant Leroy Mitchellman gazed out at a fantastic spectacle of anti-aircraft fire. Choctaw Charlie was flying in the front of the third box of ten aircraft. Ahead and to each side the blue of the sky was almost obliterated by red, yellow and white bursts of flak. At the end of the line, a B-17 suddenly swung out of formation and dropped back. Then it steadied out, about 300 feet below Choctaw Charlie's starboard wing. Both sickened and fascinated by the sight, Mitchellman watched while the fire raging in the nose-canopy began to stream back into the fuselage. On and on flew the B-17, held level by the burning pilot in some tremendous effort of will, while men began to leave it. He saw one, two, three go through the bomb bay, and another from the waist opening. All four parachutes opened, but he could see no others. There was nothing that willpower could any longer achieve on that flight-deck. Gradually, its port wing now one enormous sheet of yellow flame, the stricken B-17 turned on its side and fell vertically down through four miles of sky like a burning arrow. It passed quite swiftly from the angle of Mitchellman's restricted view. On the open heathland where it struck fifty-five seconds later, German engineers methodically noted next day that it had made a hole nineteen metres deep. Nothing remotely identifiable was left of the six men who had remained inside.

The voice of Choctaw Charlie's bombardier came back on the intercom.

"Switches one, two, three, four OK. Open bomb doors."

A whine from the hydraulics.

"Bomb doors open."

"Keep the clutch in, lieutenant. I'm going to get 'em all in there. Hold her, hold her."

"Hurry it up, Hal, for Christ's sake. It's like being in a goddam shooting gallery."

"OK, OK, hold her . . . bombs going—*now*."

The bombardier's indicator flickered 6-5-4-3-2-1 as the six 500-pounders successively left the toggles. He shouted "Close bomb-doors" the instant the pointer touched 0. The answering throaty murmur of the hydraulics was lost in a howling surge from the engines as the pilot turned hard right and climbed out of the flak, trying to hold his box position as the group re-formed. He counted seven left out of ten as they began to leave the flak of Hanover behind them. Now for the damned fighters. There'd been enough of them on the way in, *Staffel* after *Staffel* of yellow-nosed 109s, but they'd swung away as the boxes entered the flak corridor in front of the rubber factory.

In the waist, Mitchellman was looking out from his Plexiglass bubble. The B-17 formations were ragged and dispersed now, and two planes were streaming smoke and, occasionally, flame. Even as he watched, one of them, on the far right of Choctaw Charlie, erupted soundlessly in a great incandescent ball of white fire as flames reached its petrol tanks.

The urgent voice of the upper-turret gunner sounded in his earphones.

"Two 109s, two o'clock, Lieutenant."

Then the pilot.

"OK, watch them. Don't get excited. Don't—"

The voice of the tail gunner:

"Fighters, five o'clock. Three—no, four—"

The tail gun began to chatter, followed by the upper-turret Brownings. In the waist position Mitchellman, peering desperately out, could see no fighters, but he caught a momentary glimpse of a mottle blue-green fuselage and a yellow nose flashing past his window as Choctaw Charlie yawed frantically left. There was a thunderous, splintering drumming somewhere forward, followed by an acrid smell. The pilot's voice came again, a little shrill.

"I can smell oil."

Three voices simultaneously:

"The right engine's throwing oil."

"The hydraulics are out, Lieutenant."

"I've been hit, Lieutenant."

That last was the upper-turret gunner's voice. And then, faintly:

"My God, I've had it."

After that, nothing. The tail gunner was shouting again:

"Fighters . . . eleven o'clock, one o'clock, two o'clock. God damn it, they're all over the sky. And, God, they're Spitfires. And P-47s . . . Look at those lovely babies, Lieutenant. Look at 'em . . ."

"All right, all right, cut the chatter. OK, boys, we've got the escort. We'll fly a little low. I'll feather the outer. We'll have to leave the box."

"There's a B-17 dropping back, Lieutenant. Looks like he might be from the 97th. Not from our group, anyway. He's a right friendly guy. Looks like he's goin' to cover us back."

"Are there any more 109s?"

"Can't see any, Lieutenant. I reckon they're busy with the escort."

"Can anybody get up the crawlway to the upper-turret to take a look at Jim Broster?"

The bombardier's voice answered.

"I'll go."

The tail gunner:

"That B-17's comin' up behind. His waist-position looks closed. Maybe he's been hit himself."

"Maybe."

The bombardier, from the crawlway:

"I guess Jim Broster's dead, Lieutenant. He got it in the chest. The bones are kinda stickin' out."

The pilot replied, irritably:

"All right, all right, there's no call to chatter about it . . ."

Mitchellman stared out from the waist of Choctaw Charlie. Gradually the dark bulk of the escorting B-17 came into the edge of his vision. As the tail gunner had said, its waist position was closed. It was about 100 yards out on the flank, and he could see men in the nose-canopy looking towards him. He raised a hand to them, and they waved back. He spoke into his microphone:

"That's a black B-17, Lieutenant. I thought all the 97th ones were green, like ours—oh, my God."

In the same instant, the upper-turret guns of the escorting B-17 swung towards Choctaw Charlie and opened fire methodically at point-blank range. The first burst smashed into the nose canopy, cutting the head cleanly from the co-pilot's body and drenching the pilot with spurting blood from the severed arteries in the neck.

"Jesus Christ," Mitchellman was screaming. "He's gone bloody crazy. He's firing at us . . ."

At a steepening angle, trailing smoke and sparks, Choctaw Charlie crossed the German coast and headed for England.

"What's got into you, then?" said Vandamme.

Expertly, he flicked the jeep down the winding East Anglian road towards the US Eighth Air Force bomber base at Polebrook.

"Horses for courses," said Croasdell shortly.

"What do you mean?"

"I'm not a field man, Gene. I'm a pilot, first and foremost—and now I seem to have become a desk intelligence man."

"But he's giving you a chance to stop being a desk intelligence man."

"Look, Gene, I'll be no bloody good in the field. I hate the idea."

"Scared of it?" said Vandamme quietly, after a pause.

"Yes. And scared of making a fool of myself, too. Aren't you?"

"Of course."

"Well, I'm not going to play at secret agents. I want to get back to a squadron as soon as I can, where I've friends on the ground and enemies in the air, and the friends wear red-white-and blue and the enemy wears black crosses."

"But they don't, do they?" said Vandamme.

"Sometimes the enemy wears red-white-and-blue, nowadays, it seems. And what happens if you refuse to take on this new job?"

Croasdell hesitated.

"They could grade me LMF."

"What's that?"

"Low Moral Fibre—I'd lose rank, get some rotten job . . . Maybe even lose my commission, though they'd have a tough time doing that."

"I thought you wanted to get back to a squadron?"

"I do."

"Well, this LMF caper doesn't seem a good way of going about it."

"They mightn't find it too easy to grade me LMF," said Croasdell obstinately. "Not with this."

He tapped the ribbon of the DFC on his chest.

"And if he tried, I'd kick up a hell of a fuss. I reckon I'd stand a chance of getting back to a squadron, just so's they could shut me up."

Vandamme looked at him impatiently.

"What's the matter with you? Give you a new idea and it frightens you. You'd like a nice cosy little war, all fought from inside your goddam squadron or your goddam regiment or your goddam ship. Join the club, old boy, and don't do anything to disgrace it. Wear the badge, and keep it shiny."

The intensity in Vandamme's voice startled Croasdell. He looked at him covertly. The American's lips were set in a downward drooping line, his eyes narrowed, watching the road ahead. Croasdell glanced at the jeep's speedometer. They were doing seventy-two miles an hour along a straight stretch of road.

"No need to take it out on the jeep," he said quietly. "Or are you aiming for take-off?"

Vandamme looked at the speedometer and suddenly laughed, easing his foot on the throttle.

"Why're you so het up about it?" said Croasdell. "It's not exactly going to win or lose the war whichever way we decide, is it?"

"I've decided."

"Oh?"

"I'm willing to try it." Croasdell said nothing, for a while. They passed through a village which he recognised as being just outside Polebrook. Ahead of them, in the late summer afternoon, a few people were standing on the village green, looking upwards. Vandamme slowed down and pulled the jeep into the side of the road. The two men got out, and shaded their eyes, looking into the bright blue of the sky. Low above the tree-lined skyline appeared the unmistakable shapes of Flying Fortresses, echeloned in flights of four, circling the airfield.

"Back from a mission, I guess," said Vandamme. "And I guess they didn't have too good a time. There seem to be some holes in those flights."

"There's a lot less come back than went out," said a middle-aged woman standing beside the jeep. "I know there are . . . We count them, you see," she added in explanation.

"Out and back. My daughter's got a boyfriend at the base. He flies in the Fortresses."

"He'll be OK," said Vandamme.

"Yes, he's all right," said the woman. "He wasn't flying today."

Croasdell and Vandamme got back into the jeep, and drove the remaining mile-and-a-half to the airfield. The security at Polebrook was relaxed but efficient. Both Vandamme's and Croasdell's identity papers were checked thoroughly before the white-helmeted military police at the gate barrier finally lifted its double bar to allow the jeep through. They drove on towards the administration buildings. With a tremendous roar, a B-17 came down low overhead, heading for the nearest runway. Its No. 3 engine—the starboard inner—was trailing sparks and was feathered, Croasdell noted, and as it lumbered in, wheels down, it was possible to see blue sky through the great hole in the forward sweep of the tail fin. It made a bad, bumpy landing, and long before it had rolled to a stop, two ambulances, bells ringing, were following it down the runway.

They were walking towards the US officers' mess when Vandamme suddenly checked and changed direction towards the tall round bulk of the control tower.

"I'd like to see the rest of this mission land," he said. "You go on and get yourself a drink. There's plenty of RAF boys come in here—you won't have any trouble."

"No, I'll come with you," said Croasdell.

"Trouble is," said Vandamme, "I've got a kind of a thing about the B-17. I flew the old B-17 D in the 19th Group in the Philippines, before I switched to fighters, and before the Nips knocked most of the rest of the B-17s out on the ground.

"It was kind of an article of faith with the Army Air Corps, the B-17. It had a rough start—crashed on a demonstration flight a few years ago, and killed both test pilots. Lucky there were some guys in the Air Force could see what these big babies could do, given the chance."

"They're certainly tough planes," said Croasdell. "But daylight bombing . . . well, I suppose you can only find out the hard way. You're going to have some pretty heavy losses. We have bad enough losses at night—and that's when the Germans can't really bring their full fighter strength to bear. Not on the scale he can by day, anyway."

"What we need," said Vandamme wistfully, "is a real long-range fighter. Not a Spitfire or a P-47. Something that can go all the way there and back, and stay just as fast as the 190s and the 109s. And there's something we don't need."

"Yes?"

"We don't need," said Vandamme, "goddam Germans flying B-17s that were made in Seattle or Long Beach or Burbank. Especially we don't need Germans flying B-17s with US markings."

"Do you really think many of them do?"

"Wonder-boy did," said Vandamme stubbornly. "He didn't come over just for the ride. And I aim to find out why—Jesus, look at that . . ."

A B-17 came into view, high over the airfield perimeter. It was flying at about 1,500 feet, far too high for a landing approach, and it appeared to be on fire from nose to tail. Men were running out of the administration buildings below it, standing, looking into the sky. Over to their left, a ground crew working on a B-17 inside a hangar climbed down from its wings and came to the hangar door. The B-17 flew straight on across the field, trailing a long black plume of smoke, shot through with flame.

"Put her down, put her down," Vandamme was saying. "Oh, Christ, boy, get her down. He's climbing. Look, he's trying to climb. What the hell . . .?"

"He's trying to get some room to bale out," said Croasdell. "But I shouldn't think he's got much left in the way of flaps. Look . . . there's a man now."

A dark speck had left the Fortress's waist position, tumbling through the sky. Both men watched the falling man.

Infinitely slowly, it seemed, the white silk of the parachute streamed behind him, gradually opening to full canopy, no more than three seconds before he hit the ground. Somewhere in the distance another ambulance bell began to clang.

"That was close," said Vandamme. He peered upwards, shading his eyes against the glare of the sky. "Are there . . .?"

"I think he's the only one," said Croasdell.

"What about the boy who's flying it?" said Vandamme. "What the hell's he doing? Why doesn't he—look, he's getting the nose up. She'll stall, she's going to stall . . ."

The burning B-17 was rearing upwards, over the centre of the field. The great Wright Cyclone engines howled on full boost, but they could not defy the laws of aerodynamics. The B-17 faltered, seemed to hang in the air for a long, terrifying moment, and then fell sideways to the ground. One wing struck first. The great bomber turned over like a burning catherine-wheel, and blew up in a crumping explosion. The heat and the shock-wave reached the onlookers a second or so later. Firebells clanged. Vandamme turned away. His voice shook slightly and his face was white.

"Why didn't that guy bale out with the other one?" he said. "Why did he try that crazy climb?"

Croasdell did not reply for a long time, and when he did his voice sounded flat, almost resigned.

"He wasn't crazy, Gene. He climbed deliberately, because he knew she'd stall right in the middle of the airfield."

He swung round and pointed back over the distant gate.

"You can see where he was heading. Polebrook village. He couldn't turn her, I imagine, and he wasn't going to bale out and leave her pointed at a village. He was a pretty good pilot. He'd worked it all out."

They walked back, past the base medical section. Bells clanging, an ambulance was drawing up outside the doors, and medical orderlies were busy easing a stretcher out of the back. The man who lay there was blackened by flame from head to foot, his flying kit charred, his face terribly blistered, his head virtually hairless. He was conscious.

"That's the one who jumped," said Vandamme.

"Colonel," said the man on the stretcher weakly. "Colonel Vandamme. Remember me? Mitchellman. Sergeant Mitchellman. We were together at Luzon, 'bout a year ago. Don't you recognise me?"

Vandamme swallowed.

"Sure, sure, I recognise you," he said. "But what—"

"Colonel, sir, I guess they're goin' to shoot some morphia in me in the next five minutes. And not before goddam time, either. But there's something you all ought to know . . ."

"Yes?"

"You know what got us in Choctaw Charlie? It was a B-17 from the 97th. Came up alongside, no more'n eighty yards away, and poured .50 calibre into us . . . like a goddam maniac. That's what got us. It wasn't the Krauts. It was the 97th."

The orderlies began to carry him inside. Mitchellman's eyes, in his blackened, hairless face, sought Vandamme's again.

"I guess . . . Louis . . . the lieutenant . . . he didn't . . .?"

"He the pilot?"

"Yeah."

"No, he went straight down in the middle of the field. Didn't get out."

Mitchellman sighed, bubbling slightly through the cracked, blistered lips. His eyes closed.

"That was always one thing Louis was scared of . . . puttin' a B-17 through the middle of some Limey kids' school . . ."

The orderlies carried him inside, and Croasdell and Vandamme walked on towards the officers' mess. Just before they got to the door, Croasdell spoke.

"All right, all right," he said irritably.

"OK, OK," said Vandamme. "Come and have some real whisky, first."

I'm always wrong about this British guy, he thought. I'm probably wrong about the whole damned lot of them.

"Do you know when you'll be back?" said Joanna, drying the dishes.

"Not the faintest," said John Croasdell from the living-room. He was bending over the table, beside Gene Vandamme, looking at a map.

"We're on special stand-by from tomorrow morning—fully operational. The usual drill, darling—you know, no leave, no day-pass, no 'phone calls."

"Any use asking why?" she said.

"No," said Croasdell.

Damn, damn, damn, she thought. It's been heaven, the last fortnight, having them here. Well, heaven and hell, in a way. The trouble with being an RAF wife was that the one you loved could never be out of sight, out of mind. If your husband was in the desert with the Eighth Army, say, well, you worried about him, of course, but you could always kid yourself that he wasn't doing anything very dangerous at that particular moment, anyway. But an RAF wife always knew. Often enough, if she lived near the base—as she did herself—she literally saw him go off to battle. And waited for him to come back. And now John and Gene back on ops—some sort of ops, anyway. She knew Gene was keen to go. He'd had that little lift to his step, the last couple of days—the way he had when he and John had shot down that Heinkel everybody was being so cagey about. But John . . . you could never tell, with John. He'd had a bad time when he was shot down, three years ago. He could be very edgy, still . . . and the last couple of days he'd been so impassive, so hard to read, so non-committal that she'd known something was happening. I suppose that, physically and mentally, I'm as close to John as I've ever been, or will ever be, to another human being, she thought. But in lots of ways he'll always be a mystery to me.

And Gene? In a way—she said the word to herself with a curious sense of revelation—she felt love for Gene. Sexual attraction, certainly—but more than that, perhaps. He probably had more sexual attraction for her than John himself had, she knew. But he was a different kind of man from John—a bit spoiled, she supposed. Too much money too young—he'd said it to her himself. If you start off with a father who's vice-president of a railroad, you miss some of the advantages in life that men like John had. John had to fight for everything he'd got. It had made him tougher, more sophisticated, more truly male, in a way, than Gene.

Gene hadn't as much as touched her hand since that day in the churchyard. She'd caught him looking at her once or twice, and she'd wondered if John had noticed anything. Not—she lifted her chin a little—that there'd been much to notice. But it would be awkward if he had. He and Gene seemed to be working together on whatever it was they were doing, and there was no room for little green monsters. But John hadn't noticed, she was sure. He was far too self-absorbed. It was one of the reasons that made her look at Gene. What was it the psychologists said? Propinquity is the greatest sexual stimulant of all.

"I've got a bottle of wine in the jeep," said Vandamme, appearing in the kitchen doorway. "I thought we might have kind of a celebration supper."

"Celebration?"

" 'Cos we're back on ops, honey."

"Wine?" said Croasdell. "What kind of wine?"

"Californian," said Vandamme. "Red. A guy I know flew in with it from Stateside, yesterday."

"What do you mean, Californian? That's not wine, that's just grape juice."

Vandamme went out to the jeep and came back with the wine. Croasdell took the bottle and uncorked it, looking at it critically. He poured a glass and drank a little.

"Well, I've tasted worse grape juice. Californian, eh? I've never heard of it."

"The trouble with you British, Croadsell, as I told you the other day, is that you close your minds to anything new."

"Nothing new about grape juice, old boy. They could probably make a fair grape juice in the Stone Age. The whole art of civilisation has been to find how to make it into wine."

"If you two connoisseurs have finished the lecture," said Joanna, "there's the equivalent of a week's meat ration waiting on the table. And I'd like a very large slug of the grape juice. I've had a rough day."

"Here you are, honey," said Vandamme, filling her glass. "Take a drink of sunshine. All the way from the San Fernando valley."

"What's the meat, Joanna?" said Croasdell. "This grape juice mightn't suit it."

"The meat," said Joanna, "is all the way from the South Pole, I imagine. It's whale. We get whale off the ration, you know."

"War," said Croasdell, "is hell."

TOP SECRET
United States Strategic Air Forces
Office of the Chief Intelligence Offier

MEMORANDUM:
Subject: Enemy-operated B-17s: Their Use and Menace

1. British bombers and fighter planes which have fallen into the hands of the Germans, and have been rebuilt by them, amount to a sizeable figure. For a long time, Rechlin has been rebuilding and testing Wellingtons, Stirlings, Spitfires and others.
2. Except on very rare occasions, these planes have been put to little use in active combat role against the British. The very nature of British operations precludes the Germans gaining any real tactical advantage by the use of such equipment at night.
3. The enemy has turned his attention increasingly in recent months to the acquisition and rebuilding of US B-17 and B-24 bombers.
4. The use of B-17s by the enemy does offer possibilities for him which under present conditions seem worth trying. The limited use to which they have so far been put is recorded in the attached digest (analysis of mission reports from April 1943 to the present).
5. As can be seen from these reports, the Germans first used the Fortresses for observation, staying a safe distance from the range of our .50 calibre guns. Since then, they have closely observed our tactics. When cloud or other openings appeared, they have jumped right into the midst of our formations, and by R/T have notified other enemy planes and ground stations of our every move.
6. Not having sufficient .50 calibre ammunition, the *Luftwaffe* has re-equipped its B-17s and B-24s with what appear to our crews to be 20mm cannon.
7. Positive identification that a B-17 is an enemy plane has not proved as easy as one might expect. On Mission 86,

a B-17 joined our formation bearing the painted identification signal of the day on its vertical stabiliser.

8. The absence of heavy bomb load enables enemy Fortresses to outmanoeuvre our heavily-laden planes.
9. Intrusion into our Fortress formations by enemy-operated Fortresses can not only break solid formations but can direct fighter and flak activity against disrupted formations or crippled planes.
10. The ability of the Germans now to put into action a number of B-17s and B-24s which are hard to distinguish from ours, and to use them in unexpected ways, presents a menace as yet hard to assess—but one with which we may have to deal any day.
11. It is recommended that copies of this report be forwarded to the appropriate Operations, Training and Armament divisions for immediate consideration.

FRANK D. LASKER
Colonel, Air Corps
Chief Intelligence Officer

Copies to: General Paul Hamel
AOC Royal Air Force Fighter Command
Royal Air Force Bomber Command
Royal Air Force Coastal Command

14

"And now," said Colonel Frank Lasker, "we come to Mission 77."

He rustled his papers, and a little stir of interest ran through the other three men seated at the green baize-covered table in the long intelligence room at Polebrook. Mission 77 was not a mission they were likely to ignore. In any case, Frank Lasker was not a man who'd let them ignore it. He was Chief Intelligence Officer for all US bomber groups in the United Kingdom. Top Air Force commanders such as Eaker and Spaatz and Arnold listened very carefully to what he had to say: copies of his reports went to the commanders of the Royal Air Force, and—sometimes—to the Prime Minister himself. Few men of such comparatively low rank could command such an audience.

"Mission 77," he read in his flat Wisconsin voice. "Three hundred B-17s despatched: 199 succeeded in bombing. Ninety-two hit the rubber processing plant at Hanover: 54 hit the U-boat yards at Hamburg: 53 bombed targets of opportunity. There were diversionary raids by B-24s from Eighth Air Support Command—and by RAF Typhoons and Bostons."

He looked up for a moment at the three listening men. One of them was an RAF Intelligence liaison officer—a wing commander.

"The RAF hit the fighter fields round Hanover," he said. "Photo-reconnaissance shows a lot of damage. But we had heavy losses—very heavy losses."

He paused, running his eyes down a column of figures.

"The targets at Hanover were the two main factories of

Continental Gummi-Werke, and we laid 209 tons of high explosive on them. Intelligence estimates reckon there'll be a reduction of around 20 per cent in capacity there for the next six weeks. Results at Hamburg look pretty good, too, though we've no intelligence evaluation yet. Hamburg's still in a hell of a mess from the two RAF night raids, and there's been too much smoke and low cloud over the target for photographs.

"We lost," he said, "twenty-four B-17s—thirteen of them to enemy fighters, seven to flak."

"And the other four?" said the RAF man.

"I'll come to those in a minute," said Lasker. "At the moment, they're scheduled as 'Causes Unknown'."

"The mission was unescorted, of course?" said one of the other two USAAF officers.

"That's so," said Lasker. "Except . . . we tried out three YB-40s in the escort role."

"And . . .?"

"Results evaluated as poor," said Lasker quietly.

"The YB-40?" said the RAF wing commander, "That's the new Fortress you've designed as a sort of flying arsenal, isn't it?"

"That's so," said Lasker again. "We dreamed it up to try to solve our escort problem. Basically, it's a B-17F that doesn't carry bombs, but does carry fourteen .5 Brownings instead of the standard ten, and extra armour. And Vega, the company that builds it, tried to solve the forward fire problem—you'll know, sir, that the B-17s have always had a weakness here? They tried, as I say, to solve the forward fire problem with a two-gun chin-turret, right under the nose."

"But you say results were poor?"

"That's what we're getting from the crews, as of now. The extra armour makes it heavier and slower than the B-17s it's escorting—especially on the trip home, when the bombers have got rid of the bomb load and are a hell of a sight lighter themselves. The YB-40s lag behind the formations—

I guess it looks as though they'll need special escorts of their own."

He smiled wryly.

"I'll come now to the four B-17s that went down for 'causes unknown'. Now these were B-17s that were observed by other crews on the way back from the mission—two from Hanover, two from Hamburg. Each had gotten some damage—but not the kind of damage which would put down a Fortress. A Fortress, gentlemen, is a very rugged ship, as all of you know. But there's one thing these four had in common. They'd all had to leave formation. They were over the sea, there was no flak, and no fighters. Two of them were seen to be 'escorted' by other B-17s—ships that in each case were assumed by other B-17s to be from some other group. You know how it is—with 200 B-17s streaming back over the North Sea, and the formation well chopped up by flak and fighters, the groups get pretty mixed, and there's no way they can all know each other."

He paused and eyed each of the other three carefully, shuffling a new clip of papers which he had taken from a grey Air Force folder. Each of the other officers had a similar folder in front of him.

"I assume," said Lasker, "that you've each read your copy of this Intelligence digest, which is my own analysis of crew reports from 21 April until this date. I would like each of you to return your copy at the end of this conference—in fact, it is General Hamel's order that you do so. This information carries the highest security classification. Meanwhile, I'll just remind you of some of the salient points . . ."

Rather unexpectedly, he took a pair of spectacles from his pocket and adjusted them carefully on his nose. None of the other three present felt inclined to smile.

"We can start," said Lasker, "with Interpretation Report No. L 86, which begins on page three of your digests, after the operational summaries. I quote: " '. . . A Fortress was first photographed at Rechlin on 21.4.43 (Interpretation Report No. L 75) and on that date was seen with a group of

German aircraft near buildings on the northern boundary. The later photographs show the Fortress near the north-west hangars used for repair work. It is painted a fairly light colour and service wing markings are visible near the edge of the wing . . .' "

He looked up.

"That, gentlemen, was the first report we had of a B-17 in enemy hands. Since then, collating mission reports from Mission 53 on May 1—it was an attack on harbour installations at St Nazaire—up to Mission 77, which we've just discussed, there have been twenty-three sightings of completely unidentified B-17s reported by Eighth Air Force bomber crews.

"There was also"—he flicked through his papers—"the Eighth Bomber Command Intelligence memorandum dated April 28, dealing with new Rechlin photographs, which said, and I quote: 'Among the aircraft identified on the aerodrome are several Wellingtons, a Stirling and a B-17 of this Command. There have been two engagements and three encounters during RAF raids this month with aircraft identified as Wellingtons and a Halifax . . .' "

He looked across at the British officer.

"We've certainly had these reports ourselves," said the RAF wing commander. "And, as you know, Air Marshal Shevlin is fully informed about them. But the whole matter, as you say, is absolutely top secret. The effects on crew morale could be disastrous. It's bad enough for your boys by day, but—if you'll forgive my saying so—it's a damned sight harder to sort out friend from foe by night."

Lasker nodded.

"The most comprehensive report of enemy-operated B-17s we have," he said, "comes from Mission 67, attacking a convoy off the Frisian Islands. I quote again: " 'A heavily-camouflaged B-17 was seen flying over the Elbe estuary. Its colour was lighter than our aircraft and windows of waist guns were closed . . . At time of attack on convoy, three B-17s suspected of being enemy aircraft were seen headed towards Germany. There were four other reports of single B-17s, suspected enemy aircraft, flying in vicinity of, or attempting to join, our formations . . .' "

He closed the file.

"We lost eighteen B-17s that day—and we're not sure exactly how or why some of them went down. It was a higher loss than usual—eighteen out of 167 planes attacking. That's more than ten per cent. We couldn't go on long with a loss ratio like that."

"Presumably," said the RAF wing commander, "you've called this conference because you now have something a bit more concrete to go on? Something more specific than these crew reports?"

Lasker frowned.

"I'd call these crew reports very, very specific. But yes, we do have new evidence that the enemy is increasingly using our own planes—and especially the B-17s—against us. A B-17 crashed at Polebrook yesterday, on returning from Mission 77. There was one survivor—the right waist-gunner, a Sergeant Mitchellman. He's got 40 per cent burns, and I was told an hour ago that he's probably on the way out, poor guy. But before he went into surgery he told an officer of this Command that his ship was fired on by a B-17 of another group—a black B-17, he said. He thought it was from the 97th. Now we've been over this matter very carefully, as you may well imagine. One: all the surviving ships of thc 97th have been accounted for, and none has reported an engagement of this kind. Two: none of the ships flown by the 97th is, or ever had been, black or even dark-grey. All are standard USAAF olive-green. Three: we had a further crew report at the debriefing after Mission 77 which indicates enemy B-17 activity during that mission. I quote:

" 'A single strange B-17 joined a First Wing formation over Germany and stayed with it until the formation was about five minutes off the German coast. At that time two twin-engined fighters appeared and the single strange B-17 joined them and headed inland . . .' "

The senior of the two American air officers spoke for the first time. He was a young brigadier-general commanding a bomber wing, and his voice was troubled.

"You know, Frank, that there's no way we can keep this whole thing under wraps? It just isn't going to be possible to stop the boys talking. Hell, they're talking already. All sorts of people will have heard Mitchellman sounding off—medical orderlies, doctors, nurses, the lot. And people gossip. More than that—there's been a lot of scuttlebut already, for weeks past."

"I know," said Lasker.

"One thing puzzles me," said the RAF man carefully. "Why do they have so many B-17s? Why this particular type of aircraft? I mean, we've had reports of Stirlings and Halifaxes and Wellingtons—there was even a Breguet 69 attack bomber, complete with French markings, used in an attack on Lyneham on September 18, 1940. I looked up our own Intelligence files after I read your digest: There was a Stirling shot down over the Alps not long ago under some very dodgy circumstances, and another over Essen. But if your reports are accurate—and we've no reason to suppose they aren't—they've got B-17s on a far greater scale than they seem to have RAF aircraft. Well, why? I mean, I don't want to impute anything, but—"

"You're damn right you don't want to impute anything," said the American brigadier-general angrily, but Lasker interrupted him swiftly:

"No, General, sir, our friend here is talking sense. They do seem to have a hell of a lot of Fortresses and B-24 Liberators, too. Exactly the same point occurred to me, and I came up with what seemed to me to be the answer. The answers, maybe, because I reckon there are two.

"First, as we've already noted, the B-17 is a very rugged ship. Oh"—he held up a hand as the RAF man began to bristle—"I know the Lancasters and Stirlings are good ships, too. But there's one difference. We fly by day and you fly by night. Not entirely true of either of us, but largely true. Agreed?"

The RAF man nodded slowly.

"You're a pilot, sir, a good one, judging by the fruit-salad on your chest. You'll know that if you're over Germany or France or wherever, with say two engines out and flaps that don't work properly, you've got a hell of a sight more chance of putting a ship down in a decent belly-landing when you can see where you're putting her, by day, than if exactly the same thing is happening over a blacked-out countryside at night. You've only got to get into a jeep and take a ride round the base here to see what I mean. There are plenty of belly-landed B-17s, that just about made it back after some mission. Nearly all those planes will fly again. We've got a colonel at the 444th Sub Depot, for instance, who's real good at cannibalising planes. I was down there the other day, because I wanted to see exactly how the Germans might be doing it at their end, and he's right now joining the rear end of one crashed B-17 to the front end of another. I'm damn sure that over there they've got specialists like that."

"It's a good point," said the RAF man thoughtfully.

"Second," said Lasker, "the Germans seem to be concentrating on salvaging B-17s, in particular, for some reason we don't yet understand. And converting them."

"Converting them?" said the brigadier-general.

"The intelligence digest I prepared did not contain, for security reasons," said Lasker drily, "the most interesting fact of all. As you know, only one of these enemy B-17s has come back into our hands—the one that crashed at Mersea. Pregnant Portia, the ship was called. There was damned little left of Portia after she blew, but your boys at Farnborough"—he nodded towards the RAF squadron leader—"tried to put together what was left. They did a fine job—and they came up with one very interesting fact. The bomb bays had been altered—made longer. And although there wasn't much of the release mechanism to judge from, the Farnborough boys reckoned that Pregnant Portia had been re-rigged to carry a single bomb—something, they said, of around, maybe, 4,500 lbs. But she wasn't carrying it when she came down."

"That'd mean changing the bomb sight as well," said the brigadier-general. "Had that been done?"

"We don't know, General. There just isn't enough left of the bomb sight to judge. It was pretty well melted in the blaze, but it did seem to be of a standard Norden sight."

The brigadier-general got up from the table and walked to the window. Far over to his right, he could see the twin olive-drab fins of a B-24 Liberator outlined against the paler green of the boundary hedge as the big plane taxied out to the runway. He watched it, but his mind was far away. After a moment or two, he swung back to the others.

"What the hell are they playing at, then?"

It was the RAF wing commander who answered.

"You've had some trouble lately with air-to-air bombing, haven't you, sir. Captured aircraft flying above your formations, and dropping clusters of fragmentation bombs into your aircraft? I read it in some recent debriefing reports."

The general nodded.

"Well, sir, it occurs to me that if the Germans could devise a big bomb that could be accurately fused and timed—and they're not exactly slouches at that kind of engineering—it could be a pretty horrifying weapon if it was dropped into the middle of one of your boxes. It might be expected to knock down, say, three or four Forts—or even more—at one go. And where better to drop it—or them, I suppose—than from another false Fortress formation, echeloned a bit higher, that nobody—they hope—suspects . . .?"

"You could be right."

The general turned to Lasker.

"But, Frank, do you seriously think they've got enough B-17s to fly a whole box?"

"They may have more than that, sir."

"Jesus!"

"There are other uses they have for them, as well, General. They seem to be using B-17s and B-24s to shadow our formations to report height, speed and the rest—long before we're in radar range. They bring them over to drop agents—the one at Mersea was most likely doing just that. And they're picking off stragglers—like Choctaw Charlie on Mission 77 the other day. But, on the other hand, they're doing some pretty dumb things, too. Even they can make mistakes."

"What kind of dumb things?"

"Well, they often seem to paint their Trojans a non-standard colour. Should make 'em easier for our boys to pick out. And another thing . . . you have a look back through that digest, and you'll see that again and again in those 23 sightings, the waist-windows of these phoney Fortresses were closed. It's nearly always commented on in the debriefings."

"Why would they do that?"

"There could be a lot of reasons, General. It can't be easy to train crews for this job. Now the waist-positions are probably the least effective gun positions in the ship, with the smallest field of fire. So if they're cutting down on crews, that's where they're gonna cut first. Then again, it's likely they're short of .5 calibre ammo. They don't make that calibre themselves, they'll have to use a lot of what they capture for gun practice if the gunners in these ships are going to hit what they open up on—and I reckon they've decided to reduce both crews and guns. In one way it favours them, of course."

"How's that?"

"Makes 'em lighter, more manœuvrable. They aren't carrying bombs, anyway, naturally. Gives them a good performance edge over our own ships."

The room shook slightly as the B-24 which the brigadier-general had watched passed low overhead, climbing away to the east. For a moment or two, it was impossible to hear any human voice pitched below a shout. Lasker waited until the echoes washed away, and then spoke again.

"The main reason I asked all of you to meet here today was because I'd like to have your comments on a couple of recommendations I'm going to make to Command at Eighth Air Force."

"Recommendations you're *going* to make?" said the brigadier-general drily. "So our comments are just for the record. That sure sounds the way you operate, Frank."

For the first time since the meeting had begun, Lasker smiled. But his voice was serious as he went on:

"Each of you gentlemen," he nodded towards the two Americans—"commands a bomber wing. And you, sir"—he turned towards the RAF officer—"are here as representing the RAF. What I have to say affects you all."

He doodled absently for a moment with a pencil on his desk.

"You see, we're sure that we've got to give orders that fire should be opened on suspect aircraft."

"But—" said the US colonel. It was the first word he had spoken during the meeting.

"Oh, God knows, I can see a heap of objections," said Lasker. "But this whole Trojan system they're using—'Trojan' is what we're code-naming their operation in our own files, incidentally—is getting way out of hand from our point of view. We're losing ships, losing men, being intercepted before we reach targets—and soon our boys are going to feel that they're clay pigeons up there for any German who can fly a Fort or a Liberator."

"There's going to be a stack of problems the other way round, as well," said the colonel. "The boys are going to have to be mighty sure before they open up on another B-17."

"They sure will," said the brigadier-general. "But I take Frank's point. The enemy has it all his own way with these captured Forts. We'll have to figure out a way of making him a lot more scared of infiltrating our boxes. And what's more, he can afford to lose B-17s even less than we can. Because it's a damn sight harder for him to replace them."

"True," said the RAF man quietly. "But what happens if your own crews make perfectly understandable mistakes? Pretty bad for morale, if they shoot down one—or more—of your own aircraft."

"War," said the general heavily, "is the province of mistakes. Some guy said that—Napoleon, was it, or General Lee or somebody like that?—a long time ago, and he was right. But you're right, too, about morale. So we'll also have to figure out a way of dealing with that."

"From the purely practical point of view," said Lasker, "we hold one card the enemy doesn't know much about, because we've only just begun to play it, and at first sight it didn't seem too good a card in any case."

"What's that?"

"The YB-40s—the super-armed Forts. These enemy B-17s like picking off stragglers. Why don't we arrange it that in each formation there are one or two phoney stragglers . . . YB-40s? We might even arrange it so they streamed chemical smoke. Make it look like the real thing."

"And when the enemy B-17s jumped them, the YB-40s could blast straight back?" said the general reflectively. "Well, it sounds like an idea we could work on . . ."

"I've included that idea in the summary I've put forward to Eighth Air Force Command," said Lasker.

"You said earlier there were two recommendations you were making to General Hamel, Frank," said the general. "What was the other?"

Lasker smiled slowly.

"It was the name of that ship that was shot down the other day made me think of it," he said. "An idea put up to me a long time ago, by a man who's now dead."

"What name was that?" said the general. "I don't recall . . ."

"Choctaw Charlie," said Lasker. "That was the name. And it started me thinking of Indians . . ."

"Indians?"

Lasker turned to the Eighth Air Force colonel.

"Ed, how many Navajos do we have in our air crews, over here and Stateside?"

The colonel laughed.

"I wouldn't know, Frank. Some, for sure. But I can find out. I'll send a signal right now."

"You do that, Ed. Because I reckon this is a dandy of an idea."

The three men listened intently as he spoke for the next few minutes. Then the general sat back, grinning. There was a reluctant smile on the face of the RAF wing-commander.

"Well, it's worth trying," said the general. "Put it all in the file, and we'll see what Ira has to say. By the way, what code name have you used for that file?"

"Well, General, the first file, dealing with the enemy side of this whole matter, was code-named Operation Trojan, as I said. So I guess we'll call this one Operation Double-Trojan," said Lasker.

"Don't like it," said the general.

"Why not, sir?"

"I don't like code names with built-in meanings. Code names get talked about, and one day, eventually, they get back to the enemy. As soon as some bright German Intelligence officer—some guy, just like you, Frank—gets hold of an air operation code-named Double-Trojan, he's going to start thinking. And he wouldn't have to think very far, would he?"

"I guess you're right."

"I'll tell you what you could call it, Frank, and still keep a touch of your original plan. Just use the initials. Call it Operation DT."

"Stands for Delirium Tremens, in the medical books, doesn't it?" said the American colonel. "Seems a right good code name for it to me . . ."

15

"The chief problem, as I see it," said Strongman, "is that we have to produce a tandem contingency plan. Everything in duplicate, what? Only not duplicate at all, I suppose, actually. Two sets of identities, contacts, channels of communication, rendezvous, despatching and receiving points. One for Holland. One for France. Because we can't be sure that this German chap will, in fact, choose your Egmond route. Oh, I agree you've done your homework properly, and your argument seems pretty sound to me. But given the limited amount of fuel we are allowing him, it seems to us here that he may simply decide to hop straight across the Channel to France. And risk the ack-ack. So we'd better be ready for that to happen."

Croasdell and Vandamme studied him covertly. He had introduced himself as Major Edward Butler. He was a foxy-faced little man, with a small reddish moustache, who—faintly absurdly—still wore, with his uniform, riding breeches of an early pre-war pattern, and who spoke in an idiomatic, slightly affected drawl. He was, said Vandamme to himself, the kind of Englishman that Americans liked least. But he worked for MI5—British counter-espionage—so presumably he couldn't be such a phoney as he seemed.

"What date do you think the operation might begin?" said Croasdell. Butler shook his foxy little head reprovingly.

"It's already begun, old boy. Began when you arrived here a couple of days ago. You mean, I suppose, what day are we sending you off into the wild blue yonder, eh? Don't know. Not the faintest. Depends on masses of things. A lady, amongst others. And you know what ladies are, what?"

"A lady?" said Vandamme.

"Can't go into that now, Colonel. But she's basically the reason I'm here. We're all rather feeling our way on this one. You're going into the field in rather an unusual way—and there's going to be some co-operation with special Operations Executive. We've got together a sort of *ad hoc* team to work this out. You do Latin at your school in the United States, Colonel?"

"I know what 'ad hoc' means, if that's what's worrying you," said Vandamme drily.

"Ah, good. Never know, with you chaps. Nothing divides us like the language, eh?"

"I guess not."

Butler got to his feet and walked across to the great leaded window of the book-lined, comfortably furnished room where the three men sat, looking out on a green garden and low hills beyond. Out to his left, a gravelled driveway led round behind the house to a group of stables. A soldier leading a chestnut mare was walking slowly down the drive towards them. This was the Special Operations Executive country house headquarters in the heart of England. The men and women who came there for courses or to wait for operations were brought at night in blacked-out cars and by roundabout routes.

"He's got that damned girth too tight again," said Butler absently, looking critically at the mare. He walked back to his chair, and sat down once more, rubbing his hands.

"Well, to business."

Suddenly he sounded harder, colder, shrewder than he had a few moments ago, thought Vandamme. Butler took a flat black leather case from beside his chair and drew out some papers.

"I'm giving you each—or rather SOE is giving you—a set of contacts and code words for both Holland and France. The Dutch ones will do for Belgium, because the Germans allow free movement over the frontiers. Take a look through them after we've finished talking, and learn them by heart.

Then give them back to me, and we'll do a little test on them—and again tomorrow. You can't take them back to your rooms. They remain with me. They'll tell you who to contact in various circumstances, where to go, and what to say. Once you're over there, obey these instructions absolutely." His voice hardened for a moment. "The rest will be done for you. We don't anticipate a lengthy stay for you. Possibly a few days, possibly a week or a little more. Frankly, you'll have to be spoonfed when you're over there, because you've only had basic training. Not your fault, because there's not time for the months of extra training that chaps starting off on this sort of thing usually get. Now these code names are those of the people who're going to help you. All we want from you, when you're there, is expert opinion. No heroics. No Heinkels. Oh, yes," he said, noticing the surprise on Croasdell's face, "I've heard about that."

He took from the briefcase two small bundles of grey and green books.

"Now, your identities—one Dutch, one French. First, the French, though that's the one, in fact, that you probably won't need."

He passed one bundle to Croasdell, the other to Vandamme. Croasdell took the elastic band from his and spread out the three books on the arms of his chair. They consisted of a *carte d'identite* issued by the Paris Prefecture de Police, a *feuille de demobilisation* stamped 18 January 1941, and a valid French ration card. Between them, they announced that he was Jean Renaudin, born Grenoble, 10 August 1916, military service as a *caporal* in the 14th Bataillon, Armée de l'Air, stationed on detachment at Chauny, Northern Zone air headquarters in May 1940, demobilised at Soissons 29 September 1940, living now at 18 Rue Berthelet, Paris, working as a clerk in a wholesale grocery business.

Vandamme's papers, precisely similar, identified him as Pierre Blanquet, *sergent-secretaire*, *état-major* of the 4th Bataillon, 3rd Division Legère Mecanique, demobilised at Troyes, 21 September 1940. He was born at Nîmes on 8 July

1916, and he, too, lived in Paris—23 Avenue Grouchy. He worked as a clerk in the Metro station at Passy.

The Dutch papers, with similar dates of birth, gave their identities respectively as Adriaen Wynants and Martin Layster, living in Haarlem and Groningen, neither with military service behind him, and working as clerks on the Dutch railways. Green ration cards and red movement permits were included.

Butler waited while they looked through these papers, and then spoke again.

"You will also be allotted code names . . . the same, however, for either country. Or, for that matter, for any other country in Occupied Europe. You, Colonel Vandamme, will be Dreamer."

Vandamme grinned suddenly to himself.

"And you, Squadron Leader, will be Tipperary. These names will not, I say again will *not*, be written down. They've already been transmitted, as a routine precaution, to every major Resistance unit in Northern Europe, and to contacts inside Germany itself. Communicate only with me, as I am your controller. I also have a code name, which is the only way from now on in which you will address me or refer to me. My code name, for this operation, is Strongman."

Vandamme grinned again.

"OK, Strongman."

"Let's go over the outlines of the operation—it's being code-named Operation Shipwreck. Again, the technical aspects I assume you know all about, and they're not my province, in any case. If you've got questions—about the radar side, for instance—talk to the technical officers about them.

"Basically, it's simple. It's being arranged for this German chap Warnow to steal a Mosquito at West Murford airfield after dark one night very soon. You will be there—the details are all on your Operation Shipwreck orders—in another Mosquito. His aircraft will contain no working radar and its fuel gauge will show just enough fuel to allow him to take the Egmond option of the two possible routes you consider to be open to him. In fact, his fuel tanks will contain slightly less even than that shown on his gauge, but just enough to allow him, by skilful and determined airmanship, to reach some portion of the coast.

"Your own aircraft will be equipped with the latest tracking radar apparatus, and with enough fuel to allow you to follow Warnow, watch what happens to him and where he puts down, and then to return at once to West Murford. At West Murford a Lysander aircraft of SOE will be waiting, complete with despatcher officer, fuelled and ready for immediate take-off. This aircraft will return you immediately to the approximate vicinity of Warnow's grounded Mosquito —and to the nearest Dutch, or possibly French, Resistance unit to Warnow's aircraft. If there is no suitable landing place, you may have to land by parachute. You will identify yourselves to whatever Resistance unit meets you at the drop-zone, wherever that is. Almost certainly, the Germans will not try to move the Mosquito before daylight, and if everything goes right, you should be in position to watch what happens. After that, our Resistance friends—and you —will have to play it by ear.

"Now you'll notice that I said 'provided everything goes right'. As both of you know, everything doesn't always go right. This is a very offbeat operation—not the way we usually work, at all. There are a lot of imponderable factors.

"It's possible, though not likely, that Warnow will decide to ditch in the sea. If he does, I think you should try to kill him. Your Mosquito will be armed, of course. We can't recover him from the sea, and we don't want him being picked up by some rescue E-boat and being taken back to the open arms of Fatty Goering, do we?"

"It's against the Geneva Convention to shoot at downed pilots," said Croasdell quietly. "And it's also a thing which most pilots would never dream of doing."

"Ah, yes, the Geneva Convention," said Butler. His face

looked especially foxy at that moment, but Vandamme found himself suddenly reminded that the fox was a predator, and not a warm, red, cuddly creature. "Yes, I've heard about the Geneva Convention. It's not a thing we talk about much here. Don't find it goes down well with the people we get out of Dachau and places like that from time to time."

"Dachau?"

"You won't have heard of them, Tipperary, but they're a long, dirty story that I haven't got time to tell you now. You really must kill Warnow if he decides to put down in the sea. He's too important to the Germans to leave alive. We're taking a big chance letting him get back this way, but we're hoping, as you know, for an even bigger dividend. No dividend, no Warnow. That's an order, I'm afraid."

"And I'm afraid, Strongman, that you can't give me an illegal order."

Butler looked at Croasdell for a long ten seconds. "And don't forget technically a spy anyway—he's wearing false insignia. It's up to you, in the last analysis, anyway," he said finally. "It may not be operationally feasible, if and when it happens. In any case, I don't think it will happen. Warnow is the best pilot in KG 200, he won't waste an opportunity to bring back a spanking new Mossie."

He paused, eyeing each of them carefully.

"I've no doubt the whole operation seems pretty hit-and-miss to you. Well, it seems a damned sight more so to me. We don't know when or where it's going to begin, though we have some rough idea. And we don't know where it's going to end—especially, especially, we don't know where it will end. If it involves your going into Germany—and my own instinct would be to assume that it will—then you'll have to take advice, and possibly orders, from whatever Resistance unit is covering you, wherever you are. Frankly, it's a situation right outside my experience, and outside SOE experience, too. Nobody's ever tried to track a stolen aeroplane across Occupied Europe before.

"The great thing," said Butler, "is to get in and out—

fast. The longer you're there, the more your chance of getting picked up. Learn what you need to know as quickly as you can and if you have to go to Germany, don't stay an hour longer than you can help. I'll tell you now, Germany is very, very complicated. There's no Resistance in Germany, as such. But there can be . . . help. As a matter of fact, in one way, you might find Germany easier than France or Holland. You each speak decent German—at least well enough to be immigrants from the so-called Greater Reich. And Germany's full of people like that now. All you want are the German papers—and once we know exactly what you need, and where and why you want it, those can be arranged. Now, are there any questions?"

Croasdell and Vandamme shook their heads.

"Well, there's one last thing. You'll fly in civilian clothes, carrying those two sets of Dutch and French papers."

Croasdell began to speak, but Butler interrupted him.

"No, Tipperary, if you are going to wear civilian clothes on the ground, there's not the slightest reason why you shouldn't wear them in the air. For all I know, you may have to bale out of the Mosquito for some reason. If you do, I want to be certain you can go ahead with the operation, and not end up in some German *Stalag*, waiting for Red Cross parcels and thinking of the girl you left behind you."

For a moment, Joanna's face, unbidden, came into Vandamme's mind.

"That's it, then," said Butler, gathering up his papers and stuffing them into his briefcase. "I'll see you . . . well, soon, I imagine. But not before Operation Shipwreck is launched. I won't shake hands. I never do. One of my superstitions . . ."

He gave them a crooked little smile as he opened the door, and they walked out across the bare hall to the gravelled drive.

"Honestly, you'd wonder how a chap like that ever got into a decent regiment," said Croasdell when they were out of earshot. "Did you see his badges? I'm told they're very good indeed, that mob. But he seems a poisonous little twerp."

"Probably a Cambridge man," said Vandamme.

Croasdell looked at him.

"I'm never quite sure when you're fooling," he said. "But you seem to have a bloody funny idea of the British."

"You British," said Vandamme, "are a bloody funny lot."

Back in his room, Butler picked up his telephone. He gave the Director's number. The Director asked three questions, to all of which Butler replied "Yes".

"There was just a small brush with Tipperary, sir," he added.

"Yes?"

"Well, he quoted the Geneva Convention."

There was a short laugh at the other end of the telephone.

"I must say, sir, that I don't like the operation. It's not a typical MI5 job. Not a bit. Not that the SOE people haven't been helpful, because they have, in their own peculiar way."

"The only reason that MI5 is involved," said the Director, "is because it's MI5 that controls double agents. And that's not a side of things you'd want to hand over to SOE, even for one operation, presumably?"

"Good God, no."

"The lady's being very co-operative."

"She seems a co-operative sort of lady, sir, in all sorts of ways."

A chuckle.

"Don't let life make you coarse, Strongman."

"I'll try not to, sir. Though another ten days of the cooking at this place, and I won't be able to make any promises."

"Ten days, you think?"

"That or thereabouts."

There was a pause, and then the Director spoke again.

"What country-codes do Tipperary and Dreamer have?"

"None, sir, No need to give them Holland or France,

because they'll communicate through the usual channels. And we can give them Germany and even Norway if and when, so to speak . . ."

"Give them the lot, Strongman . . . no, not the lot, perhaps. All the Northern and Western Europe ones, anyway."

"You think . . .?"

"We'd better be on the safe side."

Strongman put down the telephone and began to write. He felt, as he often felt nowadays, very tired. And his chest was hurting again.

Thirty minutes later, in their room above the stables, Croasdell and Vandamme were handed, by a Marine orderly, a list. It was marked: "Country-code names: Sections 4 and 5. For Your Eyes Only: To Be Returned To Warrant Officer i/c Records at 19.30 Hours Precisely."

It read:

"France, north of east-west line through Bordeaux: Helen.
France, south of line ditto: Josephine.
Germany, east of north-south line through Nuremberg: Bertha.
Germany, west of line ditto: Claudia.
Poland: Edna.
Denmark: Shirley.
Norway: Margaret.
Sweden: Ursula.
Finland: Madelaine.
Ukraine: Maureen."

"They must think we're on a real Cook's tour," said Croasdell. "More to learn by heart—it's like being back at school."

"I once knew a girl called Maureen," said Vandamme reflectively. "She had very peculiar knees."

"Well, thank God there's nowhere called Joanna," said Croasdell. "I wouldn't have liked her to have been 'Germany; west of line ditto'."

"The trouble with you, Tipperary," said Vandamme, "is that you've got a long way to go . . ."

"Where to?" said Croasdell, suspiciously.

"To the sweetest girl you know," said Vandamme, and ducked as Croasdell picked up a pillow.

"We got that bastard," said Captain Angelo Romero. "And we got him good. He went straight down into the drink, not far out, say about thirty-five miles off Yarmouth, I guess."

"You can give me the exact fix in a minute," said the debriefing officer at Bassingbourn. "Just give me the salient facts right now, and I'll get it all down on the debrief form. How will you identify him?"

"Well, first of all he was silver. He was flying the identification signal of the day for the 965th Group—red and yellow—but he was flying it forward of the tail fin, right forward on the fairing, and not where it should have been, on the fin itself. In any case, I was over at Grafton Underwood last week, and there were about twenty 965th Group ships lined up on the field and they were all olive drab. Nobody flies silver ships."

"And?"

"Well, Captain, when he came alongside us—of course, I guess he'd no idea that Bells a'Ringin' was a YB-40—and the guys in the flight deck started waving like their radio was out. You remember, Captain, they did the same thing with Choctaw Charlie?"

The debriefing officer nodded.

"Well, of course, we couldn't see his left waist position, because he was flyin' on the left side of Bells a' Ringin', but our left waist-gunner saw him and said that the silver ship's right waist position was closed, and that there was something round it that looked like flak damage—but that it looked like phoney damage, if you get what I mean?"

"I get it," said the debriefing officer.

"I guess it was all getting pretty conclusive, and there was a bit of argument and chatter, you know, goin' on over the intercom in Bells a' Ringin' and then we saw his top turret start to move and we let him have it, straight from the left waist. Couldn't miss—the bastard was no more than fifty yards away. Then Paul in the top turret just about blew his nose off and he went straight down. We didn't see anybody get out, but we weren't so high—no more'n about eight thousand feet."

"Sounds like real good work," said the debriefing officer.

"Guess so," said Romero. "But it sure feels wrong, openin' up on a B-17. It was good anticipation by the waist gunner. I figure he's good for an Air Medal, Captain? It's his first Kraut—it ain't easy to get confirmed kills from the waist."

"I'll put it in the report," said the debriefing officer. "Now go grab some coffee."

"Sure," said Romero. "I'm in the grabbin' mood tonight. I got me a date with the best lookin' dame in Bassingbourn—and that's better than you might think."

"Don't claim unless she's confirmed," said the debriefing officer, and Romero laughed as he went out of the hut.

Left alone, the debriefing officer read carefully through the report, picked up the telephone, and made three telephone calls—the first to the headquarters of the 965th Bombardment Group at Grafton Underwood. It was four hours later, while he was lying on his bunk in his quarters, reading a magazine, that an orderly corporal came to tell him there was a telephone call.

He put on his tunic and walked across to the debriefing hut, where he shut and locked the door. Then he picked up the telephone. He spoke briefly to a junior officer at the other end, and then a voice he knew came on the line.

"Frank Lasker here. I'm afraid I've bad news. Anybody with you?"

"No, sir."

"The B-17 shot down in the debriefing report you told me of?"

"Yes, sir."

"It was one of ours. A ship from the 965th. Painted silver because there hadn't been time to paint it olive-drab—it was a replacement ship just in from Stateside. And I checked with the 965th—some of their ships did go out with the colours of the day on the tail fairing instead of the fin. Some snafu by the ground crews."

"Oh, Christ, Christ. Are there any . . .?"

" 'Fraid not. An RAF Sea-Rescue tender went straight out there and picked up two bodies. They say it was a pretty rough sea, and there's no chance of anybody being still above. The bodies they brought in have been identified. A couple of guys from the 965th—the pilot and the tail-gunner."

"What in God's name do we say now?"

"That's just it. Nothing. Nothing at all. As far as you're concerned—and as far as the crew of that ship, what's it called—?"

"Bells a' Ringin', sir."

"As far as the crew of that ship are concerned, they shot down a German. I've spoken to Intelligence at the 965th, and the RAF brass are talking to the RAF Sea-Rescue people. Now I'm telling you. You understand?"

"Yes, sir."

"Well, I hope you do, Captain, because heaven help you if you don't."

There was a pause, and Lasker spoke again. His voice sounded very tired.

"That waist-gunner—"

"Yes, sir?"

"He gets the Air Medal. I'll see to it. And the rest of the crew—they get commended in daily orders. Understand?"

"Yes, sir."

"It was bad luck, and it could happen again. We'll have to rethink the whole matter of identification. I guess this ship's radio really was out. He knew Bells a' Ringin' was a YB-40, all right. That's why he closed on him. He thought the YB-40 would escort him home . . ."

"But they said the top-turret moved."

"If you're looking at a top-turret long enough, boy, waiting for it to move, eventually it'll goddam well move. And if you've got your thumb on the firing button of your own gun, it just needs a reflex to push it down. You'll do all the rationalising afterwards."

"I guess so."

"But one thing we can do without is the groups tangling with each other over this kind of thing. It's bad enough them worrying about phoney B-17s. It's going to be hell if they have to worry about each other as well. Now as far as they're concerned, that ship was lost to enemy action."

"Yes, sir."

"I'm calling a conference of group debriefings day after tomorrow. You'll be getting a memo about it. We'll talk it through then."

"Yes, sir."

The flight-lieutenant was drunk. Not so drunk that he couldn't walk or talk, but drunk enough to make him stumble on the narrow stairs of Hannah Walters' flat.

"Ssh," she said, laughing. "I may as well hang on to what rags of reputation I've got. These walls are thin, and the neighbours can hear practically everything that goes on through them."

"In that case," he said, slurring his words a little, "they're going to have a hell of a party in the next couple of hours."

"Couple of hours, is it?" she said. "Going to be one of those nights?"

"Oh, sweetie, sweetie, come here."

He stretched out a hand as she reached the top of the stairs ahead of him, grasped her by the waist, and pulled her into his arms. She giggled as they slumped against the wall, pushing him back in a deliberate parody of reluctance, but finally letting his mouth come down on hers, pushing her head back so hard on her neck that she could hardly breathe.

He was a tall young man—not bad looking, she thought wryly as she felt his hand sliding and fumbling round her thighs, but he did nothing for her in that sort of way, nothing at all.

"No, no, not here, please, Peter—no, you're hurting . . . it's too uncomfortable. Let's have a drink, first."

"Don't want a drink. Want you."

"Well, I want a drink."

She pulled herself away, took him by the hand, and led him into the living-room.

"Go on—you go to the bathroom and I'll get the Scotch."

He wandered over to one of the doors and pushed at it.

"It's locked."

"Not that one, silly. This one."

"What's in there, then?"

"Oh, a lot of junk and stuff I keep. Nothing important."

She went into the kitchen and started mixing the drinks. She put enough of the stuff in—a bit more than they'd told her to. But she wanted it to work quickly—God, she wanted it to work quickly. Then she went swiftly into her own bedroom and changed into a loose kimono. If it didn't work quickly, she was going to have to accommodate young Peter, and he was the kind who had a tendency to tear a girl's clothes when he got excited. In a way, she wouldn't have minded nearly so much if she hadn't known Rolf was there, only about three feet away. What she'd said about the walls was true. Rolf would hear everything. Would he do anything about it? He mustn't, of course. But he claimed he cared for her and probably he did, after his own fashion. And his own fashion meant that getting back to Germany came first, second and third in his mind. So, no, Rolf Warnow would listen and maybe writhe a little, but he wouldn't do anything to prejudice his chances. She went back into the living-room. Peter had taken off his RAF tunic with those precious wings on the breast and was waiting.

"Here you are, darling. Scotch all right? Not tnat there's anything else."

"I don't want anything else. Not a drink, anyway."

She was pleased to see that he drank it at a single gulp. That way he'd be less likely to taste anything and it would work more quickly, too.

"Come here."

She was back in his arms again, and they were on the spare bed, the one she used with Rolf.

"Take those damned things off." He fumbled at her clothes.

The stuff would never work as quickly as this.

"But it's cold, and I like to—"

"Take them off, sweetie. You're not going to be cold—oh, come here."

He seemed to have hands everywhere.

"No, let me—"

"Just a—"

"No—like that. That's better."

It hadn't worked quickly enough, of course. It rarely did. She tried not to gasp, for Rolf's sake, but Peter was a big vigorous man. It was rather like being worried by a wild animal, she thought. He shouted as he finished, and if that didn't bring Rolf in, nothing would. But the door of the spare room stayed shut.

The stuff was working now, damn it. The flight-lieutenant lay with his hot face against her bare breast, one hand still tangled in the curls at the back of her head. Rhythmically, he began to snore. She eased her body from underneath him. His trousers lay in a heap at the foot of the bed. Quickly she unbuttoned his blue RAF shirt and drew it over his head. Then she walked over to the door of the spare room, took a key from her pocket, and unlocked it.

"He's well away," she said.

Warnow came out and took the tunic, shirt and trousers

from her. He looked briefly, at the sleeping man and asked:

"What about him?"

"He'll be out for hours and hours, and when he comes round he won't be in a position to make much fuss. I'll tell him the place was robbed while I was out buying something for breakfast. He'll believe it."

"He'll be in trouble without his papers."

"That's his look-out."

Warnow said no more, but began to dress in the RAF uniform. It fitted pretty well, she thought. She had chosen Peter, that night at the dance, because he was about Rolf's size.

"Let's look at his papers."

"He's a Mosquito pilot, at West Murford. That's about an hour and a half in the train. It leaves Liverpool Street in an hour, so we haven't time to waste. Let's hope to God there's no air-raid warning. Now listen, Rolf. We had supper before he . . . well, you know . . . and he told me a lot. They put the Mosquito planes round the edge of the airfield, on the northern side, because they do those flights—what are they called—?"

"Night intruder?"

"That's right—they do them often at night, and without much warning, depending on the weather, and that sort of thing. So the planes are often fuelled up, for use at short notice. Can you fly a Mosquito?"

"I can fly anything."

"Good. Will you need a flying outfit, or whatever you call it? Because I can't see how I can get one."

"I'd like one, because then I can fly high and avoid our own flak. Our flak's too damned good—it got me at Wangerooge, when I was bringing those agents over. But I don't see how you can get me a flying suit, Hanna. So I'll fly low and weave."

"Where will you make for?"

"I don't know. France, probably. It depends on the plane

and on the fuel. I might not get a Mosquito, for all we know. I might get something altogether different."

"I think it's mainly Mosquitoes there, at night. That's what Peter said."

"Peter?"

She jerked a thumb at the snoring form on the bed. For the first time, Warnow looked at him closely.

"What an oaf. I'd like to get him in my sights, one of these days. How people like that can imagine they're going to beat the *Führer* is beyond my understanding."

"Don't you think a German might have been caught in the same way . . .?"

He shrugged.

"Perhaps. With a woman like you . . ."

He took her suddenly in his arms, and kissed her once, twice, three times . . . gently, for him.

"You know," he whispered, "this . . . makes no difference. To us. To my feelings. This year, next year, I'll be back for you."

This year, next year, she thought. What was the British saying? This year, next year, some time, never. Her hands caressed the hair at the back of his neck.

"Do you really care?" she said.

"It's destiny," he said, firmly. "I've always believed in destiny. Our lives have crossed, yours and mine, and they'll never grow apart again. But there are other destinies, too. There's the destiny we all share, we Germans. We're part of that, and must all give to that. As you did, just now."

"You didn't hate me for it?"

He laughed shortly.

"Hate you? I've never respected a woman so much in my life. You make me ashamed, that I can give so little and you so much. I think . . ." he paused, as if finding it difficult to say . . . "I love you."

"I love you, John," said Joanna Croasdell. He had that

funny little half-smile on his face which meant that he was really very tensed up, she saw. "So watch what you're doing . . . whatever it is. You still don't know when you'll be back?"

Croasdell picked up the satchel which held his Air Force respirator.

"Sorry, darling, no."

He bent swiftly and kissed her.

"See you soon."

Gene Vandamme came forward from the doorway and stooped to kiss her cheek, but in a sudden movement she turned and kissed him lightly on the mouth.

"You, too," she said. "Watch what you're doing."

"Oh, we're a couple of battered old birds, John and me, honey," he said easily. "We might lose a few tail feathers, now and then, but we're mighty hard to get down. See you, and I'll bring some more of that Californian grape juice."

"You do that," she said. They were outside in the jeep now, and Croasdell, who hated goodbyes, was eager to be away. He lifted his hand, and before anyone could say anything more, the jeep moved forward, scattering the loose gravel on the little driveway. Vandamme, beside him, waved briefly. Then they turned the corner and were gone. Joanna went back into the cottage. It was, she remembered later, the first goodbye which had made her go to her room and cry.

SECRET

Army Air Force Proving Ground Command,
Eglin Field, Florida

MEMORANDUM
To: Chief Intelligence Officer, Eighth Air Force, ETO
Subject: Willie Baby

1. Here is the information relevant to your message 235/21/2.
2. (War Wearies) Willies are aircraft (B-17 and B-24) which are of no further use for combat, and can be used to carry large explosive loads (app. 18,500 lbs.). Several methods for remote control of such aircraft have been developed. In one, known as Willie Orphan, the aircraft is controlled from the ground, whereas Willie Baby is controlled from an accompanying aircraft, television being incorporated to improve accuracy.
3. The method being presently evaluated at this Command for the purposes laid down by operational planning staffs is Willie Baby. This is the only method yet suitable for a target at the range proposed.
4. The air control system used is designated the Corticated System. Only Phase 1 of this system is yet operational, though two further phases are planned, using more sophisticated television and telemeter equipment.
5. The Corticated System includes a television camera in the nose of the missile, which becomes the equivalent of providing the remote control operator with an eye looking at the area towards which the missile is flying.
6. The missile is controlled through the use of an FM radio link. It is navigated visually to within ten miles of the target and the Block 3 television is then used during the final run.
7. The visual navigation employed in this system requires good weather during the mission. The exact require-

ments for weather depend upon the type of mission planned, as this determines the distance at which the control airplane should remain from the missile in order to avoid enemy action.

8. The possible accuracy of this system was demonstrated in October 1943 when a YPQ-12A airplane, equipped with the inferior Block 1 television equipment, was expended against a thirty-foot-square target. The point of impact was only thirty feet from the target.
9. The control airplane used in the Corticated System is a B-17 aircraft equipped with the necessary FM and television equipment. It is commonly known as a Bluefish.
10. Operational evaluation of Willie Baby, and training of ten crews, continues at this Command as a matter of urgency. Four crews will be posted to Eighth Air Force, ETO, later this week.
11. You will be informed of further Willie Baby tests conducted at Eglin Field thru next week.

JOHN D. HAMLYN
Brigadier General, Air Corps
Chief Evaluation Officer

16

"We'll try it at eight miles," said Major Paul Dore. "Turn away now, Lieutenant, and let's put that Willie right where it belongs."

The pilot eased the control wheel to the right. Slowly, the B-17 turned its massive bulk, tilting its port wingtip higher into the dazzling blue of the Florida sky.

"Twenty-six thousand five-hundred feet, Major, sir," said the pilot into his throat microphone. Right on the button, he thought to himself, glancing down through the Plexiglass of the nose, where the major squatted in front of the small, glowing television console. Below the B-17, the green-and-brown chequerboard of the scrub and light forest of the 800,000-acre Eglin proving ground rolled slowly past like a hazy, shimmering map. Far, far ahead and to his left, he caught a momentary flash of sunlight on a Plexiglass canopy. That, he knew, was the Willie, now about five miles away, lumbering along at 200 miles an hour, packed with explosive, and stripped of every movable piece of equipment normally carried—turrets, mountings, gun brackets, and all routine radio fittings. From the ground, it would look much like an ordinary B-17. But no pilot sat on the flight-deck: no bombardier crouched in the nose. The man who flew that far-away B-17 sat here, in this aircraft, touching every so often the toggle switches on the radio console which moved the controls on the robot ship six miles ahead.

"Willie Mother Four to Eglin Field," said Major Dore into his microphone. "Do you read me?"

"Eglin to Willie Mother Four. I read you."

"Roger. I'm taking the Willie One down to 150 feet. Two miles out."

"Check."

Dore's fingers pushed the flaps switch on the console. Five miles away in the B-17, the flaps moved, and the trimming knobs adjusted themselves. Flatly, insensitively, but obediently, the robot B-17 wallowed down in a long slow dive.

"We're flying a 90-degree course now, Major," said the pilot.

"OK."

Dore stared fixedly at the television console mounted beside the FM radio remote control, watching the red, streaky flicker of the picture transmitted by the camera in the robot's nose. When he had first begun training on Willie Baby two months ago, the picture had been no more than an incomprehensible blur of changing light. By now he had learned to interpret it. There was a whitish patch at the upper left of the ten-inch screen. Swiftly, he flicked the switch again. The whitish pattern grew steadily bigger, until it filled half the screen.

Crouched in the nose, Dore said his familiar little prayer to himself. The patch occupied virtually all the screen now.

"OK, Lieutenant, Willie locked on. She's yours now. Try a bit of evasive action."

The pilot grinned, and Willie Mother slid down through the sky, banking steeply, one wing high, as though attacked by enemy fighters. The picture on the console blurred for a moment, but Dore was no longer looking at it. He was hanging on to a metal stanchion in the nose, looking out through the side of the canopy. Away to the left, a mushroom of dirty brown smoke and flame erupted from the ground. Dore looked back towards the lieutenant and raised his thumb. Twenty minutes later, Willie Mother Four landed at Eglin Field. Dore walked over to the Test Evaluation Office.

"Pretty good, Paul," said the duty evaluation officer as he came in.

"Seems to have been dead right for angle of approach—around forty feet short of target, though. With 18,000 pounds, that shouldn't make all that difference."

Dore shook his head.

"Trouble is that the Block 3 camera loses something close to the ground. Too much mush, I guess. If we could come in steeper, we'd be able to put a Willie right on."

"No go," said the evaluation officer. "That's the one specification Eighth have really laid on the line. 'Shallow glide—similar to a landing approach, but at maximum speed.' That's what they say."

Dore shrugged.

"Well, that's what they're getting. But what's it all for? Sounds like we're trying to put those clapped out old Weary Willies right inside something. U-boat pens, maybe?"

"Maybe," said the evaluation officer.

A light summer rain was drifting across the *Luftwaffe* compound at Rastenburg, and the armed SS sentries outside the door of Jeschonnek's office complex dripped water from their capes as they brought their Schmeissers up to the "present arms". *Oberst* Pertz raised a hand in a stiff ungainly salute, Privately, he despised saluting. It reminded him, he thought, of a lot of apes each scratching where their leader scratched. There were those who thought and those who swung their arms. One should be careful not to confuse the two.

Jeschonnek was standing with his back to him, looking out of the window, when the *Feldwebel* knocked at the door and showed Pertz in.

"Good evening, *Herr General*," said Pertz politely, but it was several seconds before Jeschonnek finally turned to him. The *Luftwaffe* Chief of Staff's tall, slim form was slightly stooped. His eyes were red-rimmed.

"You will recall the operation about which I minuted you last week, *Herr General*? The operation to recover Major Warnow?"

"Of course," said Jeschonnek. The man seemed positively absentminded sometimes, thought Pertz, annoyed.

"Well, *Herr General*, I thought you should know, that the operation will be mounted tonight. The *Abwehr* have confirmed this—I had a message from the Tirpitzhufer this afternoon. Their . . . contact . . . in London had made the arrangements. Extremely efficiently, as far as we can judge. If they work out, Major Warnow should be back under my command tonight."

"With a little luck," said Jeschonnek. Pertz looked at him sharply.

"Luck should be irrelevant in KG 200, Herr General."

"Luck is never irrelevant, in life, in love, in war," said Jeschonnek heavily. If this man, thought Pertz, worked for me in KG 200, I'd have to get rid of him. Sometimes one wondered about the poor *Luftwaffe*, torn between a fat, dreaming optimist like Goering and a neurotic pessimist like this one. Thank God for the *Führer*. At least he still knew what this war was all about.

"Well, I thought you should know, *Herr General*," he said finally. "Because, as we know, it brings *Ulysses* forward again, if we get Warnow back."

"Of course. Thank you, Pertz."

The damned man was dismissing him, Pertz said to himself. He tried again.

"The *Führer* will be pleased, *Herr General*. He puts a lot of faith in *Ulysses*."

"Men under stress often put faith in magic," said Jeschonnek. Pertz could hardly believe his ears.

"For years, men believed that alchemists could transmute lead into gold. Quite intelligent, sensible, even far-seeing men believed that, Pertz. But their belief changed nothing. Lead remained lead. It could never be gold."

"And?" said Pertz, reluctantly. Where was this discussion going to end?

"Germany needs more than *Ulysses* now, Pertz. We need a great deal, an impossible amount, of your despised luck . . ."

"Impossible," said Pertz, "is not a word I have ever heard our *Führer* use."

"Quite," said Jeschonnek.

In his room fifty feet below the Horse Guards Parade, Winston Churchill struggled to his feet from the narrow iron-framed bed where he had taken his afternoon nap and zipped up his blue-denim siren suit. He crossed to the wash-bowl and rubbed a little cold water over his face. He felt rested . . . not bad for an old man he thought to himself. He tugged on a pair of carpet slippers and walked to the great map of Western Europe on the far wall, pulling aside the curtain which covered it. He looked at it for several minutes—once taking a ruler from a drawer and making some rough mental calculation of distance. Then he drew the curtain across once more and walked to his desk. There were three buzzers at its top left-hand corner, marked respectively Detective, Butler, Secretary. He pressed the bottom one, and waited until she came in.

"Good evening," he said. "Kindly take a personal minute:

" 'Prime Minister to Chief of Air Staff:

" '1. I am informed that Operation Shipwreck, which I discussed after last Friday's meeting of the War Cabinet with the Director of Intelligence and with Air Marshal Harris is to be mounted tonight.

" '2. What arrangements have been made to safeguard the security of the operation should it not go according to plan?

" '3. I commend to your notice the reports from Châteaufort in France, from Zilistea in Roumania, and from Sola-Stavanger in Norway (which were transmitted to you on the

19th) and which appear to indicate an unusual concentration of captured machines at these airports.

" '4. I am concerned that we should not be deceived by the enemy into imagining that his use of these machines will be confined to peripheral though irritating activities of a minor character, such as the destruction of the United States B-17 bomber last week.

" '5. I cannot entirely agree with your minute relating these enemy activities to a breach of the Geneva Convention. It is true that there may be a technical breach, but for many centuries the use of enemy colours has been considered a legitimate *ruse de guerre*. I commend to your attention in this regard the activities of a number of our more celebrated naval officers during the Napoleonic wars. If, of course, the enemy extended his operations into other fields, we could reconsider our position on this.

" '6. I am greatly concerned that the enemy appears to be concentrating on the recovery of United States B-17 and B-24 machines for his purposes. The reason for this is not clear, but can only be ominous. I read with careful attention the lucid report of the Intelligence Section, United States Eighth Air Force, but remain unconvinced that it is only the inherent constructional strength of these United States machines which causes the enemy to concentrate on them in this way.

" '7. Pray let me have, for immediate attention, a résume of the effective operational ranges of these machines *in the conditions under which the enemy would fly them*, and a digest relating those ranges to targets attainable from the three enemy bases cited earlier in this minute.

" '8. Pray keep me constantly informed of the progress of Operation Shipwreck.' "

The secretary went out of the room, and Churchill turned back to the wall and once more drew the curtain from the map. He looked at it intently for a minute or two, and then shook his head. He opened the door, and the Royal Marine sentry outside came smartly to attention as the Prime

Minister ambled down the passage towards the main Map Room.

High up in the brown stucco four-storey building at 74-76 Tirpitzhufer in Berlin, Germany's spy-master, Admiral Wilhelm Canaris, looked out from his desk to where the Landwehr Canal gleamed through the green leaves of the chestnut trees. The head of the *Abwehr*, the German Intelligence Service, was a small, stocky man, with a cap of smooth white hair. He rang a small brass handbell which stood on his desk. A youngish, bald man in a grey suit came in and stood beside him.

"Ah, Helmut," said Canaris. His voice was soft, almost feminine—an unexpected voice in a man who in 1914 had served in the German sea-raider *Dresden* and in U-boats, and had ended his sea career commanding a battleship. Canaris's mind was not a Service mind, however: it was a powerful instrument of devious, Byzantine complexity. No one, not even his trusted Helmut, knew what Canaris was thinking, or what his opinions were on any subject. Did he now, for instance, support Adolf Hitler? It was a question Helmut had occasionally asked himself ever since 1935, when Canaris had arrived at the little bare room in the Tirpitzhufer. Helmut knew—though he deliberately turned his mind away from the fact—that Canaris had been in contact with the British before the war. Could there be contacts even now? There was only one constant principle which any observer could ever fix in the old man's behaviour. He steered the whole structure of the *Abwehr*, with its hundreds of agents, through the rockstrewn whirlpools of the Third Reich as though it were his own private army. The loyalties of the head of the *Abwehr* were labyrinthine, but they all led back to himself.

"Bring me the files on Siegfried and Cassandra—the immediate files, not the full ones."

"Yes, Excellency."

It was an old-fashioned title, but Helmut knew that Canaris liked to be addressed by it. When the files came, the white-haired man leafed through them abstractedly.

"How long has Siegfried been in Stockholm now?"

Why does he want the Siegfried file? thought Helmut. Siegfried—it was a most serious offence in the Tirpitzhufer to refer to an agent by any other than a code name—was the agent whose task it was, in neutral Sweden, to gather every scrap of information on Allied aircraft and flying techniques. Siegfried's reports were sent automatically from the Tirpitzhufer to the *Luftwaffe* chief technical adviser, *Oberst* Dietrich Stahl, at the testing base of Aldershof, outside Berlin. And Stahl shared them with the *Luftwaffe* intelligence unit known as Department X.

"Two years and three months, Excellency."

"*Ach, so*? And Cassandra, in London?"

"Since 1938, Excellency."

That was it, of course. Cassandra was involved in the *Ulysses* tie-up with KG 200—he, Helmut, had seen the radio flimsies. That would explain why the old man wanted the Siegfried file as well.

"Since 1938—that's a long time, Helmut."

"Yes, Excellency, but consider where she works. It's a fantastic coup to have her there at all. Almost unbelievable."

Canaris sighed, and passed a hand across his white head. If it hadn't been for the small bright eyes, he would have looked like a favourite German uncle. But the eyes were strangely unrevealing: they neither smiled nor frowned. They didn't, thought Helmut, show any emotion at all.

"Unbelievable? Yes, you're right, Helmut."

He tapped the file.

"You know about tonight's operation, of course. The plan seems excellent—very much better than we could have anticipated, a week or two ago. Yet it's curious, the way it's worked out, isn't it?"

"In what way, Excellency?"

"It all hinges on Cassandra. The original *Fall Ulysses* hinged on Cassandra, because only she could give the signal for the operation. And now look what's happened. Warnow's in Britain—and once more, it all hinges on Cassandra. To get him out. And then, even when he's out, the whole affair will go back to where it was. And still it will hinge on Cassandra."

Helmut's face was thoughtful. He was an acutely perceptive man, which was why Canaris employed him.

"But, there was no way . . . I mean, it could not be predicted that Warnow's plane would crash when and where it did. There was no way in which Cassandra could have known. Or in which the British could have known. And Cassandra herself does not know the details of *Ulysses*. Her only task is to send the signal."

Canaris said nothing for a moment. He stared quietly from the window at the rustling tops of the chestnut trees. At last he spoke again:

"When she reported Warnow's arrival, which code word did we send?"

"Goethe, Excellency, and Mozart."

"That was the 'kill if necessary' code for the month . . .?"

"Yes, Excellency."

"And she replied?"

"She replied that she thought it would be unnecessary, Excellency."

Canaris twirled a silver pencil.

"She was swift to make up her mind."

"She is always swift, Excellency."

"Of course. But . . . she's certainly doing a very good job. Without"—Canaris spoke the words slowly and deliberately —"without help from anybody."

Helmut's eyes widened.

"But, surely—"

"Surely? Surely? That's not a word we use in this business."

He handed back the file.

"A most impressive record, Cassandra's. A pity it must end."

"Why must it end?"

"Because her cover will be blown. What will happen when this RAF officer finds he has lost his uniform and papers? He will say he was with her. And she will be looked at, eventually, first by RAF Field Security, then by MI5. It's a high price to pay for Major Warnow, but apparently KG 200 think he's worth it."

"We do not take orders from KG 200, Excellency."

"No, no, of course not, my dear Helmut. But KG 200 is very much the *Führer*'s favourite child. There are times when one should let a favourite child do what it wants, don't you think?"

"And Cassandra?"

"We shall have to get her out. Or"—he gave an elaborate start as though a thought appeared to strike him. His voice altered subtly—"or, of course, she may have been able to make her own arrangements."

"I see," said Helmut.

"This is the stop," said Hannah Walters. Warnow got up from his bus seat and followed her out. The bus conductress, she was amused to see, gave an appreciative smile to the tall blond man in RAF uniform as he swung down from the platform. He looked good in it, she thought. Rolf Warnow was born to wear uniform.

They had picked up the bus at West Murford station after the train had been, unexpectedly, on time. The RAF base was about two miles out of the little East Anglia town, but there was a steady stream of traffic along the road. She was trying, for Rolf's sake, to keep an impassive face, but she was nervous. All that she had arranged with the Director was that there would be a suitable Mosquito at the north-western corner of the field. Everything else she and

Warnow would have to manage as though this were, indeed, a genuine escape . . . as to Rolf, she reminded herself, it actually appeared to be. The Director was taking no chances by arranging an easy passage for Rolf through the airfield security. It was going to be up to Rolf himself.

"I still fear that the guards at the gate will know that I am not the flight lieutenant," he said in a low voice.

"I don't think so," she said quietly. "He'd only been stationed here for five days, and you look rather like him, anyway. And it's dusk. You'll be all right."

"At any rate," he said, "there's no photograph on the identity papers. Just name and rank."

"The British don't like identity photographs," she said. "They think it's an invasion of their freedoms."

He laughed shortly, and she tucked her arm into his and walked him into the shadows past the gate.

"Don't try to go in yet," she said. "Walk with me—it will just seem we are saying goodbye."

As we are, Rolf Warnow, she thought to herself. They walked slowly down the side of the field. There was a big twin-engined machine standing close to the hedge, with a tarpaulin flung across its fuselage.

"Is that—"

"No, no, that's an Anson. God help me if that's the best I can get. It would be a sitting duck for our flak. And it has little range."

"You still don't know where to try for?"

"Not until I'm in the cockpit."

He glanced for a moment at the faint glow in the night sky where the sun had set.

"It's good flying weather, anyway. And good weather for flak. Ah, that's more like it."

"Don't point," she said swiftly. "Where . . . oh, yes. That's a Mosquito?"

"Yes," he said.

It was there, where she'd been told it would me, at the

north-western edge of the field. Warnow was staring at it hungrily.

"I think that's a plane on stand-by," he said, at last. "It's not under wraps, and there are chocks in front of the wheels, so it looks as though somebody's been warming the engines."

"He said there are always two or three planes round the edge of the field, waiting," said Hannah Walters.

"What's the name of the nearest airfield to here—a field where they fly operations from?" he asked suddenly. They were walking back towards the main gate, arm in arm, ostensibly a young man and his girl saying goodbye. She thought for a moment.

"Little Snoring," she said. "Why . . .?"

"I don't know," he said. "It might be useful." He nodded towards the perimeter barbed wire fence.

"Look how slack they are . . . it's almost too good to be true."

Oh, don't think that, Rolf Warnow, she said to herself. Don't start thinking that.

"See?" he said. "No mobile patrol, that I can see. No searchlight, either. Nobody checking on the road outside the wire. Any *Luftwaffe* airfield commandant would have a fit."

"Most of your *Luftwaffe* airfields are in Occupied Europe," she said. "There's no Resistance here."

He grunted.

"I wonder if that Mosquito's tanked-up?" he said. "If it's on stand-by it should be. We do the same thing with the JU-88s."

Casually he flicked his hand to his cap to return the salute of a passing aircraftman. She noted admiringly that he did it in exactly the right way—not too smartly, but not slackly, either. He caught her glance and said softly:

"They teach us, you know . . . all of us in the special units are taught. We watch films as well . . . such bad films, Hannah, you wouldn't believe. And we practise it. We watch prisoners in the *stalags*, too. And listen."

She knew now that she loved him, but she began also to feel for him a consuming admiration. He gave the impression of being watchful but relaxed. Any other man she knew would have been avid, desperate, to get through that gate and across to the Mosquito. Any other man might have felt ill at ease in enemy uniform—especially since, if he was caught in it, he might be shot. But Warnow strolled up and down in front the RAF police at West Murford as though he'd been in and out of the camp fifty times. His eyes missed nothing. At intervals he laughed in a pleasant, intimate sort of way—the very picture of a young man with his girl. Only the occasional WAAF who walked by ever gave him a glance. He was, she reflected, a very good-looking man.

"Those are the main administration buildings, over there on the right, I imagine," he said. "And the hangars, between there and us. And presumably that thing"—he pointed to the long low shape of a road tanker—"is going round to the refuelling bowsers. Even these idiots won't have those right beside the hangars, so they must be beyond them, where we can't see."

Navigation lights winking, an aircraft rumbled overhead in the dusk, wheels down as it came into the runway. Warnow watched it carefully.

"Beaufighter," he said. "That might do, if he leaves it somewhere convenient."

The Beaufighter passed out of sight down the far end of the runway, and did not reappear. Warnow shrugged.

"I'd rather have the Mosquito, anyway," he said. "They'll like it better over there."

"Are you sure you can fly it?" she said.

"I tell you I can fly anything. Now, listen, Hannah. I'll be back."

He's going, she thought.

"I'll be back with you . . . I swear it. I've got the lay-out here now, clear in my head. I'm going to try for that Mosquito, and if that's no good, I'll find something else."

"You realise I can't wait?" she said. "I've been seen here outside the gate with you, and if they pick you up, they'll start looking for me, too."

"Of course. I won't say what I feel. You know."

He bent and kissed her lightly on the lips. She turned and walked away from him, down the long white road to West Murford station. He watched her for a second or two, and then crossed to the RAF Regiment sergeant with the white blancoed belt and cross-straps, who stood beside the gate and the guard Nissen hut. Warnow took his identity papers from his pocket. The sergeant glanced at them cursorily.

"Nice evening, sir."

"Yes . . . too bloody nice. I'd like a quiet night."

The sergeant laughed, and handed back his papers. Slowly, methodically, he put them back in his tunic pocket.

"Can you tell me where the Station Commander's office is, Sergeant? I only arrived the other day, and I don't know my way around yet."

"Over there, sir, just to the right of the Officers' Mess. But he won't be there now, sir. He'll be in his quarters, or in the Mess."

"No, I only want to drop off a bit of bumf he wanted. Thank you, Sergeant. Good night."

"Good night, sir."

Warnow was annoyed to find that his hands were damp as he walked away up the drive towards the administration buildings. It was a reaction he had tried hard, in training, to control, because it was one which was easily noticeable by any suspicious person. But the psychologists at Rechlin had said there was nothing he could do about it. "It's a reflex," he'd been told. "And you can't control a reflex . . ." Possibly not, he thought. But you could try. He looked casually around him. There was no one near. Without checking his pace, he walked off the driveway on to the short, clipped grass of the field. The administration buildings were now at his back. Unhurriedly but purposefully, he strode on through the darkness, moving towards the Mosquito parked at the corner of the field.

"That's him," said Vandamme. "I'm sure it's him. He's been talking with that girl out there for the last ten minutes, walking up and down. I can't see her face, because she's got a head-scarf on. But she's got a nice pair of legs."

He handed the powerful Ross night-glasses to Croasdell. They were leaning against the wing of a Mosquito, deep in the shadows of a hangar about 100 yards from the perimeter fence. Each wore a civilian jacket and flannel trousers—the kind of half-shabby, anonymous clothes, they'd been told, in which they would be equally inconspicuous in towns or in the countryside. Secure in their pockets were their alternative sets of Dutch and French and Belgian papers, so that they would be able to take off again immediately in the Lysander as soon as they returned from tracking Warnow. The summer night, reflected Croasdell, was short, and there would be little time to spare. But Warnow was not likely to be flying for long.

"She's walking away now," said Croasdell. "And Warnow—if it is Warnow—is coming in through the gate."

Intently, almost hungrily, he stared through the binoculars at the tall, slim figure outside the guard-room.

"Wait . . . he's having his identity card checked. Now he's coming on . . . did you see that salute? I don't think that's Warnow. That's a real RAF type."

"He's wonder-boy, all right," said Vandamme. "Look—he's going off to the side now. He's after that Mossie. I'm losing him now . . . it's too damned dark."

"He'll have to bring her out on the runway to take off," said Croasdell. "We'd better get into the cockpit."

They settled into their seats—Croasdell's slightly forward and on the left, the pilot's position. In front of Vandamme was the console containing the twin screens of the AI Mark X radar. Vandamme switched it on: the cathode ray tubes glowed. Croasdell glanced at the engine temperature gauges. The twin Rolls-Royce Merlins had been fully warmed, and the Mosquito was ready for take-off.

"We'll have to watch like crazy," said Vandamme. "We don't want to mix up wonder-boy with some other guy taking off on a normal mission."

"That won't happen," said Croasdell. "The only man who's in on this is the CO of the RAF Regiment here. And he won't interfere unless something goes seriously wrong. The control tower has been told it's a security exercise, and that no other aircraft will land or take-off for the next thirty minutes. Anything incoming is being diverted to Snoring. It'll spoil a few arrangements with the local popsies, I should imagine."

Vandamme propped the glasses against the cockpit Perspex.

"I think he's moving the Mossie," he said suddenly. "That looks like his exhausts. Yes, there he is."

About a quarter of a mile away, the low clean shape of the moving Mosquito bulked blacker still against the darkness of the summer night. Small pink stabs of flame flickered halfway along each wing.

"I won't move out yet," said Croasdell. "This is the tricky bit, because we don't want him to see us, and on the other hand, we mustn't lose him. Is that radar OK?"

"It will be once we get above about 500 feet," said Vandamme. "As long as we get off pretty well in his track, he won't spot us. He's got no working radar, and he hasn't got eyes in the back of his head. And if he does, well, we're just another Mossie. We can drop back a mile or so and watch him on the screen . . . Jesus, what's he doing?"

Warnow's Mosquito was turning away from the runway and was taxiing slowly back behind the hangars.

"I don't get it," said Vandamme. "He can't have missed the runway, because the markers are clear enough, and anyway, the glim-lights are on."

"I suppose that *is* wonder-boy?" said Croasdell worriedly. "Not some other spare type fooling round with a Mossie?"

"There's only one Mosquito down there. It had to be arranged that way so he got the one with the rigged fuel tanks and no radar," said Vandamme. "So unless somebody else had decided—God, he's gone right behind the hangar. What in hell's he playing at? And why are you laughing . . .?"

"Don't you see?" said Croasdell. His voice, Vandamme noticed, even at that moment, was slightly shrill and his laughter a little theatrical. "Don't you see? Wonder-boy is just what he's cracked up to be . . . a real wonder-boy. Trust him to do the unexpected. He's really screwed up the Director's little plan."

"But how?" said Vandamme, bewilderedly.

"You know what's behind those hangars?" said Croasdell. Vandamme shook his head.

"The bowsers, Gene. The bloody fuel bowsers. Wonder-boy doesn't like the look of his gauge. And he's got all the nerve in the world. He's taking that Mossie along and he's going to get her tanks filled up."

"Well, I'm damned," said Vandamme quietly. "So he won't be making a crashlanding on the coast, and all those Resistance boys will be waiting for nothing?"

"That's right," said Croasdell. "Wonder-boy doesn't know it, of course, but he's just made a monkey out of the head of British Intelligence."

"A Mosquito, fully fuelled, can do around 1,400 miles," said Vandamme.

"That's right," said Croasdell again. "He'll be able to go pretty well anywhere he wants . . ."

17

Rolf Warnow sat in the cockpit of the Mosquito and forced himself to think. Every nerve inside him clamoured that he should roll the plane to the runway and take off, heading blindly south. Deliberately, he looked round him. There was no radar set—some sort of maintenance chit was stuck across the brackets where the console, he imagined, would normally be mounted. He switched on the fuel gauge: the needle kicked briefly, showing only a little fuel in the tank—enough, perhaps, he calculated, for around 150 miles. He did not know for certain how fast these Merlin engines used fuel, but he had a respect for the efficiency of British engines. Nevertheless, there was something funny about that fuel gauge. Experimentally, he switched it off and on again. On a German engine, it would have needed a second to stabilise itself—a momentary flicker, no more. And the same was true of the quite different gauges on the B-17 he'd been flying. But this gauge rose for half an inch and then stopped dead. Almost as though it was hitting some sort of barrier. He had to face the possibility that something was wrong with it. Well, if something was wrong with that gauge, which way was it wrong? Was it showing less fuel than was actually in the tanks, or more? It was obvious that his assumptions had been wrong in one respect. This Mosquito certainly was not on stand-by—not with a tank only about one-sixth full and no radar. The one thing he did not want to do was to take off, run out of fuel, and crash-land to be captured. He was too important. *Ulysses* was too important to risk that. The same applied to a forced landing in the sea.

The conclusion, he thought, a little desperately, was obvious. He had to make certain—and the only way he could make certain was by taking the Mosquito round to the refuelling point and filling its tanks. His hands began to sweat again at the thought of it. He looked out of the cockpit window. There was no one near the aircraft—no one at this end of the field at all. There were a few points of light where the blackout of the administration block was a little less than efficient, and the blue lights of a vehicle moving across the field far ahead to his right. Possibly another tanker, he thought. To his left, the runway glim-lights stretched away into the darkness, a long glowing path. Why were they switched on? Well, of course, there was plenty of traffic to and from this field—which was one reason why probably no one would pay the slightest attention when he started up and moved. The control tower, of course, would react sharply when he took off without permission—but by that time he would be moving away at about 380 miles an hour, and they'd probably just log his number and report him. There was the risk, of course, that those runway lights were on because a flight of night-fighters or bombers was due to land from some mission, but there was absolutely no way he could find out about that. Immediately, he dismissed it from his calculations. The chances of a runway or take-off collision were not to be estimated. He would have to take his chance.

He pushed the button for the starboard engine. The Merlin burst into life in a surge of power, decreasing its roar to a steady rumble as he throttled back. Then he started the port engine. Professionally, he ran his eyes along the panel. He had decided to treat this aircraft much as though it were a Junkers 88—a type which he knew well and which in many ways it resembled. The engine temperature gauges showed the glycol mixture at about 90 degrees Centigrade, which argued that the engine was already more or less warmed up. The propellers seemed in pitch. He pulled the red brake release handle, and quickened the engines. The

Mosquito strained but did not move. Damn, the chocks. She was pushing on the chocks. Cursing his foolishness, he switched off, scrambled out of his seat, jumped to the ground, and kicked them away. Once more he looked round. There had been absolutely no reaction to his engine-start as far as he could see. He clambered back into the cockpit, and started up once more, taxiing the Mosquito slowly forward, across the runway, round behind the great block of the hangars. He had been fairly certain, when walking round the airfield with Hannah, that the bowsers were round there somewhere, but he was relieved, as soon as he came round their bulk, to see the blue lights of the fuelling point. A twin-engined plane, a Beaufighter—probably the one that had landed a quarter of an hour ago—was just being towed away from it. He brought the Mosquito up alongside the bowser, switched off, and jumped down. The corporal on the bowser came across and said to him in a carefully controlled voice:

"You know that's a serious offence, sir?"

"What?"

"Bringing your aircraft up to us like that with the engines on. Have the whole lot go up one day, if you go on doing that, sir."

"Oh, I see, I'm sorry, Corporal. I'm just in a hell of a hurry. Got to ferry this thing over to Snoring and pick up my navigator. I'm on ops."

"May I have your fuel authorisation, sir?"

"Look—I haven't got one. I've just been given this kite—they're one short for their patrol. I was having a quiet Scotch in the mess—I haven't got any bloody authorisation. What do you think I'm going to do with this lot—land the thing on the road and pump the fuel into my car?"

The corporal looked at him curiously.

"You an American, sir?"

"No—why?"

"You've got a slight American accent."

"Oh, that . . . no, I'm not American, but I was brought up in Canada, when I was a boy. In Toronto. It tends to stick a bit, you know."

The corporal's voice warmed.

"Really, sir? What part of Toronto?"

"We used to live just outside South Park. We had a flat there. My father worked for Shell Oil."

The corporal began to unclip the bowser hose from its mounting.

"Here, Jeff," he called into the darkness, and an aircraftman appeared beside him. "Get the squirt into these tanks. How much, sir?"

"Full," said Warnow.

"OK, sir. Interesting that. You see, my boy and girl are out there now, and they live by South Park. Very nice family, the people who've got them. Better life in some ways than I could have given 'em myself, matter of fact. Interesting, you comin' from there."

"Your boy and girl?"

"Evacuated, start of the war," said the corporal briefly. "Better off there, anyway. Well, that's it, sir, All full up. Don't worry about the authorisation. We get a lot of spillage, as we call it. Have a good trip—and get one of the bastards for me."

"I'll do that," said Warnow.

He climbed back up into the fuselage and got into the cockpit. The corporal and the aircraftman pushed at the tail until he faced away from the bowser. Then he touched the engine switches, one after the other, and slowly rolled the Mosquito back to the end of the runway. He looked around him at every angle of the night sky. There was no sign of an aircraft, no wink of landing lights as some Beaufighter or Mosquito came in on its final approach.

Up in the tower, the take-off and landing control officer turned quickly to the warrant officer beside him.

"What's that Mossie doing at the end of Runway Two?"

The warrant officer checked a paper pinned to the tower wall.

"Don't know, sir. There's no take-off listed."

"He's starting to move. Has he flashed the letter yet?"

"No, sir."

"Well, the silly bugger's taking off, all right. Is there anything coming in?"

The radar corporal in the corner of the tower raised his eyes for a moment from his glowing screen and shook his head.

"Nothing on plot, sir."

"Well, there he goes. Get his bloody number. I'll have his guts for garters tomorrow . . ."

Below the tower, the Mosquito gathered speed. Automatically, Warnow's eyes once more swept across the instruments. Gauge still showed one-sixth full, so he'd been right —it was out of order. But, anyway, he knew now that the tanks were full. Glycol temperature 95 degrees Centigrade: fine. Propeller pitch, excellent. Now . . . open the throttles. The glim-lights of the runway began to flick by in a continuous stream, quickening as the Mosquito approached lift-off speed. Warnow was pushing forward now on the control column, until he felt the tail come up. Then he pulled back. There was an unmistakable lifting sensation as the Mosquito became airborne. A shadowy white ribbon of road unreeled for a moment under the port wing. Heading due south, wheels retracing slowly into their nacelles. Warnow's Mosquito began to climb at 2,500 feet a minute into the summer night. Below him, Croasdell and Vandamme turned on to the end of the runway. Croasdell opened the throttles, and the Mosquito began its rush down the glimpath.

In the control tower, the take-off control officer turned to his companion.

"Am I going mad?" he said. "Or is that another Mosquito, taking off without permission?"

"It is, sir," said the warrant officer heavily. "There's that security exercise you were told about, of course. It might be something to do with that—I wouldn't know."

The landing control officer did not miss the emphasis of the warrant officer's "I" and "you". The warrant officer had been kept in the dark about the security exercise, and that was something he resented. Not, he thought, that he himself knew anything much about it.

"It may be," he said in a neutral voice. "But log the numbers and the times of take-off. I'll have a little inquiry in the morning."

About him the two Mosquitoes climbed steadily south.

"Have you got him?" said Croasdell.

"There's a definite flicker," said Vandamme, straining his eyes into the glowing screens. "You could hardly call it a blip yet. But there's a lot of interference from ground mush, because he's still low."

"I'll keep about three miles back. What's the range of that thing—about nine miles?"

"About," said Vandamme. "Only don't keep anything like so far away. Once I've lost the bastard, I've lost him, and I'd never find him again. Keep near his tail until we know what he's going to do."

"Right," said Croasdell.

"I wish," said Vandamme, "that we'd had time to do more night flying."

"Would have helped," said Croasdell. Suddenly, thought Vandamme, he sounded relaxed, at ease, even cheerful.

"You never know," said Croasdell, "we might have found another Heinkel . . ."

Warnow levelled out at 2,500 feet, still heading south, and began to think. He had no flying helmet or oxygen mask, and knew that it would be foolish to go higher. This meant that he would have to cross the German coast at a relatively low altitude, pretty well a sitting duck for almost any kind of flak, light or heavy. Hannah had told him, he reflected, that the German command had been warned that he would try to fly in tonight. He placed little trust in that. There was no effective way in which literally hundreds of sandbagged flak emplacements could all be expected to identify any particular plane out of possibly hundreds crossing the coast that night. The alternative would have been to give orders that fire must not be opened at any plane at all —and that was clearly unthinkable. No, he must accept that to his own anti-aircraft guns—and to his own fighters —he was an enemy aircraft.

There were the two radar gaps at Egmond and Pointe d'Ailly, of course. But they were sometimes covered by fighters nowadays, and Warnow feared fighters more than he feared guns. He knew also that it would be better to land at a KG 200 field. There was one at Châteaufort, quite near Versailles, and another at Nantes. And there was a KG 200 detachment at Schiphol, outside Amsterdam. Regretfully, he discarded both Schiphol and Châteaufort. The airport flak would think he was a night intruder. Nantes was a possibility, though. The air defences were not so thick on the Atlantic coast, and if he flew south-west, out over Cornwall and the Scillies, and then came in from the Atlantic, he might be able to land before they got too excited. On the other hand, that meant exposing himself to the English radar right the way across south-west England—with all the increased chances of night fighter interception as soon as his Mosquito was reported missing. He thought for no more than thirty seconds, and then he made up his mind. His hands grasped the wheel, and the Mosquito banked slowly to port. It would be a long flight, and he had no maps. But he had the compass whose dial swung in front of him, and he had the moon. More than that, thank God. He was flying again.

"Look at that blip," said Vandamme urgently. "What in hell's he playing at?"

Croasdell glanced down at the radarscope. On the plan-view screen, the blip of Warnow's aircraft had changed direction. It was now moving steadily north-north-east. Ahead of their own Mosquito, clearly defined in the moonlight by its silver thread of breaking waves, Croasdell could see the shorelines of eastern England. They were crossing the coast.

"Well, it's obvious, isn't it?" said Vandamme. "That boy ain't goin' to Egmond or Pointe d'Ailly or wherever we'd arranged for him to go. He's heading straight for Norway—the one place we didn't consider he would try to reach tonight, because we didn't think he'd have the nerve to refuel."

Croasdell laughed. It sounded this time, thought Vandamme, like genuine amusement.

"You know, you can't help but admire wonder-boy."

"I bloody well can," said Vandamme.

"No, Gene, you have to admit it. He runs circles round the lot of us, without even knowing it. Think of it—there's a blacked-out, tanked-up SOE Lysander back there at West Murford, all dressed up with nowhere to go. Because if we fly back for it now—well, we'd obviously lose him for good. In any case, it hasn't got the range for Norway. And if we fly on, how are we going to get back? I reckon there's enough fuel in our own tanks to reach just about anywhere in Norway—Sola, Bergen, Trondheim, Narvik, any of the *Luftwaffe* strips. But there's not enough to get us back, because we've got no drop-tanks. They didn't put drops on because they didn't think he'd be going far, anyway—and they didn't want to cut our speed, compared with his. And, of course, wonder-boy doesn't need drops himself. He's on a one-way trip."

"Blast."

"We'll have to go on," said Croasdell steadily. His stomach crawled as he said the word, but he made himself say it. "Parachutes. We've got parachutes. If it looks feasible, we'll have to jump somewhere near where he puts down. The only alternative is to call the whole thing off now, and let wonder-boy go."

"He's down to cruising speed now," said Vandamme reflectively. "Say, around 270. We could overtake the bastard and shoot him down."

"We could—but that'd be the end of the whole plan. And anyway, we can't."

"Why not?"

"He isn't armed. They took the guns out of that Mossie."

"Oh," said Vandamme, and said nothing more.

"Are you OK on the set?" said Croasdell. "I don't want to close up too much in this moonlight because he was a fighter pilot once, and fighter pilots never forget the bit of sky behind them. And if he sees us, way out here, he'll know it's no coincidence."

"I've got him good and clear," said Vandamme. "There's no mush out here—in one way, this route makes it easier. Wait . . . wait . . . there's something coming up on the set. Down on the surface. Convoy."

A group of dimmed navigation lights appeared below the Mosquito's port wing. From somewhere ahead of them, presumably from the escort, an Aldis lamp began to blink.

"He'll be asking for the recognition signal—that must be the challenge he's flashing," said Croasdell. "And I haven't the faintest idea what it is. Let's hope to God he doesn't open up. We're nice and low, both of us, for some good deflection shooting."

The convoy fell rapidly astern without a gun being fired, but Vandamme said thoughtfully:

"I know there's strict radio silence for this op, but I think we'll have to break the rules to let them know at least where we're heading."

He picked up the radio-microphone that swung from his headset.

"What was that country-code . . . the one for Norway?"

"Margaret," said Croasdell.

"I'll let 'em have the briefest transmission I can manage,"

said Vandamme. His fingers adjusted to the SOE frequency he had been given for use in emergency.

"Shipwreck, Dreamer, Margaret," he said clearly into the microphone. He said the three words again, and then switched off the set.

"I hope that means something more to somebody back there than it does to me," he said resignedly. "By the way, you realise you're going to have to write off another Mosquito?"

"Of course."

"And that we'll be parachuting down to a Resistance—I suppose there *is* a Norwegian Resistance?—that doesn't expect us. And that there seems to be no way back, that we know of?"

"Of course there's a Norwegian Resistance," said Croasdell. "It's called Milorg. And now you've sent those code words, presumably it can be warned."

"How can it be warned?" said Vandamme. "Only wonderboy knows to within six hundred miles where he's going to put down."

"There aren't all that many places he *can* put down," said Croasdell. "The likely ones can be warned."

"Christ," said Vandamme. And then slowly:

"You know, John, only a few days ago you were all set to say you wouldn't play. Now you've got a real good excuse to call it off, and you're all-fired hot to get on with it. What's it all about?"

"I just feel in the mood," said Croasdell, "to dish wonderboy."

At a little after midnight, in the Director's flat only 100 yards from Downing Street, the red flasher of the telephone on the desk in his study began to alternate. The Director looked up from a thick clip of typescript and picked up the receiver. The red flasher indicated the use of the private line to MI 5.

"Strongman," came the slightly affected drawl from the other end of the phone.

"Yes, Strongman?"

"We had a somewhat . . . unexpected . . . message from Dreamer, ten minutes ago. He broke radio silence, justifiably, I think, to say 'Margaret'. It seems Major Warnow is bound for Norway."

"Always a strong possibility, after the report from West Murford that he'd refuelled," said the Director.

"Did you seriously think he'd refuel?" said Strongman.

"That, too," said the Director, "was always a strong possibility."

There was a momentary pause at the other end.

"They seem to be going on," said Strongman. "Tipperary and Dreamer. I'm sure they'd report if they decided to run back."

"What's the nearest Norwegian Resistance unit to Sola?"

"There's a Milorg unit at Vigestrad, just down the coast. Nothing much, though, two men and a boy . . . that sort of thing. And there's a Milorg radio post, two men always on duty, up in the lakes above Ov Sirdal. That's about thirty miles west of Stavanger. Not easy country."

"If you were Tipperary, flying that machine, and you had to decide where to bale out within reach of Stavanger, where would you try . . .?"

"I'd try the area to the west," said Strongman promptly. "It's hilly, lonely country, with good cover. Not pleasant for a parachute drop, though. I'm glad I'm not with them."

"You'd better have both those units warned," said the Director.

"I can't tell Vigestrad, because it isn't a listening night for them," said Strongman. "But Ov Sirdal will be listening in about thirty-five minutes' time."

"Tell them, and they'll have to tell Vigestrad," said the Director.

"Why are you so certain he'll land at Sola?" said Strongman. "He might try Bergen or even Trondheim."

"Major Warnow came here from KG 200 at Sola," said the Director flatly. "And it is to KG 200 at Sola that he'll return. He's simply doing it more quickly than we'd anticipated. Now . . . is that all?"

"There's one thing that's rather shaken me," said Strongman, slowly.

"Yes?"

"If you—we, I mean—thought it was a strong possibility that Warnow would refuel and try Norway, why didn't we give Dreamer and Tipperary a standby set of Norwegian papers?"

"Because," said the Director, "it was only a strong possibility. And suppose he'd flown to, say, France, and Dreamer and Tipperary had followed him, and been picked up, the *Gestapo* might have found Norwegian papers, and they'd have realised we were on to something in the Sola area."

"Only if Dreamer and Tipperary had talked," said Strongman.

"Sometimes it's difficult not to talk," said the Director.

"Well, they have got a lot on their plate, sir. One of them doesn't speak Norwegian, they don't know how, when, or with whom the Milorg Resistance people will contact them. I wouldn't put their chances at more than fifty-fifty. Seems a bit rough. Not our sort of thing at all."

"It was a bit rough over Berlin, a couple of days ago," said the Director quietly. "We lost thirty-nine Lancasters. It was a bit rough over Schweinfurt the other day, when the Americans lost sixty Fortresses. It's a rough war."

The *Himmelbett* radar station at Egersund first picked up the blip of Warnow's Mosquito, moving north, ten miles out to sea. For about a minute, the *Gefreiter* on the *Wurzburg* set was not quite sure that the blip was a plane. The Mosquito was made of wood, and wood bounced back a much fuzzier image than metal. But he had seen Mosquitoes on his set before, and he didn't take long to decide. He looked up and spoke swiftly to the duty *Hauptmann*.

"One Mosquito, Sector Dora-Dora, moving north, sir." The *Hauptmann* walked over and looked at the screen. Then he picked up the telephone and spoke direct to the operations room at Sola-Stavanger, forty miles to the north.

"We can make you an offer, Joachim," he said. "A Mosquito . . . he should be in Sector Dora-Kurfurst in a minute . . . moving north."

"He's behaving rather curiously, sir," said the radar *Gefreiter*. "He's moving quite slowly, and keeping exactly parallel with the coast. Not trying to come farther in."

"My *Gefreiter* says he's flying along the coast, but slowly —for one of those damned things, anyway, Joachim. He could be in trouble."

"Many thanks."

The operations officer at Sola pressed the scramble buzzer. The alarm began to honk hoarsely, and down below him a yellow-nosed ME-109 taxied out to the runway, moving quickly into take-off. Three minutes later it banked at the end of the field, and came back low over the tower, climbing out to sea. Back in the tower, the operations officer was thinking. There had been that vague general warning about any single aircraft yesterday . . . and this one was behaving strangely. Almost as if . . . he picked up the microphone:

"Bodo calling Mosel One. Course 070 to intercept."

The acknowledgement came at once.

"Victor, victor."

"And don't be in too much of a hurry, Heinz. Just watch what he does before you open fire. Have you got that?"

"Victor, victor."

Staring into the glass panel in the cramped cockpit of the 109, *Leutnant* Heinz Altpeter asked himself what in heaven's name Sola control thought he was up to. Watch what he does, indeed. He'd got the Mosquito blip on his own radar now . . . and a few moments later he got a visual. The Mosquito was ambling steadily along, a dark shape against the aurora glow of the northern night sky, at about 260 miles an hour—a most un-Mosquito-like performance. Engine trouble, possibly. He banked to the right, and prepared to dive for the attack. The Mosquito was slowly waggling its wings from side to side, and as he watched, its wheels came down. Altpeter took his gloved thumb from the firing button. Wheels down was the international signal for surrender. Laughing to himself, he reflected that there were a few people who'd shot a Mosquito down, but he, Heinz Altpeter, was going to be the only one who'd captured one. He took up position astern of the Mosquito, eyes watchful, guns ready, as it turned into the coast and began its let-down towards Sola . . .

Vandamme's voice was urgent.

"There's another blip on the scope. I guess they've scrambled a fighter. Hey, what are you doing . . .?"

Croasdell was banking the Mosquito away, turning north-west.

"That Hun fighter mustn't see us," he said. "He won't at the moment, because this AI Mark X set is better than anything they've got. That's why you spotted him first. Remember, if he sees us, eventually Warnow's going to realise he's been followed."

"But damn it, I've lost wonder-boy now," said Vandamme disgustedly.

The Mosquito flew steadily north-west, while the gap between them and Warnow widened it about ten miles a minute.

"Look, Gene, we don't need to track him any more," said Croasdell. "We know what's going to happen to him. Either that Hun fighter will shoot him down, or he'll take him back and make him land at Sola. He's almost certainly been scrambled from Sola—and it looks to me as though Warnow was making for Sola, anyway. So you can forget your precious radar—as far as wonder-boy's concerned, anyway."

"You're not just a pretty face," said Vandamme admiringly.

"There's one thing I don't like," said Croasdell. "It's getting too damned light. There's not much real darkness up here at this time of year."

He began to bank, turning back towards the coast.

"If we don't want to be seen jumping, we'd better get back over the land as soon as we can. There's no radar station that I've ever heard of between Stavanger and Bergen, so if we come in low over Hangesund we won't be pin-pointed. And we'll have to find somewhere pretty deserted in the countryside behind Stavanger and then bale out."

"Then what?" said Vandamme.

"We shall see," said Croasdell. I've never, he thought to himself, been so frightened in my life. Beside him, Vandamme had produced a spanner and was methodically undoing the locking-nuts on the radar console. There were four of them, and as he took the last one off, he slid the heavy console out from its metal tray on to his knee. Then he pushed back the canopy and the cockpit was filled with whistling, rushing, cold dawn air.

"How far are we out now?"

" 'Bout four miles."

"That'll do. Just bank her a little."

The Mosquito's port wing dropped. Vandamme pushed the console up to the top of the canopy, shoved with all his strength, and watched it drop swiftly away into the grey light above the waves.

"That," he said, "takes care of that..."

Two minutes later they came in over the land, flying at about four hundred feet. Croasdell was growing more and more uneasy—the lightness in the sky to the east seemed to be increasing every minute. The moon was down. He climbed to four thousand feet, worrying about the mountains ahead. There was still snow glimmering on the upper slopes: all over Europe, it had been a hard winter. He banked the Mosquito hard right as a tree-covered peak appeared ahead through the half-darkness. They flew on and on, spreading their wings through dark, shadowy valleys. Occasionally they passed over a single light or a group of two or three, cottages or hamlets where some Norwegian family was already awake. People down there, he knew, would be listening to the thunder of the Merlins, and wondering. At last they came out of a valley to find ahead of them a small lake and an area of open, rocky scrub. Croasdell circled once at about 1200 feet and made up his mind. He circled again, climbing while he and Vandamme struggled into their parachute harness.

"This is as good as anywhere," he shouted, for the whistle of the wind through the open cockpit canopy made it difficult to hear. Vandamme put his mouth close to Croasdell's ear.

"We must go out virtually together," he yelled. "Otherwise we'll land miles apart and lose each other."

Croasdell slowly turned the Mosquito on to her back, pointing her, upside-down, back towards the mountains they had come through. Vandamme did not hesitate. He swung up a thumb, grinned and was gone. Levering himself from his seat, conscious in those last seconds of the glimmer of the lake far away to his left, Croasdell followed him. The tail plane caught his shoulder a glancing, painful blow as he dropped clear. For one hideous moment, he thought that it was all going to happen again the way it had done on the Spit three years ago. Then the wind was howling around him and he was turning slowly over in the slipstream of the Mosquito, whose glowing exhausts were receding to the west. With a jerk his parachute opened. Below and to his left, he saw the great white mushroom of Vandamme's parachute. They were drifting rapidly in towards the sandy shores of the shining water of the lake, but they were too low to drift far. A moment later, Croasdell landed on rough, heather-clumped ground with a jarring thump and a stab of pain as the Ross glasses he had looped round his neck were rammed into his chest. His shoulder, too, was hurting. Gasping, he punched the button of the quick-release harness, and ran over to where Vandamme was struggling in enveloping sheets of silk, about seventy yards away. They were about a quarter of a mile from the lake. It was cool rather than cold, and it was getting lighter and lighter. Cursing, Vandamme was getting out of his harness. He saw Croasdell and grinned.

"So far," he said, "so good. All we have to do now is get back."

Far to the west there was a flash, followed some seconds later by a muffled boom from high up on a mountain-side.

"There goes the Mossie," said Vandamme. "I don't know about you, but I feel lonely."

"I must congratulate you, Miss Walters," said Strongman. They were talking at his desk in the room he used in London. "A most efficient operation. Major Warnow, by the way, was predictably unpredictable to the end."

"In what way?" said Hannah Walters. I mustn't let him think I'm too interested, she said to herself.

"Well . . . oh, I suppose you'll have to know soon enough, so you may as well know now," said Strongman. "Major Warnow . . . acquired . . . some fuel and flew to Norway."

"Oh?" said Hannah Walters. She hesitated. "Is he . . . did he . . . ?"

"He landed safely," said Strongman, "if that's what you mean?"

"Yes . . . well, now when do I go? And how do I go?"

"Go, Miss Walters?"

"To Argentina. That was our bargain," she said impatiently.

"Miss Walters, you came here in 1938 as a German agent. Nine months ago we discovered you at work. At that point we offered you a choice. One, you could be sent for trial and eventual execution. Two, you could work for us. Understandably, you chose the second alternative. Your services have been exceptional, but are not yet over."

"You said—"

"I said I would make arrangements for you to leave this country when the present operation is successfully completed. It isn't. You have one more service to perform."

"But . . ."

"Miss Walters, you are in no position to say 'but'. You will really have to do as I say, won't you?"

If she hadn't known him, she would have thought that his voice was kind.

"Go back now to your flat—you will find that the Military Police have removed your young flight-lieutenant. Have some sleep. And perhaps"—he looked at her closely—"a good cry . . ."

"Surely you can see," she said furiously, "that the *Abwehr* will wonder why I'm not being picked up, since that stupid flight-lieutenant will obviously name me. My cover is blown. I'm no use to you any more."

"That," said Strongman, "is up to me. And as for Admiral Canaris, well, we shall have to tell him a story, shan't we?"

He rose and opened the door for her.

"Good afternoon, Miss Walters."

Without replying, she went out of the room. He returned to his desk. Suddenly he looked older, more tired. He poured a glass of water from the carafe, and grimaced as he drank it. It was luke-warm. He had that pain in his chest again, and—as sometimes happened nowadays—he felt his age. He picked up the thick sheaf of typescript once more and began to read, making an occasional mark in red ink at the margins.

18

Colonel-General Alfred Jodl, Chief of Staff of the *Oberkommando der Wehrmacht*, the German Armed Force's High Command, stood at the window of Pertz's office, looking thoughtfully out into the sunlight of Rastenberg. Outside, on a concrete path leading towards a thick belt of trees, Hitler's great Alsatian dog Blondi, held on a leash by an SS sergeant, padded by on her daily walk. He watched them, his heavy face impassive, until they passed out of his field of vision. Then he turned to where Pertz was standing quietly beside his desk. "What time is it?"

"Ten o'clock, *Herr Generaloberst*."

"In one hour it is the *Führer's* morning conference. And I have much to do."

"The *Reichsmarschall* asked to be present at our meeting, sir."

Jodl sighed.

"Well, I wish—ah . . ."

There was a stir in the outer office, and a moment later Goering's bulky form filled the narrow doorway. Pertz and Jodl clicked their heels and saluted: Jodl's salute, Pertz observed from the corner of his eye, was the old Imperial German salute, a hand to cap, and not the Nazi raised arm. Goering did not appear to notice. He was affable.

"I am sorry to have kept you waiting, gentlemen. *Generaloberst*, I suggested to Pertz here that you should join us this morning because he's going to demonstrate something to me which I think you should now see too. But first, I think you want to discuss Operation *Elefant*?"

Jodl nodded.

"Yes, *Reichsmarschall*. I can show you most easily on the map."

He crossed to the great map display on the wall behind Pertz's desk, running his finger down the long Eastern Front from the Baltic, down the hundreds of river miles of the Dvina, the Berezina, the Dnieper, until he reached the cluster of coloured pins which surrounded the Soviet city of Nikopol, north of the peninsula of the Crimea.

"You see," he said grimly, "how our front moves west, all along the line. But today we're concerned with the Nikopol bridgehead. Look at it . . . seventy-five miles long, and five, six miles perhaps, in depth. Then our backs are up against the Dnieper. And all round us . . . the Plevna marshes, as full of partisans as a rotten tree stump is full of weevils."

He turned away from the map.

"That bridgehead is going to have to go. It's being held by Schorner with 40th Panzer Corps. He's a good man, but he can't work miracles. He's outnumbered four-to-one by Chuikov's Eighth Guards Army, and he won't keep them out for more than another two or three days."

"Does the *Führer* . . .? asked Goering.

"The *Führer* will be told this morning," said Jodl wearily. "But there is a further complication."

"Indeed?"

"We have been experimenting at Nikopol with a modified version of the *Elefant Panzerjager* . . . you remember, the original Porsch prototype Tiger tank that we decided to adapt as a tank-killer when we chose the alternative Henschel design for the Tiger?"

Goering nodded.

"There are eight technicians from the Porsche works inside the bridgehead at Nikopol," said Jodl. "One of them is Professor Lilienthal. And there were also two scientists from the *Heereswaffenamt*—Hacker and Koll.

Goering whistled softly.

"Lilienthal? Isn't he the one who . . .?"

"Yes," said Jodl. "With Koll, he's been working on the new marks of the Panther tank. We mustn't lose him. Or some of the others."

"Can't they get out by road?" said Goering.

Jodl shook his head.

"There's still a road open, true. But it's covered by Stormovik fighter-bombers every hour of daylight, and by the partisans at night. They might get through, but they might not. And it's too important a matter to risk any 'mights'."

Goering glanced interrogatively at Pertz.

"So it's going to be a job for your new Andromeda *Staffel*?"

"Yes," said Pertz. "I have already issued the order."

"When? Tomorrow?"

"Yes."

"Do you think," said Jodl, "that you can get them all out? I warn you, conditions are bad. There is a landing strip, but it's under mortar fire."

"They're as close as that, are they?" said Goering, surprised.

"Chuikov isn't . . . yet. But the damned partisans are. They've got a multibarrelled Katyusha that they bring up at intervals. Schorner says he believes they have vehicles," said Jodl.

"Can't our fighters . . .?"

Jodl smiled grimly.

"There are no fighters at Nikopol. No *Luftwaffe* fighters, anyway. No shortage of Russian fighters, though. That's why we can't fly these people out in a couple of Heinkels. It's going to be up to you, Pertz."

Pertz said nothing. There was an awkward little pause, and then Goering rubbed his hands together briskly.

"Well, that's that, for the moment, at any rate. I've got something more cheerful to show you, *Generaloberst*. Something you've heard of, but of which you don't know the details."

"*Ulysses*?" said Jodl. There was a flicker of interest behind the stolid features.

"Precisely," said Goering. He crossed the room, opened the door, and spoke briefly to the SS warrant officer outside. A few moments later, the man came back into the room, wheeling a large trolley. The card and pasteboard model on its top brought Jodl immediately to his feet. He turned to Pertz.

"This is the . . .?"

Pertz nodded. Goering smiled.

"Show the *Generaloberst* how you will do it," he said.

Pertz bent over the model beside Jodl.

"Here . . . and here . . . and here, sir. Those will be for the special bombs with the new fuses. Here . . . and here . . . and there, too. Conventional bombs, but pinpointed, of course. Well, not conventional bombs, really, I suppose. They're meant to go deep . . . deeper than usual. They have a name for them in KG 200. They call them foundation-lovers."

Goering guffawed, but Pertz kept his face straight as he said the words. *Oberst* Adolf Pertz was not a man who cared much for even a mildly dirty joke.

"These bombs . . . where are they being made?" said Jodl.

"Zherzinsk," said Pertz. "All the bombs for *Ulysses* have been built there, at the Special Weapons plant. They were designed in Marienfelde, of course, by the Bomb Section of the *Luftwaffenamt*.

"Have *been* built, you say?" asked Jodl.

"Yes, sir, I think only one batch now remains to be completed."

"Just as well. I wouldn't give Zherzinsk more than a couple of months before the Ivans are in it. God knows, it seemed far enough behind the lines when the plant was set up, a couple of years ago."

He sighed.

"Well, at least it was well out of range of the British and

the Americans," said Goering. "And the Russian bombers didn't bother about it. They've got a lot to learn, about strategic bombing."

"They'll learn," said Jodl.

He bent once more over the model. Then he shook his head slowly, and turned to Pertz.

"It seems . . . impossible. How can your people do it? What speed do they come in at?"

"About 250 miles an hour," said Goering.

"Two hundred and forty-three," said Pertz.

"You can do astonishing things with the right aircraft and the right training," said Goering. "Admittedly, we've learned something from the enemy. Especially the use of these big aircraft in a low-level—almost a ground-level—role. The great thing about the B-17 is that it's such an exceptionally stable platform for the bomb-run. Of course, there are problems. At that height, they're an enormous target. And you can see"—he pointed at the model—"that there's not going to be much room to spare when they go in."

Jodl did not like Goering. Hardly any German officer of the regular army did, he thought to himself. But every so often, he reflected almost unwillingly, the *Reichsmarschall* sounded as though he still knew what he was talking about.

"There are other advantages for the B-17," Pertz was saying. "Obviously, the fact that it is a B-17 means that we can get it—or rather them—comparatively near to the target before the British or the Americans realise what's happening. Second, it's by far the easiest plane in which to adapt the bomb bays for the special bombs. When we tried the same thing with the JU-88, we lost two good pilots—because when the JU-88 is carrying the special bomb, it's stalling speed changes catastrophically. The B-17 has the extra reserve of power that we can't get in any German plane. The only comparable plane would be a Lancaster—and we do not have a single one. We have eight Stirlings—

unsuitable for this operation, as the Technical Branch at Rechlin reports—but no Lancaster."

Methodically, Jodl began to fasten his black despatch case.

"If you succeed—"

"We shall succeed," said Goering.

"If you succeed," continued Jodl, "the effect on the war would be considerable."

"No doubt of it."

Jodl turned to the door.

"Then good luck. And we can do with some luck. If we had a few of those divisions that are sitting now behind the Atlantic Wall, we wouldn't be worrying so much about places like Zherzinsk. Or Nikopol, for that matter."

His hand flicked to his cap. Goering nodded, smiling. Jodl went out. Goering rose to his feet, struggling out of the padded office chair, and walked up to the model. He looked at it almost unseeingly, the smile gone from his face.

"They sit in London and order German women and children to be fried," he said. "Have you seen the reports, the reports from Hamburg? The reports from the *Gauleiter* of Cologne, what's his name, Grohe? Firewinds, firestorms they call them, sweeping through the streets at 800 or 1,000 degrees Centigrade. Do you know what is happening to our people there? That they are dying because there's no air to breathe, and frying because the very streets melt under them as they run? As soon as the RAF turn for home at night the Americans are over by day. And sometimes the *Führer* blames me for this. I tell you, we will write an epitaph on the heart of every American airman. We'll make the day of *Ulysses* one at which the world will hold its breath."

Pertz said nothing. Goering's chest heaved, and his face shone with sweat. At last he walked back to his seat. Pertz watched him carefully, and waited for half a minute before he spoke again.

"And yet, *Herr Reichsmarschall*, the excellent thing about the plan is that even if the main part of the operation should fail, then the diversionary operation offers enormous possibilities, considered entirely by itself."

"You mean Colchester?" said Goering.

"Exactly."

"Well, we're using half the force for Colchester, of course," said Goering. "But it's an easier target than the other."

"True, but we've taken a few leaves out of the enemy's book, after all. We're doing what they did at Augsburg and the Mohne Dam and Ploesti. We're bombing full-scale mock-ups."

"In Norway, you mean? At that lake, what's it called?"

"Innsjo Vaktel. We bomb it each day, when the weather is suitable."

"How about security?"

"It's a full-scale target, but in plan only. There's no construction of the actual target, only the detailed lay-out on the ground. Or in this case"—he smiled briefly—"on the water. Nobody seeing it from the lake shore could imagine what it is. You would have to fly over it to guess. Even then, it would only be a guess. And nobody will ever fly over Innsjo Vaktel and return to England."

"What about the pilots doing the rehearsing?" said Goering.

"I don't think there's anything to worry about there," replied Pertz. "From the air, unless you know what the target represents, it's extraordinarily difficult to identify what it is. It looks simply like a complicated jigsaw, with the various aiming points painted on it in different colours. And if a crew in one of our captured B-17s has worked it out . . . well, they're all in the Special Mess now. Fully operational and with no contact outside the Sola base."

"So none of them know?"

"Just Warnow. And von Altmark will be told tomorrow, since he's to command the Colchester diversion."

Goering looked up quickly.

"How is Warnow, by the way? That was a smart piece of work, getting him back. And with a Mosquito, too."

"We have to thank the *Abwehr* for that," said Pertz. "Warnow is well, sir, and as eager for *Ulysses* as the rest of us."

"Good," said Goering. "Because nothing, nothing must go wrong with *Ulysses* . . ."

Directive No. 38

From: Reich Kommissar, Byelorussia
To: Deputy Administrator, Regional Office
Generalbevollmachter fur den Arbeitseinsatz

a. *Labour situation*
The unparalleled demands of the war in the East mean that we must continue to mobilise many millions of foreigners for work in the total war economy of the *Reich*. This labour force will be expected to work at maximum capacity. In general it is not desirable that it should be contaminated by Jews, who will be shipped, as before, for treatment and disposal at scheduled camps.

b. *Exceptions*
It is a fact that in the general area of Byelorussia, Jews form an especially high proportion of specialists needed for certain tasks in the armaments factories of the *Reich*. Jews with special qualifications, therefore, will continue their work in such factories, and will remain unselected for camps until reasons of age or health make it desirable to transfer them.

c. *Inspection*
GBA officials will at once inspect specialist Jews at armaments factories in their area, and will send for immediate disposal any man or woman whose work is no longer repaying the *Reich* for its generosity in this matter. Officials are authorised to make arrangements for such disposals without further reference to this office, or to the region office of the *Ostministerium*.

Heil Hitler!
WILHELM KUBE
Reich Kommissar

19

The GBA inspector sat reading Kube's Directive No. 38 in his little glass-panelled office at the *Reich* Special Weapons Factory at Zherzinsk. It was not a large factory, but its output—mines, bombs, experimental torpedoes—was highly secret. Its task was to assemble and fuse weapons designed at other factories in the *Reich*—to assemble and store them here, out of reach of the British and American bombers who were making life so unpleasant in the *Reich* itself. Though soon enough, thought the inspector gloomily, it would be Soviet tanks they'd be worrying about, not American bombers.

He looked along the line of ten women working below his office window. It was a bomb line. He stared down thoughtfully. These were the new special bombs they were sending to Norway every twenty-one days—curious-looking things, he thought, though he knew nothing of bomb technology. This was the last batch. They had pointed, needle-like noses, and large and elaborate tail-fins—almost like stunted little aeroplanes with the wings at the back. And they were heavy—somewhere around 2,000 kilogrammes, he guessed.

The delivery date for them had to be met, or heads would be on the block. Well, his head wasn't going to be one of them. He would weed out some of those damned Jewesses who weren't pulling their output weight, and send off a few of the less fit ones for disposal before he was accused by higher-ups of getting soft. But which ones? He looked along the line again. There was that horse-faced one at the end. She could go, for a start. But there'd better be at least one other. Down below him, a woman dropped a small copper ring which she was fitting on to the firing cylinder of a bomb fuse for these new winged things. He picked up a pair of Zeiss glasses from his desk and focused them on her. She was looking round furtively, to see if anyone had noticed. The woman next to her was standing protectively, masking her hand as she crouched swiftly to the floor to pick up the ring. Ah, yes, there was the hand again now. Well, look at it. Look at those fingers. Arthritis, no doubt of it. She could be the other one, then. These Jewesses were only here because they were so good with their fingers. So clumsy fingers meant disposal. He went down the wooden steps and walked to the end of the line, where the horse-faced woman stood.

"Don't go back to the mealhouse when you finish tonight. Report to the transport compound. You're leaving."

She looked at him wordlessly, her eyes filled with tears. He turned and went to the woman who had dropped the copper ring. Yes, he'd been right. Her fingers were swollen.

A low moan of terror shook her. She began mumbling in her dreadful pidgin German.

"No, *Herr Direktor*, please. Please."

The inspector was not a harsh man, by his own standards, but he hated scenes. The woman beside her also spoke.

"Please, *Herr Direktor*, allow her to stay. She is my mother. We work well together."

He looked at her for a few seconds. He was not, he thought again, a harsh man.

"Let me see her hands."

The daughter picked up her mother's left hand and spread it on her own palm.

"Stop playing games," he said impatiently. "The other hand."

He looked at it impassively. A Jewish hand, he thought, I don't want to touch it.

"Look at the fingers. Swollen. She can work no longer."

The mother clutched at him and he stepped back sharply.

"Please, *Herr Direktor*, it will pass. I'm very good with

my hands. Very skilful. The swelling will pass, in a day or so."

"You think this is a hotel where we can feed you and clothe you and wait for your fingers to heal, do you?"

Nevertheless, he hesitated. She was right. The hand wasn't too bad. A couple of days rest would probably help it. The daughter watched him silently. He could almost feel the coiled tension of her. He made up his mind. There was no point in messing about.

"Report to the transport compound," he said. "You're leaving."

The older woman shrieked, but the daughter made no sound as he walked back up the steps to his office.

Eva Karpinski made no move to interfere when the burly works foreman came into the fuse-shop to take her mother outside. The older woman, too, was now more subdued, with only an occasional burst of muffled weeping. The eyes of mother and daughter met, briefly, as they parted: that was all. Eva's mind was racing. Somehow she must get to her mother. Her mother must not be left alone to face whatever it was that lay ahead. There had been sorts of rumours . . . death, medical experiments, brothels. Brothels? Surely not a brothel, not at her mother's age? But you never knew . . .

Mechanically, but carefully, she adjusted the small copper ring to its exact whorled position inside the six-inch-long cylinder of the fuse. Only someone with exceptionally delicate fingers could perform this task, and she doubted whether there was any machine tool in Germany capable of doing it. Eva and her mother, two years before, had painted porcelain in the ceramic factory at Minsk. That, she knew, was the reason—the lucky accident of physical skill—that had kept them both, and a handful of other women, from being packed on to the trains which, at that time, pulled out nightly, wedged with moaning people being transported west. Carefully her fingers stroked the ring into place. You had to be careful at this point, because the edges of the ring were covered with extremely sharp, jagged serrations, and apparently if you cut your finger inside the cylinder of the fuse, it was a serious matter. Once, a couple of months ago, they had found a smear of blood inside a fuse ringed by Valentina Vrodsky, and Valentina Vrodsky had not been in the line next day. Or ever again.

The trouble was that she, Eva, was so fit. They'd send her to the camp with her mother if only she were ill. But how could she become ill, in a day. They watch us like hawks, she thought. Even the rings we screw into the cylinders are counted. We get so many rings: we must pass out so many cylinders. And they search us as we go out, to make sure we hide nothing. Nothing sharp.

She put the ringed fuse back on the slowly moving production belt, and picked up the next cylinder. The sharp serrated edges of the ring—rather like a jagged, razor-edged slice of cucumber, she thought—rested lightly in the almost imperceptible pressure of her fingers. Like a slice of cucumber. Suddenly she felt excited. As unobtrusively as possible she looked around her. The *Direktor* was up in his box. She could see the thinning top of his oily black head. He was writing. Swiftly she put the ring in her mouth and swallowed it, gagging slightly as it passed down her throat. It cut her at once. She could taste the blood in her mouth, but she swallowed it. There would be more symptoms soon.

She put the fuse-cylinder, unringed, on to the moving production belt. That, she thought, is one bomb that won't explode.

The rumour was that they were for some very special kind of air attack. They looked it. They were like no bombs she'd ever seen. She was sure the devastation and casualties they could cause must be appalling. Well, at least the only deaths the fuse she had just sabotaged would cost would be *Luftwaffe* lives that might be spent getting a dud bomb to its target. Even a slave worker could hit back . . . sometimes.

The pain came later that evening, worse, far worse, than she'd imagined. The woman who, now that her mother was gone, occupied the next iron-framed bed in the dormitory, called a guard. The guard called the factory doctor. He arrived in his braces, grumbling at being dragged from his supper. He looked at the writhing Eva, and said:

Appendicitis. Or some form of intestinal blockage. She needs surgery. At once."

An hour later, after supper, he telephoned the *Direktor*. The *Direktor* was scathingly amused.

"Surgery? What do you think this is, a private nursing home for Jews? You know the orders as well as I do. If she can't work, she goes to the camp. Can she work?"

"Of course not."

"Can she travel?"

"Well . . . she can lie in the back of a truck."

"Then she goes, tonight, with the others from the lower factory. Nine of them altogether. What's the point of wasting good German surgery on that one? If she can't work, she goes to the camp."

Eva Karpinski died, two hours and forty minutes later, from intense internal haemorrhage in the back of the truck.

They didn't bother to operate, so no one knew about that ringless fuse.

A few days later, Eva's fuse was on its way to Stavanger-Sola to be added to KG 200's 'Operation *Ulysses*' stockpile, and nobody at the Zharzinsk Weapons Factory ever knew what happened to Eva's mother.

"Well, what the hell do we do now?" said Vandamme. He and Croasdell had just made as good a job as possible of hiding their parachutes in the tangle of scrub on the slopes above the lake. They pulled branches and bracken and slabs of peat-moss over the bundles of silk until Croasdell was satisfied. The parachutes were not completely hidden, but they would not be seen easily. The lake seemed lonely, and there was no road beside its shore. With any luck, it would be days or weeks before anyone was up here to give the scrub even as much as a casual glance. It was now fully light—a cool, greyish morning.

"I thought I spotted a road over the other side of the ridge as we came in," said Croasdell. "We'd better get within reach, and then lie up and keep our eyes open."

"Keep our eyes open for what?" said Vandamme disgustedly. Both men felt flat in the sudden reaction from the uncertainties and excitement of the last few hours.

"We've got," he said carefully, "French and Belgian and Dutch papers. Maybe you're thinking we'll meet some French or Dutch Resistance guys on the road? Jesus Christ."

"Well, it'd be a bloody good thing if we met him, I agree," said Croasdell more cheerfully.

"Who?"

"Jesus Christ, of course. He could start off by raising you from the dead."

Vandamme laughed, unwillingly.

"It's not as bad as it looks," said Croasdell. "You sent the 'Margaret' codeword. They know we're in Norway. They're bound to have informed the Norwegian Resistance—you remember the lecture that little cavalry twerp gave us? He didn't talk much about Norway, I agree, but he did mention Milorg. They run a lot of radio stations round here."

"Yes, but how the hell does Strongman know where we are? All we sent was 'Margaret'. That covers the whole of the goddam country."

"Strongman's not a fool—Sola was always the most likely place in Norway for Warnow to make for. So Strongman might well expect us to be down somewhere in the Stavanger area. He'll have told all the local units. They'll find us. What we've got to do is to make sure it isn't the Germans who pick us up first."

"Or the Quislings. After all, let's not forget there are a few Norwegians who think Adolf Hitler's a great guy. Your Strongman did just about remember to mention them in the thirty seconds he thought was enough to brief us about Norway."

"He's not *my* Strongman," said Croasdell, irritated. "All right, then, we'll keep a sharp eye out for Quislings."

"You think they'll carry a goddam banner saying 'I love Adolf Hitler'?" said Vandamme sarcastically. "Just so's we can identify 'em easy . . ."

The sky was becoming a washed-out blue, with a watery sun emerging intermittently from scurrying clouds. They walked west, over a bare landscape, covered with scrub and moss, in which there was, as yet, no sign of human life. Once a large elk, perfectly camouflaged against some stony outcrop, got up a few yards in front of them and crashed off snorting through a broad swathe of bracken. A falcon swung in the sky, braced aerodynamically against the gusts of wind. Both men had worried that the crash of the Mosquito, which as far as they could determine might have been rather more than ten miles away, might bring out some small patrolling aircraft like a Fieseler Storch to look for the wreck. But in the sky, only the hawk moved.

After an hour and a half's steady walking, they breasted a long low ridge. There below them, suddenly stretched a long ribbon of tarmac motor-road, winding over the horizon, south-west towards where, they knew, lay Stavanger. It was wet and shiny in the intermittent rain. Even as they crouched on top of the ridge, Vandamme said urgently: "Get down." They stretched in the mud. Cautiously, Croasdell raised the Ross glasses he had used—it seemed a century ago—to watch Warnow at the airfield in Essex on the previous night. Far along the road, in the direction of Stavanger, a moving cloud of spray jumped into the lens. As it drew steadily nearer, he could see that it was a half-track vehicle, painted in grey-green mottled camouflage. A helmeted driver and an officer in a peaked cap sat in the front: in the back, above the thumping tracks, squatted six German infantrymen. They did not glance up towards the ridge as they passed.

"Probably going to have a look for what's left of our Mossie," said Croasdell, thoughtfully. "I reckon this road must wind round behind us, through the mountains where she came down."

"That flash where she hit last night looked real high," said Vandamme. "Those boys'll have some climbing to do. I hope they get as wet as I am."

"Do you know," said Croasdell thoughtfully, "I think that's the first time I've seen a German—apart from the odd prisoner—in this war? I've seen shapes, behind canopies and cockpit hoods in aircraft. But never a man with a face, if you know what I mean? How about you?"

"The same," said Vandamme. Just for a moment he remembered the death-dive of the man who had jumped, parachuteless, from the Heinkel off Lowestoft.

"Of course," he added, "we did see wonder-boy. Through the glasses, at the field, before he took off."

"Oh, him?" said Croasdell. "I don't count him as the enemy."

"Oh?"

"No, he's just a sort of . . . opponent."

They were getting steadily wetter, lying there on the reverse slope of the muddy ridge above the road. The rain was thin but penetrating. After a little, Croasdell said hesitantly:

"I think we ought to walk along the road a bit, but away from Stavanger. Because there are bound to be more German troops—even a checkpoint, possibly, nearer to the airport and the town."

"How near do you reckon we are, then?"

"Who knows. It all went by so quickly when we were in the Mossie. Twenty miles, maybe."

Vandamme grunted.

"Seems risky on the road. It only needs another German patrol, and we've had it."

"We ought to be able to see them coming, though, if we move carefully. And there's a ridge on either side. If we see something, we can always get up on to one or the other. The point is, we have to establish contact with something or somebody friendly. In spite of the Quislings you're so worried about, Strongman said practically the whole Norwegian people were fed up to the teeth with the Nazis. So we'll have to look for a farm and take a chance that somebody there will put us in touch with Milorg."

"Or a village, maybe."

"No, not a village. Even if there's only one Nazi supporter in a village, that'd be enough to scupper us, because you can never keep anything quiet in a small group of people. We want a lonely farm."

They walked steadily along the road, their wet trousers slip-slopping rhythmically against their damp legs. There was no more sign of human beings: no smoke rose from any isolated homestead: no vehicle passed. Only the road itself wound steadily across a brownish, misty, undulating moorland. An occasional crow, pecking at the roadside verge, got up and flapped heavily away. Once, off on the left side of the road, they saw a heron-like bird standing in a small pool. Nothing else. Vandamme kept watch in front of them, worried that the German half-track which had passed an hour before might soon reappear on its return journey. Croasdell turned regularly to scan the road behind them, in case of traffic coming from Stavanger. And so it was Croasdell who, after more than an hour of steady walking, saw the first faint movement on the road far behind them. Quickly the two of them scrambled from the tarmac up on to the high ridge which rose a hundred yards to their left. They wedged themselves into a patch of rough scree, and Croasdell focused the Ross glasses on the patch of road where he had seen something. But the lenses were blurred by the rain, and by the time he had cleaned them with the cuff of his shirt, whatever it was he had glimpsed had disappeared into one of the long slow dips along the road. Anxiously they waited, uncertain whether they themselves had been seen, and whether they should go higher up the ridge so as to give themselves more leeway if they were to be pursued. Finally, something came out of the dip, about three-quarters of a mile away. Croasdell swung the glasses on to it.

"Well, look at that," he said, after a few seconds, and passed the binoculars to Vandamme.

"Pony and trap," said Vandamme briefly. "Just like the kind of thing we use in trotting races, in Connecticut. But wider, I guess."

Steadily the little vehicle moved nearer, pulled by a slowly-trotting grey horse. One man sat in the back. He wore a small green hat with a feather in it, and smoked a pipe. Croasdell noted that the man's head turned repeatedly from side to side. He was keeping careful watch on each side of the road.

"He's looking for something," he said at last. "And it could be us. There's damn-all else around here for him to bother about."

"Maybe he's a bird-watcher."

"Seems a bloody funny way to watch birds."

"Maybe he's a Quisling."

"I'd have thought the Germans could manage better transport for their chums than a pony and trap. I think he's worth talking to."

They scrambled down to the road and waited for the man in the trap to come abreast of them. He reined in and stopped, looking at them curiously, and taking his pipe from his mouth.

"God morgen," he said slowly. Croasdell answered.

"God morgen."

Perhaps this hadn't been such a good idea after all, thought Croasdell. Suddenly all the Norwegian he knew had gone out of his head, and he didn't have the faintest idea what to say next. The man spoke again:

"Hvor kommer De fra? Reiser De alene?"

Why does he want to know if we're alone? thought Croasdell. He replied quickly and firmly:

"Nei. Jeg er sammen med noen venner."

He pointed vaguely over the ridge. If he thinks we've got friends, he thought, it will do no harm. The man went on looking at him inquisitively:

"Hvilken del av Norge kommer De fra?"

"Bergen."

"Ah?"

Croasdell swallowed. The man seemed inquisitive, but not suspicious. Almost friendly, in fact. They were going to have to take a chance. He swallowed again and said carefully:

"Hvor kan jeg finne Milorg? Kan De hjelpe oss?"

"Milorg, eh?"

The other laughed shortly. He put his pipe back in his mouth and took a pull before he spoke again:

"Har de et identitetskort?"

Desperately Croasdell felt in his pocket and pulled out his Dutch identity papers. The man looked at them carefully, his lips moving soundlessly as they framed the foreign words. Then he handed them back and smiled.

"You are speaking Norsk very badly."

It was a full two seconds before Croasdell realised that the man was now talking English. He was holding out his hand.

"Dreamer." He pronounced it "Dremmer".

"And Tibba . . . Tibba . . . I cannot say it." He laughed.

"Tipperary."

"So."

He motioned to them to get into the cart. They sat on a box-like structure, behind him, their feet resting on a large sack of carrots. Slowly, the grey horse jogged forward.

"For two hours I have been looking," he said. "The warning did not come on the radio until last night. Not enough time. And then, your plane came down over the Strelshammer."

He pointed back towards the mountains which rose blue on the horizon.

"We thought you would be nearer to the plane."

An enormous feeling of relief was sweeping over both Croasdell and Vandamme. They had been very, very lucky, Vandamme said to himself. And Croasdell had been right. They'd had to take a chance, and it had come off. In the same instant, driving along in a cloud of spray on the road three-quarters of a mile ahead, he saw the German half-track. The driver saw it, too. With a flick of the reins, he turned the horse into the side of the road, leaning heavily to the nearside until the little cart tipped. Then he kicked out the carrots.

"Get out," he hissed. "Start to gather them. And try to say nothing."

As the half-track, slowing, drew alongside, he stood in the road, arms on his hips akimbo, glaring angrily at the Germans, cursing them roundly in Norwegian. Behind the cart, Croasdell and Vandamme desperately gathered carrots. The officer in the peaked cap gave them a cursory glance, and then said something sharply to the German driver. The big vehicle gathered speed, its churning tracks scattering the pony cart with mud. The pony-cart driver ran a few yards up the road, shaking his fist. One of the helmeted soldiers in the back waved derisively. Gradually the half-track dropped from sight into one of the undulating dips of the road behind them.

"Whew," said Vandamme, wiping his forehead. Croasdell noticed that he was still, absurdly, clutching a carrot. His own hands were trembling. The pony-driver seemed unmoved.

"They disturb us little, the Germans," he said. "They have men out looking for the radio stations, you understand? But they do not disturb the farmers and the foresters. One should not try to be too friendly to them, nevertheless. Nearly all the folk round here are *jossinger.* The Germans would think it strange if I had smiled at them. We are never more than correct."

"Jossinger?" said Vandamme.

"Our name for those who hate Hitler," said the other, simply.

The grey horse trotted on, and after a mile or so turned off on to a track which led up over a flanking ridge. All three dismounted to help the old animal over the difficult ground. They had walked for about three-quarters of an hour, across stony outcrops scattered with heather and gorse and small stunted pines, until they entered an area where the trees changed abruptly to firs, and grew in solid ranks, side by side. About five hundred yards into this fir forest they came out on the side of a hill. Below them was a small wooden house, at the top of a slope descending to a small lake—a pool rather, thought Vandamme. A boy was walking up the path from the water. He carried a trout-rod, and he was slight and fair-haired, perhaps sixteen years old. He ran forward when he saw the older man, and then stopped shyly a few yards away. The trap-driver spoke in Norwegian but Croasdell could follow what he said:

"I found them, back along the road. What time is the broadcast?"

"At ten tonight."

"Good. We can tell them then what we require. Papers, for a start."

He turned to Croasdell and Vandamme.

"We have not met properly, have we, Dremmer and Tibba . . . I still cannot say it. I am Sverre Sars, head forester of Egermoss."

He waved a hand towards the deepening belt of Douglas firs which lapped over the ridge behind them.

"And this is Trygve. He works for me in the forest, and he is my son. He speaks better English than I."

The four of them shook hands.

"Thank God we met you," said Croasdell earnestly. "We cannot stay long in Norway, and you can put us in contact with the local Milorg unit."

The other's eyebrows lifted. Suddenly he laughed, and the boy laughed with him.

"The local Milorg unit?" he said. "You are in contact now. We are here, all of us, Trygve and me . . . we are the local Milorg unit."

"You've been told about *Ulysses* today, Frido?" said Warnow. They were walking down the line of the heavily-camouflaged hangars behind the airfield at Sola. A brisk wind, a little chilly for summer, blew in from the waters of the fjord and, beyond that, the North Sea.

"Yes," said von Altmark, but he didn't pursue the subject. He looked affectionately at Warnow.

"You know, Rolf, I can hardly believe it. That morning, when you didn't come back from Colchester, I . . . well, I hung your picture in the Mess. Yours and Peter Behrends."

"You've moved mine now?" said Warnow.

"Yes. But not Behrends."

Warnow walked on a few paces before speaking again.

"Behrends . . . died."

Von Altmark looked sharply at him.

"In the crash?"

How many times shall I be asked that question? thought Warnow. But I will not lie about it. I am not ashamed. I would have done it to myself. I would have ordered him to do it to me, had it been necessary.

"His back was broken," he said. "And his stomach torn out, more or less. I finished it for him."

"Was there no chance?"

"I think not. But in any case, I couldn't risk him talking."

"Behrends would never . . ."

"Of course not. Never knowingly. But a man might say something, under anaesthetic, in delirium . . . something he is powerless to control."

"I see. But Rolf?"

"Yes?"

"Why, when I asked, didn't you just tell me he died in the crash? I could never have known otherwise. And now

—if you could see your own face, Rolf—just telling me is tearing you to pieces."

"It is not. I don't like to remember it, true. Who would? But soon, very soon, you must fly your own command, to Colchester, Frido. You've been a fighter pilot mostly, until you came to KG 200. You're the best pilot in the *Geschwader*."

"Except you."

"Perhaps. But that is not the point. The point is that commanding a group on a mission like Colchester is not like cutting around the sky in a fighter *Staffel*. You have to give yourself totally to your command. Nothing else matters—not even the things that, in quieter days, you may have been brought up to believe. Supposing I had left Behrends to die in some Tommy hospital? Supposing he had, without knowing it, talked—given the whole of *Ulysses* away? Apart from me, he was the only flier in KG 200 who knew the operational plan. What would that have made me? I will tell you. A commander who would not be fit to lead men. A man who put his personal mental comfort before their safety, and their ability to carry out their mission. A traitor to the *Führer*."

Von Altmark sighed.

"Sometimes I wish I still flew in an ordinary *Geschwader*."

Warnow seized him by the shoulder. They had come round the corner of the line of hangars, and were walking up the field.

"Never say that, Frido. I thought when I flew in Loerzer's lot over the Channel in 1940 . . . I thought I knew it all. But I didn't. It was schoolboy stuff—more like fencing with the buttons off than like real war."

"It seemed enough like it to me."

"No, Frido. Anybody can do that sort of thing, anybody who can fly a 109 fairly well, and who's got a good eye and a bit of commonsense. I'm talking about war. Real war. The best of all activities."

"You can't mean that?"

"I do. What else can offer as much? In four weeks over the Channel in 1940, I learned things about myself that it would have taken me forty years to learn any other way—that I might *never* have learned any other way. But in a few months with KG 200, I've learned more. A lot more."

"What, from Adolf Pertz?" said von Altmark, incredulously.

"Don't dismiss Pertz so easily," said Warnow. "He's never shot down a plane in his life, but he's more use to the *Führer*, and to Germany, than a couple of fighter *Geschwaders*. I've learned more from him than ever I learned from Loerzer. Think, Frido, think. What are the most important principles of war?"

Von Altmark was silent.

"You see," said Warnow, "you don't think about war at all. All you think about is fighting. But that's not enough. We won't make Germany safe by winning Knight's Crosses and German Gold Crosses. The principles of war matter. There's only one that really counts. Surprise. And that's our job, here in KG 200. It's the absolute essence of what we do. Our job, our primary task, is operations with special weapons. War is fought with weapons, Frido, but it's won with special weapons. How did the English beat the French at Creçy, all those so many centuries ago? With the longbow. A special weapon. How did the Tommies upset Ludendorff in 1918? With the tank. A special weapon. And how are we going to beat Churchill? Well, God knows, you've seen some of the things we're working on here. The new fighters, with the squeeze engines . . ."

"They call them jets," said von Altmark.

"Yes, the jets, I tried one at Rechlin, two months ago. Experimental airframe, twin-engined. Like riding a damned rocket. But, how it could move. Two hundred kilometres an hour faster than anything the Americans or the British have got. We're going to get an evaluation *Staffel* here in KG 200 as soon as they enter preproduction."

"Well, that'll be more like it, I suppose," said von Altmark doubtfully.

"Did you have another go at the Mistel?" said Warnow.

"I did. What a cow! I nearly had my own picture up in the Mess. I cut out at 900 feet, missed the field by a thousand yards, but I put the thing down on the road. Like flying a pregnant swan."

Warnow laughed.

"Nevertheless, if only we had the Mistel really operational, we could probably do *Ulysses* with them at a lot less cost than the way we're going to do it now. But *Ulysses* is really a dream operation—and you know who worked it out? The Adolf Pertz you've got so little time for."

"I didn't say—" said von Altmark.

"Just look at *Ulysses*," Warnow went on. "The security alone is a model of what it should be. Have you ever known anything more secure than KG 200 at this moment? Or any other moment, come to that. I'm sure there are very few officers in the whole *Luftwaffe* who know that our peculiar *Geschwader* even exists. We've got a wing of operational B-17s that even the enemy don't know we've got—though I suppose they've realised that we've picked up one or two. Pertz said we'd let them see a couple at Rechlin, just to convince them that we're only using them for evaluation purposes. Surprise? By God, we've got surprise all right."

"It certainly surprised me," said von Altmark thoughtfully. "*Ulysses*, I mean. It looks so impossible. But you couldn't really call it a special weapon. It's more of—"

"It's special because nobody's ever dreamed of trying it before in this way. In the whole history of air war, nobody's ever carried out an operation like this. You'd have to go back to ancient times. And the superb thing about it is, just at this moment when the British and the Yanks are pouring their stuff on the *Reich*, that its so—hey, look, there she is."

He pointed to the low, graceful shape of an aircraft parked ahead of them, at the door of a hangar. The plane wore the patchy grey-brown-green camouflage and dull red-and-blue roundels of the RAF. It was the Mosquito Warnow had flown from West Durnsford.

"She's going to Rechlin for evaluation next week," said Warnow proudly. "Only the second we've got—and she seems a bit different from the first. No proper radar set, though, more's the pity."

"Oh?" said von Altmark.

"It had been dismantled for some maintenance reason," said Warnow. "And there was something wrong with the fuel gauge, too. I had to fill her up."

"Really? That must have been pretty dodgy."

"Not as bad as it sounds. They run a real circus at their airfields. Lousy security, all very casual. It makes you wonder how they manage to do as well as they do."

"They can fly," said von Altmark.

"Yes, they can do that," said Warnow, slowly. "Pretty near as well as we can. But that shouldn't be enough."

"Where did you manage to lie up in London?" said von Altmark, curiously.

"You're not supposed to ask. With . . . a friend."

"I see."

"I'll be going back to see her, one of these days."

"Her, was it? Nice."

Warnow walked on towards the Mosquito without replying. Von Altmark looked at him inquisitively.

"Surely, Rolf . . . oh, I don't believe it. Don't tell me she's got you . . ."

"We're not the only ones who're fighting for Germany, you know," said Warnow. "Others do it in different ways. The two I took over, as part of that rehearsal trip to Colchester—they died just as surely as if they'd been in uniform. And Han—the girl I met. The kind of woman you can't forget."

"I see," said von Altmark. "Well, well . . ."

I would never have believed it, he thought. I think my old Rolf is in love. Must be a very remarkable woman.

"Pretty?" he said.

"Melts my knees," said Warnow, simply. "But more than that. She's like the other half of me."

I wonder what his chances are of getting out, if he's still alive when the whole Hitler dream finally caves in, thought Hannah Walters. If I'm in Argentina, and they let me have a little money, maybe he could join me. He'd be a prisoner-of-war, of course, for a few months. But not forever. Perhaps we can meet again. It could all come right . . . just. And meanwhile, what is it Strongman wants me to do? He's a bit like Canaris, she said to herself, in the way he looks at me. Probably anybody doing that job was a bit like Canaris. Neither of them ever looked at her body . . . well, they *did* look at it, but not in a personal sort of way. They seemed simply to be assessing the effect they thought it might have on other people. Suddenly she ached for Warnow.

Twenty-seven miles away outside the cottage in Essex, Joanna Croasdell leaned her bicycle against the wall, unlocked the front door and went in. She looked eagerly at the mat, but there was no letter. I wonder where they are, she thought. They. I keep thinking of "them". A few weeks ago, I would only have thought of John. Could a woman love two men? Not according to any magazine I've ever read, she told herself, amused. But life wasn't like magazines.

20

Flying in a loose arrowhead formation, the four Petlyakov bombers, red stars gleaming on their twin tail-fins, flew steadily north over the grey-capped waters of the Karkinitskiy Zaliv. The pilot of the rear machine of the arrowhead listened critically to the bellowing roar of the twin 1,000-horsepower M-105 engines. He was cruising at 270 miles an hour, well below maximum speed. There were only 270 gallons of high-octane fuel in his eight wing tanks. That gave him a range of 720 miles at cruising speed, and he had no intention of splashing down into the waves of the Karkinitskiy on the return trip. He pushed back his hair, cut in a careful Russian quiff, from his forehead. He sat alone in his armoured seat. No navigator squatted behind him on the forward facing fold-up seat, and there was no ventral gunner in the little turret at the rear of the fuselage, behind the wing-root. He wiped his forehead again, reached down, and pulled on his close-fitting Russian flying helmet with its Viking-like wings of defensive armour. Ahead of him, the lead machine of the arrowhead began to lift . . . 6,000 . . . 7,000 . . . 8,000 feet. Obediently, the others followed. No instruction came over the inter-aircraft frequency. That, reflected *Oberleutnant* Hans Hauffe, would have been against standing orders.

He glanced ahead and to his right. There, right on station, flew his friend Udo Ganschow. His PE-2, like Hauffe's, was painted green and mottled brown, with dull silver patches showing through where the camouflage paint had worn away. There were red stars on the tail-fins and the rear side-fuselage, but none on the wings. All that relieved the drab, sinister effect of these purposeful machines were the two badges painted on the nose. Each bore a red flag and a scroll with a CCCP motto. They were the Guards Unit emblem and the Order of the Red Banner, won by the Soviet 27th Air Bombardment Regiment over Stalingrad in 1942.

Ahead of Hauffe's PE-2, the aircraft of Major Sepp Diercks, the flight leader, suddenly waggled its wings. Swiftly, Hauffe looked up through the cabin window, searching the sky. He saw them almost at once, high and to his left, in the eleven o'clock position. They came down like three little blunt-nosed gnats—a flight of stubby Polikarpov I-16s. Steadily the four PE-2s flew on. One of the I-16s peeled off from the flight, and came down alongside Hauffe. He looked quickly behind him. The other two cruised watchfully, 1,000 feet above and to his rear. The Russian in the I-16 was looking at him intently, no more than twenty yards out on his right. Hauffe stretched his lips into a smile, and raised a clenched fist. The Russian looked at him a second longer, and then raised his own arm in reply. The I-16 swung sharply away, climbing to rejoin its companions. Then the fighter flight turned sharply, moving in the other direction, west across the Ukraine. Hauffe wriggled uncomfortably in his seat. He found he was sweating. Episodes like that had happened before, and no doubt would happen again. They were something you learned to live with, he thought, when you flew with KG 200. But you could never take them for granted. Those three I-16s were from the 201st Soviet Air Fighter Regiment—out-of-date planes, whose use seemed to indicate that Russia was dredging up everything that could fly to support the new drive on the Ukraine. But out of date or not, those three I-16s would have made short work of four PE-2s, flying unescorted and with no manned guns.

Half an hour later, Hauffe glimpsed the broad silver ribbon of the Dnieper below his starboard wing. The four PE-2s were much lower now, flying at about 1,500 feet. Hauffe looked down. It was a landscape of marshy lowlands—small, desolate-looking pools, stunted trees, patches of greyish swamp grass. There seemed little life in it, but once, moving along the edge of a stream bed, Hauffe saw a group of twenty horsemen. Three or four of them looked up as the PE-2s roared above them. One of them waved a carbine. Partisans, thought Hauffe grimly. Just for a second, he wished he were behind the guns of the ME-19 he had flown in a regular fighter *Geschwader*, two years ago.

Here was the air strip, looming up ahead now. It didn't look much, by heaven. Sepp Diercks was strictly following standing orders. They swept above the strip once, line ahead now. Then, six miles away, they turned in succession and began the final approach. Hauffe came in at the end of the line, flying through the loose brown dust kicked up by the other three. He locked the wheels down, flicked a glance to the airspeed indicator. It read 200 kilometres an hour. Throttle back . . . but not too much. These Peshkas, as the Russians called them, landed fast . . . at 175 kph. Bring them in 10 kph slower, and you were liable to hit the ground like a stone. His wheels touched. There was a jarring thump. The Peshka bounced back into the air, touched down again. This time it stayed down. Hauffe pulled the brake handle, and the PE-2 rolled to a standstill at the end of the strip. Carefully, he turned and taxied back to where the other three were lined, already prepared for take-off. In the same instant, a fountain of earth and mud erupted from the ground three hundred yards to his right. It was followed in rapid succession, by six or seven similar explosions grouped around the first. The strip was under mortar bombardment.

There were three tumbledown cottages beyond the airstrip, with a group of trenches arranged around them. From his cockpit, Hauffe could see a steel-helmeted mortar crew, squatting in the nearest trench, thumping away with a mortar in reply to the partisans' Katyusha. And from the cottages, a strange procession was emerging. Four men in civilian clothes, four in uniform, and two others carrying one on a stretcher. They were escorted by a party of soldiers led by an infantry captain with one arm in a sling. As they passed the line of aircraft, three men fell out at each, and began to clamber in. Hauffe waited at the end of the line. The two men with the stretcher, he saw now, were medical orderlies. The man on the stretcher was a civilian. He was unconscious, and his face was streaked with blood. Beside him walked an older man, white-haired, with glinting gold pince-nez. He looked unutterably tired, but he smiled as Hauffe clambered down over the wing to help them. He brought his heels together formally, looking carefully at the badges on Hauffe's collar.

"Lilienthal," he said. "Thank you for coming. I presume" —he smiled again, with an effort, "that you are *not* a Soviet lieutenant?"

"*Oberleutnant* Hans Hauffe, Herr Professor," said Hauffe swiftly. "We must hurry."

So this is the great Lilienthal, he said to himself. The man who was a German legend, who'd designed everything from prewar Grand Prix cars to cruiser tanks—and was now working, it was said, on a gun that would bombard London.

Lilienthal was speaking again. He nodded towards the form on the stretcher.

"Can you get him in? This is my colleague in the *Heereswaffenamt*, Engineer Hacker. He is far gone."

Hauffe swung to the orderlies.

"You'll have to put him in the rear turret. Take your jackets off and wedge him in as best as you can. He may get thrown about a bit in the flight back."

The man on the stretcher opened his eyes as they took him from it, holding him under the armpits. His lips moved, and Lilienthal bent over him to listen. Hauffe could just hear the hoarse whisper.

"Koll . . . where is Koll?"

Lilienthal pointed down the line of PE-2s to Udo Ganschow's aircraft.

"Don't worry about him. He's in that one there. We'll all be safe in the Crimea in a couple of hours."

The other groaned as the orderlies pushed him into the rear turret. One of them turned to Hauffe and shook his head warningly. Lilienthal clambered, grunting heavily, into the navigator's seat behind Hauffe. The PE-2's starboard engine burst into life. Then the port engine. Above their roar, Hauffe could just hear three more crumping explosions as the Katyusha ranged on to the trees out to the right of the strip. One by one, the big bombers took off, climbing swiftly into the grey, cold spring afternoon. Below, in the swirling dust, Hauffe saw the ant-like figures of the German infantry running back to the shelter of the three cottages.

It was exactly one hour later, at the edge of the Dnieper estuary, that Major Pavel Nefedov, Hero of the Soviet Union, 28 confirmed kills, spotted the four PE-2s. He was moving through the sky above the Ukraine at approximately 400 miles an hour in his Yak 9 *Ulutshennyi*, sitting behind 1,600-horsepower of engine, and a 20mm ShVak cannon and two 12.7mm machine-guns. As soon as he saw them, he dived. He looked hard at the third in line. Flying south, to the Crimea, were they? And the only Guards Air Bombardment Regiment in this sector was the 27th. Plenty of German targets in the Crimea, of course. But why were they unescorted? The 27th would never send a single flight all the way from Krasnovil without protecting fighters. Or would they?

He flew closer. The pilot of the third machine gave him a friendly wave. From this range, he could even see the smile on the man's face. But what was that behind him? It looked like a man wearing a broad-peaked *Wehrmacht* cap. Abruptly, Nefedov swung the Yak higher, and looked at the rear turret. The man in its seat was wearing civilian clothes. And the PE-2 wasn't flying slightly tail-down, the way they always did when they had a full-load in the forward bomb-bays. A funny mission this was, flying south with no bombs and a civilian for rear gunner. And a *Wehrmacht* soldier for navigator.

Another man might have hesitated, even then, but Major Pavel Nefedov had not become a Hero of the Soviet Union by hesitation. He climbed the Yak high above the speeding four, moving into an attacking position, and dived at the third in line. The ShVak cannon hammered briefly, and the PE-2's port wing drooped as the shells smashed into the wing-roots. The bomber staggered, port wing down, and began its long plunge. Thirty-five seconds later it hit the waters of the estuary in a fountain of spray and a cloud of steam. Nefedov turned immediately to the last in line, and prepared to repeat the attack. But this was the end of his patrol, and the blue "ammunition expended" light was glowing on the Yak's instrument panel. Angrily he turned away, landing forty minutes later at the fighter base at Olginka. He strode over to the debriefing hut, but brushed aside the questions of the young Soviet Air Force lieutenant.

"I want to see Major Budakov, the squadron intelligence officer," he said. "I have a special report to make . . ."

At exactly the same moment, *Oberleutnant* Hans Hauffe brought his PE-2 in to land at the KG 200 base at Simferopol, in the Crimea. He taxied to the main building, and an ambulance came out for Hacker. Lilienthal got stiffly down from the navigator's seat and smiled painfully.

"I'm told you're called the Andromeda *Staffel*?" he said. Hauffe nodded.

"I'm afraid I'm no substitute for a beautiful Andromeda," said Lilienthal wryly. "But I shall remember you . . . Theseus."

He stopped smiling, and said earnestly,

"I saw what happened—to the aircraft with Koll in it. I suppose there is no . . .?"

"None," said Hauffe.

"Poor Koll," said Lilienthal. "I lost a friend."

For a moment, Udo Ganschow's face came back into Hauffe's memory.

"Each of us, Professor," he said, "has lost a friend."

21

"I tell you it is too risky yet to go down to Sola, anywhere near the airfield," said Sverre Sars earnestly, in his heavy, pedantic English. He ticked off the points on his fingers.

"First, you speak Norsk stiffly. Grammatically correct, but stiffly. And Dremmer"—he nodded towards Vandamme, who was listening attentively—"speaks hardly any."

"Second, even a Norwegian is at risk down there, because the security, once you get that side of Stavanger—the airfield is a few miles down the road—is very strict.

"Third, you haven't even got your papers yet. I spoke today, on the telephone, with Elsa Sturlason. She has them. She will try to bring them tonight. The Halifax dropped them two days ago.

"Fourth, it's true that most people round here are *jossinger*. But there are quite a few pro-Nazis in the towns. Members of the Norwegian branch of the party . . . some of them in the state police. There are checks on buses, trains, quite often. You wouldn't stand a chance without papers."

"Then what the hell are we doing here?" said Croasdell. "The whole thing's half-baked."

"Wait . . . don't be in such a hurry. Elsa Sturlason says she has some information for us. She's in a good position to know."

"Oh?"

"Her sister works in the sergeants' canteen at Sola. Oh, not the secret part—only Germans work there. But she sees enough, hears enough. You can't hide aircraft, not entirely."

"What sort of aircraft does she see?"

"She is a cook, Tibba. I am a forester. I can hardly tell

the name of a car I haven't seen before, much less an aeroplane. Nor can she. But——"

"Yes?"

"Some, she says, carry British or American markings. She has seen them returning, often late in the evening—and before they can be placed into their special sheds."

"Returning from where?"

Sverre Sars shrugged.

"The north. We have had reports . . . But tonight you will meet also Niels Raknes, who will tell you more. He has seen them, in the north."

"Who's he?" said Vandamme.

"He is manager of a silver mine at Kvar, above Namsos. Far to the north of here. The Sola planes go there once, twice a week."

"What do they do?"

"I know not. Raknes comes to Stavanger seldom. His business is mostly in Oslo, and in Drammen. He supplies the firms which make knives, how do you say it?"

"Cutlers," said Croasdell.

"So. Indeed, cutlers. Silver knives. They sell well in Germany."

"You mean he helps the Germans?"

Sars frowned.

"I would not let Raknes hear you say that, Dremmer. His son is in England, with King Haakon's men."

Restlessly, Croasdell got to his feet. The little wooden house, with the reindeer horns above the door, and the reindeer skin rugs on the floor, was becoming a prison to him. And to Vandamme also, he suspected, though the American made no complaint. After three days here in the mountains, they had done nothing. Tonight, at least, they would get the newly-forged papers which had been dropped from England—giving them new Norwegian identities with which they could hope to travel. Except that the most interesting area to which they could travel—Sola, where Warnow had taken the Mosquito—was apparently barred to them. He felt frustrated, eager to get back to England. Even their return seemed a gigantic, almost impossible project, though Sars kept telling him it could be arranged. And every time he asked just how it could be done, the Norwegian shook his head and said: "Wait."

He walked outside, on to the small back porch of the house, and looked up at the trees above him. A movement up there caught his eyes. He stepped back sharply, and then realised that it was the boy Trygve, snug in his usual position in the rocks, peering out with binoculars at the track which wound down past the little lake. They had seen no one else since they arrived, but both father and son kept intermittent watch by day. Just beyond Trygve, in a wooden chest concealed in a carefully-camouflaged hole, was the radio set which they used to give and receive messages. Sverre and Trygve Sars operated one of three radio stations organised by Milorg in an area of about 100 square miles—the others, according to Sars, being on the coast, placed to watch shipping and naval movements.

He went back inside the house and moved restlessly over to the bookshelf. Neither of the Sars was much of a reader, it seemed. All he had been able to find was a Bible, in Norwegian; a coastal survey, in Norwegian; and a book about the diseases of trees, in English. There was also a single copy of an old British *Punch* magazine. Vandamme, he noted sourly, was reading this again—for the fourth time. Vandamme caught his look, and said equably:

"I'm exploring the whole field of British humour. If ever I go back to college when this is all over, I'm going to get a doctorate in British humour. It's always been assumed that nobody could ever get a doctorate in British humour, because it hadn't got enough depth to be studied in depth, if you get me?"

"Very funny," said Croasdell.

"There you go, you see. You think that's funny?"

He tapped the copy of *Punch*.

"I guess you think this is funny, too? I guess I'm fortunate. I'm probably the only man trying to get a doctorate in humour who's been stranded on a mountainside with one copy of *Punch* and a book on tree disease. It gives me a hell of an unusual start . . ."

"Very funny," said Croasdell again.

"Wait a minute," said Vandamme. "I'll just write that down . . ."

Niels Raknes and Elsa Sturlason came in the late dusk of the summer evening. Apparently he had picked her up in Stavanger, with a motor-cycle and side-car which he garaged near the Cathedral for local journeys when he came down from Namsos. He concealed it, Sars said, off the main road below the track which led over the ridge to the little house.

The woman Elsa was small, in her mid-thirties, pale, with slightly faded blonde prettiness. She worked in a shop in Stavanger. Raknes was a big, bluff man, well-dressed by wartime standards, with a shrewd but affable manner, and a pair of sharp questing eyes. He looked, to Vandamme, like a man whom it would be hard to get the better of in a deal. The six of them ate one of the strangely mixed meals that Sars provided—bacon and oatcakes, honey and coffee. Elsa Sturlason picked, bird-like, at her supper: Raknes ate heartily. Then they talked.

"They were working on four, perhaps five, of the big planes with four engines at Sola today," she said. "They could not be seen—they have built screens round the airfield. But I know they were there."

Four engines—they must be Allied planes, or Focke-Wulf Condors, thought Croasdell. Nothing else in Germany was four-engined.

"How do you know how many planes they worked on, if you can't see?" he asked.

"They send to the canteen for sandwiches and beer," she said. "My sister Ulla says they asked for twenty sets. They work about four men to a plane—the mechanics, I mean. So there must have been four or five."

"Were they the big American planes?" said Vandamme.

"I think so," said the woman. "Usually after they have ordered the food, they work on the planes all night, in the secret sheds. You can see the chinks of light in the tears in the screen. And they will fly the day after tomorrow."

"How do you know that?"

"Because Ulla says they have ordered forty ration packs for that morning. That's the amount for five planes—when they fly north. They come back in the evening."

Raknes stirred in his seat in the window, his head outlined black against the pale light from the lake. Sars got up and drew down a blind. Then he lit the two bright paraffin lamps.

"They are bombing a lake," said Raknes.

"Bombing a lake?" said Croasdell, incredulously.

"Yes. I did not think so at first, because although the lake is no more than eight miles from my mine, I heard no explosions. But one of my boys—one of the boys who works in the mine—got in and found a bomb."

"Got in?"

"Exactly. The area is guarded. There are signs saying it is mined, all round Innsjo Vaktel. That's the lake."

"It means, in English, Lake of the Quail," said Sars. Raknes laughed.

"Why, I do not know. I have never seen a quail there."

"This bomb the boy found—what did it look like?"

Raknes felt in his pocket and produced a piece of paper.

"He drew it for me," he said. "It was stuck in a piece of damp ground, behind the lake. I think perhaps they searched for it later, but could not find it. My boy said it was buried halfway up in mud. It was about five metres long, and about two metres were buried. He could not dig it out, and in any case, of course, he could not have carried it."

"Let me see that drawing," said Vandamme to Croasdell.

"Hell of a big bomb," said Croasdell. "But not dropped from very high, if there were only three feet of it in the mud. And look at that tail-assembly. Almost like little stubby wings, but too far back to fly it."

"And it certainly isn't radio-controlled, or anything like that, if this drawing's anything like accurate," said Vandamme. "Look at the thing. It's just a smooth cylinder, tapering towards the front, with that tail on the end."

"Presumably a dummy," said Croasdell. "They must all be dummies. A thing that size would create a pretty big bang if it was dropped live. And presumably more than one is dropped. How many of these things do you reckon a B-17 could carry, Gene?"

"No more than one," said Vandamme slowly. "It might lift two, but there's no way of fitting them into the bomb bays. Even to carry one, you'd need a big modification on the bomb bay. But I reckon one would be possible."

"This is the only one you found?" said Croasdell.

"Yes. All the others have gone into the water, or on to the bridge."

"The bridge?"

"We call it that, those of us who have seen it. But it may not be a bridge. It is a collection of, how do you say, floats? Bridge boats?"

"Pontoons," said Croasdell.

"So. Pontoons . . . in the middle of the lake. But they do not connect with the shore."

"And that's what they're bombing?"

"Yes. They have a steel net under the pontoon. And then, when the planes have gone, they have soldiers in a boat who come out and take back the bombs from the water. Perhaps to drop again. Who knows? Sometimes the bombs are stuck in the pontoon itself."

Croasdell looked at Vandamme.

"Well, what have we got? They're bombing some sort of pontoon target on a lake in the north—a target which may or may not be a bridge. Even if it is a bridge, it's presumably some sort of model. They're using dummy bombs, which argues that they want extensive practice, and can't afford to blow the thing up with the first few hits. What do you think?"

"Agreed," said Vandamme. "And one more thing—it also looks, from the way that bomb was stuck in the mud, as though it's low-level bombing."

"I think we ought to have a look," said Croasdell. "We will at least have achieved something if we can find out something about this side of the business."

Elsa Sturlason opened her square leather shopping bag.

"Milorg at Egersund gave me your papers," she said. "The Halifax dropped them." She passed them each a small bundle—a Norwegian passport, a grey-green travel permit for general journeys, issued by the State Police in Oslo, a ration card, and a sheaf of Norwegian money. Croasdell's passport said he was Jens Vogt of Kristiansand and Vandamme's that he was Johan Sorensen, of Oslo. Each of them was listed as a forestry apprentice. "Good," said Sverre Sars gravely, "because with such papers and such work you have reason for travelling from one end of Norway to the other."

"Can we get up to this Quail Lake?" said Vandamme. Sars pursed his lips, and looked at Raknes.

"To Innsjo Vaktel?" he said.

Raknes nodded slowly.

"You can go from here to Trondheim by train," he said. "At Trondheim change to the line for Namsos, and at Namsos I could meet you with the truck from the mine. We can think of a reason . . . let me see."

He paused with a finger to his mouth.

"I have it. We are having much trouble with subsidence on the slope above the mine. There is much loose shale, and it slips down into the road. We can say, if we are asked, that you are coming to the mine to see if it would help to plant young trees on the slope—to act as anchors for the loose soil and stones, you understand? That would be understandable. But I do not think we will have trouble with the Germans in getting to the mine. They are used to traffic there. It will be more difficult to get in to Innsjo Vaktel, though if we are to be there on the day of the bombing, it may be easier. When they bomb, they take away the forest patrols. But always they look from the air, with the little, slow planes."

"The Fieseler Storch?" said Croasdell.

"Perhaps. I am not airman."

He looked at Sverre Sars.

"I think it would be best if you came with them, old friend," he said. "They'll need help on the trains."

"Of course," said Sars. "In any case, I am the one who can answer the questions about forestry. They know about aeroplanes. I know about trees."

He looked hard at Raknes.

"We will meet you at Namsos station, off the Trondheim train, the day after tomorrow."

Raknes nodded.

"I shall be there."

After he and Elsa Sturlason had gone, Croasdell looked at Sverre Sars.

"The day after tomorrow, you said? That gives us tomorrow in which to look at Sola. We have the papers now."

Sars shrugged.

"If you wish it. You have come a long way, and perhaps for little. We will go tomorrow morning. As it happens, the papers which the Halifax dropped for you are suitable for this. You are listed as forestry apprentices. There is a small forestry school, at Sandnes, on the road beyond Sola. If we are questioned you will have good reason to be there. It is fortunate your papers listed you so."

Fortunate? Vandamme thought of Strongman's small, foxy face. Fortunate? Well, perhaps . . .

They were silent in the truck which took them down to Stavanger next morning, driven by a redheaded man who had greeted them each with a vice-like handshake, but who had said virtually nothing. Sverre Sars had jerked his head at him as he climbed into the back of the truck.

"*Jossinger*," he said and then seemed to slide into some deep reverie. Croasdell and Vandamme, neither of whom had slept much during the night, sat watching the metalled road reel by, without speaking. At last the truck stopped on the outskirts of Stavanger, and they got stiffly out. A few people were about, walking head down in the light, drizzling rain. They followed Sars across the road to a small yard beside a house. Behind them, the truck whined into gear and lurched away. There was no one in the yard, but three bicycles were standing against the far wall. Sars pointed to them.

"For us," he said simply. Carefully, they mounted and wobbled off into Stavanger. It was, thought Vandamme ruefully, the first time he'd been on a bicycle since he was seventeen. They pedalled slowly through the little town, past the green-caped policeman on the raised dais outside the black bulk of the cathedral, out through the thinning ribbon of houses to the south . . . the road to Sola. There was little traffic—an occasional old French or German saloon, a couple of *Kubelwagen* trucks in dazzle-camouflage splashing past them, a dripping squad of German infantry marching with an NCO along the road back into Stavanger. No one paid them any attention, and it was with a sense of shock that Croasdell and Vandamme followed Sverre Sars round a bend in the road and saw the road block. It was a temporary affair—a half-track slewed across the road, and a small side-road behind it, so that it could reverse enough to allow traffic to pass if the officer in charge so decided. The soldier on top of the half-track squatted behind a Spandau machine-gun, mounted on a tripod. He looked competent and alert. Beside the half-track, a small table had been set. A German officer sat there. He appeared to be having his breakfast, and an orderly was pouring him a cup of steaming coffee as the three rode slowly up and dismounted, straddling their bicycles. A sergeant came forward, and said something to Sars. He spoke bad Norwegian, but Croasdell caught the words for "papers" and "business". Sars replied at once, but not in the Norwegian accent Croasdell had heard him use to Raknes and Elsa Sturlason. This was a thick, heavy, country intonation and it was obvious the sergeant didn't understand him. Impatiently, the German held out his hand and asked for the papers once more. Sars nodded, and produced his own. The sergeant looked at them carefully, and Croasdell heard him say questioningly:

"Sandnes?"

Sars nodded, smiling, and began to say something else. On an impulse, Croasdell came forward and offered his own papers. The sergeant glanced at them, and said again:

"You also are going to Sandnes?"

"Yes," said Croasdell. "With Sverre Sars."

The sergeant held out his hand for Vandamme's papers. Impassively, the American handed them over. The sergeant looked at him and asked a question which Croasdell could not hear. Vandamme nodded vigorously. The sergeant looked again at the papers for a moment, then turned away, laughing. He shouted to the driver of the half-track, which began to ease back a few feet on the road. The three of them straddled their bicycles once more. Suddenly there was a shout from the officer's table, and the officer himself rose, dabbing at his mouth with a napkin, and walked slowly over. He was a small dark *Leutnant*, who flicked his legs with a cane. He stopped beside them, and spoke to the sergeant in German. At least, thought Vandamme, I'll know what people are saying.

"Where are they going?"

"To the forestry school at Sandnes, sir."

"Why?"

"These two"—he pointed to Croasdell and Vandamme—"are apprentices. The old man is an instructor."

"Where are they from?"

"Dirdal . . . up in the hills above the town, sir."

"Hm. Tell them not to leave the road, and not to stop on the road. Or they will answer to me."

"Yes, sir."

The sergeant repeated the instruction in his execrable Norwegian, looking at each in turn. They nodded vigorously. He turned and lifted his hand to the half-track, and the three bicycles wobbled off down the road. As soon as they were out of sight, the other two rode up abreast of Sars.

"Whew," said Vandamme. "When that officer came over, I thought . . ."

"Occupation troops," said Sars contemptuously. "If he was any good, he'd be on the Russian front."

"What did the sergeant ask you, when you nodded?" said Croasdell. "How did you understand him?"

"I didn't," said Vandamme simply. "It just seemed to need a nod."

"He was making a joke," said Sverre Sars. "He asked you if you would spend your life with trees."

Croasdell and Vandamme looked at each other and laughed weakly.

"Must have been that book I was reading yesterday," said Vandamme.

They rode slowly on, across a broad flat countryside, dotted with an occasional clump of silver birch. The high wall surrounding the Sola airfield came into sight long before they reached it—rearing fully twelve feet from the shallow perimeter ditch, completely masking the field from sight.

"Over on the other side, beyond the turn for Sandnes, there is a gate," said Sars. "There is a guard-house there, and a checkpoint. But on this side, just the wall."

Croasdell slowed his bicycle, and began to dismount. There were small holes in the wood-and-canvas screen, and he thought it would be worth putting his eye against one. But even as he began to swing his leg across the saddle, Sars leaned from his own bicycle and grasped at his arm.

"Do not be a fool, Tibba. Look . . . there are guard houses on the fence. They will see you at once."

Croasdell looked along the fence. It was true. Three hundred yards ahead, a small wooden tower sprouted above it.

"We cannot stop, Tibba. The Germans have thought of that. We must ride on and take the Sandnes road."

Somewhere beyond the screen, an engine exploded into a hoarse, growling roar. It was followed by another, and another, and another. More faintly, other engines began to start. Then one by one, they cut out again, and the silence washed slowly back.

"Hear that?" said Vandamme quietly. "Those were Wright Cyclones . . . B-17 engines. I know the sound of those babies better than my mother's voice. Those were Cyclones, on test."

"How many?"

"Two, perhaps three. Or it might have been four, even. Difficult to tell about the ones in the distance."

"Well," said Croasdell, "we've learned one thing for sure. There are definitely—what on earth is that?"

Low over the perimeter fence in front of them staggered one of the strangest flying machines any of them had ever seen. At first glance, it looked like a three-engined biplane with the top wing shorter than the other, and with a needle-shaped nose jutting out from the centre of its triangular-grouped propellers. It yawed slightly, passing no more than fifty feet above their heads as it climbed slowly away into the grey morning sky. Peering upwards, Croasdell noted that the nose was composed of two twin needles, each with a bright yellow point at its end. From the rear it became obvious that it was not one but two aircraft—a single-engined fighter mounted on top of a big twin-engined bomber.

"It's that Mistel thing the Director showed us," said Vandamme slowly. "But his model sure didn't have that nose."

"Hollow charge warhead," said Croasdell briefly. "I'm sure that's what it was. The sort of thing you call a bazooka—and two-barrelled, at that. And those yellow things at the end were detonators."

"ME-109 atop a JU-88," said Vandamme reflectively. "And the JU is the guided missile. But did you see how the thing wallowed? That boy was having a rough time flying it . . ."

"Stop talking now," said Sars urgently. "And do not seem interested. They are looking at us from the guardhouse."

A helmeted soldier leaned out from the guardhouse window and watched them all the way down the road as they cycled slowly past. A quarter of a mile farther on, they came to a small white sign which said: "Sandnes, 3km." They pedalled slowly in the direction it pointed.

"Can we cut across from here and get on to the main road back to Stavanger?" said Croasdell. Sars shook his head reprovingly.

"We can, but we must not. We have told the road-block we are going to Sandnes," he said. "Therefore it is to Sandes we must go. The officer may check."

"I guess you're right," said Vandamme resignedly. "Oh, well, another few hours on trees . . ."

"I don't know about you," said Croasdell, "but it seems to me we've already found plenty to think about."

On the same morning that Sars and Croasdell and Vandamme cycled to Sandnes, Warnow and von Altmark half a mile away on the other side of the perimeter screen walked slowly down a long line of bomb-trolleys inside one of the reinforced concrete hangars at Sola. On the trolleys, in pairs, lay the long sharp-nosed, stubby-winged bombs which, a week before, had left the Special Weapons factory in Zherzinsk.

"They're strange-looking babies, aren't they?" said Warnow, running his hand along the smooth grey-metal casting of one of them. It lay beneath the open bomb bay of a B-17, deep in the floodlit hangar. A fitter was feeding belts of ammunition into the top-turret Brownings: two others were installing a bomb sight far forward, in the nose-canopy. On the metal behind the canopy, shining yellow in the surrounding olive-green camouflage, in newly painted scrolled letters, was the B-17's name "Happy Hanna".

Von Altmark glanced at Warnow.

"This is your B-17, isn't it?"

Warnow nodded.

"You chose the name?"

"Yes."

Von Altmark stole a look at Warnow's face, and decided to ask no more questions.

"It sounds right," he said. "A good name."

"Yes," said Warnow, without any particular inflection to his voice. "A good name."

They walked back from the hangar to the special mess. The *Luftwaffe* sentry at the door sprang to rigid attention, but then unhooked his Schmeisser machine-pistol and pointedly asked Warnow and von Altmark for their passes. They took them from the breast pockets of their tunics, and showed them.

"Showing off, that lad," said von Altmark, as they opened the mess door. "If he doesn't know the *Gruppe-Kommandeur* and his deputy by now, he wants his head examined."

"Just doing his job," said Warnow briefly. "That's all any of us can do."

It was quiet in the mess. Most men were reading. A few stood round the piano, listening to a young red-haired *Leutnant* playing softly.

"What's that he's playing?" said Warnow.

Von Altmark looked at him curiously.

"You mean you don't know?"

"No. I've told you before—I'm tone deaf."

"It's Chopin . . . one of the *études*, I think."

"Chopin? A Pole? Would they be playing Chopin in an American mess?"

"I don't know. Well, perhaps not . . ."

"Then we can't have Chopin here."

He crossed to the piano.

"Franz . . . let's have something else, eh? Something a bit less serious."

The *Leutnant* looked up at Warnow, frowning slightly.

"What's wrong with Chopin?"

"Nothing. But let's have a song they sing over on the other side. You know that's the way we're supposed to think . . ."

The *Leutnant's* face flickered for a moment, and then he said smoothly:

"A song they sing on the other side? Well, how about this . . ."

His fingers began to stroke out the old tune that all of them knew, the song they'd heard and sung, some of them, on dusty airstrips in Cyrenaica and Crete. There was a hush, and then a roar of laughter. A score and then another score of young voices took up the cheap haunting refrain:

"Unter der Lanterne,
Vor dem grossen Tor . . ."

There was a momentary flash of anger in Warnow's face, but he was determined not to show it in his voice. The singing grew louder for a moment, until the voices dropped in that theatrical last line:

". . . Lili Marlene."

Warnow held up his hand and gradually the voices died away. The *Leutnant* was looking at him blandly.

"You said a song they sang on the other side, sir. Well, they sing this one, I'm told. It's better than theirs."

Warnow looked at him for a moment. The young man met his eye.

"True," said Warnow. "They do sing 'Lili Marlene'. But they don't sing it in German. They sing it in English. So if you sing it in this Mess, sing in English. Does anybody know the English words to it?"

There was no reply. The group around the piano began to break up.

"Play something else," said Warnow. "You play well."

It wasn't he reflected, the kind of victory he wanted to score. The *Leutnant* was shutting the lid of the piano.

"I don't think I'll play any more, sir," he said. "I can't think of anything I want to play . . ."

Someone was tapping Warnow on the shoulder. He looked round.

"Come and have a drink," said Werner Lutz. "And I'll tell you how I missed that damned pontoon last week. When you weren't around."

They went to the bar, and Lutz ordered two John Collins.

"There's only one thing I like about the Americans," he said, "apart from *Fraulein* Betty Grable, and that's their drinks. I've come to the conclusion that all that our *Reich* needs to make it a perfect system is gin. We drink too much *Schnapps*."

Warnow laughed, and looked around him.

"Everybody seems a bit edgy," he said. "What's got into them?"

"They've been in the special mess too long," said Lutz promptly. "They're getting tired. Quite understandable. And all this business of enemy uniforms, enemy books, enemy magazines—and now enemy songs—well, it gets on their nerves just before an operation."

"I see," said Warnow, slowly.

"It's different for you," said Lutz. "First of all, you've been away. Oh, I know it wasn't pleasant, but it was at least a change, Rolf. They've had three months of steady continuous training, flying four-engined bombers at zero feet, dropping dummy bombs on bits of wood in a lake. And that's another way in which you're different, Rolf. You know the target, don't you?"

"Yes," said Warnow.

"Well, we don't. All we know is that a lot of us aren't going to get back from trying to hit it. A big bomber at that height is a sitting duck, and you know it. And, of course, the boys discuss likely targets all the time. I've heard some wild theories—one of them that we were going to land on an Atlantic ice-floe, pick up fuel dumped by U-boats, and fly on to bomb New York."

"Nonsense," said Warnow.

"Of course it's nonsense," said Lutz. "But it's the kind of nonsense that gets about in the absence of the real facts."

"I see what you mean. Perhaps it's time I did something about it."

He climbed on to a small bar table.

"All right, boys . . . if you'll give me a couple of minutes. I've got some news for you. You're probably getting tired of waiting."

There was a brief murmur from the crowd of upturned faces.

"Well, I am too. And you're probably wishing you were back with your own *Geschwader* some of you, on conventional operations. What I want to say to you is: Don't wish that. Never wish that. To be in KG 200 is a privilege. No, don't laugh . . . look around you. Who do you see . . .? Werner Lutz, here, who flew in Spain with the Kondor Legion, who's flown with the Richard Wagner Concert deep into Russia from Zilistea in Roumania. No, Franz, it wasn't an orchestra . . ."

There was a little buzz of laughter.

"It was the most brilliant undercover operation we've ever conducted against the Ivans, and it was an operation that demanded super-pilots. A real KG 200 job."

"Super-pilots?" said Lutz. "You should have watched me miss that pontoon last week."

"Too many John Collins," said Warnow. "And then there's Frido here. Fifty air victories. And Dieter Arndt, who sank a cruiser off Crete a couple of years ago. And Hans Sonerland, who took a JU-88 in at ground level to the Mosquito factory at Hatfield, and delayed production for three months. They're not here because they're tired of fighting. They're here because, like the rest of you, they're part of a very special KG 200 operation—an operation that's going to use some of the best pilots, the best navigators, the best bomb-aimers, and the best air-gunners in the *Reich*."

They were all silent now, looking up at him. He had every scrap of their attention.

"The trouble with being in KG 200," said Warnow, "is that everybody thinks you can work wonders. They're all after us—*Oberkommando der Luftwaffe*, the *Abwehr*, the ordinary *Luftflotten* who want a bit of special help, the test people at Rechlin . . . all of them. They're after us because we're willing to fly, and fight, anything that can get into the air—and some things that can't. I mean," he said, looking poker-faced down at the crowd, "the Mistel".

There was a roar of laughter.

"Now it's been irritating for you to have all this emphasis on talking, thinking, being like the enemy. But that's an important part of the operation, I assure you. You don't need to be very perceptive to have gathered that we're going to fly a mission as Americans—in an American formation, in American planes, in American uniforms, and talking to each other on plane to plane radio like Americans. Exactly like Americans. There's only one way to do that. Practice. And that's what we've been doing.

"And that's not the only practice, either, as you know well enough. I know it's been boring, flying with only a couple of yards' tolerance, in exact lanes, and dropping dummy bombs from a precise height at a precise speed. But when you see what we're going to do, you'll understand why all this trouble has been taken. And you'll wish you had had more practice, not less.

"No, I can't tell you what the target is. Not today. That is the *Führer*'s order. But I can tell you something. We are sending eleven of our B-17s on this operation. The crew will be chosen on the basis of the results achieved in practice. And the operation will be in two parts. One part will take six B-17s. It calls for precise bombing, low-level bombing. That section will be commanded by *Hauptmann* von Altmark. The other section takes the remaining five B-17s. The crews will be chosen from those who have the best record on the pontoons in the lake. That section will be commanded by me. And that section will write an unforgettable name in the history books of this war—a name that will not be forgotten."

There was complete silence in the Mess.

"So go back and read your English magazines, and drink your American drinks—and perhaps, Franz, even play an American song. One more bit of news, though. This week's practice will be the last. And to give you a little taste of what it's all about, after we've done the practice runs, I'll come in again. I want you all to circle and watch, because the bomb I drop won't be a dummy. It'll be the real thing, and that'll be the end of that damned lake pontoon."

He jumped off the table, and turned to Lutz, who looked at him quizzically.

"Well, Rolf, I think we can say now that we're not bored any more. Perhaps it's all going to be worth the trouble, then?"

"It's not just we who've taken trouble," said Warnow slowly. "There are others . . . others you'll never meet, who take trouble, too. There's been a lot of effort put into getting those B-17s."

22

The silver mine, thought Vandamme, looked remarkably like something out of a Western film. He sat at a wooden trestle table in the little office, drinking strong, hot coffee from a tin mug, and felt relieved to be there. There had been plenty of strain for Croasdell and Sars during the rail journey—but more, he reckoned, for him, since he was the one who spoke hardly any Norwegian.

There had been two police controls on the trains—one between Stavanger and Trondheim and one between Trondheim and Namsos. The first one had been a fairly perfunctory affair by a couple of bored State policemen, who'd taken a casual look through their bags and at their papers. He'd pretended to be half-asleep, and they hadn't given him a second glance. Luckily, the three of them had a compartment to themselves.

The second check, on the first section of the Namsos journey from Trondheim, had been altogether different. They had stopped in the station at Stjordal, and the train had been thoroughly gone over by four armed State Police and a couple of civilians—one of them a small fussy man in a shabby suit with a Norwegian Nazi Party badge in his lapel, and the other a better-dressed man with a sallow face and thinning dark hair and an indefinable something about him that had fairly shouted that he was Gestapo.

The compartment had been crowded, and everybody in it had been so frightened—the women being told to empty their bags and the men to stand with their hands on the luggage racks—that nobody had thought it strange that he hadn't said a single word. The S.O.E. people in London had done a damn good job on his papers, anyway. The State policemen who looked at them—he imagined that the Gestapo man didn't read Norwegian well enough—hadn't suspected anything. But at least one poor devil in the next compartment had run into trouble. They'd seen him being led away—probably fortunate for them, he thought, since it had given the searching party something to crow about.

Croasdell and Sars were walking past the window. They'd been sitting on one of the timber joists above the main tunnel of the mine. Ten men worked here normally, Raknes said. But today was Sunday, and only a watchman was on duty. He was a boy called Knut, and he had spent the night reconnoitring Innsjo Vaktel. He came in now, with Croasdell and Vandamme and Sars. Raknes, who had been writing at a desk in the corner of the room, came over to them.

"We will go to Innsjo Vaktel early tomorrow. There is hardly any darkness up here at this time of year—at best, a sort of dusk. This means that they can fly the small search planes at almost any hour. But there is less activity early in the morning—and in any case, it is best for us to be in position well before the bombers come."

"Do they always come at the same time?" asked Croasdell.

"They follow a routine," said Raknes. "They arrive each time—eighteen times we have seen them—a little before noon."

"We're about 500 miles from Sola," said Vandamme reflectively. "Say, two-and-a-half hours in a B-17 at an economical cruising speed. And they may be doing the occasional formation exercise on the way. Say, three hours. Yes, noon would be about the time to expect them. That'd mean they'd be back at Sola by late afternoon. It's only human nature to want to have a quiet night at the base."

"Is there a good place we can lie up, to watch?" said Croasdell.

"There is a place in the rocks, about 200 metres from

the lake," said the boy Knut. Like almost every Norwegian they had met, he spoke English.

"Isn't that a bit close, if they're bombing?"

"No," said the boy. "The bombs do not explode. And they are very . . . good . . . with the aiming. Only once have I found one on the shore. The one"—he looked at Raknes—"that I drew for you."

Raknes nodded.

"I think we must sleep. We have much to do in a few hours."

The first Storch came over while they were bumping down the track from the mine, twenty minutes after they'd started. The light was a curious bright twilight. The pilot, thought Croasdell, would have no difficulty in seeing them. He noticed that Raknes kept the truck's sidelights switched on as they lurched down the narrow, stony road. The little plane made two passes over them—the second so low that they could clearly see the pilot's goggled head. He waved briefly as he swept above them, and then climbed away into the midnight sun glow of the sky.

"He will think nothing," said Raknes contemptuously. "There are trucks on this road many times in a week."

They drove on. He and Croasdell sat wedged in the front with Raknes. Sverre Sars and the boy Knut squatted uncomfortably in the back. It was a bare, undulating landscape—not a very convincing landscape for foresters to be interested in, thought Croasdell—though the State policeman to whom Sars had explained their journey in the train had made no comment. There were a few stands of trees—silver birch, small stunted pines, an occasional clump of battered firs. But in general, it was a bare, moon landscape, covered with lichen-smothered rocks. Raknes noticed Vandamme looking at them and said: "That is reindeer food."

"What, the rocks?"

"The moss. Without it they die. See there . . . a herd."

On a long slope to the right stood a small herd of grazing reindeer. Vandamme counted three antlered stags and about a dozen does. The road was winding downhill now, and the landscape was changing. There were more and more trees—not the uniform fir plantations of the south, but birch, pine, and some stunted, mis-shapen oaks. A Storch came over at about fifty feet and flew ahead of them down the road before banking away and climbing off to the west.

"That is good," said Raknes. "He will not be back for twenty minutes, and that should give us time."

He stopped the truck beneath an overhanging, gloomy clump of pines, and they clambered down. Sars came round and got into the driving seat. Raknes spoke to him briefly in Norwegian, and he nodded. Then Raknes came back.

"Come," he said. "Into the forest."

Grinding its gears, the truck moved away, leaving them standing beside the road.

"Won't the Storch see that there's nobody in the back now?" said Croasdell.

"Four miles up the road," said Raknes, "there is a farm. Sars will stop there, and leave the truck openly beside the barn. The pilot will think we are all inside. And Sars will meet us back here, in five hours. Come."

"Why not meet at the farm?" said Vandamme. "Wouldn't that be safer?"

Raknes shrugged.

"The people at the farm are *jossinger*, you understand. They help us. But they are not Milorg. We cannot involve them too much."

"I see," said Vandamme.

They had been walking for about an hour through the thick trees, completely shielded from observation from above, when they suddenly glimpsed the pale blue of the morning sky ahead, and found the trees beginning to thin. A few minutes later, moving cautiously, they came out on the spine of a long ridge. Raknes made them stop in the trees, and went forward, cautiously, to crouch on the line of the ridge and look down. He watched for several minutes before he beckoned them out of cover. They ran up and squatted beside him. He pointed downwards.

"There," he said, "is Innsjo Vaktel."

Vandamme, for the rest of his life, never forgot his first sight of the lake. It stretched about 300 feet below them, and seemed immense, glittering in the morning sunlight far towards the horizon. In the middle of this nearer end was moored an extraordinary construction. He looked at it for several seconds and turned to Croasdell.

"What in hell . . .?"

Croasdell was staring, fascinated.

"It's like a piece of a jigsaw puzzle," he said. "But it's absolutely enormous. It must be the best part of five hundred yards long. I've never seen anything like it."

"It reminds me of something," said Vandamme. He sighed. "But I don't know what."

"Some kind of lay-out," said Croasdell thoughtfully. "Docks, perhaps? The trouble is that we aren't high enough to get a proper plan view. The angle's too oblique at this height. What are those circles—the white circles painted on the wood?"

"I think they aim at those with the bombs," said the boy Knut. "I have seen bombs sticking in the circles."

Raknes was looking round carefully. He gestured to them to be silent, and listened for a few moments. Then he nodded, satisfied.

"We must move quickly. I cannot hear the plane now, but it may be back soon. And we must cross open ground to get to the hide in the rocks."

They scrambled down through the loose stones and pebbles on the side of the ridge that dropped towards the lake. Once on its sandy shore, Vandamme noted the criss-cross track marks of some small armoured vehicle. Raknes saw him examine them and said:

"It is here they pull in the steel net. With a winch . . . to recover the bombs."

A few minutes later they climbed into a natural *sangar*

of yellowish rocks, about 150 yards from the water at the end of the lake. There was just room for the four of them, wedged side by side, lying on their stomachs. The overhang of the rock shielded them from observation from above—something they had reason to be grateful for, Croasdell thought wryly, when the Storch came back half an hour later and circled the lake. Apparently satisfied, it flew away. They lay waiting. Once in a while, a fish jumped in the lake ahead, and inside the *sangar* the mosquitoes were busy. A flight of ducks took off in an arrowhead formation. Croasdell wished dearly that he had the Ross glasses—but Sars had forbidden him to bring them with him on the train.

At 11.30 precisely, by Croasdell's watch, there was a faint rumble of sound, somewhere ahead of them. A flock of small birds rushed shrieking above the lake. And then, fifty feet up, flying seemingly straight at them down the lake, came the first B-17, the pale northern sunlight sparkling on its Perspex nose-canopy. The long, finned cylinder of the single bomb fell away above the pontoons, striking somewhere within one of the chalked or painted circles. One by one, three more B-17s followed, all bombing in the same way. Only one bomb missed its circle, striking at the edge of a pontoon and ricocheting into the water in a fountain of spray. Successively the four B-17s roared over the *sangar*, climbing away above the ridge behind them.

"Lord Almighty," said Vandamme, as the echoes of their passing died away. "Did you ever see anything like that? Who would have believed you could do that with a B-17?"

"Did you see the way those bombs fell?" said Croasdell thoughtfully. "Almost horizontally—the nose can't have been more than a few degrees down when they hit. A bit like torpedoes."

"That'll be why they've got those tail assemblies," said Vandamme. "Well, I guess the show's over. And we haven't learned so much, after all."

Raknes had crawled a few feet feet out of the *sangar* and was staring at the sky.

"Wait," he said urgently. "They have not gone. They are circling. I have not seen this before."

Vandamme looked up. The B-17s were flying in line ahead, banking in a steady, tight circle above the lake.

"And not high, either," said Vandamme. "Two thousand . . . two thousand five hundred feet, maybe. We'd better watch out. From that high, they'll pick us up."

"There's another one coming," said Croasdell suddenly. Again they heard the distant rumble of engines, and then a fifth B-17 appeared over the edge of the lake. It flew directly towards them, no more than thirty feet up, a sight of enormous four-engined splendour and technical power as it passed over the construction in the middle of the lake. Again the single bomb fell, speeding at a slight descending angle to the exact centre of the pontoon. The B-17 roared overhead, so low above them that they felt the wind of its passing. For an instant, outlined against the Plexiglass of the nose canopy, they saw the bomb-aimer looking back towards the pilot on the flight-deck.

"Did you see that?" said Vandamme admiringly. "That was flying, real gen-u-ine flying, that was. Like he was on rails. And he put that baby right in the middle of the pontoon. I would never—Oh, my God!"

The centre of the pontoon erupted in a great incandescent ball of fire. Moments later the heat wave hit them, the hot blast of it seeming to suck the breath from their lungs. The fronds of the sparse bracken round the *sangar* wilted. They crouched with their arms across their eyes, seared by the breath of the bomb. After a second or so, Croasdell peered cautiously out. There were still gusts of hot wind from the furnace of the pontoon, which was slowly sliding beneath the surface. Around it, the waves of the lake were boiling in clouds of steam. Faintly, above the hiss and crackle of the heat, they heard the dying rumble of the departing B-17s.

"About an eight-second delay on the fuse," said Croasdell quietly. The lake was subsiding now, and a few pieces of wood were all that remained of the centre of the pontoon structure. About 150 yards of it seemed to have been totally consumed. The boy Knut and the man Raknes stared out from the *sangar* with frightened eyes, but they followed Croasdell and Vandamme to the lake shore. Vandamme stooped and put a hand in the water. Even here, sixty yards from the pontoon, it was warm to the touch. The surface was covered with dead and dying fish, and patches of bubbles were breaking on the surface. A piece of wood lay close in to the shore. Croasdell paddled out and picked it up.

"Look at that. It's more than burned . . . it's sort of disintegrated by heat. And did you notice—there wasn't really much noise? That was just about the most effective incendiary I've ever seen."

"And the biggest," said Vandamme soberly. He picked up a large sliver of heat-melted wood.

"I reckon I'll take this back and let the technical boys have a look at it."

Croasdell nodded.

"They must have decided to try out a live one. Which means they had no further use for the pontoon. Which means—"

"Which means," said Vandamme, "that rehearsal days are over. They're ready to do whatever it is they're planning to do."

He paused, thinking.

"Funny thing, though. Only one of 'em had a live bomb. I wouldn't have liked to be the guy. He'd have looked a pretty dumb cluck if he'd missed."

"Missed?" said Croasdell. "Not him. You saw the way that plane was flown—twenty per cent better than any of the others. The thought of missing never even crossed that pilot's mind."

"I see what you mean," said Vandamme, slowly.

"Obvious, isn't it?" said Croasdell. "That was wonderboy."

He turned to Raknes.

"We must return to England. I know you can report what

we have seen on the radio, but I think our scientists should examine these pieces of wood."

Raknes nodded.

"We will return to the meeting-place. Now, and quickly, before the soldiers come to the lake. And soon, also, the little plane will be over, to take photographs."

"How in hell are we going to get back?" said Vandamme wearily.

"As you came, on the train to Trondheim, and then down the line," said Raknes, surprised.

"I don't mean that. I mean back to England," said Vandamme. Raknes shrugged.

"You must ask Sverre Sars."

And it was Sverre Sars who answered the question, several hours later, at the silver mine. All the men were tired. They had reached the rendezvous early, and had been forced to lie up for an hour-and-a-half, waiting for the truck. The plane had been over almost continually—not, as far as they could see, looking for anything specific, but busy probably on photographic tasks over the lake. Most disturbing of all, a small tank with a winch in place of its turret had come down the road towards the lake, and its crew had stopped to brew coffee only about fifty yards from where they lay in hiding beside the road. After half-an-hour, it had continued its journey. Altogether, the five of them were glad to be safely back at the mine.

"Back to England?" said Sverre Sars. "That should not be too difficult."

"Oh, no," said Vandamme sceptically, but Sars smiled.

"We can send you by post," he said.

Croasdell and Vandamme stared at him.

"I mean what I say," he said. "First, we send you to Sweden. Then you go home by post—from a neutral country, you understand."

He laughed at the expression on their faces.

"I will explain. Twice each week, since the beginning of this year, the British mail plane flies in from Scotland. It is a British Overseas Airways plane—but in type it is a bomber. The sort of bomber in which you came to Norway."

"A Mosquito," said Croasdell. "Well, I'm damned. I never knew . . ."

"So," said Sars. "It takes from England freight and diplomatic mail: it flies back with ball bearings where it would normally carry bombs. It is used because it flies too fast and high for the Germans to catch it."

"But it can't carry us," said Croasdell patiently. "It has room only for two—a pilot and a navigator. No more."

"You have enough ball-bearings in England this week, I think," said Sars, laughing. "This time, instead of ball bearings, it will carry you."

"What, in the bomb bay?" said Croasdell. "We couldn't breathe."

"There is oxygen provided," said Sars. "It has been done before, many times. There is just room for two."

"Where does it fly from?" said Croasdell.

"Bromma, in the south of Sweden."

"How do we get there?"

"There is a Swedish ship captain I know, who is in Stavanger this week. He likes the British, and he also likes money. He will take you, but it will not be a short voyage. He must call at Fredericia, in Denmark, where, of course, there is a German administration. And then through the Mecklenburger Bucht to Sondemunde, outside Rostock. And then to Karlskrona in Sweden. A small ship, with general cargoes, you understand. But you will have no difficulty. You have Norwegian passports, and I will give you Norwegian Nazi Party badges in case you need them."

"But Rostock?" said Croasdell. "Rostock is—"

"Yes," said Sars evenly. "Rostock is in Germany."

"So Dreamer and Tipperary are returning in the mail Mosquito?" said the Director. He sipped once more at the damned lukewarm water. His mouth always felt dry nowadays.

"Good idea of Milorg," said Strongman at the other end of the phone. "You saw the transcript of last night's broadcast? Fascinating stuff they seem to have."

"Let's hope it's enough," said the Director. "When will they be back?"

"They'll be calling at some port in Denmark on Thursday," said Strongman. "Then Rostock—well, Sondemunde, actually, but it's only a couple of miles down the coast. That's on Friday. And they sail for Sweden next day. With luck, they should be on the Sunday Mosquito."

"Good," said the Director wearily. "No . . . wait. Rostock? When?"

"Friday, sir."

"Cancel that, at once. Not Rostock. Send that message now, priority."

There was a pause, and a rustle of paper. Then Strongman's voice came back on the line.

"Can't be done, sir."

"Why not?"

"According to the latest Milorg message—I've got it here—they sailed three hours ago. They'll be somewhere in the entrance to the Skagerrak by now."

"I see," said the Director.

23

"You will have to go ashore," said the little bald Swedish captain in his carefully-phrased, ponderous English.

"It is the order of the port commandant. All ships' crews must go ashore. Look, my friend . . ."

He seized Croasdell's elbow and led him to the porthole of his cabin.

"You see why? They are moving troops. Somewhere up to the Ostfront. Up the coast—to Riga, perhaps. They do not wish anyone to see what they are moving—especially not neutral ships like mine, with crews that may talk. So all ships' crews must go ashore tonight, and they will put their own police on board as guards. I tell you, you must go with the others to Rostock, to the seamen's hostel. There is no danger. You have Norwegian passports and party badges. You will not be expected to speak German. And tomorrow you come back with the others and we sail for Sweden. Good?"

Croasdell looked moodily out of the porthole. A big camouflaged German transport ship, of about 9,000 tons, was moored at the end of the deepwater jetty at Sondemunde. Beyond it launches were ferrying out parties of steel-helmeted troops to two smaller transports. The trucks on the single-track railway along the deepwater jetty were shrouded in canvas, under which bulked spiky, awkward-looking shapes. Guns, thought Croasdell. Or rocket launchers. He was scared at the thought of setting foot in Germany. So, he imagined, was Vandamme. Everything had gone almost unbelievably smoothly until now. When they called at Fredericia in Denmark the German port authorities had come aboard, but he and Vandamme had kept out of the way. A glass of *akwavit* with the captain, and the Germans were gone. But here, in Sondemunde, there had been trouble. There was a big troop movement taking place—something which the Germans did not want curious eyes to watch. So all crews were being accommodated in Rostock for the night. It was bad luck.

"I am telling you, there is no problem," said the captain. "They will not even look at your papers. They only want for you to be in Rostock for tonight. Tomorrow you will be back here."

He gestured expansively through the open cabin door to the well of the companionway which led to the upper deck. The *Vetlanda* was a fairly scrubby little coaster, around 3,000 tons, but the little bald captain was proud of her.

"You must go," he said again. "If the harbour police find you on board when the others of us are gone, I shall lose my port licence. And my work, you understand?"

Croasdell nodded. Vandamme turned from the porthole and said:

"I guess he's right, John. I can't say I like the idea, but we can't stay here alone. It probably won't be too bad."

"I fix," said the captain, relieved. "You go with Lundquist, the third mate. He will take you to the seamen's hostel."

It was an hour before dusk when they left the ship. And open trucks provided by the harbour authorities took them two miles down the coast to Rostock. The road was full of military traffic—most of it moving in the opposite direction, towards Sondemunde—long lines of squat grey lorries, motor-cyclists weaving in and out. They passed several towed guns, a group of three or four medium-sized tanks, and a sectionalised bridge divided between three eight-wheeled trailers. The civilian traffic was much sparser—an occasional small Opel saloon, a few cyclists, and once a white bus loading with workers from factory gates on the outskirts of the port of Rostock.

Fortunately, thought Croasdell, the seamen's hostel area was not far into the city. Their truck skirted a broad park—an area of open grass and trees, with old, dignified houses on three sides, where a few children were playing, and one or two women were exercising dogs. It seemed that in Rostock, hardly a man above the age of fifteen was not in some kind of uniform. As they turned down a narrow cobbled street towards the port area, a squad of young boys, brown-shirted, with swastika arm-bands, marched by in the other direction. Their faces were set in self-consciously stern lines, they swung their arms and stared ahead. The third mate, Lundquist, a tall fair young man who had seemed sunk in some Viking introspective reverie, stirred, smiled briefly, and said, pointing: "*Hitler Jugend.* They work . . . how you say? . . . against the bombings in Germany."

"As air raid wardens?" said Croasdell.

"So. As in London."

Their Norwegian passports got only a perfunctory glance from the two overworked clerks in the administration office of the seamen's hostel, which was a barrack-like modern block, in red-brick, fronting the harbour itself. Big temporary canvas screens had been erected between the hostel windows and the waterfront, and these were patrolled by three or four elderly *Volksturm* reservists, rifles slung over their shoulders. Croasdell and Vandamme with the key they had been given, walked up the uncarpeted wooden stairs to a room on the first floor. It faced the back of the hostel—an uninviting vista of red-brick walls, downpipes, refuse bins and a single lonely plane tree.

The room was small and bare, with a white wash-hand basin in the corner, two metal-framed beds, and a cheap dressing-table with a chair in front of it so that it also served as a desk. There were two pictures on the walls—a portrait of Hitler staring grimly from above the wash-basin, and a view of Lake Constance over the nearest bed. Vandamme flopped down on the other bed.

"My face still feels raw from that goddam bomb," he

said. Croasdell nodded. The intensity of the giant incendiary at Innsjo Vaktel had scorched each of them, and neither had found it comfortable to shave next day.

"Seems a hell of a long way now, though, that lake," he said. "We've met some pretty rum people in the last few days, Gene. That chap Raknes. And the girl—woman, I suppose, really—Elsa. And the kid, Knut."

"Quite a looker once, that Elsa, I'd guess," said Vandamme.

"And Sverre Sars, of course," said Croasdell.

"That was one good guy," said Vandamme, sitting up on the bed. "I got the impression, though, that sometimes he was laughing at us."

"I don't blame him," said Croasdell. "Better laugh than cry. What a dog's breakfast it's all been!"

"Oh, I don't know. We know a lot more than when we started out."

"Not so very much."

"Maybe enough, though, to keep your Strongman happy."

Croasdell turned irritably from the window.

"He's not *my* Strongman," he said. "I wish you'd stop identifying everything you dislike with me."

"Hey, hey," said Vandamme peacably. "Don't get so het up. I don't do that—and anyway, I don't dislike the guy. He's doing his best."

Croasdell smiled.

"Sorry. Maybe you're right."

He crossed to the window.

"I wish this room wasn't at the back," he said. "Then we could see what's going on. Might be useful."

"Might be," said Vandamme. "But I sure ain't risking my neck on that waterfront to find out . . ."

They ate the sandwiches which the ship's cook on the *Vetlanda* had given them, for they had decided that the less they appeared in public, even as Norwegians, the better. There was always the chance of meeting genuine Norwegians who were genuine Nazi Party members, for Sars had told them that Rostock was much visited by Quisling's men who were sent, as a reward for co-operation, to holiday centres along the coast. When they had eaten, Croasdell and Vandamme lay on their beds and dozed.

It was dark when the thin, persistent noise of the first siren woke Croasdell. He looked out of the window, staring up at the small square of light between the red-brick walls. It seemed a fine but cloudy night. At intervals a single searchlight swept across the small patch of visible sky, but he could hear no sound of engines. He turned back to the bed and shook Vandamme by the shoulder.

"Looks as though we may get a visit from our own lot."

A moment later there was a knock at the door of the room. The fair-haired third mate, Lundquist, stood outside. A strapping redhaired girl hung on to his arm, her head tousled as though she had just risen from bed. As, thought Croasdell, she probably had. Lundquist spoke to him in Norwegian, using only one German phrase. The girl looked on uncomprehendingly, but tugged at his arm.

"You must get on your shoes, and be ready to move," he said. "That was the *offentliche Luftwarnung*."

"Move where?"

"To the air raid shelter outside. It is compulsory here in Germany. If you stay here, the police will arrest you."

"The *offentliche Warnung*?" said Croasdell, stumbling over the unfamiliar German phrase.

"The early warning . . . ah, there goes the *Fliegeralarm*."

A more strident siren began to undulate over the port. Behind Lundquist, a steady procession of men was passing down the stairs, some still buttoning their clothes, carrying ditty bags. Among them, laughing shrilly, were a few of the bar-girls of the port.

"You must be quick," said Lundquist. The girl pulled angrily at his arm. Whistles began to sound outside. He turned away, and disappeared down the stairs. Croasdell and Vandamme put on their boots and followed him. Outside, in front of the hostel, a long line of people was forming, shuffling forward steadily into the doorway of a concrete bunker at the back of the quay. There were a few children, presumably from the flats above the shops at the side of the hostel. Ahead of them were two young women with babies, One, a smiling girl with long fair hair, was trying to stop her child crying, patting it, whispering to it, jogging it up and down on her shoulder. At intervals people stared intently into the night sky.

The first flares, when they fell, were things of savage beauty, drifting down like green and yellow dragons, with sparks for tails, against the black of the night. They were followed by six or seven bright flashes, with accompanying orange glows, over to the east, at the edge of the city. The whump . . . whump . . . whump . . . of the explosions came a few seconds later. The noise of engines was clear now, and about twenty searchlights were cutting through the sky. Suddenly there was a whistling crash and a bright orange bomb exploded somewhere in the buildings behind the seamen's hostel, about 500 yards away. The ground shook. There was a nervous murmur in the queue, but no panic. The shuffling line began to move more quickly. The baby on the fair-haired girl's shoulder stopped crying, and thoughtfully sucked its thumb. Vandamme looked at the sky. It would be fully a minute before they were inside the shelter.

"What ships are those?" he asked softly. "Russian?"

Croasdell shook his head. They were at the end of the queue, and no one could hear.

"Four-engined bombers. Lancasters and Halifaxes, I'd think."

"Not many, though," said Vandamme. "Doesn't seem likely to be much. I'd say there aren't more than a dozen or so up there."

"Are you joking?" said Croasdell quietly. "That's not the main force. Those were illuminators' flares. The orange bombs were visual target markers. That's not the lot by a hell of a long way. Those were RAF Pathfinders. Give it another quarter of an hour. Then you'll hear the main force arrive."

"How many?"

Croasdell shrugged.

"Hard to say. But it's a good target tonight, Rostock. Full of troops and transports. Somebody at home must have known all about it. I'd be surprised if they've sent less than six hundred . . ."

Inside the long air-raid shelter, people were stumbling and groping for their places. The lights were blue and scanty, impossible to read by, even if anybody had brought a book. Men and women sat on the long wooden benches beside the walls, or spread coats and blankets on the concrete floor. The fair-haired girl disappeared, and Croasdell saw her a few minutes later, sitting on a blanket at the far end of the shelter, about twenty yards from him, still rhythmically jogging her baby.

The bombing was becoming more continuous now, and the shelter shook from time to time, small chippings of concrete raining down from its roof. There seemed to be more children than Croasdell had imagined. Most of them were crying. A couple of uniformed Hitler *Jugend* boys, no more than fifteen, moved among the shelterers, speaking occasionally to older people, and to mothers with children. Even deep in the shelter, when there was a lull in the crump . . . crump of explosions, it was possible to hear the steady thrum of score upon score of aircraft engines.

There was hardly any talk. A muffled weeping came from two women a few places down the bench from Vandamme and Croasdell. Somewhere beyond them, in a loud clear voice, a man was praying. Vandamme turned his head, and said quietly:

"If this goes—"

In an appalling, bone-watering, crumping roar, all the lights went out. A hot breath of explosive seared through the shelter. As soon as his stunned eardrums partly recovered, Croasdell could hear a dreadful screaming from the end of the shelter. He was lying on his back at Vandamme's feet, and the American stooped and grasped him by the shoulder. Both men were coughing desperately. In the same instant the end of the dark shelter became as light as noon. Contorted figures danced against a bright curtain of magnesium flame: for two seconds, before they were utterly consumed, Croasdell saw the shape of the fair-haired girl and her child, ablaze from head to foot, outlined against the unearthly light. The girl's mouth was open as though she was miming song, but above the frenzied shrieking all around her, no single voice could be heard. Then the flame died to a dull red glow, and she disappeared. There was a frantic jam in the one available exit. Croasdell and Vandamme were carried forward by the pressure behind them, unable to move even their hands from their sides. One of the Hitler Youth boys was trapped in the angle of the entrance. He went down just as Vandamme reached his side. The American desperately pushed his hand down to grasp the boy's but felt his fingers slip away helplessly as the heavy feet behind him poured on over the boy into the exit. Many of those at the back of this pressing crowd were themselves on fire. These had been the ones who were at the edge of the effective area of the large incendiary which had come in through the smashed roof. Some reached the exit: others fell, writhing, where they stood.

One by one, people burst from the mouth of the shelter like corks from a bottle. Outside, the light was so blinding that they had to shield their eyes. Behind them, Rostock seemed to be a towering wall of fire. The tar in the roads ran molten in the gutters. The heat was unbelievable. They seemed to be in the centre of a universe that had become an oven. The seamen's hostel was a long mass of throbbing flame. The canvas screens hiding the ships had long gone, and out beyond the quay a transport ship burned brightly, like some illuminated vessel in a firework gala.

"We can't stay here," gasped Croasdell. "We must find somewhere to breathe."

They ran desperately up the long cobbled street behind the burning hostel. Around them hundreds of people stumbled in the same direction. Every house on each side of the street was burning fiercely. At intervals, a rash of hundreds of small explosions pocked the streets as bombers above unloaded their cargoes of incendiaries. Vandamme slowed, his face and hair scarlet in the light of the flames, though no sweat could last a second in the heat.

"I . . . can't . . . breathe," he croaked.

"For Christ's sake," rasped Croasdell. "You can't stay here."

A stick of high explosive bombs dropped about a hundred yards in front. The blast flung them from their feet to the foot of a burning tree.

"God in Heaven," said Croasdell. "Look . . ."

Down the side of the street came something which looked like a medieval illustration of hell. It was a whirling firestorm, a towering dust-devil made of flame. It swept through a group of running people fifteen yards ahead. Instantly, as though snuffed out, they were scattered on the ground in little smouldering heaps of rag. As the firestorm passed over them, the corpses of grown men shrank to the size of those of children. Then, caught by some trick of wind, it veered away from Croasdell and Vandamme, and disappeared into a group of blazing sheds which had once been a garage. The most noticeable feature now was the wind. It had been a quiet, still night, but the suction from the flames of hundreds upon hundreds of burning houses was causing a strange intermittent gale to blow. On and on Croasdell and Vandamme lurched, following the running feet of those ahead of them, until they turned a corner and saw before them the open park where they had seen children playing as they came into Rostock. Hundreds of people were here, lying face down in the red light on the grass, hands over their eyes. At the far end of the park, all the trees were on fire, as was the row of old, solid houses beyond it. The popping explosions of burning branches could be heard faintly above the steady roar of flame. Croasdell and Vandamme lay there with the rest. Hours later it seemed, the sound of the engines above them slowly died away. With the others, they remained in the park, not stirring until daylight came. Then, wearily, saying nothing to each other, they set off down the road to Sondemunde.

There was a steady dribble of refugees walking out of the town, some pushing prams and carts. But there were hardly any cars. At the factory gates where the bus had loaded the previous evening was stacked a pile of what at first seemed to be old, smouldering clothes. It was only the unmistakable, unforgettable smell of roasted flesh that made Vandamme realise that the pile was of corpses—eighty or ninety men and women. Already identification parties were searching, dry-eyed and desperate in the death-heap. They walked on, and in forty-five minutes they reached Sondemunde. The little port had suffered some damage, but on a far smaller scale than the holocaust of Rostock. A haggard, wild-eyed man came down the quay towards them. It was Lundquist. He seemed hardly to know them.

"I have lost my girl," he said, over and over again. "I have lost my girl."

Vandamme took him by the arm and led him back down the quay. With a surge of relief, he saw that the *Vetlanda* was still beside the quay, apparently undamaged. They walked up the gangplank to find the captain on his way to the bridge.

"We sail," he said. "Now. We do not wait for permission. We sail now."

"Is the crew aboard?" said Croasdell. He was faintly surprised to find that he could still ask logical questions.

"Not all. But we cannot wait. Last night we had the RAF. Today we shall have the Americans. You see," he said. "I have seen this before. This spring . . . I was in Hamburg . . ."

An hour later, the *Vetlanda* stood out into the choppy seas of the Mecklenburgher Bucht, on a course north-east for the southern tip of the Swedish peninsula. Croasdell stood at the rail, looking, numbed, at the pall of smoke above Rostock. Even as he gazed, he heard the distant crump of explosions far above him. Vandamme, beside him, was looking into the sky. Deep in the slate-blue were score upon score of white, threadlike contrails, with flak shells bursting below them. By straining their eyes, they could see the tiny dots of the bombers.

"B-17s," said Vandamme. "Three or four groups, I'd say. That place is going to get more of it."

Croasdell was silent. He felt unutterably tired. And nothing, he knew, could ever be the same again.

MOST SECRET

From: Director of Intelligence

To: Prime Minister

Subject: *Kampfgeschwader* 200

Note: This memorandum is intended to amplify, in the basis of information recently acquired by investigating officers and from other sources, the earlier précis assembled by Chief Intelligence Officer, United States Strategic Air Forces, a copy of which was supplied to you by AOC Royal Air Force Bomber Command.

a. KG 200 is not a *Geschwader* in the ordinary German *Luftwaffe* organisational sense. It is an organisation, which might without exaggeration be described as a miniature air force, operating from a number of bases in Europe and Western and Southern USSR.

b. Bases from which *I Gruppe* KG 200 (the operational *Staffel*) operate include Sola-Stavanger (Norway); Bergamo (Italy); Zilistea (Roumania); Simferopol (Ukraine); Smolensk; Aalborg (Denmark); Finsterwalde and Echterdingen (Germany); Châteaufort and Nantes (France); and Thens-Kalamaki.

c. Aircraft used by *I Gruppe* are principally Allied aircraft, captured or rebuilt after crashing on enemy territory. There is a massive continuous salvage operation, with flight testing centres at Lerz, Rechlin, and Oranienberg, and reconstruction at various centres including Rotern-burg (Hanover), Essen Katenberg, Utrecht, and Creven-broich, near Cologne. The latter establishment alone receives an average of 15 aircraft daily of which some 90 per cent are Allied, particularly B-17s, Liberators, and Lightnings.

d. Types of aircraft used by KG 200 include a heavy preponderance of United States B-17 and B-24 bombers, but also appreciable numbers of RAF Stirlings and Wellingtons. In general, Allied fighters are less used, though photo-reconnaissance have disclosed examples of the Bristol Beaufighter and the Lockheed Lightning on the airfield at Berlin-Rangsdorf. It is not yet certain whether these aircraft were staging there, or whether Berlin-Rangsdorf is also a KG 200 base.

e. In our first effective contact with Soviet Air Intelligence for many months, we have a report from their operations analysis officer, Colonel Victor Nikazin, that a German unit—assumed to be KG 200—is using Tupolov, Martin and Petlyakov PE-2 bombers and SB-EK dive-bombers with Soviet markings in various areas of the Eastern Front. A German-manned PE-2 was shot down by a Soviet fighter in the northern Crimea last week.

f. Colonel Nikazin further reports that the Russians believe that the Germans have used Soviet aircraft with Soviet markings in the Mosul area. You will recall last month's pipeline sabotage.

g. In Western, Northern and Southern Europe, the use by KG 200 of captured machines bearing our own markings had until recently been confined to agent-dropping (normally at night) for which B-17s and Stirlings have chiefly been employed. In addition, there have been increasing numbers of reports of small formations of "Trojan" aircraft infiltrating our own bomber formations. This has been chiefly by day, and the formations affected have been principally of B-17s. In addition, however, two infiltrations of RAF formations at night have been reported: one over the Alps north of Turin, and one over the marshalling yards at Hamm. In each case, RAF casualties were suffered. The aircraft used were Stirlings.

h. Definite evidence has been secured by investigating officers that this pattern of use of captured equipment by KG 200 is now changing and expanding.

i. The KG 200 base at Sola appears to be one of the most important centres for new operational activity. Evidence has been collected that there are several B-17s at Sola, and that training is taking place for a bombing operation, to be conducted in Allied colours. The target is not yet known.

j. The base at Sola appears also to be used by *II Gruppe* KG 200 (the experimental *Staffel*). Examples of the composite Mistel or Huckerpack aircraft have been observed flying from the base (see separate report from Royal Air Force Experimental Establishment, Farnborough).

h. In view of the possibilities of this aircraft for interfering with our future operations on the mainland of Europe—and of the almost limitless possibilities of confusion if the enemy is able to operate entire bombing formations in our own colours—KG 200 bases we locate should be attacked to minimise their serious potential danger to our future invasion strikes.

l. Because of the immensely strong character of the German installations at Sola, which resemble a U-boat pen rather than aircraft hangars, it has been decided to attack with the method known as Willie-Baby, utilising war-weary aircraft as missiles. The attack will be code-named Operation Stand-Off.

m. To provide reasonably easy identification for Allied fighters and bombers of formations they do not personally recognise, a number of speakers of the Navajo Indian language will be included in our own B-17 formations until further notice. Challenges from ground stations, and in some cases from aircraft, will be made in Navajo. This operation is code-named Operation Forked Tongue.

n. Active consideration is being given to a similar plan for Welsh speakers in the Royal Air Force.

o. You will be kept informed of the progress of Operations Stand-Off and Forked Tongue.

Three copies:

President of the United States
AOC Royal Air Force
Commanding General, US Army Air Force

24

"What were the casualty figures for Rostock?" said Goering. He sounded, thought *Oberst* Adolf Pertz, deflated and dispirited. Pertz picked up a sheet of paper.

"The provisional figures from the *Gauleiter* of Pomerania, *Herr Reichsmarschall*, are Rostock . . . dead, 2,321 civilians, 690 army personnel. Stralsund . . . dead, 99 civilians, 156 army personnel. Sondermunde . . . dead, 45 civilians, 136 army personnel. In addition, about 8,000 people were injured with varying degrees of severity. Eight hundred homes were totally destroyed, and four troopships sunk."

Goering seemed hardly to hear. He sat at his desk, head sunk on chest. Pertz cleared his throat.

"You heard the bad news this morning, *Herr Reichsmarschall*? About General Jeschonnek?"

Goering laughed mirthlessly.

"That he shot himself, with his own Luger, in his office? Yes, I heard."

He sat there for a moment, without saying more. Pertz watched him curiously. "They say," said Pertz, "that he had cancer . . ."

Again Goering did not seem to hear.

"Poor Jeschonnek," he said at last. "He always took things too seriously . . ."

"Well, I have *some* good news at any rate," said Pertz.

"What's that?"

"*Ulysses* is ready. It can be mounted at an hour's notice. We simply await the signal. It should not be long in coming, the *Abwehr* tells me."

Goering propped his massive chin on his hand and looked at Pertz.

"Indeed?" he said. And then, almost to himself, he added: "So they'll fry our German cities, will they? Well, now we'll see who else will fry . . ."

"Well, honey, what's it all about?" said Vandamme. For a few minutes, Joanna Croasdell made no reply. They were walking through a large Oxford Street department store—one which, that week, was showing an exhibition called "It's A Lovely Day Tomorrow". In the air around them trembled the voice of Vera Lynn singing the song of the same name, and people were pressing forward, surprisingly eagerly, into the exhibition room. How shabby we all look, thought Joanna. And how pale everybody seems. Vandamme spoke again.

"There's something bothering you, Jo, dear. Or you wouldn't have asked me to meet you."

"It's John. I'm terribly worried about John."

"Well, he's back . . . all in one piece."

"He's not."

"How's that?"

"He just isn't the John who went away."

Vandamme was silent. After a moment, she plunged on.

"John can be moody, but not like this. Sometimes he looks at me as though I weren't there. I can't talk to him properly any more—and he simply doesn't talk to me at all. Oh, he speaks to me—I don't mean that. He's polite, even considerate—perhaps, even more considerate than he used to be. But he doesn't talk to me any more."

"He had a rough time . . . We both did."

She squeezed his arm affectionately.

"But it hasn't made any difference to you, Gene, has it?"

Hasn't it? he wondered. Not in the same way it had hit Croasdell, anyway. She was right. Croasdell was strange. Strongman had thought so, too, when they met. He was sure of it. Strongman had been concerned that they were caught in the Rostock raid, and congratulatory about what they'd discovered. Apparently the laboratory boys had tested those pieces of wood from the lake, and found the Germans were using a new thermite-phosphorus mixture which produced fantastic heat—a new dimension in incendiary bombs, they'd called it. Not that they were any nearer finding out where the Germans intended to drop it. Or much more about KG 200 except that they had a fair-sized force of reconstituted B-17s there—more than had been imagined. And that they operated the Mistel there experimentally—hollow-charge warhead and all.

It had been he, Vandamme, who'd answered most of the questions from Strongman, and who'd made all the right noises. He'd seen Strongman looking speculatively at Croasdell once or twice. And then, when the guy had said: "Take some leave," Croasdell had refused, and suddenly asked to be posted away from Intelligence, back to a fighter station. Strongman hadn't even seemed surprised. All he'd said was "Why?" And Croasdell had replied: "I just want to shoot down bombers . . ."

It was fine to feel Jo's hand on his arm. She still took his breath away, with that sweep of shining brown hair, and the long narrow face he could summon to his memory at any time of the day or night.

"The point is," she was saying, "that I've got something to tell John."

He looked at her again, more directly this time.

"Is it what I think it is?"

She laughed.

"It doesn't show yet, surely?"

"Of course not. But that's the kind of voice women use when that's what they've got to tell."

"How do you know?"

"I go to a lot of movies."

So now she was going to have Croasdell's baby. That was it, then. Somehow, when they had no kid, it had got to be like some kind of threesome, the last few months. But now it would be different.

"Do you think I should tell John? I know it's not fair to

ask, and I wouldn't ask anybody but you. You see, in some ways now, you know more about him than I do."

Should she tell Croasdell? Croasdell had taken that air-raid harder than he, Vandamme. Why? Maybe he, Vandamme, didn't think so deeply about things. Maybe. But it sure wasn't exactly the right time to tell him he was going to be a father.

"Leave it for a day or two. He'll be back to normal, soon enough. He's a guy who takes things seriously."

"And you don't? Is that what I'm supposed to think . . .?"

"Oh," he said vaguely, "I guess I've always been a lightweight sort."

She smiled.

"Let's go and look at this lightweight exhibition, then."

They pushed through the crowd, looking at astute designers' ideas of what the world would be wearing, and how the world would be furnishing, after the war . . . whenever that was going to be.

"I will never," said Joanna, "wear my hair like that. And I'll never sit in a chair like that. And I'll never hang anything like that on my wall."

Vandamme grinned.

"You'll wear your hair like that one day, because that's what other women will be doing. And you'll sit in a chair like that, because you'll just get used to the idea. You'll take what the commercial world hands out, more or less. But no . . . you won't hang anything like that on your wall. I wish you would."

"Why?"

"Because," he said, suddenly half-serious, "John Croasdell would divorce you if you did."

She looked at him and made no reply. They walked on to a table with a representation of an architect's idea of the new London that was to rise from the ruins of the blitz.

"It all seems very white and square, the new part," said Joanna doubtfully. "Like living in that film *Things to Come.* I don't think I like it."

"The trouble with you British," said Vandamme, "is that you hate anything new. Your husband's the same."

"It's not that," said Joanna indignantly. "It's because we don't like anything shoddy. Look at the older part, over there. Nobody felt like that about Wren or even Gilbert Scott and the Victorians."

"I bet they did. I take quite a shine to those white tower things—you don't have much in the way of high buildings in your city. Though you'll have to think hard where to build your airport. I wouldn't like to make a final approach in fog through those towers."

"We've got an airport," said Joanna.

"You're goin' to need another airport, maybe two. The air's the thing of the future, and this world's going to travel by air, come, say, 1950. It's going to mean problems for cities like New York and London. Just imagine trying to fly in over this. Can you see what I . . . Jesus . . ."

"What's wrong?"

That's it, he thought. That's what's been bothering me about that damned pontoon in Norway. There it is, right in front of me. It is, isn't it? I think it is. And it makes sense.

"What's the matter, Gene?"

"Jo, dear, I've got to make a phone call. And I guess I may have to leave you. Can you get to the station?"

"Of course. Well . . . I know a girl has to look out for herself nowadays, but I never thought I'd be stood up for a model of London."

"Jo, I wouldn't stand you up for the whole Ziegfeld chorus line. But this is important. Where's the nearest phone booth?"

"Over there."

It was empty. He dialled Strongman's number. Strongman came on the line himself.

"I left a meeting to speak to you," he said. "I'm sure you wouldn't call about something trivial."

"I think I just may know what those guys were aiming at in that lake."

"Can you come to my office now?"
"Yes."
"Where are you?"
"Near."
"I shall expect you in ten minutes."

Strongman looked at Hannah Walters, and for a moment, doubt stirred in his mind. She seemed as tense as a bowstring. Was she hiding anything? He'd been her Control for long enough to be quite sure that she genuinely longed to get away to South America. He was sure, too, that since her cover had been blown, that day so many months before, she had switched sides to work loyally for the Allies. Loyally? It was not, of course, a word which had meaning for someone in her circumstances. Yet there was something . . . something hidden, something in reserve, in this woman. She was beautiful, but it was, he reflected, a cold beauty. He would have called it a pure beauty if he hadn't known better. Strongman in all his life, had slept always with the same woman. It was the one field of life in which he lacked sophisticated experience.

He leaned forward and sipped once more at his water. That damned pain was there again in his chest—not acute, not even very uncomfortable, but omnipresent. He put it aside.

"It's your job to give the signal to launch *Ulysses*, Miss Walters? Why?"

"I have told you before. You know the *Abwehr* system. I am the clearing station for this operation."

"How do you decide when to give the signal?"

"I do not decide. The *Abwehr* tells me."

"Ah."

He forced himself to think. Really his mind seemed very confused these last few days. And his chest hurt.

"On the basis that *Ulysses* involves the use of B-17s, carrying American markings—and, it seems, in considerable numbers, it would be reasonable to suppose that the *Abwehr* will choose a day on which an American operation—a genuine American operation—is scheduled to be flown. They would then, presumably, attempt to join or mingle with it in some way? So that they could make an undetected approach to this country?"

Hannah Walters shrugged.

"Possibly. I don't know. I have told you all I do know of *Ulysses*, which is little. I do not choose the day."

"Presumably the *Abwehr* does so on the basis of information supplied by another agent in Britain—an agent who is able to tell them when suitable American operations will take place?"

"I suppose so."

"Do you know the way in which such an agent would communicate? The codes he would use?"

"Yes," she said reluctantly. Strongman rubbed his hands.

"Then we can send the *Abwehr* our own signal, can't we?"

"What would be the point of that?"

"Miss Walters, we know the approximate target, though not its precise nature. The area is not one which can be indefinitely closed while we wait. Our best chance will be to make certain that the operation will fail, by the simple process of launching it ourselves, on a day when we are completely ready for it."

She thought . . . Rolf. Was she to be spared nothing? Now, apparently, she must send him to his death. With her signal.

"That is impossible," she said. "What is to stop the other agent—whoever he is—from sending his own signal? The *Abwehr* would then receive two signals—probably naming different days. They would know at once that one was fake."

"I think not," said Strongman slowly. He sipped his water again. "If this agent is sending information as to American operations, he—or she—must be stationed in East Anglia. Almost certainly he—or she—even works at an American base, or near one. I suspect that the woman whom Major

Warnow was bringing over—and who didn't survive—was such an agent. Now it is technically possible for us to jam all radio transmissions from all American base areas for the next three days. It will be difficult, but it can be done. It has been done before. You will be able to send your own signal unimpeded from London. They will think it is from him."

"I see," she said dully. "And afterwards, can I leave this country? Can I trust you?"

"I'll keep my word," said Strongman. "Our arrangement is personal, between the two of us. A government may break its word: governments, as you know, often do. But I shall not. I'll arrange it personally."

"Thank you."

Goodbye, Rolf Warnow, she thought, I can't exchange my neck for yours, especially since you'll probably break yours soon enough, some other way. It may take me years, but in the end, everything passes. Even this will pass. I shall have to forget you.

"Let me see," said Strongman. "We might reasonably assume that since the B-17s of KG 200 which are involved in *Ulysses* are based at Sola, the *Abwehr* will want to know about American operations in the area of north-eastern Germany, so that they can fly the dog-leg down from Sola and join in. As Major Warnow did, on that rehearsal jaunt.

I wish he would stop saying Rolf's name, she thought. He consulted a file from his desk.

"There are two such operations this week. One is tomorrow, Tuesday. To Kiel. The other on Friday, to Heligoland. What are your day-words, in this week's *Abwehr* code?"

"Tomorrow," she said, "is Frederick. Wednesday is Max. Thursday is Otto. Friday is Fritz. Saturday is Willi."

"Tomorrow is far too soon," said the Director thoughtfully. "We must arrange an adequate reception. Friday would be suitable, and has the advantage of not keeping us in suspense too long. Send Fritz, Miss Walters. Send Fritz tomorrow morning."

"Very well."

He looked at her. It seemed to him that she had shuddered when he'd said the words "adequate reception".

"Miss Walters," he said.

"Yes?"

"You asked me if I'd keep my word. I shall. But you must also keep yours. Your broadcast tomorrow, of course, will be monitored, as always."

"Of course."

"Then thank you," Miss Walters, and goodnight. We'll meet again after, I trust, a successful completion. And I shall have happier things to tell you."

When she had gone, Strongman drew a clean white pad of paper towards him and wrote awhile. His narrow, face showed deep lines of strain. At last he picked up the telephone, and spoke to the exchange. He gave a number he knew well, and a name he had grown to respect.

"This is a personal call," he said, "for Colonel Frank Lasker."

Three minutes later, Lasker was on the line.

They spoke for ten minutes, and Lasker then repeated what he had been told.

"Thanks," he said. "This goes straight through to Command, right now. They'll be glad to get it. We'll fly that mission, of course, but now we'll know just what's cooking. Those KG 200 boys won't get here, and they won't get back to Sola, either."

"Good. It won't be the end of the KG 200 problem, of course, because there's a lot more to KG 200 than *Ulysses*. But I'm afraid, Colonel, that there can't be an end to the KG 200 problem as long as the war lasts."

"It'll be the end of *Ulysses*, though."

"Yes," said Strongman.

He put down the telephone and looked thoughtfully at the door. Time to go back to his room and a warm bath. Thank God for small luxuries. That woman, though. Why had she shuddered when he said "adequate reception?"

There was something she was holding in reserve. Well, she'd been warned. Her broadcast tomorrow would be monitored. As all her broadcasts were monitored. Those day-codes, though. They were very short transmissions. I wonder? he thought. I don't think she'd be such a fool, but I'll make certain. I think we'll monitor tonight, as well. He reached for the telephone, and the pain in his chest hit him like a hammer. Suddenly he could neither open nor close his fingers. He tried to speak, to shout, but no sound came. A dribble of saliva came from his mouth. He was all red, roaring pain now, crushed by it. The world was receding fast, fast, fast down a long searing tunnel. Even the pain receded after a few seconds. Lying across his desk, hand clenched on the telephone, Strongman was dead.

Hannah Walters sat in the teashop and tried to think. She had won through, then . . . she was going to South America, away from this country, this war. Strongman would keep his word. And all it had cost her was Rolf Warnow. Her face was so pale that the waitress, an elderly woman, came over solicitously to ask if she felt ill. She managed a smile.

"No, no," she said. "I'm just tired."

The waitress nodded.

"We're all tired nowadays, dear. It's the war. Seems to go on for ever."

If only it didn't have to be Rolf. The others, the ones she didn't know, who would fly in those planes . . . well, she could shrug them off. But Rolf . . . Was there any way she could stop him flying on Friday? No, there wasn't. He'd come, he'd get that "reception" Strongman had been smacking his lips over, and he'd die. And she'd be free.

But he might not die. He was the kind of flier who might manage some sort of landing, given the opportunity, in conditions when lesser fliers *would* die. But even then he would die, because if he was captured, in enemy uniform, he could be executed. Couldn't he? She was sure he could. But *would* he be executed? Need he be executed? Well, that's something she could have tried to arrange. Something she could still arrange. She'd go back and see Strongman.

She got up from the table, pushed twopence under the plate, smiled at the waitress and left. She walked down the busy street to Oxford Circus, and went in through the doors she knew so well. There was some sort of commotion going on near one of the lifts, and people were crowding forward to stare curiously. Two ambulancemen with a stretcher were coming out of the lift, followed by a tall grey-haired man with a bag. A doctor presumably. The form on the stretcher was sheeted from head to foot. Hannah Walters hated the sight of death. But as she waited there for them to pass, the corner of the sheet fell away, and for one second, the dead eyes open stared into hers. It was Strongman. She swayed, but controlled herself with a tremendous effort. She turned her back on the stretcher and went out by another exit into Oxford Street.

She was doomed. She was sure she wasn't going to South America, now or ever. A personal arrangement, he'd said. To be dealt with personally. Well, even he couldn't deal with it from whatever part of hell he'd be roasting in. She looked up at the grey London sky. I hate you, God, she said to herself. You torture me. And now, apparently, she must send the signal from which she would gain nothing, but which would send Rolf to his death. If she didn't send it, she'd be tried as an agent. Spies were hanged, often enough.

If only that foxy little man could have stayed alive a week longer. She had lived South America, dreamed South America, for so long that the thought of losing it now was like losing life itself. She couldn't stay on here, to start all over again with some other Control. Above all, she didn't want to be in London when Rolf came over to die. If this was all life had to offer, then she could do without it.

She stood at a bus stop and, at last, squeezed on to a

crowded bus. In the flat at Chelsea, she looked at her watch, and took out the transmitter, switching it on. It hummed and glowed as it always did. She plugged in the key, and those long fingers which had so delighted Rolf Warnow adjusted to the *Abwehr* frequency for the week. She began to tap the message "Frederick," she sent. A twelve-second pause, and then again "Frederick". It was, she thought, the shortest transmission she'd ever sent. Even so, it would probably be monitored though they wouldn't expect her to be sending at this time, and so she might just catch them off guard. Carefully, she packed away the set, went to the wardrobe, and pulled open the lining at the hem of her skirt. There were two tablets there, grey and round. They lay on her palm, and she looked at them for several seconds. With a sudden movement, she pressed them into her mouth, walked to the tap in the kitchen, and drank a glass of water. Then crossed to the bed and lay down. They take ten minutes to act, she'd been told at the Tirpitzhufer, that day so long ago. And then, nothing. No pain. Nothing.

Rolf, she thought. Tomorrow we'll both be dead. I have sent "Frederick" and tomorrow you will come. My life has been pointless, without purpose . . . because I have really had no purpose to serve.

She was becoming drowsy and knew it couldn't be long.

But you have a purpose, Rolf. I don't, I can't share it now. But this is the only gift I'll ever give you that isn't tainted by treachery. I have no purpose, but . . . I'll . . . give . . . you . . . the . . . chance . . . to . . . serve . . . yours . . .

In Berlin, a radio operator plugged in his key, and sent two words winging across the North Sea to Hannah Walters' silent set

"Frederick," he sent, "Frederick".

The *Abwehr* had accepted the date.

In a bedroom opposite Hannah Walters' flat in Chelsea, the radio monitor engineer lay on his bed, reading. His shirt-sleeved companion sat by the set, earphones clipped to his head, listening.

"Got a cigarette, mate?" said the man on the bed.

There was no reply from the man hunched over the set. The man on the bed swore, and lobbed an empty cigarette packet across the room. It hit the man at the set on the shoulder, and he turned inquiringly in his chair, taking off his earphones.

"What's going on?"

"Have you got a cigarette?"

Grumbling, the other got up and crossed to where his jacket hung on a chair.

"Here you are," he said, taking out a packet. "I'm not supposed to leave the set, you know."

"Get away with you, Tom," said the other derisively. "It's not her time to transmit. What are you worrying about?"

"Well, you never know," said the other, and pulled the earphones back on his head.

25

"Cassandra relayed the signal correctly, Helmut?" said Admiral Canaris, in his soft voice. Abstractedly, through the green leaves of the chestnut trees, he looked down at a barge on the Landwehr Canal. He stood at the high window of his office in the Tirpitzhufer. It would soon be time to move out from this pleasant headquarters to the concrete bunkers of Zossen, south of Berlin. The bombing was getting heavier . . . more than 1,000 tons the other night, he'd been told.

"Yes, Excellency," said Helmut.

"Curious, Helmut, that her cover was not blown after all, no?" said the old man.

"She will have told them a good story, Excellency. They believed her. She'll have to lie low for a little, perhaps. But, eventually, she can resume work."

"We shall see."

"The operation is mounted tomorrow, of course," said Helmut.

Canaris turned from the window. Watching the impassive face he knew so well, Helmut sensed suddenly that the old man was puzzled.

"Do I think that Cassandra was . . . persuaded . . . to give a false signal, Helmut? No. As a matter of fact, I do not . . . now . . . think that is so."

"I've never thought it, Excellency. But why are you now sure, yourself?"

"The date, Helmut. The date is tomorrow. If the Americans or the British had dictated the date, it would have been at the end of this week, or early next week, to give them time to get ready. Tomorrow is too soon for the British."

"I see."

Helmut hesitated. Sometimes the old man could be indulgent, sometimes he could be waspish, sometimes he could be the devil himself. But he, Helmut, wanted to know. He plunged.

"If Cassandra had sent a date at the end of the week, Excellency, what would you have done?"

There was a pause. Then, to his relief, he saw that Canaris was smiling.

"What would I have done? As always, I should have obeyed the *Führer*'s order."

"Of course," said Helmut.

Fifty feet below the Treasury building facing St James' Park, under the seven white-shaded electric lamps of the Cabinet Room, the War Cabinet was meeting. It was going to be a long session, thought Winston Churchill. He had never really become used to the slightly artificial quality of the air down here—sometimes he could swear that it was possible to smell the reinforced concrete, though "Pug" Ismay always laughed at the idea. There he was now, taking his seat. They were all coming in, past the Marines sentry at the door . . . Eden, Morrison, Attlee, Brooke, Portal and the others. And there were two Americans—one of them General "Hap" Arnold, Commander of the US Army Air Force, over here because of this B-17 affair. But it was the other American on whom Churchill's eyes rested speculatively. He knew him fairly well, he thought, but not very well. Despite his charm, the other was a difficult man to know. Churchill lit a cigar—a favourite ploy—and watched the American through the wreathed smoke while the others sat down. They talked about him a lot in Washington, of course. He was a good man to talk to—though he always seemed to hold something in reserve. Mind you, that was to be expected. Not much command experience, however. But he was good with men, very good, and he could make up his mind. More than that. He'd got, thought Churchill, what in the eighteenth century they used to call "bottom". He would be a hard man to push in any direction he didn't want to go. Well, it was going to have to be an American, one day next year. He peered through his cigar smoke at the American and wondered.

"You know, gentlemen, that today's agenda embraces the situation in Italy, and our plans for northern Europe," he said.

"First of all, however, you all know General Arnold, and on your behalf I extend to him the pleasure which we have in welcoming him. I feel that he himself will wish to re-assure you, briefly, with the, ah, operational dispositions which have been made by the United States Army Air Force in this country to frustrate the German *Ulysses* operation of which you were informed by Intelligence minute two days ago. As you will be aware, we have succeeded in, ah, so arranging matters that we have been able to, ah, encourage the German forces involved to launch their operation on a day of our choice. I am assured that there is no chance that this ingenious, bold, but terrible plan will succeed. Perhaps, General, you will now inform us of precisely how you propose to deal with these intrusive units from . . ."

He turned to the Cabinet Secretary, on his right.

"Pray, what was the designation of that enemy formation, Bridges?"

"KG 200, Prime Minister."

"Just so. Well, General?"

General "Hap" Arnold shuffled some papers and began to speak . . .

Some hours before the meeting in London, the air crew of KG 200 filed into the operations room at Sola. On the concrete wall at the far end of the room were two maps. Fixed above one map was a white-lettered board which said: *Gruppe Altmark*. It showed a section of south-east England, with the Essex garrison town of Colchester at its centre. Pinned to the map were red location arrows indicating various targets. On a table to the side were air photographs of the barracks complex at the main Colchester garrison, and other buildings as its perimeter. However, it was the other map which caused the roar of laughter from the air crews as they sat down on their hard wooden benches. The board above it said *Gruppe Warnow*. It was a large-scale map of Central London, and some humorist had pinned red location arrows to the exact positions of 10 Downing Street, the buildings to its flank, the giant clock tower of Big Ben, and the long rectangle of the House of Lords.

"I didn't think Rolf had a joke left in him," said Werner Lutz comfortably as he took his seat. He smiled.

"Maybe we've been training all this time to put one of those special eggs into Churchill's lavatory pan, eh? What's the matter, then?"

The men around him had stopped laughing. One of them was standing beside the table, and holding up an air photograph. It showed part of the area arrowed on the London map.

"You mean . . . that's the target?" said Lutz incredulously. "Seventy feet up in four-engined planes, across London, down the damned London streets, to put them there? It can't be done. Those of us they don't shoot down will crash, anyway."

"It can be done," said Warnow. "And will be done."

He was standing on the little raised dais in front of the wall maps, holding a long yellow pointer. He seemed utterly relaxed, completely confident, smiling.

"Now," he said, "you see the reason for all the security. This is the boldest, best-rehearsed, and potentially most catastrophic—to the enemy—air operation of this war. As you know, it's in two parts. *Gruppe Altmark* attacks the British army barracks at Colchester—more than 10,000 men there, some of them the key training instructors of the British Army. My *gruppe* attacks the heart of Churchill's government itself—Parliament and Whitehall. We're going to make them feel what they've made our cities feel over the past months.

"First of all, though, I'll put you out of your misery, and tell you to which *gruppe* each of you has been allocated. You know perfectly well that you're all here because you're among the best low-level pilots in the *Reich*. At least, when you came to KG 200, you were among the best low-level pilots in the *Reich*. Now you've trained with KG 200, you *are* the best. Both these operations are low-level, and both are precise. Nevertheless, it so happens that my own operation is, perhaps, going to have to be just a little more precise than Frido von Altmark's here. So, on the basis of your training records on that lake, I've chosen the four crews who will be in my *gruppe*. They are those led by Lutz, Mathy, Stross, Trobitius. The other five crews go with *Gruppe Altmark*.

"In a minute or two, we will go—each of us—in exact detail over what is expected of us on this mission. First, though, there are two points. We'll be wearing American uniform, as we have done for the past few weeks. That's because, as you'll have guessed, we're going to tag on, flying as two casualty-depleted boxes, on the other end of an American mission which is going to have a go at Kiel this morning..."

He held up his hand.

"I can't tell you how we know that. Just accept that we do know. Tagging on like this will give us an undetected radar approach to England, and, as you'll be told in a minute, it has other advantages, too. But it's very important that any American fighter pilot or bomber crew, flying near our own B-17s, sees exactly what they would expect to see. And should hear what they expect to hear. All inter-group radio conversations will be in English. There's just one concession. It could be very awkward, as you know, to be captured wearing enemy uniform. So crews will take *Luftwaffe* tunics with them, and anybody who has to bale out for any reason should put on a *Luftwaffe* tunic first. But they are not, repeat not, to be worn during the flight.

"When we get to a point which you will be told in a moment, our two *Gruppen* will diverge—Frido's going straight on to Colchester, and then turning south to land at Romilly-sur-Seine. Mine will turn south-south-east for London. One hundred and eight miles from the turn-off point to the target, thirty-one minutes' flying, under the radar at fifty feet, going up to seventy feet to bomb. That's to give you a chance to miss Big Ben, Lutz," he added, but there was no answering laugh. He paused.

"After my *gruppe* has bombed, we shall turn south to land at Orly."

"How many of us?" said a quiet voice from the benches.

"Not all of us," said Warnow evenly. "That would be too much to hope. But some of us, I am sure."

"You're the only one, then," said another voice, sourly. There was a murmur of confused conversation from the benches. Then the doors at the end of the operations room opened, and there was the momentary bustle of an arrival. Again, Warnow held up his hand. The short, tubby man who walked down the central aisle wore *Luftwaffe* uniform, but he was a man whom few of those there had ever seen.

Panting slightly, *Oberst* Adolf Pertz climbed up beside Warnow on the dais. Almost defiantly, he wore his gold-rimmed *pince-nez*. His chest, as ever, was bare of decorations.

"There is someone here who will explain to you better than I the importance of this operation. The commanding officer of KG 200 . . . *Oberst* Pertz."

Below Pertz there was a ripple of interest through the packed benches as men leaned forward, curious to see him. He looked down at the young upturned faces. He knew it was not as a fighting airman that he could appeal to these men. All he could do to win them was to give them the facts.

"Airmen of KG 200," he said. "I am proud to be here with you on a day that will change the history of the war, of Germany, of the world. You are going to destroy the British command structure, the whole way in which they run their side of the war. In addition, you are going to strike a propaganda blow against the Americans which will haunt them for a century to come. And"—he smiled—"quite incidentally, you are going to do the British Army a great deal of damage. Not a bad programme for eleven air-crews, eh?"

Below him one or two men shuffled their feet, but no one spoke. Pertz looked round the room and spoke again.

"I want you to realise what will happen when you carry out the two parts of this operation. First the so-called diversionary part, to Colchester. The six planes of *Gruppe Altmark* which attack Colchester do two things. First, they will be going in at low-level, so that everyone will see their markings. These are, of course, American markings. I must emphasise to you that there is friction and jealousy between the British and American forces in their little island—and especially so in the area of Colchester. British Servicemen regard their American allies as complacent, arrogant amateurs who are overpaid and underskilled. Now, suddenly, six American bombers—remember, they are used to seeing American bombers in the area of Colchester—are going, by a remarkable piece of carelessness or inefficiency, to unload their bomb cargoes all over the British training base, which, of course, will be totally unprepared for such an attack. Given a little luck, *Gruppe Altmark* could well kill five hundred or six hundred men, some of them irreplaceable, key training instructors. Such a disaster could not be kept quiet. Can you imagine the effect of this on the relations between the Americans and the British? Oh, oh"—he made a dismissive gesture—"of course, both the British and Americans will instantly deny that the attack was made by genuine American bombers. They will try to explain the truth that these bombers were manned by German crews. This will lead them into another swamp of propaganda difficulty. American bombers with German crews? the great British public will ask. How so? Are, then, the Americans surrendering their bombers to Germans? How can this be? And, of course, we—on Radio Hamburg and in every neutral country—will deny it. The mud will stick. Mud always sticks. That is the whole art of propaganda. It is something from which Anglo-American relations will not quickly recover. The trust will be gone. It will be hard, after this, to persuade the British Army that it must engage in operations under American command."

Pertz paused. He was sweating slightly, and his voice had become slightly shrill.

"And that, gentlemen, is only the so-called subsidiary operation. We come now to the part which concerns London. Gentlemen, the War Cabinet meets frequently, directly under the area you are bombing. You are going to destroy the house of Churchill, the secret command building under which the Cabinet meets, the House of Lords where the House of Commons—it is today in session—meets now, since we burned out the House of Commons some time ago. In addition, one of you—as a propaganda bonus—will try to bring down the so-called Big Ben, to show the world that nothing can stand for ever. This, too, will be accomplished by seemingly American bombers. This, too, will cause confusion. They will be in a terrible dilemma. Either they let the world think—as it *will* think—that this was done by crazy Americans. Or they will have to admit that in some extraordinary way, Germany has access to entire American bombing forces. More than that, key officers inside the command building—and perhaps many members of the War Cabinet—will die. The world will gasp and wonder. But one day, when it can safely be told, they will learn how this was done by you of KG 200. Today, at Rastenberg, the *Führer* is watching and waiting. Gentlemen, I salute you . . ."

A voice spoke from the back, as Warnow stood again.

"*Oberst* Pertz said, sir, that the British War Cabinet meets under the area we are bombing. How far under?"

"About fifty feet down, we understand," said Warnow.

"But in that case, sir, how can our bombs possibly . . .?"

"We have thought of that, naturally, Trobitius. As it happens, it will not concern you. Your objective is the House of Lords. We thought"—he grinned—"that would be more suitable for somebody with an aristocratic name like yours."

There was a shout of laughter from below him. He was good with men, this Warnow, thought Pertz. They were beginning to relax.

"The War Cabinet is mine," said Warnow. "There is a way to do it, and I shall be responsible. I shall not fail."

"Good old Rolf," said another voice, and there was more laughter. Suddenly Lutz stood on his bench.

"Come on, lads," he shouted. "Let's give the *Herr Oberst* something to tell the *Führer*. Let's have the old song, the good song."

He began to bellow the staccato tune, and swiftly the voices around him picked it up, crashing out the chorus.

"*Wir fahren*," they sang, "*gegen England* . . ."

26

The five blips appeared on the big screen of the *Himmelbett* radar station at Egersund, below Stavanger, at exactly 10.32 a.m. The corporal operator stared at them for a moment, and then spoke urgently to the duty *Leutnant*.

"Five big aircraft, sir. Coming in very low. They're just at the bottom edge of our scope. Around 250 feet, I'd say. They're coming lower . . . lower. Too low . . . I've lost them."

The officer crossed to the scope.

"Sure it wasn't bird flocks? I can't see anything."

"I'm sure, sir. They were big planes, Lancasters, maybe. Or B-24s or 17s. But it was a very ragged formation."

"Right, we'll take no chances. I'll tell Sola to scramble."

The three 109s scrambled from Sola took twenty minutes, without radar guidance, to pick up the five B-17 Weary Willies four miles out to sea. Using the new tactics, they concentrated first on the rear one, two above, one below. The B-17 ploughed on, undeviating in course, not changing its height or its speed. The lead 109 put in a long burst at 200 yards, turning sharply away to avoid the raking fire which usually followed a fighter pass. No fire came from the turret . . . and in the same instant, the pilot of the 109 saw that the B-17, in fact, had no turret. It was well ablaze amidships now, but still flying straight. The windows of the nose canopy were darkened as though the Plexiglass had been smoked. There seemed to be nobody on the flight-deck.

"Bodo One," he said urgently, "there's something very strange about—"

The incandescent ball of fire which blew the B-17 into thousands of small pieces forty yards from the 109's port wingtip killed him instantly. It blew the 109 above him into an uncontrollable spin, and then the blazing mass of the main fuselage wrapped itself round the third 109 as it came up to make its under-fuselage attack. The remaining four B-17s wallowed on. They had two miles to go to Sola.

There was a glint of concern behind *Feldwebel* Greiner's spectacles as he came to ponderous attention in front of *Oberst* Pertz's office desk in the KG 200 compound at Rastenberg. His left hand was outstretched, holding a flimsy grey teleprinter message. Pertz read it carefully, and frowned. He got up from his desk and waddled to the window.

"This is the first message? Since the Aalborg attack, I mean?"

"Of course, *Herr Oberst*. From the Information Co-ordination Centre at Finsterwalde. I came at once."

"Yet the Aalborg attack began an hour ago . . . an hour before this one at Orly."

"Yes, *Herr Oberst*." Greiner hesitated for a moment, and then went on. "There have been delays in getting information, *Herr Oberst*."

"Why?"

"There was a heavy British raid on Berlin last night. Many of the lines are destroyed."

"I see."

Pertz looked moodily out of the window. The Danish Resistance had attacked the KG 200 field at Aalborg—not the excellent dummy aerodrome two-and-a-half miles northwest of it, but the genuine field itself. They had been bloodily counter-attacked because Aalborg had been able to call on a whole *Wehrmacht* infantry battalion, with a couple of companies of *Panzergrenadiers* for support. But precious B-24s, and some of the rebuilt British Stirling bombers they were so short of, had been destroyed on the ground. And now there was this new attack, by the French Resistance, at Orly-Villeneuve-le-Roi, outside Paris. He looked again at the teleprinter form. It told him nothing . . . no news of casualties, damage, even of the weight of the attack. Those would come later. It could hardly be coincidence, could it? Aalborg he might just have accepted, as an attack by Danes who didn't really know what they were doing. But not Orly as well . . . not on the very same morning. The enemy were on to something. He turned to Greiner.

"Can you get through to any of the other French fields . . . Marseilles, for instance? Or Nantes?"

Greiner pursed his lips.

"I think Marseilles should be possible. The lines go through Nuremberg. But Nantes may be difficult."

"Well, try. And ask one or two of the other bases as well. The one on Schouwen—the one with the dummy field, for a start."

"At once, *Herr Oberst*."

It was twenty minutes before Greiner came back into the office. His weak blue eyes were snapping with excitement.

"There has been a Dutch attack at Schouwen, *Herr Oberst*. A mad attack. Men and boys—even some girls, I am told. Dozens have been killed."

"What damage?"

"Almost all their Flying Fortresses destroyed. In the hangars. And . . . and the same has happened at Rotterdam . . . with a similar result."

Pertz looked out of the window at the pools left in the concrete by the thin East Prussian drizzle.

"And the Schouwen dummy field?"

"It was not attacked, *Herr Oberst*. Not by the Dutch, or by the RAF."

"The RAF?"

"Fighters—Spitfires, Tempests—they came in low. Just before the Dutch attacked the real base."

No doubt now, thought Pertz. Somebody over there is putting two and two together at last.

"And in France?"

"Nothing from Nantes, *Herr Oberst*. But . . ."

"What?"

"It seems that even the local lines are down. Not just the Finsterwalde pattern through Berlin. Even the French lines."

Nantes as well, then, thought Pertz. It sounded like it.

"And Marseilles?"

"The French used mortars against the field; destroyed hangars, B-17s, B-24s, and Beaufighters. They did the same at Nice. But that isn't all, from France."

"Where else?"

"A ground attack at Vannes, and an extraordinary raid by Flying Fortresses on the St Dizier Mistel base."

"Extraordinary?"

A *Luftwaffe* corporal knocked at the open office door, and came to attention in front of the desk. Pertz stood at the window, his back turned. He did not look round. Impatiently, Greiner twitched the message from the man's hand, and read it. Then he spoke. His voice trembled slightly.

"Herr Oberst?"

"Yes?"

"Something extraordinary . . . something terrible is also happening at Stavanger. At Sola . . ."

Pertz had turned where he stood. In the pudgy, pale face, the eyes were blazing.

"At Sola. What of *Ulysses*?"

Greiner glanced at his watch.

"By now, *Ulysses* should be flying."

Pertz stretched his lips into a smile.

"God be thanked," he said. "God be thanked."

Greiner looked at him curiously. It was not a phrase he'd ever heard *Oberst* Pertz use before.

Sverre Sars was taking his morning coffee break at the Sandnes forestry school, three miles from Sola, when the earth shook and all the cups in the little school canteen jumped on their hooks. The low swelling rumble of the explosions came seconds later, and went on for a full half-minute. He went outside and looked towards the distant base. There seemed a lot of smoke but he could see nothing else. At the end of the morning, on his way back to Stavanger, he found a barbed wire barricade across the Stavanger road.

"This way is closed," said the German army corporal who guarded it. "Until further notice. You will have to go round the long way, by Harsund."

Sars stared over the corporal's shoulder at the long line of ambulances and fire engines manœuvring in the road round the main entrance. A dense cloud of black smoke hung in the air beyond the perimeter fence. He saw Elsa Sturlason's sister Ulla coming up to the barrier. She looked white and shaken. He grasped her hands.

"Go on, off with you," said the German corporal roughly. "You're not on a sightseeing tour."

"They came in, almost as though they were landing, the big American planes," she whispered, as soon as they were out of earshot.

"How many?"

"Four. I saw them. I was standing by the canteen at the other end of the administration block. I thought they were the others . . . you know, the others coming back. But these were so fast. They went straight in through the hangar doors, and blew up."

She covered her face, crying a little.

"It was terrible . . . like an earthquake. Even those hangars, all that concrete . . . it was all crushed like an egg. And so many were killed. I know they were Germans. But so many . . ."

Sars walked on in silence for a while. Then he spoke again.

"You said . . . you thought it was the others coming back. Which others?"

She looked at him, her face still streaked with tears. "The other big American planes that the Germans kept here. The ones you asked me about."

"Yes?" he said.

"They took off this morning, eleven of them. About an hour before . . . this happened."

The young American operations officer at Polebrook looked critically at the table-plot. The Kiel mission, he thought, was going well. They seemed to have got a surprise, for once. There'd been the usual heavy flak over the U-boat yards, but the two leading groups had bombed without seeing much in the way of fighters. He walked over to the radio monitor set in the corner of the room, and spoke briefly to the pretty WAAC corporal who sat there. She smiled and passed him a headset.

". . . reckon one of the 338th bought it, back there," said a crackling voice. "He was trailing smoke and his outer starboard motor was out. Didn't look good . . ."

". . . ain't seen a 109 since we crossed Wangerooge," said another voice. "Boy, this is sure a dream-ride . . ."

He nodded and gave her back the set. That Intelligence guy, Lasker, had said to call him if there was anything funny about the mission. Lasker had seemed suspicious about the mission—though he didn't seem to know why. Well, there didn't seem to be any German fighters. Was that funny? Don't be a fool, he said to himself. I wish it was always funny that way. He walked back to the table-plot and sat down. The first two groups had bombed and were turning away. Three more groups to bomb.

"Major, sir."

The little WAAC corporal was speaking to him. He went to her side.

"Yes?"

"They've got fighters round them now."

Oh, well, it hadn't lasted. Too good to last. He picked up the headset.

". . . never seen so many. Barney Kolsky's lot are really getting it. Jeez, there goes another. There's one guy out . . . and another . . . and another. All chutes open. They ain't botherin' us here up front, though."

Barney Kolsky . . . that would be Lieutenant-Colonel Barnes Kolsky, commanding the rear group.

". . . another B-17 goin' down. Those two rear groups are gettin' it hot. They ain't never done this before—they're concentrating just on the two groups at the back. Can't see much more because we're leavin' 'em fast. But I reckon there'll be some ships down . . ."

Just the two groups at the back. It didn't make sense tactically. What were the bastards up to? Well, one thing he thought. It counted as being distinctly curious. He spoke into the telephone.

"Give me Intelligence. Colonel Frank Lasker. Priority."

Lasker listened, asked to be kept informed, and thought. He'd had an inexplicable prickle of unease about this mission all morning. But surely, the Germans couldn't possibly be flying *Ulysses*? Operation Stand-Off should be taking care of Sola right now—and in any case, even if Stand-Off failed, the Germans hadn't yet got the codeword "Fritz" that would release *Ulysses* on Friday—in three days' time. British Intelligence had told him that the codeword was being sent later this morning. And they didn't make elementary mistakes.

Nevertheless . . . He picked up the telephone, and asked for a number. A few moments later, the grey-haired English lady he had occasionally met in the Director's office was on the line.

"Colonel Lasker?"

"Yes, ma'am."

"Would you identify yourself, personal code?"

Lasker did so. Her voice sounded muffled, rather as though she had a cold. Or had been crying.

"Then I have to tell you, Colonel, that Strongman is dead."

"Dead, ma'am?"

"A heart attack, last night."

"I see. Who is in charge?"

"The Director is away." She named another name.

"Is he there?"

"Not yet. He's on his way in. He was in Wiltshire when he got the news."

"Thank you, ma'am. And . . ."

"Yes?"

"My condolences. He was a good man."

"Yes. Thank you."

There was no time for shock. Had that signal been sent, or not? Or had—a thought struck him—another signal been sent? There just wasn't time to find out through unfamiliar channels. They had, at most, perhaps ninety minutes by now. He rang back to the Polebrook operations room.

"Any change in that German fighter pattern?"

"No, sir. They're still concentrating on the rear groups, as far as we can see. Especially the fourth group, because that's being so heavily engaged it hasn't got time to tell us what's happening to any others."

"Right."

Lasker had never burked a decision in his life, but this was one which, by himself, he could not take. He picked up the telephone again.

"Give me Command."

When he finally heard the voice he wanted, five minutes later, he was becoming more and more certain in his own mind. He explained briefly, while the man at the other end of the line listened.

"There's one other thing, sir."

"What's that?"

"The course the groups are flying will bring them straight back here, Colchester, Polebrook, the whole area. There's a lot of military installation round here, British and our own."

"And?"

"There's no sign, from the course I've been given, that they're trying for London. I could never understand the London end of their operation, anyway. I couldn't see how it could succeed."

"So?"

"I think we've been fooled, sir. I think we've been fooled as to the date. I don't know how, but I think we have. And I think we've been fooled about the objective. I think the target is here. I don't think it is in London."

Those last seven words were the only mistake, from first to last, that Colonel Frank Lasker made on the morning of *Ulysses*.

"You want me to authorise the interception and destruction of the fourth B-17 group."

Lasker swallowed. His face was pale.

"Yes, sir."

"We don't have our own fighters available, Frank. The stand-by group are on escort on the Bordeaux mission, and I don't intend to confuse our escort groups already on the Kiel mission with that kind of order. So it will have to be the RAF."

"Yes, sir."

"Thank you, Frank."

The man who had been speaking to Lasker was also a man who had never burked a decision in his life. He thought for a moment, and picked up the telephone again.

"Give me Air Office Commanding, Royal Air Force Fighter Command."

The voice of AOC Fighter Command was almost unnaturally even.

"You want me to shoot down a formation of B-17s?"

"Yes, Marshal."

"You're absolutely sure they *are* enemy?"

"As sure as we can be. But we can't take a chance. Anything's better than taking that chance."

"Even if our boys shoot down some of your boys?"

"If that happens, Marshal, and it may, there'll be no recriminations. I shall take full responsibility."

There was a pause, and the British air marshal spoke again.

"General, in the arrangements you made for Friday—you sent me a covering minute—wasn't there an identification signal your aircraft were going to show? A pistol flare . . . a coloured flare?"

"That's right. Green."

"Do your present crews know of it yet?"

"Yes."

"Then although it isn't Friday, they could be radioed and told to show it. Some of them, at least, will understand. It would be better than nothing."

"That's a damned good idea. I'll fix that right now."

"Good. I'll have to get cracking. We've really got no time at all. Fingers crossed."

"They are."

"There's one more vital thing. Withdraw your own fighter escorts now. If you're right, there'll be no more German fighter activity, anyway. But one thing we must avoid is clashes between your fighters and ours."

"Agreed. I'll do that, immediately."

In his office, Frank Lasker sat thinking. There were the flares . . . his general had just telephoned to tell him about that. A good idea of the British. What else could he do, to sort out friend from foe. The possibility of terrible error was frightening . . . there was always the chance, almost too awful to contemplate, that he was finally, disastrously, murderously wrong about the whole thing. Once more he picked up the telephone. He rang the RAF base at West Durnsford.

"Duty officer?"

"Yes, sir."

"Are Colonel Vandamme and Squadron Leader Croasdell on the station?"

"Yes, sir. In the mess."

"Let me speak to Colonel Vandamme. Urgently."

Vandamme was sitting almost alone in the mess, desultorily reading a copy of *Esquire*, when the call came through. In the far corner, a tall red-haired RAF flight-lieutenant called Burns, whom he knew slightly, was idly throwing darts into the board. Croasdell stood at the window, hands in pockets, watching mechanics arming and refuelling five Spitfires which had just landed from a Channel sweep. The crews, Vandamme guessed, were either debriefing or already on their way out of the aerodrome for their evening out. He went out to the telephone cubicle behind the bar.

"Vandamme?"

"Yes."

"This is Lasker."

"Colonel, sir, what can I do for you?"

"Vandamme . . . you saw those B-17s didn't you? At that lake . . ."

"Innsjo Vaktel, Colonel."

"That's it. Would you know them again?"

Vandamme laughed.

"They're much like any other B-17s. No . . . wait a minute. There was one—much paler green than the others. I'd know that one, if I saw it."

"Good. Then I want you to fly and see if you can see it. And take Croasdell with you."

"Colonel, sir?"

"Listen to me, Vandamme."

Lasker talked for one minute. At the end, he asked Vandamme.

"What fighters have you got there?"

Vandamme looked out of the window.

"There's a flight of Spitfires just refuelled," he said slowly.

"That's dandy. Get on to the operational frequency immediately you take off."

"Am I cleared to fly with the RAF again?"

"I'll see to that. Just you get up there and report."

"OK."

"Can you switch me through to the station commander on that phone?"

"Yes."

"Then do that. And then get moving."

Vandamme ran through to the mess. He grabbed Croasdell by the arm and said urgently:

"Come on, boy. We're being scrambled. Intelligence reckon that wonder-boy's lot will be over any minute now. They want us to get up there and see what we can see."

"Wonder-boy? I thought his big day was supposed to be Friday."

"So did everybody else, I guess."

They were joined by Burns.

Vandamme explained. They ran out to the dispersal hut to pick up flying helmets and suits.

"Hang on," said Burns. "I'm coming, too. Corporal," he shouted to a man looking at them from the wing of a Spitfire. "Are these crates armed and fuelled?"

"The four on the end of the line are, sir," said the NCO. "Standing orders."

"Then wheel three of them out, Saunders. We're scrambling now."

"Yes, sir."

The corporal ran into the hangar, shouting. A thought struck Burns.

"Have you flown a Spit before, sir?" he asked Vandamme.

"A few times," gasped Vandamme. He stopped by the first Spitfire. Men were already pushing it away from the hanger line.

"We had them on evaluation at San Diego, couple of years back."

"Good. But these are VBs, sir. Quite a lot hotter than what you'd be trying out a couple of years ago. You'll want a bit more take-off speed, and they're tighter in the turn."

"Thanks."

Croasdell came by, his face grim. It was always grim nowadays, thought Vandamme, as he levered himself into the Spitfire's cockpit. He raised his hand, and Croasdell smiled briefly, and raised his own as he took the next Spitfire in the line. The rigger was standing beside it. Croasdell jumped up on to the port wing, and clambered into the cockpit. It felt, he thought bitterly, like home. He raced through the cockpit drill. Trim OK . . . flaps up, mags off tank full, wheels locked, radiator open for the heat of take off. Above him the rigger leaned in to fasten his shoulder straps, and then jumped down. Oxygen connected . . . right

"All clear," he called. The rigger waved back.

"Contact."

Croasdell's thumb went down successively on the two black buttons on the right of the instrument panel. The Rolls Merlin engine burst into its shattering 1,400-horse-power roar. His eyes flicked to the panel. Oil pressure climbing . . . 50. Here we go. He pushed the throttle knob, released the brakes, and rolled the Spitfire towards the run-way. A red Verey light sprouted from the control tower. He was last in line. There went Burns . . . a good pilot that, with six kills behind him . . . a lovely take-off. There went Gene . . . not bad, not bad, considering he didn't know Spits. A bit longer getting off than was proper, but not bad at all. Now it was his turn.

The Merlin roared louder and louder. He pushed the throttle knob right down, and the concrete began to blur beneath his wheels . . . 60 . . . 70 . . . 80 . . . 90. He pulled back lightly on the stick, and the Spitfire rose into the air like a gull. Below him, as he banked towards the coast, he glimpsed the hangars and the maintenance crew looking up. His wheels slowly retracted into their nacelles, as he pushed forward the undercarriage lever. The three Spitfires were climbing in a staggered line of three, in which he was bottom and last. Croasdell touched the button of the gunsight and checked the electric light image on the glass. Then quickly he tried his guns. The cannon thumped and the Brownings hammered. He switched on his radio. He outranked Burns, but Burns was flight-leader, since West Durnsford was his station. Almost immediately, Burns was speaking:

"Hallo, Blue leader here. Course 030, height 12,000. We should hit trade in about six minutes."

"Blue, two, Roger." Vandamme's voice.

"Blue, three, Roger," he said himself.

The green checker-board of East Anglian fields was receding into the haze below them. Somewhere down there was Joanna . . . she might even have heard him pass her. He knew he'd given Joanna a rough time lately. The trouble was . . . he kept seeing that girl, the one who'd burned with her baby in the Rostock shelter. He'd been so pig ignorant about war . . . he'd thought it was a matter of fighting hard, and behaving well and trying to keep your nerve—or get it back—and acting properly under stress. And that wasn't it at all, was it? It was appallingly, blindly, horribly cruel, whichever side you fought on . . . too often the destruction of the innocent by the ignorant.

A West Durnsford voice crackled in his earphones.

"Blue leader, vector one-eight-zero. You should see our own trade in three, repeat three, minutes."

"Blue leader, Roger." Burns' voice, flat and calm. He dipped the Spitfire's port wing and followed Burns and Vandamme out in a slight turn, scanning the sky ahead.

Somewhow, he'd found he couldn't talk about Rostock to Joanna. If he'd felt he could, he would have—and damn the security. But he couldn't. One day he supposed, she'd want to have kids of her own. How could he face them . . . his own kids? After Rostock? Six thousand feet. He plugged in his oxygen and adjusted the mask.

"Trade . . . twelve o'clock high."

Vandamme's voice, with Burns acknowledging.

"Blue leader, Roger."

There they were, straight ahead, about a thousand feet

higher . . . echeloned silver dots, rapidly swelling into recognisable B-17 Fortress shapes. One or two were trailing smoke, but these first two groups didn't look too badly hit. He hoped Burns had enough sense to stay clear. Some of those boys in the top-turrets would be a bit trigger-happy by now.

West Durnsford again:

"Blue leader, five trade have turned away from main force. They are on course, five-three-zero, and losing height. You are ordered to investigate."

"Blue leader, Roger."

No sign of any other fighters. Presumably they'd be engaging this fourth group Vandamme had been told about. That group wasn't visible from here—it must be at least thirty miles back.

West Durnsford again.

"Blue leader, your trade is going down fast. We can't hold it on the scope. They must be damned nearly on the deck . . ."

Burns again.

"Last vector, please."

"One-three-two."

"Roger."

Following Burns, the Spitfires of Croasdell and Vandamme turned sharply right, swinging south towards London.

At Polebrook, Frank Lasker turned from the table-plot.

"What was that about five turning away?"

The operations officer reached out with a pointer and moved a counter on the table.

"There, Colonel. And that's the course."

Lasker stood rigid.

"What's happening to that fourth group?"

"The RAF fighter wing from West Malling's on them. I guess those Germans, if"—he looked quickly at Lasker—"they are Germans, aren't goin' to make it."

Lasker didn't seem to hear. They've fooled me, he was thinking. Or, at least, they've partly fooled me. They've split their force. The RAF are doing just what they were told. They're shooting down the fourth group—and that's OK because the Germans wiped out our fourth group and put in one of their own. But they had a fifth group, that I didn't reckon on.

"I was wrong," he said aloud. He swung on the operations officer.

"What's the nearest fighter force to those five?"

"The three Spits they scrambled from West Durnsford. That's Colonel Vandamme and two others, sir."

Gene Vandamme, if ever you flew, you've got to fly now, said Lasker to himself.

"Have you got their frequency?"

"Yes, Colonel."

"Order them to engage those five."

"But, Colonel . . ."

"That's an order. I'll tell Command."

"Yes, Colonel."

"And alert the London Defence Command. Tell them . . . no, goddam it, ask them . . . to warn their anti-aircraft people."

"Right."

Five minutes later, 6,000 feet above Clacton, the three Spitfires recrossed the coast.

"We're going to be lucky to spot that trade if it's down near the deck," said Burns' voice in their earphones. "Even the low-level station at Hopton's lost them now. They must be damned well clipping the bloody grass."

"Blue two," said Vandamme. "If I reckon right, they'll be on a course of something like two-zero-zero."

"Blue leader. You think you know the target?"

"I know the target."

"Blue leader. Well, everybody else has lost the bastards. We'll try it your way. How are you for fuel?"

"Not too good," said Vandamme.

"Me, neither," said Croasdell.

"OK, gents. Two-zero-zero. Here we go."

Exactly nine minutes later, speeding far below them over the industrial haze south of the Thames, they saw the shapes of the five B-17s flying in arrowhead formation. Burns saw them first.

"Tally-ho. There they are, seven o'clock low. Let's get down there."

Croasdell pushed forward on the stick. His stomach seemed to drop away, straining on the straps that held him in his seat. The Spitfire dived faster and faster. The needle of the airspeed indicator flickered past the 480 mark. God, he thought, how long will the airframe stand this? The top turrets of the five B-17s below him began to wink in unison.

Vandamme's voice.

"There it is . . . that light-green bastard. I remember that one at the lake."

Right then, wonder-boy, thought Croasdell as the rear B-17 began to fill the space between the electric light bars on his sights. Here I come . . .

27

Seventy miles to the north-east, Frido von Altmark turned irritably to his radio operator.

"What do you mean, you can't understand? He's talking English, I presume?"

"That's just it, sir. I'm not sure what he's talking."

Von Altmark glanced from the flight deck window. They were dead on station, flying a couple of miles behind the third group of B-17s. Another couple of B-17s had dropped back to join him. He gave them a friendly wave, but his heart was beating faster. They were YB-40s . . . the super-armed B-17s that were intended to protect formations.

"Have they challenged us?"

He waved back at the YB-40 again, lifted his hands above his head in a parody of friendly triumph.

"I don't know what they're saying, sir."

"Let me hear."

The operator passed him the headset. He eased his own to his neck and held one earpiece to his head. A voice was speaking urgently, but it was a series of clicks and grunts and hisses, like no voice he'd ever heard.

"Answer him in English. And make it good."

The operator went at once into a mid-West drawl.

"Mighty good to see you boys. I guess it's kind of a holiday for you, just flyin' over the ocean, no goddam bombs to drop, and no flak, either. Still, you stick around and we'll buy you a highball when we reach base."

"What does he say?"

"Nothing, sir."

A voice in von Altmark's headphones. Ruge, the top-turret gunner.

"The group ahead seems to be dispersing. They're spraying off in all directions. I've never seen anything like it. And those YB-40s have turned away. We're all by ourselves, sir. Our group is alone in the sky."

"Try him again, in English," said von Altmark urgently to the operator.

Ruge's voice came again.

"We're not alone any more. Fighters, eleven o'clock high. Spitfires, Tempests . . ."

The air-to-air and ground-to-air Navajo voices continued communications in their precise robot-like dialect and there were broad grins on a lot of dark-skinned black-haired faces.

Fifty feet over northern Kent, Warnow's B-17 Happy Hanna drilled on. Slightly behind him and to his left, he could see the olive-drab shape of Lutz's B-17: to his right, that of Trobitius. Behind those, he knew, would be the aircraft of Mathy and Stross. The five B-17s seemed to be clinging to the ground like low-flying birds, reeling the contours under them, while the pilots watched the landscape hurtling towards them in a broad, moving swathe.

"Twelve minutes to target?" he asked into his throat microphone. Forward in the bombardier's compartment Buttman, the bombardier, nodded. Beside him sat Steiger, the navigator, busy with a map and a ruler. Steiger's voice came now.

"Here's the railway crossing at Reigate," he said. His voice was calm, with an undercurrent of excitement. "First Turning Point . . . *now*."

Warnow lifted the B-17 twenty feet, banked slowly right with his right wing-tip close to the ground, and settled back to fifty feet, heading almost due north.

"Ten minutes to target," said Steiger.

No flak yet, except for that destroyer off the coast, thought Warnow. We've taken the Tommies by surprise. Not like Frido . . . poor Frido.

Everybody aboard Happy Hanna was fairly tense, having heard the battle—after they turned off—between the RAF Spitfires and *Gruppe* Altmark. It had sounded bad for Frido's lot—they'd been caught still some way from the coast, and he doubted any would get to Colchester. But *Gruppe* Warnow seemed to have slipped through the net. Or rather . . . under the net. He wasn't so far from Hannah now . . . she was down there somewhere, in the haze of London ahead. Perhaps she'd hear him coming. Well, they weren't bombing near Chelsea, anyway. And one day . . . still no flak.

Even as the thought flicked across his mind, he saw the barracks ahead, with khaki-uniformed men clustered round a mobile gun position. The top-turret gun of Happy Hanna began to clatter, but its tracer was far above the British gun. Lautenschlager, up in the top turret, couldn't get the depression on his guns to bring them to bear. Experimentally, as the barracks hurtled nearer, he tried dropping the nose a little to give Lautenschlager more chance, but there simply wasn't room for manœuvre. Now the flak gun was blinking, seemingly, straight into his eyes. A long, low curl of tracer came lazily towards him, suddenly speeding to whiplash speed out to his right. In the same instant, he passed over the gun position, so low that he seemed almost to scrape the sandbag emplacement, and he heard the tail-turret gunner open up behind him. He looked out to his side. They seemed all there. He spoke on the inter-aircraft frequency.

"Everybody all right?"

"We were hit somewhere low and forward."

Trobitius's calm voice, from the B-17 on his right.

"Doesn't seem to be affecting our flying. I'm going to—"

"Lord of Heaven."

That was Lautenschlager, in the top turret. In the same instant, he saw from the corner of his eye the momentary droop of Trobitius' wing, the shower of sparks on the ground where it touched, the way the great bomber reared into the air, and flailed along the ground in an explosion of earth and flame. Seconds later, in the Plexiglass of the nose canopy, the reflection of the giant explosion glared, though they were already three-quarters of a mile away. A voice from Happy Hanna's tail turret:

"Must have set off the bomb. The swine couldn't miss, not head-on, a target of that size."

"Windsor Castle, Second Turning Point now," said the navigator, unemotionally.

There they were, the stone towers ahead to his left. He took Happy Hanna up to a hundred feet and banked right.

"Three minutes to target," said the navigator.

"I'm ready," said Buttman from the bombardier's compartment.

Then Lautenschlager's voice, a little shrill.

"Spitfires, back and high. One . . . two . . . three."

His turret began to clatter again. Suddenly, there was an appalling, jarring vibration far back in Happy Hanna, and a smell of cordite.

"Tail gunner, are you all right?" said Warnow sharply. He eased Happy Hanna down to eighty feet, watching his trim. There was no reply from the tail.

"I think we're burning, somewhere at the back. There's a lot of smoke."

That was Lautenschlager once more. And then, urgently:

"Here come those pigs again . . ."

"That's fixed that bastard," said Vandamme savagely, pulling back on his stick and watching as the outer right B-17 of the formation ploughed majestically into the railway banking below him in a sheet of flame. Jesus, these were sweet little ships. But who would have thought he'd have used one to knock down a B-17? He turned tightly, almost standing on one wing, two hundred feet up, and set his sights on the next ship in line. His fuel-exhaustion light was showing, and he knew there wasn't much time. Three left—since that Limey flak gun had got one. Burns was in trouble. Ahead and to his right he saw Burns' Spitfire roll on to its back. There he went now, his chute streaming. He was low for baling out. Did it open? He couldn't see.

The leading B-17 was filling the electric light bars on each side of his gunsights. He pressed the twin firing buttons and the cannon and machine-guns drummed. Pieces of the B-17's fuselage hurtled past the nose of his Spitfire, and there was an orange glow from the rear. For a moment, as he saw the olive-green stretch of the long graceful body below his port wing, he read the name painted on it . . . Happy Hanna. That sonofabitch has a nerve, he thought irrelevantly. He's spelled Hannah the German way, without the 'h'. The Rolls-Merlin coughed, picked up, coughed again, and was silent. Suddenly he could hear the wind, see the propeller slowly turning. Out of gas. He looked down quickly below him. He had two hundred feet in which to find a suitable field.

Trobitius gone, Mathy gone. And Stross? He couldn't see or hear Stross. From far behind him, there was a red glow in the Plexiglass. Stross, too, then. Happy Hanna was hard to hold. The burst that had killed the tail-gunner and set fire to the rear had done something to the tail trim. Gently but firmly, Warnow's hands held the controls. He looked carefully at his instruments.

"Northolt airfield," said Steiger's voice. "Dead on for target."

A blur of runway, men running, open hangar doors, three Spitfires lined up for take-off. If only the tail-gunner had been there, he could have warmed those swine up. Then more roofs, a railway line, a bridge, more roofs, a road, two red buses. Behind and to Warnow's right flew Lutz, still untouched.

With a comet tail of flame and smoke, Happy Hanna wallowed on flying like a burning arrow towards Whitehall.

Two of them left, thought Croasdell, as he banked tightly above Ealing. And two of us gone. Burns got out, but I hope Gene's all right. There they were, like toys, below him. The lead one was streaming smoke and sparks.

"That baby hasn't got long," said Croasdell aloud. "I'll take the other—the way I got the outer left one back at Reigate."

They've come a long way round, wonder-boy's lot, cutting a wide turn through Southern England to approach London from the west. I wonder why they feel that they've got to have a go at Whitehall from the west? thought Croasdell as he pushed forward the stick. They'd have saved a lot of time with a straight run.

He was approaching the rear undamaged B-17 at what seemed astonishing speed. The bomber was full in the sights now, and its top turret was winking. Five hundred yards . . . three hundred . . . two hundred. Croasdell pressed the firing button. A long burst, and then he broke the Spitfire away to the right. In the same instant he saw four of his cannon shells pock the B-17 . . . one on the closed waist-gun position, one on the port under-carriage nacelle, and two smashing into the Plexiglass of the flight deck. Without apparent manœuvre, the B-17 went into the ground, carving through a long line of trees and bushes, burning, broken-backed. There was the crump of an explosion, and something hit the Spitfire. Glycol coolant spattered the windscreen. The engine screamed harshly.

Croasdell looked down. His ammunition indicator had entered the red position. His fuel exhaustion light had been showing for the past forty-five seconds. He was going to have one chance at that lead bastard, and one only. Look at him . . . right down on the deck, tail on fire, driving that damned thing along as though it were on rails. That's wonder-boy, that is, he said to himself. And by God, he's done it. Here's St James' Park. The Rolls-Merlin coughed briefly, but picked up. Croasdell began his dive. His tanks must be nearly bone-dry, but the angle of the Spitfire would sluice the remaining petrol forward into the engine. In the same second, there was a shocking, numbing blow to his legs. The back plate of his seat kicked like a mule. The cockpit filled with smoke.

There were four seconds left in which Croasdell could have baled out. But in front of him the B-17, so large that it filled the whole glycol-spattered windscreen of the Spitfire, came steadily on. For a moment he saw the hunched figure at the controls. His hands went down on the firing buttons and his guns fired their last burst and fell silent, empty. The Spitfire was rolling now, forty feet up, one wheel sticking into the air as it headed, upside down, for the ground. In that last second of his life, Croasdell said one word aloud: "Joanna . . ." And he saw, as he struck, the burning girl and her child in the shelter at Rostock.

"I got him, I got him . . ."

Lautenschlager's voice, excited and triumphant. Warnow could no longer answer. The last burst from the Spitfire had smashed in a long destructive swathe up from the bombardier's compartment, where the navigator Steiger sat dead. Beside him Buttman, unwounded, was calmly calling out the last-second adjustments.

"Twenty seconds to target . . . Right a fraction, right, right . . . that's it . . . You all right, Rolf?"

Warnow tried to speak, but his shattered jaw would not obey his brain. His oxygen mask, partly severed by a sliver of metal, hung on his chest, soaked with blood. For a second he put his hand up to the agony of his face. There seemed to be no jaw there at all.

Buttman's voice again.

"That's it, that's it. Lovely . . . Hold her at that . . . ten seconds to target . . ."

He was flying by instinct now, because he could see little more than a red blur in front of him. The wind howled back through the holes in the Plexiglass, whipping the blood off his chest. Happy Hanna, he thought, you are hard to hold, hard to hold. Like a lover with his mistress, he stroked her controls, responsive to every quiver in her burning fuselage. He knew now that he was dying, and that all that was left was this hurtling union of brain and flesh and metal.

Buttman was counting.

"Five . . . four . . . three . . . two . . . BOMB AWAY."

Out to the right as he touched the rudder, loomed the tower, far above him, of Big Ben. Through his dimming eyes, he saw the silver ribbon of the Thames. He was going now, but he heard Buttman's excited voice.

"That was dead right, Rolf. We put it to within a foot. We've never done better, not even at the lake. Not another pilot alive could have done it . . ."

Behrens said that, thought Warnow. I remember that Peter Behrens said that . . .

At 200 miles an hour, the burning body of Happy Hanna hit the Thames alongside Westminster Bridge and Parliament.

There was a momentary explosion of flame, and a towering wall of water rose. Then a hissing cloud of steam. A minute later a single wheel floated, turning slowly, in an eddying vortex of oil. Nothing else came to the surface.

28

"All in all, General, we must count ourselves to have been, ah, extraordinarily fortunate," said Winston Churchill, staring critically at a rose-bed. With his companion, he was taking a stroll through the lawns and shrubberies of Chequers, the Prime Minister's country home.

"General Arnold tells me," said the American beside him, "that as far as we can check from the debriefings, your RAF boys got all the KG 200 B-17s, and didn't hit any of ours. A fine piece of work. Could have been nasty."

"I thank Providence it wasn't," said Churchill, soberly. He pulled idly at a rose, and spoke again:

"Have you been informed of the details of what happened?"

"Not fully, sir."

"The bomb . . . the only one that hit, dropped directly into the stairwell above the War Cabinet room. Through the door facing St James' Park, like some sort of torpedo. A remarkable piece of airmanship. General Arnold tells me he believes that it can only have been a fluke . . . I reserve judgment.

"The chemists tell me that had the bomb exploded, the heat generated—far greater, I am told, than that of any normal incendiary device—would have sucked all the air from the Cabinet rooms . . . indeed, from the entire network of our underground chambers. The War Cabinet would have been left, so to speak, breathless . . . a most disturbing idea. I am sure this device was deliberately and accurately dropped on to its intended target. All doubtless other targets around us had been set for those other enemy aircraft which were . . . unsuccessful."

"And yet the one bomb that hit its target actually failed?" said the American.

"Yes. It seems that when the device was dismantled, the fuse was found to be defective. A vital locking ring was missing, so that the timing spring could not be released. An extraordinary, but most fortunate, omission."

"What an irony," said the American. "All that effort, all those lives, all that flying . . . for nothing. And the last pilot—did the whole thing right, and still it's all for nothing, because some factory hand fouled a fuse."

"I think not, General," said Churchill slowly. "I am informed that these devices are assembled at a forced-labour establishment in occupied Russia, out of reach of our bombers. Perhaps . . ."

He paused.

"We have taken steps to deal with KG 200. As you know, there have been air strikes and Resistance operations against their bases in many parts of Europe, and we have reports that the ingenious device you used at Sola—"

"Willie Baby—our Weary Willies," said the American.

"Just so. Willie, ah, Baby, did very considerable damage to the Sola and other installations. It is, I think, appropriate that worn-out B-17s should, with their last breath so to speak, have taken some retribution for sister aircraft that the *Luftwaffe* captured and used against us."

"I have heard KG 200 called an octopus. I prefer to describe it as a hydra—you remember, the many-headed monster. The hydra had one invariable characteristic."

'What was that?" said the American.

"As fast as you struck off one head," said Churchill, "it grew another. Perhaps, however, we have struck off enough heads to inhibit further growth for a time."

He pulled a heavy gold watch from his siren-suit and looked at it closely.

"I think it is time for luncheon. You were right, General,

when you said war was full of ironies. Not least that on this occasion, but for a missing fuse-locking-ring, much of the War Cabinet would have been destroyed . . . with you and General Arnold as an unexpected bonus. They could hardly have known that you would be at our meeting. Well . . . after luncheon we have much to discuss . . ."

The American laughed.

"True. A bonus. I take that as a compliment, sir," said General Eisenhower.

"There's just one more thing I want to say, Jo," said Vandamme awkwardly. He stood at the door of the cottage in Essex. His driver waited on the road with his jeep, engine running.

"Yes, Gene?" said Joanna. She looked pale, he thought. She'd taken a beating in the last few days. And soon there would be the child. Maybe, of course, that was good . . . better than nothing left of Croasdell at all.

"The baby," he said. "In case anything ever happens to me, I've made some arrangements. I've made them now—they're done, so there's no argument. It's a financial arrangement, in trust for you and the baby, at Chase Manhattan in New York City. My lawyers will get in touch."

"You can't," she said incredulously. "I can't possibly . . ."

"You can and I have," he said crisply. "End of discussion."

"You're very kind," she said unsteadily. For the first time she saw that he was angry with her.

"Jo, if you ever say that again, that I'm kind to you or John's kid . . . I'll . . ."

She put her hands on his shoulders and kissed him.

"Tell me about it next time we meet," she said.

AUTHORS' NOTE

KG 200—*Kampfgeschwader* 200—existed. It was a secret fighting force of World War II, so secret that individual units within it were unknown to each other; so mysterious that even today, most of the diaries and documents dealing with it are, according to both Allied and German authorities, either "missing" or "destroyed". Yet it presented the Allies with one of the most dangerous threats of the war, and the unravelling of its intricate web of operations became top priority.

This book is fiction, but based upon investigations and hitherto unpublished information in fourteen countries. Despite the disappearance of official KG 200 records, documents, orders, records of prisoner-of-war interrogations, and Intelligence reports confirming the story, were found. Former members of KG 200 were traced, though the picture each could, or would, reveal was always limited, for personnel were deliberately kept in the dark about the activities of their comrades. And most, after all these years, were unwilling to talk . . . an attitude less surprising when one takes into account the fact that their former commander, *Oberstleutnant* Werner Baumbach, the *Luftwaffe*'s greatest and most decorated bomber pilot, failed to mention a word about KG 200 in the autobiography he published after the war!

All this reticence may in part be due to the fact that a number of KG 200's activities flouted the Rules of Land Warfare, Article 23 of the conventional law of war, for example, states:

In addition to the prohibitions provided by special Conventions, it is especially forbidden to make improper use of a flag of truce, of the national flag, or of the military insignia and uniform of the enemy, as well as distinctive badges of the Geneva Convention.

Yet even the Department of History at the United States Air Force Academy in Colorado answered initial research enquiries with: "Sorry to report that none of us here has any knowledge whatsoever of *Kampfgeschwader* 200 or its employment. If they were flying B-17s and B-24s then assume their mission was highly classified and hence that whatever war records were obtained came through Intelligence channels and may not even yet have been declassified."

In spite, however, of the silence of so many of those involved, the missing records and continued secrecy, the almost incredible story did eventually fit together to form the factual basis for this book.

Many of the most fantastic, the most unbelievable incidents here described, actually happened.

APPENDIX

The destruction or disappearance of virtually all of KG 200's war records prevented detailed documentation of all its activities by the Allies, but the following are the wide range of aircraft known to have been regularly flown by the organisation:

B-17s (Flying Fortresses)
B-24s (Liberators)
Wellingtons
Stirlings
Spitfires
Mosquitos
Beaufighters
P-51 Mustangs
Lockheed P-38 Lightnings
Lockheed Hudsons
Douglas DC-3s
FW-200
S., .75
JU-88
JU-188
JU-252
JU-290
HE-111
Fieseler Storch
DO-24
HE-115
JU-352
AR-196
AR-232
Soviet Tupolov bombers
Martins
Petlyakovs
PE-2s
SB-RKs
Polikarpov I-16s

The following are some of the bases definitely established as KG 200, confirmed by German documents:

Germany

Burg (Mistel base)	Berlin-Rangsdorf
Kolberg	Berlin-Finsterwalde
Munchen-Riem	Berlin-Gatow
Burg / Magdeburg	Hildesheim
Tutow	Wildpark-Werder
Ort	Wesendorf
Boitzenburg	Stendal
Garz	Luebeck-Blankansee
Finnow	Holzkirchen
Dedelstorf	Karlshagen

France

Orly Villeneuve-le-Roi	Nantes
Marseilles	Vannes
Nice	St Dizier

Holland

Gorkum	Rotterdam

Denmark

Aalborg	Tirstrup

Austria

Wiener-Neustadt

Norway

Stavanger-Sola

Roumania

Zillistea

Greece

Athens-Kalamaki

Italy

Pergamo
Villefranca

Russia

Simferopol
Smolensk
Kharkoff
Vitebsk

Poland

Danzig-Hexengrund

THE UNHOLY

The greatest evil of our century
No one can escape its chilling power

Michael Falconer Anderson

Violent death and mindless terror stalked the streets.
The hooligan on the train died screaming as he was torn limb from limb . . .
Two lovers sneaking into a darkened lane ran when they saw the horror coming – and then one of them had vanished . . .
A police sergeant ploughed his car into a crowd of children – children who did not exist . . .
A nurse felt something embrace her and bend its filthy lips towards hers . . .
When newspaperman Jon Hammond saw the corpses mounting as terror gripped his town, he knew he must find the source of the evil. For the magnet of the horror lay hidden somewhere in the peaceful countryside, reaching out tendrils of cold evil, stalking the land for screams . . . and souls . . . and blood.

MAKING FRIENDS
A powerful saga of love, loyalty and revenge

Cornelia Hale

It looked like a perfect marriage. Misty Mason was a beautiful, blonde American girl, intelligent and loving. Sir William Courtney was a top journalist, a sophisticated English aristocrat with a lovely country house. They were very much in love. Misty knew she had never been happier than in the early months of their marriage, as a newly-wed setting up home in Washington.
But behind William's easy charm lay generations of aristocratic breeding and insistence on doing one's duty. And Misty's own youth and beauty hid a smouldering passion for revenge for the tragedy hidden in her family's past.

DANECLERE

The powerful saga of a great house and its courageous mistress

Pamela Hill

To the great house comes
Honor Thwaite, a farmer's daughter from a Puritan background who brings a rich dowry when she marries
Richard Sawtrey, lord of the manor, but an ineffectual husband, ruled by
Mrs Anna, his mother, who governs Daneclere with a will of iron
Francis Wolffe, the sinister and unscrupulous bailiff
Barbary Mountchurch, the highborn maiden who becomes his mistress
Jeremy Whyteleaf, and his siblings, all tainted with their father's evil
but brooding over them all there is Daneclere itself, the great house around which their lives centre.

'An entertaining lusty saga'

Publishers Weekly

ONE LITTLE ROOM
A heart-rending story of two sisters and the man they love

Jan Webster

Brought up in straitened circumstances by their uncaring and bitter mother, sisters Catherine and Christie-Ann fall in love with the same man, struggling small-time journalist Colum Brodie. But Catherine is determined to escape from the poverty of her childhood. She turns him down and instead marries an English army officer, Edward Elkins. Christie-Ann first comforts Colum, and then marries him.

But little does she know that there is a secret bond between Catherine and Colum, the basis for their enduring love. And Catherine, ambitious and strong-willed though she is, finds that her lasting passion for Colum threatens both marriages and becomes only stronger with the passage of time.

THE CARETAKER WIFE

Can a marriage of convenience become an affair of the heart?

Barbara Whitehead

For Lieutenant Richard Welby, thirty-year-old Caroline was a bride of convenience. The death of his spendthrift but beautiful wife had left him with a broken heart, five children and a mountain of gambling debts. He needed a wife to care for his family and his estates while he sailed against the French with Nelson's fleet.

At home, the newly-wed Caroline coped with horrendous debts, a run-down house and children who had been terrified by their nursemaid's dabblings in black magic. With her usual competence, she took control and brought order out of chaos. But by now, Caroline was more than half in love with her handsome husband. Could her marriage of convenience, coolly and sensibly entered into, ever become the love match she longed for?

'She writes with warmth and charm, a quick ear for dialogue, and her characters have real blood in their veins. A distinguished debut . . . very enjoyable'

Eastern Daily Press